USA TODAY bestselling [...] London, England. She is [...] sons—which gives her rath[...] insight into the male psyche—and also works as a film journalist. She adores her job, which involves getting swept up in a world of high emotion, sensual excitement, funny and feisty women, sexy and tortured men and glamorous locations where laundry doesn't exist. Once she turns off her computer she often does chores—usually involving laundry!

Millie Adams has always loved books. She considers herself a mix of Anne Shirley—loquacious, but charming, and willing to break a slate over a boy's head if need be—and Charlotte Doyle—a lady at heart, but with the spirit to become a mutineer should the occasion arise. Millie lives in a small house on the edge of the woods, which she finds allows her to escape in the way she loves best: in the pages of a book. She loves intense alpha heroes and the women who dare to go toe-to-toe with them. Or break a slate over their heads…

THE CEO'S IMPOSSIBLE HEIR

HEIDI RICE

HIS SECRETLY PREGNANT CINDERELLA

MILLIE ADAMS

MILLS & BOON

First Published in Great Britain 2022
by Mills & Boon, an imprint of HarperCollins*Publishers* Ltd,
1 London Bridge Street, London, SE1 9GF

www.harpercollins.co.uk

HarperCollins*Publishers*
1st Floor, Watermarque Building,
Ringsend Road, Dublin 4, Ireland

The CEO's Impossible Heir © 2022 Heidi Rice

His Secretly Pregnant Cinderella © 2022 Millie Adams

ISBN: 978-0-263-30066-6

01/22

MIX
Paper from
responsible sources
FSC™ C007454

This book is produced from independently certified FSC™ paper
to ensure responsible forest management.
For more information visit www.harpercollins.co.uk/green.

Printed and Bound in Spain using 100% Renewable Electricity
at CPI Black Print, Barcelona

THE CEO'S IMPOSSIBLE HEIR

HEIDI RICE

MILLS & BOON

To my dad, Peter Rice,
where my love of Ireland—and Irish heroes—began.

CHAPTER ONE

ROSS DE COURTNEY STRODE into the ancient chapel, having landed his helicopter five minutes ago on a clifftop on the west coast of Ireland.

The chapel was nestled in the grounds of his soon-to-be new brother-in-law's imposing estate—and currently decorated in glowing lights and scented winter blooms, and packed with a crowd full of people he did not know.

Soon-to-be, my arse.

A few of the assembled guests glanced his way as he headed down the aisle towards the happy couple who were in the midst of saying their vows—the groom dressed in a slate-grey designer suit and the bride, Ross's foolishly sweet and trusting sister, Katie, in a flowing white concoction of silk and lace.

His footsteps echoed on the old stone but were silenced by the thuds of his own heartbeat and the fury squeezing his chest.

Katie had asked him—very politely—in a message yesterday not to attend the ceremony. It was the first time she'd deigned to return any of his calls or messages for months. She had 'things to tell him' apparently—important things that needed tact and delicacy to convey—about her newly acquired fiancé, the Irish billionaire Conall O'Riordan who Ross had met exactly once, five months ago now, at the opera in London.

Tact and delicacy, my arse.

The man was a thug, a ruthless, controlling thug who, just like the first man Katie had married—when she was just nineteen and the boy had only a few weeks to live—was not nearly good enough for her.

He'd done the wrong thing, then. Objecting to Katie's foolish decision to marry Tom and then standing back and waiting for her to see reason. And of course she hadn't, because Katie was a romantic. So she'd gone ahead and married Tom. Tom had died, and Ross and Katie hadn't spoken for five years, until that fortuitous night at the opera in December. When her Irish fiancé—who Ross did not know from Adam—had all but attacked him.

Well, he wasn't making the same mistake twice. This time he refused to see his sister hitch herself to another man who might hurt her.

Maybe he had no right to intervene in her life. She was twenty-four now, not nineteen. And the truth was, he'd never been much of a brother to her... Mostly because he'd never even known of his half-sister's existence until she was fourteen and her mother—one of his father's many discarded mistresses—had died. He'd tried to do the right thing then, paying for expensive schools and then college and publicly acknowledging her connection to the De Courtney family. Something his father in his usual cruel and selfish way had resolutely refused to do while he was still alive.

Even though they'd never been close, he couldn't let her marry O'Riordan, without at least making his feelings known.

More heads turned towards him as he approached the altar, the words of the ceremony barely audible above the thunder in his ears.

Personally, he would not have chosen to do this on the day, at the ceremony, like some scene straight out of a gothic novel or a Hollywood movie. But Katie had left him with no choice. She hadn't replied in any detail to the texts and emails he'd sent her trying to re-establish contact after their disastrous reunion at the opera five months ago. Her insistence she was going ahead with this wedding because she was madly in love with O'Riordan hadn't reassured him in the least.

Had the man cast some kind of a spell over his sister, with his money and his looks—or worse, was he a man like their father, who exerted a ruthless control over the women in his life?

The ceremony was reaching its peak when a young woman caught his eye, standing to the right of the groom holding the hand of a little boy dressed in a miniature suit.

Her wild red hair was piled on top of her head and threaded through with wild flowers.

The shot of heat and adrenaline and recognition that blasted into him was so fierce his steps faltered—and for one hideous moment he was back at the Westmoreland Summer Ball four years ago, dancing with the beautiful woman who had enchanted and mesmerised him that night.

Is it her?

He couldn't see her face, just her back, her bare shoulders, the graceful line of her neck, the seductive curve of one breast, the slender waist and long legs. He dragged his gaze back up, and it snagged on her nape again, the pale skin accentuated by the tendrils curling down from her hairdo.

He shook his head, tried to focus, the heat so real and all-consuming it momentarily obliterated his common sense.

Don't be ridiculous. It can't be her. This is your memory playing nasty tricks on you at a time of heightened emotion, which is precisely why you avoid this kind of drama, wherever possible.

The girl, whose name he'd never even known, had captivated him that night. Her quick, caustic wit delivered in a musical Irish accent and her bright, ethereal beauty—all flowing russet hair, translucent skin and piercing blue eyes—had momentarily turned him into an intoxicated and rapacious fool.

The heat kicked him squarely in the crotch as he recalled what had happened later that night, in the estate's garden. The fairy lights had cast a twinkle of magic over her soft skin as he'd devoured her. The subtle scent of night jasmine and ripe apples had been overwhelmed by the potent scent of her arousal as he'd stroked the slick heart of her desire. Her shattered sobs of pleasure had driven him wild as he'd eventually plunged into her and ridden them both towards oblivion...

They'd ended up making love—or rather having raw, sweaty, no-holds-barred sex—against an apple tree, not thirty yards from the rest of the party.

But what had seemed hopelessly hot and even weirdly romantic—given that he was not a romantic man—had turned first into an embarrassing obsession... After she'd run off—deliberately creating some kind of hokey Cinderella fantasy, he'd realised later—and he'd searched for her like a madman... And had then hit the cold, hard wall of reality three weeks later, when she'd contacted him on a withheld number, believing she could extort money out of him with the calculated lie he had got her pregnant.

And thus had ended his hot Cinderella fantasy.

Except it hadn't quite, because he still thought about her far too much. And, damn it, still had this visceral reaction when he spotted random women in crowds who had similar colouring or tilted their heads in a similar way. It was mortifying and infuriating, and seriously inconvenient. How typical he should be struck down by that deranged response now, when it could cause him maximum damage.

'If any man or woman knows of any lawful impediment why these two should not be joined in holy matrimony, speak now or for ever hold your peace.'

The priest's voice rang out, jolting Ross out of the memories and slamming him back into reality.

He dragged his gaze away from the offending bridesmaid's neck and forced the heat in his groin into a box marked 'get over yourself'.

He stood for a second, suspended in time, furious at being forced into such a public display, but at the same time knowing he could not let this moment—however clichéd—pass. Katie had left him with no choice.

'I object,' he said. And watched Katie and the mad Irishman swing round.

Gasps echoed throughout the crowd. And Katie's eyes widened. 'Ross? What are you doing here?'

Her groom's brows drew down in a furious frown. One Ross recognised from five long months ago at the opera the first time the man had laid eyes on him. The concern for his sister's welfare, which had been twisting his gut in knots for seven hours during the flight across the Atlantic, turned to stone.

You think I give a damn about your temper, buddy? No way am I letting you marry her until I know for sure you're not going to hurt her.

'What am I doing here?' he said, as conversationally as he could while the concern and the fury began to strangle him. 'I'm stopping this wedding until I can be sure this is what you really want, Katie,' he said, glad clarity had returned to his thoughts after the nasty little trick his memory had played on him.

But then the strangest thing happened: instead of saying anything, both Katie and her Irish groom turned to their left—ignoring him.

'Carmel, I'm so sorry,' his sister whispered.

'Mel, take Mac out of here,' the madman said in a voice that brooked no argument.

But then Ross turned too, realising the comments were directed at the young woman he had spotted a few moments before.

Recognition slammed into him like a freight train.

Her fierce blue eyes sparkled like sapphires—sheened with astonishment. The vibrant red hair only accentuated the flush racing over her pale features... And stabbed him hard in the chest.

The heat raced back, swiftly followed by a wave of shock. The concern that had been building inside him for hours now, ever since he'd made the decision to fly across the Atlantic, then pilot a helicopter to this godforsaken estate in the middle of nowhere to protect his sister, turned to something raw and painful.

It is her.

'Mammy, who's yer man?'

Ross's gaze dipped to the little boy standing beside her. The childish voice, tinged with the soft lilt of the boy's homeland, cut through the adult storm gathering around them.

The shock twisted in his stomach and his heartbeat slowed, the emotions rising in his chest becoming strangely opaque—almost as if he had walked into a fog and couldn't find his way out again. He took in the child's striking blue-green eyes, round with curiosity, his perfect little features, and the short blond curls rioting around his head, but all he could see was himself, aged about four, in the only picture he'd ever seen of himself as a child with his mother. Before his hair had darkened. And she had died. A photo his father had taken great pleasure in burning in front of him, when he was being sent off to boarding school.

'Stop snivelling, boy. Your mother was weak. You don't want to be weak too, do you?'

'What…?' The word choked out, barely audible as his gaze rose back to the woman's face, the horror engulfing him. 'How…?'

No. No. No.

This could not be true. This could not be happening. This was a dream. Not a dream. A waking nightmare.

He pressed his fingers to his temples, his gaze jerking between her and the child.

This toddler could not be his… His mind screamed in denial. He had taken the ultimate precaution to prevent this eventuality. He would not believe it.

She wrapped her arm around the boy's shoulders, to edge the child behind her and shield him from Ross's view.

'It's okay, Mac,' she said, the smoky voice he recognised edged now with anger but no less seductive—her stance defiant and brave as she straightened to her full height, like a young Valkyrie protecting her offspring. 'This man is nobody.'

He stepped towards her, determined to do… Something!

Who the hell are you kidding?

He had no clue what to do! The shock was still reverberating through him with such force, his sense of time and place and his usual cast-iron control had completely deserted him.

A strong hand on his shoulder dragged him back a step. 'Get away from my sister, you bastard.'

He recognised the madman's voice, could hear Katie's straight afterwards, begging them both to calm down, but all he could do was stand and stare as his hot Cinderella lifted the child into her arms and headed towards the vestry.

She's running away from me again.

For a moment he was back in the orchard, still struggling to deal with the shattering orgasm as he watched her panicked figure disappear into the moonlight.

But instead of scrambling to throw off the drugging afterglow while zipping up his trousers so he could charge after her, this time, he stood frozen to the spot. The boy's gaze met his as the child clung to his mother's neck. The neck that had driven him wild all those years ago... And again just moments before.

'You need to leave.' The groom tugged him round. 'You weren't invited and no one wants you here.'

'Take your hands off me,' he managed as he broke the man's hold.

He swung back. He had to follow her, and the boy, but his movements were stiff and mechanical. His racing heart punched his chest wall, the residual surge of heat—always there when he thought of her—only disturbing him more.

O'Riordan grabbed his arm this time. 'Come back here, you son of a...'

Ross turned, his fist clenched, ready to swat the bastard like a fly, but he couldn't seem to think coherently, or coordinate his body, so when he aimed at the man's head, he missed.

The answering blow shot towards him so fast he had no chance to evade it. Pain exploded in his jaw, his head snapping back.

The fog darkened.

'That's an impressive right hook,' he murmured, holding his burning face, a metallic taste filling his mouth as he staggered backwards.

The cries of assorted guests and Katie's tear-streaked

face were the last things he was aware of as he collapsed into an oddly welcome oblivion.

But as he dropped into the abyss, one last coherent thought tortured him.

How can she have given me a child...when I can never be anyone's father?

CHAPTER TWO

'GET OUT OF my way. You said yourself there are no signs of a concussion, so I would like to leave now.'

'But Mr De Courtney, I think it's best if you rest a while. You're clearly exhausted.'

'I'm not staying.'

Carmel O'Riordan stood in the hallway of Kildaragh Castle's east wing, stricken by the buzz in her abdomen at the sound of that deep, authoritative voice as Ross De Courtney argued with the paramedic Con had called after their uninvited wedding guest had been carried to this bedroom on the second floor.

She sank back against the wall, eavesdropping on the conversation, and tried to get up the guts to walk into the room… And confront her past.

The wedding had gone ahead, and now the reception was in full swing downstairs. But she still hadn't got over the shock of seeing Ross De Courtney again. Or discovering that Mac's father—a man whose identity she had never revealed to anyone, least of all her brother Conall—was also her new sister-in-law's brother.

She pressed damp palms to the thin silk of her bridesmaid's dress. Her fingers were shaking, because she couldn't get the picture out of her head of Ross's face, those sharp iridescent blue-green eyes going wide with surprise then dazed with shock as he'd looked upon her son—*their* son—for the first time twenty minutes ago.

Would that memory be lodged in her brain now for all eternity? Like all the others that had derailed her so many times in the last four years?

The sight of Ross De Courtney—tall and debonair in a dark tuxedo illuminated by the soft glow of torch light in an apple orchard, his gaze locked on hers, his touch tender and yet insatiable. His scent musky and addictive. His voice low with command and thick with desire. Each recollection gilded by the devastating heat and the wayward emotions that had intoxicated her.

She'd been such a fool that night, having gatecrashed Westmoreland's famous ball on the outskirts of London with her college friend Cheryl. All the way there in the car Cheryl had borrowed, they'd been busy joking about finding a billionaire to marry.

But then the joke had turned on her.

Ross De Courtney had been so handsome, so hot, so sophisticated and so into her—enjoying her bolshy sense of humour, never taking his eyes off her... He'd made her feel special and so, so grown up. After years of being desperate to feel like a woman instead of a girl, and finally get away from her brother Conall's overprotective custody, it had been so easy to believe it had all been real... Instead of a trick of the sultry summer night, her idiotic naiveté and her hyperactive hormones, which had homed in on him the minute she'd walked into the party and seen him standing alone. Ross had been moody and intense and hopelessly exciting—like Heathcliff and Mr Darcy and that vampire fella from *Twilight* all rolled into one.

She could still feel his touch on her skin, that sure, urgent excitement that had flowed through her like an electric current and made her do stupid things.

But then she'd run away, like an immature little fool.

And hadn't even given a thought to protection until three weeks later, when her period had failed to arrive.

'Now where the hell are my shoes?'

The brittle words from inside the room cut through Carmel's brutal trip down memory lane.

She swallowed around the lump forming in her throat and curled her fingers into fists to stop them shaking. She couldn't stand in the hallway for ever. She needed to face this man. Truth was, she probably didn't have that long before Conall came barging up the stairs to 'protect' her. Katie might have an amazing effect on her brother, but even she wasn't going to be able to hold him back for ever when he was in 'mother bear' mode.

Her brother had crossed so many lines. He'd hired a damn private detective to discover the identity of the man she had always refused to name. When he'd discovered Ross De Courtney was Mac's daddy, he'd then hired Ross's sister Katie as an event planner for their sister Imelda's wedding to her childhood sweetheart, Donal, in December. But he'd never really intended for Katie to plan a wedding. What he'd *really* been about was finding a way to get vengeance on the man who had fathered her son. A vengeance Carmel had never asked for and Conall had no right to claim.

But then, instead of getting vengeance on Ross, Conall had fallen in love with Katie. And now Ross was integrated into her and Mac's lives—for ever—by virtue of his relationship to Conall's new wife.

The fact that neither Con nor Katie had thought to tell her any of this before *their* wedding had infuriated her downstairs. But now all she felt was numb. And scared.

Ross De Courtney had rejected Mac before he was even born. Had accused her of lying about the pregnancy in a single damning text—the shock of which had taken her years to overcome. But she'd never forgotten a single

word of his cruel instant reply after she'd worked up the
courage to inform him of her pregnancy.

If you're pregnant, the child isn't mine. So if this is an attempt to extort money from me you're all out of luck.

How was she going to protect Mac from that rejection
now? When Ross De Courtney was so closely related to
her brother's wife?

But he hadn't looked dismissive or angry twenty minutes ago when he'd first set eyes on Mac. He'd looked
absolutely stunned.

She needed to get to the bottom of that look, because
it made no sense. Not only that, but that devastating text
didn't make quite so much sense now either.

He'd accused her of terrible things, it was true, things
she hadn't done. But there was no mistaking, she had
come on to him that night.

He hadn't stolen her innocence, as her brother Conall
liked to assume. She'd offered it to him, willingly.

She'd flirted with him mercilessly. She'd revelled in
the role of virgin temptress and the way he'd made her
feel. But as soon as the afterglow had faded, and the emotional impact had come crashing in on her, she'd run—
like the little girl she was.

Virgin temptress, my butt. Virgin eejit more like.

All of which left enough grey areas now to make her
question the conclusions she'd drawn about her child's
father. What if he wasn't the out-and-out villain she'd
assumed him to be? Whatever way she looked at it, the
man was Mac's father. Had she been a coward to avoid
addressing that reality in the years since? Coasting along
on the assumption he didn't want to know his son thanks
to one text. What if he had genuinely believed Mac wasn't
his? She hadn't even considered that possibility before.

Had simply assumed he'd wanted to be rid of her, hadn't wanted to live up to his responsibilities and had found the cruellest possible way to dump her and forget about that night.

But what if the truth were more complicated?

She tapped her clenched fist against the door. 'Can I come in?' she said, steeling herself against the inevitable reaction as she stepped into the room, without waiting for a reply.

She hadn't steeled herself enough.

Sensation blindsided her as Ross De Courtney's head turned, and those vivid eyes fixed on her face. She took in his dishevelled appearance—the half-open shirt speckled with blood revealing a tantalising glimpse of chest hair, the scuffed trousers, the shoeless feet, the roughened chestnut hair furrowed into haphazard rows, and the darkening bruise on his jaw.

She drew in a sharp breath to reinflate her lungs.

How could the man look even more gorgeous now than he had that night? How was that fair?

He didn't say anything, he simply stared at her, the harsh line of his lips flattening. There was no antagonism there, but neither was there welcome. And it occurred to her for the first time that, however incredible their one night together had been—and it *had* been incredible—Ross De Courtney had always been impossible to read.

He'd been focussed solely on her that night, but she'd never for a moment known what he was thinking. And that disturbed her even more now.

'Ms O'Riordan, perhaps you can talk some sense into my patient.' The middle-aged paramedic who stood beside Ross spoke and she noticed him for the first time. 'I believe Mr De Courtney should rest a bit...'

'It's okay...um... Joe, is it?' she said, gathering enough of her wits about her to read the poor harassed paramedic's name badge. 'You can leave us. If Mr De Courtney shows any signs of blacking out again, I'll call you immediately.'

The older man glanced at his reluctant patient, then nodded. 'Fine, I'll be leaving you to it, then.'

The door closed behind him with a dull thud, which reverberated in her chest.

Was she the only one who could feel the awareness crackling in the air like an electrical force field? The last time they'd been alone together, she'd still been struggling to cope with the after-effects of an orgasm so intense she was sure she must have passed out herself for a moment.

An orgasm from an encounter that had produced the most precious thing in her life.

The significance of that now though, and the fact she could still feel the residual heat from that encounter so long ago, only increased her fear. She clamped down on the agonising swell of sensation and the tangle of nerves in her gut as she held out her hand to indicate one of the suite's armchairs. A hand she was pleased to see trembled only slightly.

'Do you want to take a seat, Mr De Courtney?' she said, drawing on every last ounce of her composure to maintain some semblance of dignity.

'*Mr* De Courtney?' he said, his tone more sharp than surprised. *'Really?'*

'I'm trying to be polite,' she snapped as the strain took its toll.

Seriously? Did he want to make this even tougher than it was already?

'Why?' he asked, as if he really didn't know.

'Because my mammy insisted upon manners at all times, and I'm trying to live by her example,' she snapped back, because an inane question deserved an inane answer. 'Don't be an *eejit*. Why do you think?'

'I don't know,' he said, looking a lot more composed than she felt. 'That's why I asked.'

'Okay, then, if you want plain speaking it's because polite seemed preferable to punching you on the jaw again,' she said, even though it wasn't aggression she felt towards him but something much more confusing.

There were a myriad emotions running through her, and not one of them was as simple as anger. Unfortunately.

He looked away, then tugged his fingers through his hair. 'I wouldn't blame you if you did,' he murmured, the resignation as clear as the frustration.

'Why would you say that?' she asked, far too aware of the livid bruise spreading across his jaw. 'Con shouldn't have hit you. He had no right.'

However confusing her emotions were towards this man, she had a new appreciation of him now after asking his sister Katie downstairs if she thought her brother was a bad man… Because she had needed to know his sister's opinion before she confronted him.

And Katie's reply, while angering Conall—who had decided Ross De Courtney was a villain of the first order—had been a lot more nuanced. Apparently she and Ross had been estranged for five years—after her marriage to her first husband, which Ross hadn't approved of. But she had pointed out he had acknowledged her as a teenager as soon as he discovered her existence and paid for a string of expensive schools and governesses. So, although they had never been close, it had surprised Katie when Conall told her that Ross had refused to acknowledge Mac.

Ross had come to Kildaragh to stop the wedding. Carmel had no idea why exactly but, given the obvious animosity between him and Conall as soon as he had appeared, she suspected it stemmed from some misguided desire to protect his sister from a marriage to her brother. The man had no knowledge of why her brother had reacted so aggressively towards him all those months ago when they first met, so that much at least made some sort of sense.

'He had every right,' Ross said, as his gaze locked back on hers. He searched her face, sending that disconcerting heat through her again. 'He's your brother.'

'That's madness,' she said, suddenly a little tired of the big brothers' code of honour. What gave men the right to make decisions about the women in their lives? And wasn't it beyond ironic he should support Conall's Neanderthal behaviour—given that he appeared to have come to Ireland to protect his sister from the same. 'Con did not have the right to interfere in my—'

'Is the boy mine?' he cut into her diatribe, slicing right through her indignation to the tender heart of the matter.

It hurt her to realise he didn't sound happy at the prospect, merely resigned.

She straightened.

'Yes, Mac is your son,' she said, refusing to be cowed by his underwhelming reaction.

Mac was the best thing to have happened to her, ever. A sweet, kind, funny, brave and bold little fella who was so much more than just someone's son. Maybe this man didn't feel the same way about him. But then he didn't know him… And, she had realised in the last hour, she had to take some of the responsibility for that. 'We can do a DNA test if you still don't believe me,' she snapped.

'That won't be necessary,' he said, taking the offer at face value and apparently unconcerned by the caustic tone. 'He looks just as I did at that age.'

He sat down heavily in the chair she had indicated. Not sat, so much as collapsed, as if all the breath had been yanked out of his lungs. He ran his fingers through his hair again, scraping it back from his forehead.

She noticed the exhaustion for the first time, in the bruised smudges beneath his eyes, the slumped line of his broad shoulders. And despite the anger she wanted to feel towards him, all she could feel in that moment was pity.

Because he didn't look resigned any more, he looked shattered.

She took the seat across from him, her legs shaky now too. She thought she'd been prepared to deal with this rejection again. Might even have hoped for it, as she made her way up to the suite, with every possible outcome from this meeting bouncing through her brain. Did she really want to allow Ross De Courtney a role in Mac's life? Wouldn't it be better if he didn't want to be Mac's father? Had no interest in getting to know him? Then she wouldn't have to deal with all the messy emotions of forming a relationship with a man who had devastated her once already. Or figure out if he should be a part of Mac's life. Because no matter whether he was Mac's biological father, that didn't give him any rights, in her opinion, unless she decided he was worthy of that place.

Wouldn't it be much easier not to have to make any of those decisions? To just go on as before?

But somehow, seeing his reaction, all she felt was devastated that he had no concept of how precious Mac was.

'Why were you so convinced I was lying,' she asked, attempting to keep her thoughts on Mac—and what was best for him, 'when I texted you?'

His head rose and she saw something flash in his gaze before he masked it. Regret? Sadness? Pain? It was impossible to tell.

He stared back at his hands, now clasped in his lap. His shoulders tightened into a rigid line. And she sensed the battle being waged. He didn't want to answer her question. But then he scrubbed his open palms down his face, cursed softly under his breath and straightened. The look he sent her was both direct and dispassionate.

'I did not believe the boy could possibly be mine, because I had myself sterilised, a decade ago, when I was twenty-one years old to avoid this ever happening.'

'You… What? But… *Why?*'

Ross could see the horror on Carmel O'Riordan's face. A face that had haunted his dreams for years, but, now it was in front of him, caused so many mixed emotions. All of them so far outside his comfort zone he was struggling to think with any clarity whatsoever.

She looked radiant, he thought, grimly. That vibrant russet hair, lit by the sunlight coming through the castle's casement windows, which made the red and gold tones even more vivid than they had been that night. Her pale skin was sprinkled with freckles he hadn't noticed four years ago in the moonlight. Had she covered them with make-up?

'Why would you do such a thing at such a young age?' she asked again.

He dragged his gaze away from her beauty. He'd fallen under that spell once before, and it had led them both here.

'A lot of reasons,' he said. Reasons he had no intention of elaborating on. He hadn't even wanted to tell her of the procedure he'd had done as soon as he could convince a doctor he knew what he was doing. But he figured he owed her the truth, to explain—if not condone—the mistakes he'd made four years ago. 'Anyway, my reasons are irrelevant now, because the procedure obviously didn't work.'

Once he got back to New York, he would have himself properly checked out. He'd never done any of the follow-up appointments. At the time he'd told himself he was far too busy, dealing with taking over the reins of De Courtney's and trying to drag it into the twenty-first century after his father's death. But looking back now, he could admit he'd found the constant prodding and poking emasculating—which would be ironic if it weren't so pathetic. He'd made the decision he did not ever want to get a woman pregnant, but he'd seen no need to dwell on it. He'd been a young man after all, foolish and impulsive and arrogant. As long as he could still get an erection, he had been more than happy after the effects of the operation had worn off.

And now he was a father. Responsible for another human life, who shared his DNA, and who would carry on the De Courtney line whether he wished it to be carried on or not. Although even that seemed a total irrelevance now. The reasons he'd based his decision on so long ago were all completely beside the point now that a little boy existed with his face and his blood...

'You don't...' He looked up to see her already pale skin had become ashen. 'You don't have some kind of genetic disease, do you? That you didn't want to pass on?'

'No.' *At least, not a biological one.*

'Oh, thank goodness.' Her shoulders slumped with relief. And he realised she had been terrified for her son. He waited for her to repeat her question about why he'd done it, but she surprised him. 'Do you think you might have other children you don't know about?'

The tremulous question, delivered in a gentle whisper, forced him to engage again, and answer her, when the thing he most wanted to do was disengage.

It had always been so much easier to deny his demons even existed, and now he was going to be forced to face them by a woman who could turn his insides to molten lava with a single breathless look.

The heat swelled and glowed in his abdomen, as it had an hour ago, when he'd got fixated on the back of her neck.

What was that even about? How could he still want her, when she had just turned his life upside down and inside out?

Nice try, you bastard. It wasn't her that did this, you did it to yourself. By being an arrogant, careless, entitled idiot who thought he could control his own fate.

'No,' he murmured. 'There won't be any others. You're the only woman I've ever had unprotected sex with,' he added, then stared back at his hands, aware of the pulsing ache in his jaw from her brother's punch as he clenched his teeth against the tidal wave of shame.

Exactly how desperate had he been to have her that night? Why hadn't he observed any of the danger signs, when he'd become so enchanted, so mesmerised, so addicted to her sultry smoky laugh, her quick wit and irreverent humour, that soft melodic accent, the earthy scent of her arousal?

Carmel O'Riordan was a stunning woman. Even more beautiful now than she had been then—but what the heck had got into him that night to make him forget every one of his own rules? And so quickly? Why had he been focussed solely on the need to plunge into her, to claim her, brand her, make her his? Because his behaviour had been nothing short of deranged, and he was very much afraid he still hadn't got a good firm grip on his attraction to her even now.

'Well, I guess that's good to know,' she said.

She brushed the tendrils back from her face, the nervous gesture oddly endearing.

He unlocked his jaw, to say what he should have said as soon as she came in.

'I owe you an apology, for that text,' he said. 'It was

unforgivable.' He threaded his fingers through his hair for about the five thousandth time that day gathering the courage to get it all out. 'And I owe your brother an apology too.'

Her brows launched up her forehead. 'Why on earth would you owe Con an apology?'

'I came here today to talk some sense into my sister, convinced Conall O'Riordan was a violent, volatile, controlling man who might do her harm, based on our one chance meeting in London months ago. I'm guessing now that at the time we met at the opera he already knew my connection to you, and his nephew?'

She nodded. 'Yes, apparently he did, he hired a private detective to find out your identity after I refused to tell him who you were. The arrogant—'

'I see,' he said, to halt her insults, not sure why the fact she hadn't divulged his name all those years ago should make the ache in his jaw move into his ribcage.

Why hadn't she told O'Riordan who he was when she found herself pregnant and alone? And why hadn't she ever followed up that text to demand a DNA test? All this time she had been surviving without any support from him... And okay, perhaps she didn't need his financial support—after all, her brother was a wealthy man—but still, the child had always been his responsibility, not her brother's. No wonder the man had looked as if he wanted to castrate him all those months ago in London. He'd had good cause.

'It doesn't matter how your brother discovered my identity,' he continued, rubbing the spot on his chest where the ache had centred.

He'd spent his whole life, determined not to be like his father, not to be as cruel or callous or controlling. Ross had prided himself on always keeping things light and non-committal with women, which was why his reaction to Carmel O'Riordan had bothered him so much. But he could see now how low he'd set the bar for himself, and with that text to Carmel—when she had informed him of her pregnancy—he'd failed to rise even to that pitiful level.

'The way your brother spoke to me that evening was not unprovoked as I had assumed. Nor was it born of a desire to isolate or control my sister's associations with me. Instead, he was motivated by a desire to protect you from a man he knew had wronged you, terribly.' He cringed inwardly. Good lord, the ironies just kept piling up. 'Which makes my presence here—and my attempt to interfere in your brother's marriage to my sister—wrong on every level.'

He stood and grabbed his jacket off the bed, the battle to maintain a semblance of control and ignore the claustrophobic weight starting to crush his ribs all but impossible. He needed time and space to deal with the emotions still churning inside him. Only then would he be able to figure out the best way to make amends, to her and her family and the boy. 'Which is my cue to leave, hopefully with more dignity than when I arrived,' he said. 'Although that could be a problem as I can't locate my shoes,' he added, the pathetic attempt at humour falling flat when her huge blue eyes widened and her brows rose further up her forehead. 'Perhaps you could speak to the paramedic and find out where he put them?'

'Wait a minute…' Carmel leapt to her feet—and placed her hands on her hips in a stubborn stance that accentuated her stunning figure in the slinky bridesmaid's dress.

The ache sank into his abdomen. *Great.*

'You're leaving?' she demanded. 'Just like that? Are you mad?' she said, her accent thickening.

Why did that fiery outrage only make her more irresistible? When he'd never been a man to appreciate any form of discord. Especially not with women he was dating... Not that he was dating her, he reminded himself, forcefully.

'What about Cormac?' she said.

'Who's Cormac?' he asked.

'Your son,' she snapped back with all the passion he could see sparking in her eyes.

Yes, of course.

He frowned, wondering how he had managed to forget about the huge elephant in the room, which was now pressing down on his chest again like a ten-ton weight. Score two to the heat pulsing in his pants. Yet more reason to be exceptionally wary of it.

'My legal team will be in touch as soon as I return to New York,' he said, determined to be as fair as he could be.

There was no way to repay her for what he had done, but he wanted to be as generous as possible. In fact, he would have to insist on it.

'If you'd like to make an accounting of your expenditure up to now, I will pay you the full amount...as I consider the error that resulted in your pregnancy to be mine. You can rest assured the maintenance I will pay for you and the boy going forward—and the trust fund I will set up for him—should ensure you and he will never want for anything ever again.'

CHAPTER THREE

AN ACCOUNTING? THE ERROR? What the actual...?

Carmel could feel her head exploding. She was so furious with the man in front of her, talking in that crisp, clear, completely passionless tone about her beautiful little boy—*their* beautiful little boy. Did he believe making an accounting of profit and loss would absolve him of his responsibilities as Mac's father? *Really?*

The outrage queued up in her throat like a stick of dynamite, stopping any coherent words from coming out of her mouth. She glared at him as he spotted his shoes under a chair and slipped them on, obviously intending to simply walk out of the door.

As he stepped past her she threw up her hands and slammed them against his chest, knocking him back a step. The ripple of reaction shot down her spine, at the flex of muscle and sinew, the whiff of his familiar scent—woodsy aftershave and soap—that got caught in her throat right beside the dynamite.

'Where do you think you're going?' she growled as the outrage exploded out of her mouth.

'Manhattan,' he offered.

'But you can't just go, this isn't over. I don't want an accounting. When did I ask you for money?' she shouted as her outrage grew like a wild beast.

She gripped his shirt front, far too conscious of the

awareness in his eyes and the electric energy flowing between them as his muscles tensed.

'You didn't,' he said, still calm, still dispassionate, even though the fire in his gaze was telling her he was as affected by the contact as she was.

He gripped her wrists, disengaged her hands from his torn shirt, but the feel of his thumbs touching her thundering pulse points sent her senses into overdrive—only making her more mad.

'But that's hardly the point,' he added, letting her wrists go to step away from her, as if she were a bomb about to detonate. 'I owe you a considerable amount for the boy's upkeep.'

'The boy has a name. It's Mac, or Little Mac, or Cormac when he's being naughty and I have to get stern with him.' She was babbling, but it was the only way to keep the outrage and the hurt at bay.

He blinked, as if the information was a complete anathema to him. 'I see,' he said, but she knew he really didn't see. There was so much she wanted to tell him about his child. Did he really not want to know any of it?

'And he doesn't need your money. What he needs is a father.'

He stiffened then, and his jaw tensed, his expression guarded. But she could still see the fire in his eyes. 'I'm afraid I can't offer him that,' he said, still not saying their child's name. 'I'm not capable of being anyone's father, other than in a financial sense.'

Oh, for the love of...

She cursed under her breath, suddenly sick of his platitudes and evasions.

'How could you possibly know that if you've never even tried?' she asked, exasperated now as well as angry.

Why did he have himself sterilised as a young man?

He hadn't given her an explanation, clearly hadn't

wanted to. But she found it hard to believe such a momentous decision could have been a frivolous one.

But still, he hadn't said he didn't *want* to be a father, he'd said he wasn't *capable* of being one. Which were two very different things. Maybe she was clutching at straws here, wanting to see more in him than was there. But there was a definite disconnect between a man who would fly thousands of miles to disrupt a wedding to save his sister from a man he believed might abuse her and the man who had barely spoken to the same sister in years. It made no sense. And Carmel had always been someone who had looked for sense in everything... Ever since her mother had taken her own life and everyone—her brother included—had resolutely refused to talk about it.

She hated secrets. She had always believed that talking about stuff openly and honestly was the only way to get to the heart of the matter and fix what was broken. Which was precisely why being unable to talk openly and honestly to her family, and more importantly her son, about his father over the last four years had been so damaging.

That ended now.

She had made mistakes too. Instead of allowing his one brutal text to make her a coward, and shielding her heart from more pain, she should have followed it up. Demanded to know why he had reacted so callously...

Well, she wasn't running any more.

'I don't need to try, when I know I won't be any good at it,' he said, through gritted teeth now, clearly holding onto his temper with an effort.

Good. Temper was better than the calm, controlled mask she'd been treated to so far—with his brittle apologies and his complete failure to explain his motivations. He was going to have to do a lot better than that before he'd be rid of her.

'How do you know?' she tried again.

'Because I just do,' he said, as stubborn as ever.

'Well, I don't believe that.' He'd never even met Mac, so how could he possibly know whether they would bond or not? But she didn't say as much. Because she had no intention of letting him bond with her precious child before she knew a lot more about him. But one thing she did know was that she was not about to let him buy off his paternal responsibilities as Mac's father either. The way he had clearly done with his fraternal responsibilities when he found out about his sister's existence. According to Katie, Ross had paid for expensive schools, tutors, governesses, even college, but he had never given her much of his time.

'No one knows if they'll be any good at parenthood until they have to do it,' she added. If all he felt right now towards Mac was responsibility, that was at least a start. Something they could work with. 'You have to learn on the job. Do you really think I thought I could be a mother at nineteen?'

His eyes widened and he winced. 'You were *nineteen* that night?' He ran his fingers through his hair, the blood draining out of his face. 'Good God, you were a child.'

'Nonsense,' she shot back.

He's worse than Conall. Men and their white knight complexes!

'I was a woman fully grown, with a woman's wants and needs...' Maybe she'd been naïve and foolish, and more than a little starstruck by him. But she'd known full well what she was doing and she'd enjoyed every second of it. Until the emotional consequences had hit home. 'And I believe I proved it rather comprehensively. As I recall, you were as well satisfied as I was that night,' she added, something about his concern making her feel like that reckless girl again. 'In fact, I should probably thank you,' she added, unable to stop herself from rubbing it in. 'I've heard tell from friends that a woman's first time is rarely as good as you made mine.'

'You were a virgin as well?' He hissed the words, shock turning to horror.

'Not for long,' she said, feeling like the badass she was when he cursed and slumped back into the chair.

Holding his head in his hands, he groaned. 'I'm surprised your brother didn't take out a contract on me after he found out my identity,' he said. 'Right now, I'd like to take one out on myself.'

The abject regret in his voice, the flags of shameful colour on his tanned cheeks had her going with instinct and reaching out to touch his shoulder. 'There's no need to take on so over it,' she said. 'When I was the one who came on to you?'

Yes, she'd been a little younger than him and hopelessly inexperienced, but she'd wanted to lose her virginity that night. And it had been spectacular, so she had no regrets about that much.

'Did you?' he said, his brows flattening in a grim line.

The doubt in his tone should have annoyed her more. She'd known her own mind that night, and she refused to let him take that power away from her just because he'd been her first and she'd been younger than he thought. But his gallantry was also intriguing. For a man who professed to be incapable of parenthood, he seemed to have a strong moral code.

'I'm not sure you did,' he said. 'All I can remember is I wanted you more than I'd ever wanted any woman before as soon as I set eyes on you. Damn it, Carmel, I took you against a tree your first time. Without using protection and without properly checking how old you were. It sickens me to even think of it.'

'You asked me my age twice, and both times I lied,'

she supplied, her heart pulsing strangely alongside the
heat that refused to dim at the force in his statement.

*'I wanted you more than I'd ever wanted any woman
before as soon as I set eyes on you.'*

So she *had* been special to him, at least in one respect.
Good to know she wasn't the only one who had been
blindsided by their physical chemistry.

'You did everything short of asking me for my ID,' she
continued. 'As I had a very good fake one on me, even if
you had, it wouldn't have done any good.'

'If I asked you twice, I must have suspected you
weren't telling me the truth,' he said. 'Can't you see how
wrong that is?'

'No, I can't.' She stood and strode across the room,
suddenly needing to move, the pulsing at her core threatening to become as distracting now as it had been then.

It didn't matter if their chemistry was still strong, in-
dulging it again was not an option. Not when their son
would be caught in the middle. All of which meant talking about the events of that night—however satisfying
she found it to goad him—probably was not a good idea,
because it brought those needs and desires back into sharp
focus.

She had a vibrator to quench that thirst now. She didn't
need him. Or any man, and it would be best if she remembered that.

'But anyway, we're getting off the point,' she said,
suddenly desperate to turn the conversation back to the
matter at hand.

'What *was* the point exactly?' he asked.

'That I'm not going to let you give me or Mac any of
your money.'

'What? That's preposterous.' He stood and crossed
the room towards her. She held her ground, determined

not to be swayed—even though she didn't know another man who wore righteous indignation as well.

Really, had he ever looked hotter? With his torn shirt and the stormy expression in those vivid aquamarine eyes finally making him look how she had always remembered him. Gone was the dispassionate control of moments ago, the brittle apology and the chilling cruelty of that text. This was the man she had met that night—exciting, forthright, determined and, oh, so passionate.

Okay, passion is so not the issue here, Mel.

Getting past that chilling control was what mattered, because she wanted to know him, not the masks he wore.

'On the contrary, we've just established how much I owe you,' he said. 'Not just for the child but also for what I did to you that night.'

The child? Why couldn't he say their son's name?

'In fairness, we've established no such thing,' she pointed out. 'All we've established is that you have a white knight complex almost as overdeveloped as my brother's. And that you think you can rid yourself of your paternal responsibilities to Mac by putting them into a neat little box called expenses paid. Well, I'm telling you, you can't.'

'What the hell does that even mean? I'm the boy's father. I have a responsibility towards him. And to you for what I took from you that night.'

'And as I've told you just now, you took nothing from me that I was not willing to give. And you gave me the most precious thing in my life in return, so you can consider that column already paid off.'

'Stop being deliberately facetious.' He glared at her, his expression thunderous. 'That's not what I'm offering and you know it.'

Oh, yes, it is, Ross, why can't you see that?

She stifled the wave of sympathy at how emotionally obtuse he appeared to be. And went for the jugular.

'If you don't wish to have a relationship with Mac, I'll certainly not force you to have one. The last thing I want is a father for my son who isn't interested in being one.' She knew what that was like, because her own mother had struggled to bond with her and Imelda and even Con. It hadn't been her mother's fault. But that didn't alter the awful effect her mother's emotional neglect had had on her and her siblings.

Con had closed himself off to emotion, Imelda had become lost in her own fantasy world. And she'd become wild and difficult, and hopelessly self-destructive. Because buried deep in her subconscious had been the certainty there must have been something terribly wrong with her if her own mother couldn't love her. Of course, she had come to see more clearly, after becoming a mother herself, it was her mother's depression that had robbed them both of that crucial connection.

She would never willingly subject her son to the same neglect, if something similar afflicted Ross that he was unwilling or unable to address. But that said, there was enough that didn't add up to make her wonder if Ross *could* be a father despite his protestations...

'Then what are we even arguing about?' he asked, even more exasperated.

'Simply this. If you're not prepared to be a father to Cormac, you can leave now and never see or speak to him or me again. But if you do that, I will not allow you to give him money. No maintenance, no trust fund, no generous allowance. Mac needs a daddy, not a piggy bank. You can be both, or you can be neither. And that's my final word on it.'

'*Your* final word?' Ross had to clench his teeth to stop himself from yelling, so frustrated, and frankly furious, he would not have been surprised if actual steam had started pouring from his ears.

Good God, she was the most incorrigible, intractable and stubborn woman he'd ever met. So intractable she seemed determined to harm herself as well as her son's best interests simply to make some asinine point.

'Yes,' she said, her chin popping out as if she needed to reiterate said asinine point. 'Take it or leave it.'

Right now, what he'd like to do was kiss that stubborn pout off her lips until she...

He cut off the insane direction of his thoughts as the damning heat spread through his system like wildfire.

Great, he was actually losing his mind. It was official.

He turned his back on her and crossed the room to stare out of the window. The waves crashed onto the rocks below them, echoing his turbulent mood.

Terrific, even the damn landscape is mocking me now.

He dragged his fingers through his hair, trying to calm his breathing, and dowse the heat once and for all so he could think.

At this rate, I'll be lucky if I'm not bald by the end of today.

He shoved his hands into the pockets of his trousers, far too aware of her standing behind him, waiting for an answer.

Unfortunately, she had him over a barrel. Even if she didn't know it yet.

Because there was no way in hell he could simply walk away from this situation, now. Not with his sense of honour intact. Not after everything that had transpired four years ago—and his damning role in it. Because that really would make him as much of a monster as his father.

He'd destroyed Carmel O'Riordan's innocence four years ago.

Perhaps she had been willing and able to make her

own decisions despite her youth and lack of experience...
But he had exploited the physical connection between
them ruthlessly, kissing and caressing her fragrant flesh
in every place he knew would stoke her desire to fever
pitch. That her artless, eager response had managed to
set fire to his own libido—until he'd lost every ounce
of his usual caution—was ultimately his responsibility
too, because she'd had no idea at the time what she was
doing to him.

To compound his crimes, he had then treated her ap-
pallingly with that knee-jerk text and there was also the
boy to consider. A helpless, innocent child who hadn't
chosen this situation. The only way he could live with
himself was if he provided the boy—his son—with all the
support he could ever need. Financially, at least.

So how did he persuade her he was not capable of
being a father, that her son would be much better off without him in his life? He supposed he could explain the truth
about his legacy, the barren emotional landscape of his
own childhood. But he had humiliated himself enough for
one day already with the confidences he'd been forced to
share. And he suspected even if he told her the truth about
his upbringing and how unsuitable it made him for the
role she wished him to consider, it wouldn't be enough.
Because Carmel O'Riordan appeared to be as stubborn
as her brother's right hook.

Not only that, but he had no desire to unearth memories he had buried a lifetime ago.

He blew out a breath, struggling to calm the wayward
emotions churning in his gut and find a tangible solution
to the impasse. His gaze focussed on the rhythm of the
surf, as it crashed against the rocks below, then retreated
down the beach of the small cove.

The spring sunshine glinted off the water, the vibrant
green Ireland was famous for carpeting the cliffs and

spreading over the castle's gardens. A few guests from the wedding were milling about near the entrance to the chapel. His gaze snagged on a small child with a couple, the woman noticeably pregnant. His heart stilled, his exhaustion and frustration momentarily forgotten as he watched the child, so active and carefree, dashing backwards and forwards as the man—a strapping redhead who looked uncomfortable in his suit—chased after him while the woman directed the action and appeared to be finding it extremely amusing. He squinted, the gritty fatigue making his eyes smart.

Wait a minute, is that boy...?

He turned swiftly away from the window, the pressure on his chest increasing, to find Carmel watching him with a disturbing intensity—almost as if she could see into his thoughts.

Good luck with that, he thought, careful to keep the turmoil of emotions off his face.

And suddenly, he knew the only solution to this impasse was to show her exactly what kind of emotional connections he was and was not capable of.

With her hip cocked and her arms crossed, her stance accentuated her lithe figure. The sun shone off her haphazard hairdo and gave her fair skin a lustrous glow. But this time, instead of steeling himself against the inevitable spike to his libido, he welcomed it.

He could do sex. He couldn't do commitment. He never had—which was why that energetic, carefree little boy was much better off without a man like him in his life. That was the truth of the matter, and the only truth Carmel O'Riordan needed to understand.

She was clearly a smart and forthright woman. It was one of the things he'd found so compelling about her that night, her ability to speak her mind with wit and courage and refreshingly little thought to the consequences.

It had amused him and intrigued him and aroused him immensely, perhaps because he had always been forced to guard his own emotions so carefully.

But—although she'd had to grow up far too fast in the years since—she still seemed to be hopelessly naïve about men.

'I think the problem we have, Carmel, is that you don't know me,' he ventured. 'We've had one...' *Exciting? Mind-blowing? Cataclysmic?* He cleared his throat, to give himself time to search for the appropriate adjective. 'Diverting night together. And not much else. Perhaps you should spend some time with me? Then you'd realise I'm not a man you would want in your life long-term.' He stepped closer and touched his thumb to her cheek. She sucked in a breath, her eyes darkening, as he hooked one errant tendril behind her ear, then forced himself to drop his hand. The contact had been electrifying, just as he had expected it would be, making his point for him admirably. 'Nor am I father material.'

It was a dare, pure and simple. A dare he doubted she would accept.

The spark was still there, waiting to explode all over again. And given what that had led to last time, how could she afford to risk reigniting the flame?

She gave her head a slight shake, as if she had gone into a trance and was waking up again. He watched the emotions flit across her face—surprise, confusion, yearning...and panic as the penny dropped.

Bingo.

However naïve she was, or inexperienced she had been then, she knew full well they would both be playing with fire if she accepted his offer.

He pressed his hands back into his pockets, to resist the powerful urge to touch her again. And ignored the strange ambivalence at the realisation she would not accept his impulsive offer.

But then her true-blue eyes sparkled with the same recklessness he had once admired so much and her lips pursed in a thin line of determination.

'I accept, I think that's a grand idea,' she said. 'Spending time with you in your home would be the best way to assess your lifestyle as well as your suitability to be a daddy to Mac. I can come with you today if you'd like as Mac is already supposed to be spending this week with my sister, Immy, and her husband, Donal, while I finish a commission. Would it be okay if I brought my paints with me, so I can work?'

'You want to come with me? Today?' he said, astonished not just by her reckless decision, but also by the brutal wave of arousal. 'And stay for a week?'

'Yes. Where do you live?' she asked.

'New York,' he croaked, the blood diving south as he envisioned her in his condo in Tribeca. It was a big space, but hardly big enough to house them both without him being far too aware of her presence. He'd never invited any woman into his home for any length of time. Sleepovers at his apartment and the occasional weekender at his estate in the Hamptons were fine, but nothing more than that. When it came to women, he preferred to hold all the cards. But it already felt as if he had somehow dropped the ace.

'Really? I've never been to New York before. I've heard it's glorious.' She pushed her hair back from her face, the flush lighting her cheeks and the nervous gesture suggesting she wasn't as composed as she was making out—which was some consolation, but not much.

'I'll need a bit of time to pack and square things with Mac and my family.' She huffed out a breath. 'Especially Conall. When do you want to leave?'

He stared at her. She was actually serious. She intended to come and spend a week with him in New York.

A part of him knew at this point he should call her bluff. Rescind the offer, because he had no real desire to open up his life or his motivations to her scrutiny, but something stopped him. Perhaps it was the emotional fatigue finally getting to him after the seven-hour overnight journey to Ireland on a mission to protect the sister he'd barely spoken to in years. Perhaps it was the shock of seeing the woman who had haunted his dreams for so long again and discovering he was a father, against all the odds. Or maybe it was the residual heat still humming in his groin. But whatever it was, he couldn't seem to think anything but... *To hell with it*. Perhaps this really was the best way to persuade her he could never be a father to her son.

'I'd like to leave as soon as possible,' he said. If she was coming, she needed to know her visit would be on his terms, not hers. 'Can you be ready in an hour?'

'Give me two,' she said. 'I'd like you to meet Mac before we leave. We won't tell him who you are. Not yet. But it should keep us both focussed on why we're doing this.'

Ya think?

Exactly how naïve was she? Did she really think him coming face to face with the boy would be enough to kill this incessant heat?

'Sure,' he said, deciding meeting the boy would be a good first step in persuading her he knew absolutely nothing about children.

But as she left the room, his gaze snagged on the subtle sway of her hips in the figure-hugging bridesmaid's gown and the heat swelled again.

Wonderful. The next week is going to be nothing short of torture and you have only yourself to blame.

CHAPTER FOUR

'YOU'RE NOT GOING. I won't allow it. Have you lost your mind?'

Mel glared at her older brother, feeling her hackles rising fast enough to break the land-speed record. If there was one thing Conall had always been an expert at, it was making her mad.

'Er...hello, Con? I'm a grown woman, and this is not your decision,' she replied, channelling a certainty about the trip she didn't remotely feel.

With Con's tie and tuxedo jacket gone and his skin slightly flushed from one too many toasts during the wedding feast, he should have looked more relaxed, but the muscle twitching in his jaw was suggesting the opposite. He'd stayed away from her meeting with Ross, given her the privacy she'd asked for. And she had to give him credit for that—or rather give Katie credit for it. Because she suspected Con's new wife had managed to drum some sense into him, and also provided a gorgeous distraction. Her new sister-in-law stood beside Con now, looking completely stunning in her wedding dress—and apparently not remotely concerned at the two of them for ruining even more of her special day with their family drama.

'You're also a mother,' her brother added, his tone darkening. 'Have you thought of that, now?' he finished, slicing right to the heart of her insecurities. Another of her brother's specialities.

She'd never left Mac for more than a night before. But they'd been building up to his week staying with Imelda and her husband Donal for weeks now—because her work had exploded in the last few months, and she had an important commission to finish. Conall was right, it would be impossibly hard to leave Mac for a week, but she also knew full well the separation was likely to be much harder for her than her son.

Mac had always been a supremely confident and out-going child. And she had her family to thank for that. They'd always been close-knit as siblings, having been orphaned when she and her sister were only eight and six and Con a young man of eighteen. They'd had a fair few rocky moments and some major blow ups in the years after her mother's death—with Conall as their guardian giving up what was left of his youth to become a mother and father to both her and Immy. But when she'd come home from London pregnant and alone that summer— and broken by Ross De Courtney's rejection—Imelda and Con hadn't hesitated to step up and help her heal. Sure, they'd judged, especially Con, but they'd also of-fered their unconditional support. Because of them, and now Donal and Katie too, Mac understood he was part of a much bigger unit than just the two of them. Surely that explained why he was such a robust, well-adjusted little guy, despite being the son of a nineteen-year-old single mum who'd had no clue what to do when he'd first been put into her tired arms after six excruciating hours of labour.

She knew how lucky she was to have such a solid, un-wavering support network—and she was grateful for it. But she also knew that if there was a chance Mac could have a father of his own, she wasn't wrong to explore that possibility. She'd already spoken to Imelda in detail about her plans to contact Mac every day over a video app—and if Imelda reported any signs of distress, she would come straight back to Ireland on the next flight.

But having Con look at her with that accusatory glare in his eye had her confidence wavering.

'Of course, I know that, Con,' she said with a firmness she didn't feel. 'But I'm doing this for Mac to see if there's a chance Ross can be a father to him,' she said, but she could hear the defensiveness. And the questions she hadn't wanted to address—ever since Ross had touched her and the yearning had exploded inside her—whispered across her consciousness.

What if spending time with Ross De Courtney made that hunger worse? A hunger she'd had no practice in controlling because, not only had she never felt such a thing for another man, she'd never had sexual relations with any other man either.

'Ah, so going off to spend a week with your ex-lover is in your son's best interests now, is it?' Conall said, scepticism dripping from every word. 'That sounds mighty convenient to me.'

She stared at him, wanting to be furious with his implication, but not quite able to be... Because, what if he was right? And that shocking blast of heat and yearning *was* the real reason she'd decided to accept Ross's invitation? An invitation that she was sure had been born of frustration rather than intent.

She'd hate herself if she was subconsciously harbouring some secret notion to get Ross De Courtney into her life, as well as her son's. It would make her sad and pathetic and weak. And totally misguided. Because if the man wasn't father material, he certainly wasn't cut out for any other form of committed relationship. But worst of all, it would remind her of the little girl she'd once been, wanting her mother to love her, even though she could not.

'Conall, stop,' Katie said gently but firmly, interrupting the panicked questions multiplying in Carmel's head. 'Carmel has every right to make decisions for herself and Mac without having to deal with the third degree from you.'

'For the love of…' Con swore under his breath. Katie barely blinked. 'Katherine, why are you siding with her now?' Conall asked, sounding aggrieved. 'Maybe your brother isn't the total gobshite I thought he was,' he added, because Carmel had shared with them Ross's reasons for thinking he couldn't possibly be Mac's father—the news of his vasectomy at the age of only twenty-one having stunned them both into silence. 'But he's still not a man I'd trust with my sister for a week in a foreign country,' he added, speaking to his wife as if Carmel weren't standing right there, before levelling her with a look that teetered uncomfortably between concern and condescension. 'The man's a player, Mel, and a billionaire one at that, who's never had a serious relationship with anyone in his life, not even with his own sister,' he added. 'On that evidence, I'm not convinced he could ever be a halfway decent parent to Mac…'

'Fair point,' she interrupted him. 'But I want a chance to find out for my—'

'I get that,' Con said, cutting off her explanation. 'You want Mac to have his daddy in his life if at all possible. And maybe De Courtney will surprise us on that score. But is jetting off to New York with him so you guys can spend a cosy week…' he lifted his fingers to do sarcastic air quotes '…"Getting to know each other" really the way to go? What does that even entail? Are you going to be sharing a bed with him now?'

'Conall!' Katie gasped.

At exactly the same moment Carmel shouted, 'That's none of your business, Con.'

Of all the pig-headed, intrusive... How dared he?

Outrage flooded through her system, pushing away her doubts—and the echoes of that sad little girl—to remind her of the woman she had become. 'But just so you know, the answer is no.'

She was being ridiculous, she decided. So *what* if she was still attracted to Ross De Courtney? Surely it was to be expected. After all, he was the only man she'd ever had sex with. And he was... She took a steadying breath, aware of the liquid weight that had been there ever since he'd walked back into her life two hours ago now. Well, the man was a total ride and he always had been.

But the important thing here wasn't Ross De Courtney's hotness, it was the fact that she wasn't that starstruck, needy, reckless nineteen-year-old any more—nor was she the little girl without a mother's love. She was a mother herself now, with her own thriving online business doing pet portraits—and she'd had her heart broken once before by Ross. In short, she was all grown up now. She'd worked hard to build a life for her and her son, and there was no way she'd throw it all away for some cheap thrills. However tempting.

'Fine, I'm sorry.' The muscle in Conall's jaw softened and he had the decency to look contrite. 'I overstepped with that remark,' he murmured. 'It's just...' He drew close and gathered her into a hug. 'I'm your big brother. And I don't want to see you hurt by him again.'

She softened against him, the comforting scent of his cologne and the peaty smell of good Irish single malt whiskey gathering in her throat. Banding her arms around his waist, she hugged him back, aware of how far they'd come since that miserable Christmas morning when Con had found their mother dead...

She'd pushed her brother away so many times in the years after that dreadful event, especially as a teenager, when she'd acted out at every opportunity—to test his commitment, she realised now. They'd had some epic shouting matches as a result, but he'd always stuck regardless. Because Con wasn't just pig-headed and arrogant with a fiery temper that matched her own, he was also loyal to a fault and more resilient and hard-wearing than the limestone of the cliffs outside.

Her eyes stung as she drew back to gaze up at his familiar face. 'You've been much more than just a big brother to me, Con. So much more. And I appreciate it. But you've got to trust me on this. I know what I'm doing, okay?'

He drew in a careful breath and let it out slowly, clearly waging a battle with himself not to say any more on the subject. But at last he nodded. 'Okay, Smelly,' he said, using the nickname he'd first coined when—according to family legend—he'd had to change one of her nappies.

She laughed, because he knew how much she'd always hated that fecking nickname. Trust Con to get the final word.

But then he cupped her shoulders and gave her a paternal kiss on the forehead. 'I do trust you,' he murmured. 'And anyhow, if he hurts you again, I'll murder him. So there's that,' he added, only half joking, she suspected.

She forced her lips to lift in what she hoped was a confident smile as her eyes misted.

Now all she needed to do was learn how to trust herself with Ross De Courtney.

Grand! No pressure, then.

CHAPTER FIVE

ROSS STOOD ON the grass near the Kildaragh heliport, next to the company Puma he'd piloted from the airport in Knock to get to Conall O'Riordan's estate without delay what felt like several lifetimes ago, and braced as the O'Riordans headed towards him, en masse.

Carmel had changed out of the silky bridesmaid's dress into a pair of skinny jeans and a sweater, which did nothing to hide the lush contours of her lean body.

He stiffened against the inevitable surge of lust and shifted his gaze to the child—whose hand was firmly clasped in hers. The boy was literally bouncing along beside her, apparently carrying on a never-ending conversation that was making his mother smile.

The pregnant lady and the man he had spotted earlier in the gardens—who Ross had been informed by Katie were the other O'Riordan sibling, Imelda, and her husband, Donal—followed behind them. Conall O'Riordan, Ross's sister, and two footmen carrying a suitcase and assorted other luggage, brought up the rear.

He nodded to Katie as the party approached. He'd spoken to his sister ten minutes ago—a stilted, uncomfortable conversation, in which he'd apologised for disturbing her wedding and she'd apologised for not telling him sooner about his son's existence.

His sister sent him a tentative smile back now, but as

Carmel approached him with the boy Katie held back with her husband and in-laws, making it clear they were a united front. United behind Carmel, and Ross was the outsider.

His ribs squeezed at the stark statement of his sister's defection. Even though he knew it was his own fault. He'd never been much of a brother to her, to be fair. He should have repaired the rift between them years ago. But thoughts of his sister disappeared, the pang in his chest sharpening, as Carmel reached him with the child.

'Hi, Ross. This is Cormac,' she said. She drew in a ragged breath. 'My son,' she added, her voice breaking slightly. 'He wanted to say hello to you before we left.'

'Hiya,' the little boy piped up, then waved. The sunny smile seemed to consume his whole face, his head tipped way back so he could see Ross properly.

Ross blinked, momentarily tongue-tied, as it occurred to him he had no idea how to even greet the boy.

Going with instinct, because the boy's neck position looked uncomfortable, he sank onto one knee, to bring his gaze level with the child's. 'Hello,' he said, then had to clear his throat when the word came out on a low growl.

But the boy's smile didn't falter as he raised one chubby finger to point past Ross's shoulder to the helicopter. 'Does the 'copter belong to yous?' he asked, the Irish accent only making him more beguiling.

Ross glanced behind him to buy himself some time and consider how to respond, surprised by the realisation that, even though this would most likely be the only time he would ever talk to his son, he wanted to leave a good impression... Or at least not a bad one. 'Yes, it belongs to my company,' he said, deciding to stick with the facts.

'It's bigger than my uncle Con's 'copter,' the little boy shot back.

Ross's lips quirked. 'Is it, now?' he replied, stupidly pleased with the comment.

At least I've managed to best Conall O'Riordan with the size of my helicopter.

The little boy nodded, then tipped his head to one side. 'Does it hurt?' he asked, his fingertip brushing across the swollen area on Ross's jaw.

Ross's throat thickened, the soft, fleeting touch significant in a way he did not understand. 'A bit.'

'It looks hurty,' the boy said. 'Mammy says it's naughty to hit people. Why did Uncle Con hit you?'

'Um, well...' He paused, completely lost for words. The tips of his ears burned as a wave of shame washed through him at the thought of how he and O'Riordan had behaved in front of this impressionable child. What an arse he'd been to take a swing at the man. 'Possibly he hit me because I tried to hit him first,' he offered, knowing the explanation was inadequate at best. 'And missed.'

'Cormac, remember Uncle Con told you it was a mistake and he's sorry.' Carmel knelt next to the boy. 'And I'm sure Ross is sorry too,' she added, sending him a pointed look.

Ross remembered how she'd mentioned she always addressed her son by his full name when he was being disciplined. But the child seemed unafraid at the firm tone she used, his expression merely curious as he wrapped an arm around his mother's neck and leaned into her body.

'I am sorry,' Ross said, because her stern look seemed to require that he answer.

'Yes, Mammy, but...' the little boy began, turning to his mother and tugging on her hair. 'Still it *was* naughty now...'

'Mr De Courtney, we'll need to leave soon if we're going to make our departure time from Knock,' his co-pilot interrupted them.

'Okay, Brian, thanks.' Ross rose back to his feet. 'If you wish to say your goodbyes, I'll wait in the cockpit,' he said to Carmel, suddenly eager to get away from the emotion pushing against his chest—and the child who could never be a part of his life.

'Okay, I'll only be a minute,' Carmel said, the sheen of emotion in her eyes only making the pressure on his ribcage worse.

He dismissed it. What good did it do? Being intrigued by the boy? Moved, even? When he wasn't capable of forming a relationship with him?

'Goodbye, Cormac,' he murmured to the child, ignoring the fierce pang stabbing under his breastbone.

'Goodbye, Mr Ross,' the boy replied, with remarkable gravity for a child of such tender years. But as Carmel took her son's hand, to direct him back towards her family and say her goodbyes, the little boy swung round and shouted. 'Next time yous come we can play tag. Like I do with Uncle Donal.'

'Of course,' he said, oddly torn at the thought he'd just made a promise he would be unable to keep… Because there would never be a next time.

'I think, in the circumstances, it would be best if we call a halt to this trip. I can have the helicopter take you back to Kildaragh.'

Carmel swung round to find Ross standing behind her in the private jet they'd just boarded at Knock airport. He looked tall and indomitable, and tired, she thought as she studied him. She waited for her heartbeat to stop fluttering—the way it had been for the last thirty minutes, ever since she had watched him speak to their son for the first time. She needed to get that reaction under control before they got to New York.

'Why would it be best?' she asked.

They'd travelled in silence after she'd bid goodbye to Mac and her family, the noise of the propellors too loud to talk as Ross had piloted the helicopter down the coast to Knock airport. She'd been grateful for the chance to collect her thoughts, still reeling from the double whammy of seeing Ross talk to Mac—and saying goodbye to her baby boy for seven whole nights.

She knew something about luxury travel—after all, her brother was a billionaire—but even so she'd been impressed by how quickly they'd been ushered aboard De Courtney's private jet, which had been waiting on the tarmac when they arrived. But she'd sensed Ross's growing reluctance as soon as they'd boarded the plane, the tension between them only increasing. The smell of new leather filled her senses now as she waited for Ross to reply.

His brow furrowed. 'Surely it's blatantly obvious after my brief conversation with the boy—this trip is pointless?'

'I disagree,' she said, surprised that had been his take away from the encounter.

Certainly, he'd been awkward and ill at ease meeting his son. That was to be expected, as she would hazard a guess he had very little experience of children. But she had also noticed how moved he'd been, even if he didn't want to admit it. And how careful.

'Mac likes you already,' she said, simply.

His frown deepened. 'Then he's not a very good judge of character.'

'On the contrary,' she said, 'he's actually pretty astute for a three-year-old.'

He shoved his hands into the pockets. 'So you still wish to accompany me?' he asked again.

'Yes, I do. If the offer is still open,' she said, suddenly knowing the conversation they were having wasn't just about their son. Because the air felt charged. On one level, that scared her. But on another, after seeing him make an effort to talk to his son openly and honestly, it didn't.

Perhaps he was right. Perhaps this trip was a lost cause. After all, a week was hardly long enough to get to know anyone. Especially someone who seemed so guarded. But she was still convinced she had to try... And she was also coming to realise that there was more at stake here than just her son's welfare.

Didn't she deserve to finally know what had made her act so rashly all those years ago? She'd thrown herself at this man that night, revelled in the connection they'd shared, and a part of her had always blamed herself for that. Maybe if she got to the bottom of why he had captivated her so, she might be able to forgive that impulsive teenager for her mistakes. And finally let go of the little girl she'd been too, who had looked for love in places where it would never exist.

She waited for him to reply, her breath backing up in her lungs at the thought she might have pushed too hard. It was one of her favourite flaws, after all. And knowing she would be gutted if he backed out now and told her the trip was off.

The moment seemed to last for ever, the awareness beginning to ripple and burn over her skin as he studied her.

His eyes darkened and narrowed. Could he see how he affected her? Why did that only make the kinetic energy more volatile?

'The offer is still open,' he said, at last, and her breath released, making her feel light-headed. But then he stepped closer and touched his thumb to her cheek. He slid it down, making the heat race south, then cupped her chin and raised her face. 'But I should warn you, Carmel. I still want you,' he said, his voice rough with arousal. 'And that could complicate things considerably.'

Her lips opened, her breath guttering out, the anticipation almost as painful as the need as her gaze locked on his and what she saw in it both terrified and excited her. It was the same way he had looked at her all those years ago—focussed, intense—as if she were the only woman in the whole universe and he the only man.

She licked arid lips, and the heat in his gaze flared.

'Do you understand?' he demanded.

She nodded. 'Yes, I feel it too,' she said, not ashamed to admit it. Why should she be? She wasn't a girl any more. 'It doesn't mean we need act on it.'

He gave a strained laugh—then dropped his hand. 'Perhaps.'

'Mr De Courtney, the plane is ready to depart in ten minutes if you and Ms O'Riordan would like to strap yourselves in,' the flight attendant said, having entered the compartment unnoticed by either of them.

Ross's gaze lifted from her face. 'Thank you, Graham. I'm going to crash in the back bedroom. Make sure Ms O'Riordan has everything she needs for the duration of the flight.'

The attendant nodded. 'Of course, sir.'

Without another word to her, Ross headed towards the back of the plane.

She gaped. Had she just been dismissed?

The attendant approached her. 'Would you like to strap yourself in here and then I can show you to the guest bedroom when we reach altitude?'

'Sure, but just a minute...' she said, then shot after her host.

She opened the door she had seen Ross go into moments before. And stopped dead on the threshold.

He turned sharply at her entry, holding his torn shirt in his hand.

Oh. My.

She devoured the sight of his naked chest, her gaze riveted to the masculine display as the heat blazed up from her core and exploded in her cheeks.

The bulge of his biceps, the ridged six-pack defined by the sprinkle of hair that arrowed down beneath the waistband of his trousers, the flex of his shoulder muscles—were all quite simply magnificent.

'Was there something you wanted?' he prompted.

'I… Yes.' She dragged her gaze to his face, the wry twist of his lips not helping with her breathing difficulties, or her burning face. She sucked in a lung full of air and forced herself to ask the question that had been bothering her for nearly an hour. 'I just wanted to ask you, what made you kneel when you met him? Mac, that is?' she managed, realising the sight of his chest had almost made her forget her own son's name.

He threw away his shirt, clearly unbothered by his nakedness. 'Why do you want to know that?'

'It's just… You say you don't know anything about children. But it was thoughtful and intuitive to talk to him eye to eye like that. I was impressed. And so was Mac.'

'Hmm,' he said, clearly not particularly pleased by the observation. 'And you think this makes me a natural with children, do you?' he said, the bitter cynicism in the tone making it clear he disagreed.

'I just wondered why you did it,' she said, letting her own impatience show. The jury was still out on his potential as a father, and she only had a week to decide if she wanted to let him get to know her son. But she didn't see how they could make any progress on that unless he was willing to answer a simple question. 'That's all.'

'I'm afraid the answer is rather basic and not quite as intuitive as you believe,' he said, still prevaricating.

'Okay?' she prompted.

He sighed. 'My father was a tall man. His height used

to intimidate me at that age. I didn't wish to terrify the boy, the way my father terrified me. Satisfied?'

'Yes,' she said, the wave of sympathy almost as strong as the spurt of hope.

Perhaps this didn't have to be a lost cause at all.

He began to unbuckle his belt, his gaze darkening. 'Now I suggest you leave, unless you want to join me in this bed for the duration of the flight.'

'Right.' She scrambled out of the room, slamming the door behind her.

It was only once she had snapped her seat belt into place that it occurred to her she was more excited by his threat than intimidated by it.

Uh-oh.

CHAPTER SIX

WHAT AM I even doing here?

Carmel stood at the floor-to-ceiling window of Ross De Courtney's luxury condo and stared through the glass panes of the former garment factory at the street life below as Tribeca woke up for another day.

The guest room she'd been given was a work of art—all dramatic bare brick walls and vaulted arches, steel columns, polished walnut wood flooring and minimalist furniture, which included a bed big enough for about six people, and an en suite bathroom designed in stone and glass brick. The room even had its own roof terrace, beautifully appointed with trailing vines, wrought-iron furniture and bespoke lighting to create an intimate and yet generous outdoor space.

The views were spectacular, too. At seven stories up she could see the tourist boats on the Hudson River a block away and the New Jersey waterfront beyond, to her left was the dramatic spear of the One World Trade Center building, and below her was the bustle and energy of everyday New Yorkers—dressed in their trademark uniform of business attire and trainers—flowing out of and into the subway station on the corner or dodging the bike couriers and honking traffic to get to work, most of them sporting go-cups of barista coffee.

She knew something about luxury living from the

glimpses she'd had of her brother's lifestyle. But Ross De Courtney's loft space, situated in the heart of one of Manhattan's coolest neighbourhoods, was something else—everything she had thought high-end New York living would be and more. But the edgy energy and purpose of all the people below hustling to get somewhere—and the stark modernity of the exclusive space she was staying in—only made her feel more out of place. And alone.

She'd been here for over twenty-four hours already, after arriving on the flight across the Atlantic. And while she'd spent a productive day yesterday—in between several power naps—exploring Ross's enormous loft apartment, the local area, and setting up a workstation with the art supplies she'd brought with her in the apartment's atrium, she'd barely seen anything of the man she'd come here to get to know.

She sighed, and took a sip of the coffee she'd spent twenty minutes figuring out how to brew on his state-of-the-art espresso machine after waking up before dawn.

Thank you, epic jet lag!

He'd dropped her off late at night after their flight and a limo ride from the airport, during which he'd spent the whole time on his phone. Once they'd arrived at the apartment, he'd told her to make herself at home, given her a set of keys and a contact number for his executive assistant, and then headed straight into his offices because he apparently had 'important business'.

And she hadn't seen him since.

She didn't even know if he was in residence this morning. She'd tried to stay up the previous evening, to catch him when he returned from work, but had eventually crashed out at around eight p.m., New York time. And slept like the dead until four this morning. She hadn't heard him come in the night before, and there had been no sign he'd even been in the kitchen last night during her adventures with the espresso machine this morning.

Is he avoiding me?

She took another gulp of the coffee, the pulse of confusion and loneliness only exacerbated by the memory of her truncated conversation over her video messaging app with her baby boy five minutes before.

'Mammy, I can't talk to yous. Uncle Donal is taking me to see the horses.'

'Okay, fella, shall I call you tomorrow?'

'Yes, bye.'

And then he'd been gone, and Imelda had appeared, flushed and smiling. 'Thanks so much for letting us have him for the week, Mel,' she'd said as she cradled her bump. 'We need the practice for when this little one arrives and he's doing great so far. He went to bed without complaint last night.'

'Ah, that's grand, Immy,' she'd replied, stupidly tearful at the thought her little boy was doing so well. Even better than she had expected. And a whole lot better than her.

She missed him, so much.

Not seeing his face first thing when she woke up had been super weird. Especially now she was questioning why she'd flown all this way to get to know a man who didn't seem to want to know her. Or Mac.

'You must contact me if there's any problem at all,' she'd told her sister, almost hoping Imelda would give her the excuse she needed to abandon what already seemed to be a fool's quest. 'I can hop straight on a flight if need be.'

'Sure, of course, but Mac's grand at the moment, he hasn't mentioned missing you once,' Imelda had said, with typical bluntness. Then she had sent Carmel a cheeky grin. 'How's things going with Mac's uber-hot daddy?'

'I'm not here to notice how hot he is, Immy,' she'd re-

plied sternly, aware of the flush hitting her own cheeks—
at the recollection of Ross without his shirt on in the close
confines of the jet's bedroom. 'I'm here to get to know
him a bit better and discuss Mac with him, and his place
in his son's life. That's all.'

'Of course you are, and that's important for sure,' her
sister had said, not making much of an effort to keep the
mischievous twinkle out of her eyes—which was even
visible from three thousand miles away. 'But sure there's
no reason now not to notice what a ride he is at the same
time.'

Oh, yes, there is, Immy. Oh, yes, there is.

She pressed her hand to her stomach, recalling the
spike of heat and adrenaline at her sister's teasing before
she'd ended the call, which was still buzzing uncomfortably in her abdomen now. Trust Imelda to make it worse.

The loud ring of the apartment's doorbell jerked her
out of her thoughts. And had hot coffee spilling over her
fingers. She cursed, then listened intently as she cleaned
up the mess and tiptoed to the door of her bedroom to
peek out.

If Ross answered the door, she'd at least know if he
was here. Then she could waylay him before he left again.
Perhaps they could have breakfast together? Although
the thought of Ross De Courtney in any kind of domes-
tic setting only unsettled her more.

The bell rang a second time and then she heard something else… Was that a dog barking?

Surprise rushed through her, which turned to visceral
heat as the man himself appeared on the mezzanine level
above and padded down the circular iron staircase from
the apartment's upstairs floor. In nothing but a pair of
shorts and a T-shirt, with his hair sleep-roughened and
his jaw covered in dark stubble, it was obvious the doorbell had woken him.

The buzz in Carmel's abdomen turned to a hum as he scrubbed his hands down his face before walking past her hiding place to the apartment's front door.

Her gaze fixed on his back as he began the process of unlocking the several different latches on the huge iron door and the dog's barks became frenzied.

The worn T-shirt stretched over defined muscles, accentuating the impressive breadth of his shoulders. Carmel's gaze followed the line of his spine to the tight muscles of his glutes, displayed to perfection in stretchy black boxers.

Then he opened the door and all hell broke loose.

Surprise turned to complete astonishment as a large, floppy dog bounded into the room, its toenails scratching on the expensive flooring, its barks turning to ecstatic yips.

'Hey, boy, you missed me?' Ross said, his deep voice rough as the animal jumped to place its gigantic paws on his chest. What breed was that exactly?

A smaller person would surely have been bowled over by the dog's enthusiastic greeting, but Ross braced against the onslaught, obviously used to the frenzied hello, and managed to hold his ground as the huge hound lavished him with slobbering affection.

Ross De Courtney has a dog? Seriously?

She waited, expecting him to discipline the dog, but instead he rubbed its ears and a deep rusty laugh could be heard under the dog's barking.

'Relax, Rocky,' he said, eventually grabbing the dog's collar and managing to wrestle it back onto all fours. 'Now, sit, boy,' he said, with all the strident authority of a Fortune 500 Company CEO. The dog gave him a goofy grin and ignored him, its whole body wagging backwards and forwards with the force of its joy.

'Rocky, sit!' The incisive command was delivered by

a small middle-aged woman dressed in dungarees and biker boots—her Afro hair expertly tied back in a multi-coloured scarf—who must have brought the dog and followed it into the apartment.

The dog instantly dropped its butt, although the goofy grin remained fixed on Ross as if he were the most wonderful person in the known universe.

'How the heck do you do that, Nina?' Ross murmured, sounding disgruntled as the woman produced a treat and patted the dog's head.

Carmel grinned, feeling almost as goofy as the dog, her astonishment at the animal's appearance turning into a warm glow.

Ross De Courtney has a dog who adores him.

'Practice,' the dog trainer said as she unloaded a bowl, a blanket and a lead from her backpack. After dropping them on the kitchen counter, she gave the dog a quick scratch behind the ears before heading back towards the door. 'You've gotta show him who's boss, Ross. Not just tell him.'

'Right,' Ross replied, still endearingly disgruntled. 'I thought I was.'

'Uh-huh.' The woman snorted, her knowing smile more than a little sceptical. 'Dogs are smart, they know when someone's just playing at being a badass.'

They had a brief conversation about plans for the coming week—Nina was obviously his regular dog walker and sitter and had been looking after Rocky while Ross was out of the country—before the woman left.

Carmel stood watching from behind the door to her room, aware she was eavesdropping again, but unable to stop herself. A bubble of hope swelled under her breastbone right next to the warm glow as she observed Ross interact with his devoted pet. Talking in a firm, steady voice, he calmed the animal down, rewarded him every time he did as he was told, and fed and watered him, before pouring himself a mug of coffee and tipping a large helping of psychedelic cereal into a bowl. The rapport between Ross and the animal—which Carmel eventually decided was some kind of haphazard cross between a wolfhound and a Labrador—was unmistakable once the dog stretched out its lumbering limbs over the expensive rug in the centre of the living area for a nap.

Questions bombarded her. How old was the dog? How long had it been his? Where had he got it? Because it looked like some kind of rescue dog. Definitely a mongrel crossbreed and not at all the sort of expensive pedigree status symbol she would expect a man in his position to own if he owned a pet at all. Especially a man who had insisted he didn't do emotional attachments.

The bubble of hope became painful.

Maybe it was the jet lag, or the emotional hit of her earlier conversation with Mac, or simply the weird disconnect of being so far away from home—and so far outside her comfort zone—with a man who still had the power to make her ache after all these years… But this discovery felt significant. And also strangely touching.

That Ross De Courtney not only had a softer side he hadn't told her about. But one he'd actively refused to acknowledge.

Ross gave a huge yawn, and raked his fingers through his hair, carving the thick chestnut mass into haphazard rows.

The swell of emotion sharpened into something much more immediate. And the hum in her abdomen returned, to go with the warm glow. She cleared her throat loudly, determined to ignore it.

Ross's head lifted, and his gaze locked on her.

The heat climbed into her cheeks and bottomed out in her stomach.

'You're up early,' he said, the curt, frustrated tone unmistakable. 'How long have you been standing there?'

The easy camaraderie he'd shown the dog had disappeared, along with his relaxed demeanour. He had morphed back into the brooding billionaire again—guarded and suspicious and watchful.

The only problem was, it was harder to pull off while he was seated on a bar stool in his shorts with a bowl of the sort of sugary cereal Mac would consider a major treat. She'd seen a glimpse of the man who existed behind the mask now and it had given her hope.

She walked into the room, brutally aware a second too late she hadn't changed out of her own sleep attire when his gaze skimmed over her bare legs—could he tell she wasn't wearing a bra? The visceral surge of heat soared.

But she forced herself to keep on walking. Not to back down, not to apologise, and most of all to keep the conversation where it needed to be.

'Long enough,' she said. 'So just answer me this, Ross. You have the capacity to love Rocky here.' The dog's ears pricked up at the sound of his name and he bounded towards her. She laughed at the animal's greeting, surprised but also pleased to see that up close he was an even uglier dog than she'd realised, one ear apparently chewed off, his snout scarred and his eyes two different colours—one murky brown, the other murky grey. 'But you don't have the capacity to love your own child? Is that the way of it?'

'It's hardly the same thing,' Ross managed, furious she had spied on him, but even more furious at the spike of arousal as his houseguest bent forward to give Rocky's stomach a generous rub and her breasts swayed under soft cotton. 'A dog is not a child,' he added, trying to keep his mind on the conversation, and his irritation. And not the surge of desire working its way south.

He'd stayed at work until late in the evening last night, catching up on emails and doing conference calls with some of De Courtney's Asian offices precisely so he could avoid this sort of scenario. He'd had plans to be out today as soon as Nina dropped off Rocky, but he'd overslept. And now here they were, both virtually naked with only a goofy dog to keep them sane. While he'd missed his pet, Rocky wasn't doing a damn thing to stop the heat swelling in his groin.

'I know, but surely the ability to care and nurture is not that different,' she said as he tried to keep track of the conversation and not the way her too short nightwear gave him a glimpse of her panties as she bent over—and made her bare, toned legs look about a mile long. 'All I'm saying is if you have the capacity to care for Rocky here, why wouldn't you have the capacity to care for Mac?' she said, scratching his dog's head vigorously and laughing when Rocky collapsed on the floor to display his stomach for a scratch—like the great big attention junkie he was.

Heck, Rocky, show a bit of restraint, why don't you?

'Hey, boy, you like that, don't you?' she said, still chuckling, the throaty sound playing havoc with his control. The dog's eyes became dazed with pleasure.

He knew how Rocky felt as he watched her breasts under the loose T-shirt—which shouldn't have looked seductive, but somehow was more tantalising than the most expensive lingerie.

Is she even wearing a bra?

The dog's tongue flopped out of the side of its mouth as it panted its approval, in seventh heaven now from the vigorous stomach rub.

Terrific, now he was jealous of his own dog.

He remained perched on the stool, grateful for the breakfast bar, which was hiding the strength of his own reaction.

She finished rubbing Rocky's belly, patted the animal and then rose, to fix that inquisitive gaze back on him. The forthright consideration in her bright blue eyes only made him more uncomfortable and on edge. Almost as if she could see inside him, to something that wasn't there... Or rather, something that he certainly did not intend to acknowledge.

'You didn't answer my question,' she said as she walked towards the breakfast bar.

He kept his gaze on her face, so as not to increase the torture by dwelling on the way the T-shirt barely skimmed her bottom.

When exactly had he become a leg man, as well as a breast man, by the way?

She perched on the stool opposite, hiding her legs at last.

This was precisely why he hadn't wanted to have her in his condo. Intrusive questions were bad enough, but the feel of his control slipping was far worse.

She cleared her throat.

'What was the question again?' he asked, because he'd totally lost the thread of the conversation.

'If you can form an attachment to Rocky, why would you think you can't form one to Mac?' she repeated, the flush on her cheeks suggesting she knew exactly where his mind had wandered. Why did that only make the insistent heat worse?

He took a mouthful of his Lucky Charms and chewed slowly, to give himself time to get his mind out of his shorts and form a coherent and persuasive argument.

He swallowed. 'A child requires a great deal more attention than a dog,' he murmured. 'And Nina spends almost as much time with Rocky as I do. Because I happen to be a workaholic.'

It was the truth.

He didn't have much of a social life, and that was the way he liked it. When he'd first taken over the reins of De Courtney's after his father's death he had resented the time and trouble it had taken to drag the ailing company into the twenty-first century, but he'd soon discovered he found the work rewarding. And he was good at it. Especially undoing all the harm his father had done with his autocratic and regressive approach to recruitment and training, not to mention innovation. The fact the bastard would be turning in his grave at all the changes Ross had made to De Courtney's archaic management structures was another fringe benefit. He'd never enjoyed socialising that much and had only attended those events where he needed to be seen. He had no family except Katie and he'd hardly spoken to her in years, and he had very few friends in New York—just a couple of guys he shared the occasional beer or squash game with. It was one of the reasons he'd moved to the US—he preferred his solitude and as much anonymity as he could have at the head of an international logistics conglomerate. And that just left his sex life, which he had always been careful to keep ruthlessly separate from other parts of his life.

All of which surely meant he wasn't cut out to be a father. No matter how easily he had bonded with Rocky, after finding the pup beaten and crying in a dumpster behind the apartment two summers ago. And he'd made a spur-of-the-moment decision to keep him.

But that hardly made him good parent material, not even close.

'That's true,' Carmel said, and nodded. 'A child does need your full attention at least some of the time. And I've already figured out how dedicated you are to your job.'

Something hollow pulsed in his chest, right alongside the surge of desire that would not die.

'I also live in New York, which would mean any time

I could give Mac would be limited,' he added, determined to press home the point—despite the hole forming in his chest.

Her pensive look faded, and her lips curved upward, the blue of her irises brightening to a rich sapphire. The hollow sensation turned to something raw and compelling.

'Do you know? That's the first time you've called Mac by his name,' she said, her voice fierce, and scarily rich with hope.

'Is it?' he said, staring back at her, absorbing the shock to his system as he struggled not to react to her smile.

Good grief, the woman was even more stunning when she smiled. That open and forthright expression of pure uninhibited joy was a lethal weapon… How could he have forgotten the devastating effect her spontaneous smile had had on him once before? The driving need to please her, to hear her laugh, something that had effectively derailed all his common sense four years ago.

He'd known it would be dangerous bringing her here. But the hit to his libido was nowhere near as concerning as the chasm opening up in his chest at the first sign of her approval.

'I think it's a very positive sign,' she said.

'I wouldn't read too much into it if I were you,' he said, trying to counter her excitement. But even he could hear the defensiveness in his voice.

Where was that coming from?

He didn't need her approval, or anyone's. He didn't need validation, or permission for the way he had chosen to live his life—avoiding forming the kind of emotional attachments she was speaking about. That hollow ache meant nothing. He'd stopped needing that kind of validation as a boy, when he'd discovered at a very young age his father didn't love him—and never would. That he was simply a means to an end. He didn't consider it a weakness, he considered it a strength. Because as soon as he'd finally accepted the truth, he'd worked on becoming emotionally self-sufficient.

And, okay, maybe Rocky had sneaked under his guard. But he didn't have room for any more emotional commitments. Why couldn't she accept that?

He opened his mouth to say exactly that, but before he could say any of it she said, 'You haven't said whether you want to be a father or not. Just that you can't be one.'

'I had a vasectomy when I was twenty-one,' he said, but even he could hear the cop-out in his answer. 'I think that speaks for itself.'

'Does it?' she said, far too astute for her own good, looking at him again with that forthright expression that suggested she could see right into his soul... A soul he'd spent a lifetime protecting from exactly this kind of examination, a soul that suddenly felt transparent and exposed. 'Because I'd say your reasons for having that vasectomy are what's really important, and you haven't explained them to me.'

'I didn't want to be a father,' he said flatly, but the lie felt heavy on his tongue, because she was right. It had never been about whether or not he *wanted* to be a father. He'd never even asked himself that question. It had always been much more basic than that. It had always been about not wanting to get a woman pregnant.

She crossed her arms over her chest, looking momentarily stricken by his answer. But then her gaze softened again. 'But now you are one, how do you feel about Mac?'

'Responsible. And terrified,' he said, surprising himself by blurting out the truth.

'Terrified? Why?' she pushed. The bright sheen of hope and excitement in her gaze—as if she'd made some important breakthrough, as if she had found something he knew wasn't there—only disturbing him more.

'That I'll do to him what my father did to me,' he said. 'And his father did to him. There's a legacy in the De Courtney family that no child should have to be any part of,' he said, determined to shut down the conversation.

But instead of her backing down, instead of her realising he was a lost cause—that he couldn't offer their son what didn't exist—the glow in her eyes only softened more.

'What did he do to you, Ross, that you would be terrified now to have a child of your own?' she asked.

The probing question, the glow of sympathy made the pain in his gut tangle with the need. And the hollow ache twisted—turning to impotent fury.

What right did she have to ask him questions he didn't want to answer? To probe and to push, to open the raw wound of his childhood and make that pain real again?

'He did nothing to me that I didn't get over a long time ago,' he said, his voice a husky growl, wanting to believe it.

'I don't believe you,' she said, her voice coming from miles away, through the buzzing in his ears. But then she reached across the breakfast bar and covered his hand with hers. Her touch—warm, deliberate, provocative, unashamed—ignited the desire like a lightning strike, turning the fury to fire.

He flipped his hand over and grasped her wrist before she could withdraw her hand. She jolted. Her pulse thundered under his thumb but her eyes darkened, the need there as visceral and volatile as his own.

He might have been embarrassed at how much he wanted her. But he could see she wanted him too. Why the hell had he worked so hard to ignore it? Giving into it again had seemed fraught with problems, but, frankly, how could this be any more problematic than it already was?

She was the mother of his son. And nothing was going to change that now. However much he might want to turn back the clock and take this commitment away—it was too damn late. Had been too damn late four years ago, when he'd plunged inside her without using protection and created a life.

She was right about that much at least. All his efforts to deny this connection weren't going to make it not so. That little boy *did* deserve a father. However inadequate he might be for the job, he would have to stop hiding. But he'd be damned if he'd bare his soul while he was at it. And he'd be damned if he'd deny the other connection they shared any longer—which had been taunting and tormenting them both as soon as he'd spotted her at the wedding.

Keeping hold of her wrist, he got off the stool and walked round the breakfast bar, not even sure what he planned to do any more, but feeling his emotions slipping out of his grasp again.

He stood in front of her, and tugged her off her stool, the force of his passion throbbing painfully in his boxers.

'I've got a child now and there's no changing that,' he admitted, knowing he'd been a coward not to acknowledge that before now. 'And you're right, whatever my misgivings, he deserves at least as much of my attention as Rocky. But right now, I don't want to talk about that.' And he certainly had no intention of ever sharing with her why he had struggled to come to terms with that truth. His childhood was ancient history. Unearthing it now would only make this transition more difficult.

Oddly the concession didn't fill him with panic as it had before. The child was bright, sweet, unbearably cute. He could never be a full-time father to the boy, and he would need to learn on the job, but maybe she was right about that too. She had been forced to figure it out. And if he could love Rocky, maybe he could find room in his heart to do a much better job than his father. Surely at the very least he couldn't possibly do as much harm. And he owed it to the lad to try. And to stop running.

'Because all I can think about is having you again.' He let his gaze roam over her face, then lifted one hand to cradle one heavy breast. He felt the nipple pebble into a hard peak beneath his thumb.

Yup, no bra.

'And tasting every damn inch of you that I didn't get to taste the first time,' he added, giving her fair warning.

He let her wrist go, giving her the choice.

But instead of pulling away, she looked him straight in the eye and then lifted up on tiptoes. She cupped his jaw, the trembling in her palm belied by the purpose in her eyes when she whispered against his lips, 'You don't scare me, Ross De Courtney.'

Then she clasped his face in her hands and pressed her lips to his.

He groaned as the fuse that had been lit long ago flared, sensation sparking through his body and turning the throbbing erection to iron. The need to claim her, to brand her as his, exploded along his nerve-endings, flooding his body like a river breaking its banks.

Grasping her waist, he lifted her into his arms, and carried her towards her guest bedroom, aware of the dog's playful barking through the pounding desperation.

His tongue thrust deep into the recesses of her mouth, gathering the sultry taste he remembered and taking control of the kiss.

He couldn't give her anything of real value. But he could give her this.

CHAPTER SEVEN

THE DOOR SLAMMED, cutting out the dog's bark. And Carmel found herself in her room alone with Ross, and the staggered sound of her breathing.

He let her go, her body sliding against the hard planes and angles of his, aware of the strident erection brushing her belly as she found her feet.

He kept his hand on her hip, holding her steady, her lips burning from the strength of his kiss.

This was madness. She knew that. But as she searched his face the pain she had glimpsed had been replaced with a fierce hunger. And the only way she could think of to free herself from that devastating feeling of connection was to feed it.

'Be sure,' he said, his voice as raw and desperate as she felt as his thumb brushed across her stinging lips with a tenderness, a patience she hadn't expected after that furious kiss.

'I am.' She nodded, struggling to speak around the lump jammed into her throat.

This was passion, desire, chemistry, part of a physical connection that had blindsided them both once before—it didn't need to mean more than that.

'Good,' he said, the word low with purpose.

But as his thumb trailed lower, slow, sure, steady, to

circle the nipple poking against the cotton, her breath released in a rush and her knees weakened.

Holding her waist, he bent his head to fasten his lips on the aching tip and suckle hard through the fabric.

She thrust her fingers into his hair as moisture flooded between her trembling thighs.

Don't think. Just feel.

Every sense went on high alert as he lifted the wet T-shirt over her head, threw it away.

He swore softly, seeing all of her for the first time.

She folded her arms over her naked breasts, the rush of shyness stupid but unavoidable. Her body wasn't as tight and toned as it had once been. Before Mac. And he was the first man now, the *only* man to ever see her naked.

'Don't...' He groaned, the rough tone part demand, part plea. 'Don't hide yourself from me,' he said, but made no move to touch her.

He wanted this to be her choice, she could see it in his eyes, the battle to hold himself back, to wait, as compelling as the need.

Don't think. Just feel. This is chemistry, basic and elemental, pure and simple.

She forced herself to unfold her arms and drop them to her sides. She arched her back, thrusting her breasts out, giving him the permission he sought. Refusing to be ashamed. Refusing to make this more than it was. Or ever could be.

This wasn't about the life they'd made together. She understood Mac had to be separate. Or she would be lost again, the way she had been once before. And she couldn't afford to be devastated again, by his rejection. She couldn't give him that power. Not now, not ever, when her little boy needed her whole. Always.

He scooped her up and placed her on the bed, then

hooked his thumbs in the waistband of her panties and drew them down her legs.

She lay fully naked now, panting, as his gaze roamed over her, burning each place it touched. She could hide nothing from him, the bright morning light through the windows showing every flaw and imperfection the pregnancy had wrought on her once perfect skin.

His fingertip touched the silvery scars on her belly, and she squirmed, feeling more exposed than she ever had before, the desire retreating to be replaced with something raw and disturbing.

But when his head rose and his eyes met hers, emotion swirled in the blue-green depths.

'I want… I want to see you naked too,' she managed, trying to find that assertive, rebellious girl again. The girl she'd been that night, bold and determined before the emotion had derailed her.

He let out a laugh, low and strained. Then levered himself off the bed and stripped off his T-shirt. The masculine beauty of his chest looked even more magnificent, if that were possible, than it had in the jet. The ripple of muscle and sinew, the defined lines of his hip flexors and the sprinkle of hair circling flat nipples and trailing through the ridged board of his abs were as breathtaking as they were intimidating. But then he dragged his shorts down.

The strident erection sprang out. And her breath backed up in her lungs.

How did I ever manage to fit that inside me?

The panicked thought only seemed to intensify the liquid fire at her core.

He climbed on the bed, clasped her chin in firm fingers to raise her gaze. 'What's wrong?'

The heat flooded her cheeks. She blinked and licked bone-dry lips, clearing the rubble in her throat.

'No…nothing. Everything's grand.'

A bit too grand really, she thought wryly. Not sure whether she wanted to laugh or cry at how gauche she felt.

He didn't know that he was the first—the only—man she had ever seen naked. That he was the only man who had ever been inside her. And she didn't want him to know, because that would only make her feel more vulnerable. And more like the frightened, overwhelmed girl she had been that night.

You're a woman now. Totally. Absolutely.

It didn't matter how little experience she still had of sex. She'd grown up in the years since that night in all the ways that mattered.

So stop blushing like a nun, you eejit.

'It's just… It's been a while now, since I've had sex,' she said, attempting to cover her gaffe. And feel less exposed to that penetrating, searching gaze. 'Being a mother is a full-time job.'

His lips crinkled in a rueful smile, only making her feel more gauche. The heat suffused her face like a forest fire.

'I can only imagine,' he murmured. 'Would you like me to slow down?'

She nodded, the emotion closing her throat and making her eyes burn, the comment reminding her of how he'd been that night. Passionate and provocative, yes, but also cautious and careful with her, until the need had overtaken them both.

Don't read too much into it. He's a pragmatic, methodical man. Why wouldn't he want to make it good for you?

'Tell me what you like,' he said.

She had no idea what she liked, but before she could come up with a creative lie he took the lead. His fingers skimmed down her body, circling her nipples.

Her back arched, the sensation shimmering again, the

mortification forgotten as he bent to lick at one turgid tip, then the other.

'That…' she choked out, bowing back, lifting her breasts to him, the need surging again—sure and relentless and uncomplicated. 'I like that a lot.'

The gruff laugh rumbled out of his chest and through her body. But before she had a moment to wonder what was so amusing, he captured the pebbled peak and suckled.

She launched off the bed, the sensation arrowing down to her core, making her writhe and squirm as he held her steady and played with the too sensitive peaks, nipping and sucking and licking until her tortured groans became sobs.

At last he lifted his head, to blow across her swollen breasts, the contact too much and yet not enough. Then he grasped her hips, and began to lick a trail down her torso heading towards…

Oh, God… Oh, no. Will he taste me there?

His tongue caressed, circling her belly button, trailing lower still.

'Ah… Oh, God… Yes…' Her sobs became moans, the need so intense now she could barely breathe, no longer think, the twisting deep in her belly tightening like a vice.

Holding her hips, he angled her pelvis. 'Open for me, Carmel. I need to taste all of you.'

Her thighs loosened as if by his command, and his tongue found the heart of her at last, licking at the bundle of frayed nerves, sending shockwaves through her body.

She sobbed, panted. One long finger entered her, stretching the tight, tender flesh. Then two, while his lips remained fastened on the core of her pleasure, the vice tightening to the verge of pain.

She bucked against him, riding those delving fingers, impaling herself, ignoring the pinch to let the pleasure build.

She cried out as his mouth suckled, the waves building and building, the vice cinching into one unbearable torment. Fire tore through her and she cried out as the wave crashed over her at last, blasting through every fibre of her being, sending her high, only to drop her down to earth, shattered and shaking, sweating and worn through.

Her eyelids fluttered open, to find him above her staring down, his eyes dark with a dangerous heat.

'You are so responsive,' he said. 'I adore watching you come.'

'I adore you making me come,' she said back, and was rewarded with a deep chuckle.

She hadn't meant to be funny, but somehow his amusement relaxed her. 'Do you have a condom?' she asked, desperate to feel him inside her now.

He nodded, the silent look reminding her of their aborted conversation about his vasectomy. The vasectomy that hadn't worked.

She'd touched a nerve there, she knew, asking him about his reasons for it. But when she'd reached for him a moment later, seeing the pain he'd been so determined to hide, it hadn't just been in sympathy. A part of her had wanted to ignite the heat, so she could forget that terrifying tug of connection.

He reached past her, delved in the bedside table, and found a foil packet. She watched, still shaky, still shattered, but oddly pleased to see how clumsy he was, how frantic he must be to have her too—to deny that connection as well—as he sheathed himself.

'I can't wait any longer,' he said.

She cupped his cheek, felt the stubble rasp against her palm, almost as raw as her emotions. 'Then don't,' she said, her voice sounding far away as the pounding in her ears became deafening.

Angling her hips, he notched himself at her entrance

and pressed inside, the slick heat from her orgasm easing his way despite the tightness.

At last, he was lodged deep, so deep she could feel him everywhere.

'Okay?' he asked.

'Yes,' she murmured.

And then he began to move. Slow at first, but so large, so overwhelming.

His harsh grunts met her broken sobs as the fire built again, even faster and hotter than before. She clung to his broad shoulders and focussed desperately on the sound of their sweat-slicked bodies.

The waves gathered again, like a storm now, sensation driving sensation, every nerve-ending raw and real and unprotected, the pleasure battering her.

He shouted out as she felt him grow even bigger inside her, touching every single part of her, but as she broke into a thousand tiny pieces she was very much afraid this time he had shattered more than just her body, because she could still feel the deep, elemental pulse of connection in her heart.

CHAPTER EIGHT

THE AFTERGLOW DID nothing to stop the thunderous pulsing in Carmel's ears as Ross rolled away from her, then left the bed and walked into the en suite bathroom without a word.

The residual pulse of heat at the sight of his naked backside, the defined muscles flexing, did nothing for her galloping pulse. Or her shattered state of mind.

She dragged the bed's duvet up to cover herself.

Had she just done something phenomenally stupid, because, despite two staggering orgasms in the space of less than ten minutes, the emotions were still charging through her system—too raw, too real—and the yearning hadn't diminished in the slightest.

She could hear the water running in the en suite bathroom. Should she get up? Get dressed? With her body still humming from his caresses?

But worse than the physical impact on her body—which felt a little bruised now, after the intensity of their joining—was that devastating feeling of intimacy.

She had thought she wouldn't feel that again. Despite her lack of experience she wasn't a virgin any more—and she had new important priorities in her life now. But somehow, where she had hoped for mindless pleasure, what she'd got was far more dangerous. His care and attention had brought back so many memories from their

first night. He had been focussed on her pleasure first
and foremost then too, and it had made her yearn for so
much more. For things she couldn't have and shouldn't
need any more.

He appeared in the doorway, a towel slung around
his hips.

The inevitable blush spread across her chest and suffused her cheeks.

Wow, awkward, much? Perhaps she should have considered this before she had chosen to jump into bed with
him. Because the easy out—to lose herself in sex—now
appeared to be anything but.

Then again, she was fairly sure she'd stopped thinking all together the moment he'd grasped her wrist, the
purpose and passion in his gaze searing her skin.

'How are you?' he asked.

'Grand.' She blinked, mortified by the foolish sting of
tears. She kept the duvet clasped to her chest and struggled to sit up, feeling far too vulnerable in her prone position on the bed.

It was a bit late for regrets, but one thing she couldn't
bear was for him to think this interlude had meant more
to her than it should. She'd made a conscious decision to
sleep with him again, and it had been mind-blowing. She
refused to regret that decision now. She could handle the
fallout now the afterglow had faded—because she wasn't
that emotional wreck of a girl any more. She couldn't be.

'I should probably get to work on my commission,'
she said, hoping he would take the hint and leave—so
she could get what had happened into some kind of perspective. It was just a physical connection. No more, no
less. Why should it interfere with their shared priorities
now as parents?

After all, before they'd jumped each other, Ross had
made a major concession there. By finally admitting he

needed—even wanted—to have a relationship with his son. That was huge. And so much more important than anything else. She still didn't really understand why he had struggled so to accept his place in Mac's life, or indeed why he had wanted a vasectomy so young... What exactly had his father done to him, to make him so convinced he should never be a parent himself? But surely it was best she didn't know the whys and wherefores. Didn't probe into that lost look, which had resonated so strongly with the girl she'd been. She needed to protect herself now—couldn't let that needy girl back in. So all she really needed to know about that look was that he was prepared to move past it.

Instead of taking the hint, though, and leaving, Ross padded across the room's luxury carpeting and sat next to her on the bed. 'You're an artist, right?' he asked.

She swallowed, and nodded, surprised, not just by the intensity in his gaze, but the way it made her feel.

She'd told him about all her hopes and dreams that night—at the time, she'd been in her first term at art school with grand plans of becoming the next big thing on the Irish art scene—and he'd listened with the same intensity. In the years since—after she'd had to give up those dreams, or rather tailor them into something more useful—she'd dismissed his interest that night too. The thoughtful questions, the admiration in his gaze when she described her passions, had become just an effective means to get into her panties... And his technique had worked perfectly, because nothing could be more seductive to a girl who had lost her father at the age of six, and been at loggerheads with her brother ever since her mother's death two years later, than the wonder of uncritical male attention.

'So you found your dream?' he asked now, surprising her again. He remembered that too?

She gave a rough chuckle. 'Well, not precisely. I had to drop out of the Central Saint Martin's School of Art. And when I got back into the studio after Mac's birth, I had to make a living. But I like what I do.'

He frowned. 'What is it that you paint?'

'Portraiture. I specialise in dogs, actually. I love them and luckily for me so do my clientele. People are willing to pay quite a lot for a good likeness of their pet.'

His eyebrows rose but only a fraction. 'Do you and Mac have a dog?'

Her heartbeat clattered against her chest wall, her ribs squeezing. This was surely the first specific question he'd ever asked about their son. 'Mac adores dogs, but we can't afford one just yet. So he's happy hanging out with Imelda and Donal's two hounds when we need a doggie fix. I think he'd love to meet Rocky one day,' she ventured.

He nodded. 'I'm sure that can be arranged. Although I'd be concerned Rocky might knock him down. Rocky's quite big, Cormac is quite small and I'm still working on Rocky's manners.'

It was a thoughtful, considerate thing to say, so she couldn't resist asking.

'How did you end up picking him? He's a rescue dog, right?'

'Yeah. I didn't really pick him...he sort of picked me.'

'How so?' she asked, intrigued by the flags of colour on his cheeks. And trying not to let her gaze dip to his chest—which was having a far too predictable effect on her hormones again.

He sighed. And looked away.

'He was dumped in a trash can at the back of the apartment building as a puppy. Someone had beaten him quite severely. I heard his cries. Took him to the shelter. Two weeks later I rang to find out if he'd been successfully placed. And he hadn't. He's not the prettiest dog, as you probably noticed, but he's got a big heart.' He shrugged, as if his connection to his dog was a small thing, when she suspected it was massive. 'I'm not a sentimental man, but it seemed a shame to let him die after he'd fought so hard to stay alive.'

'I see,' she said, deeply touched by the story.

Ross De Courtney might believe he couldn't make emotional attachments, but Rocky proved otherwise.

'Is that why you called him Rocky? Because he's a fighter?'

'Yes,' he said, but then his intense gaze fixed back on her face. 'The marks, on your stomach, how did you get them?'

The blush reignited at the unexpected question—as she recalled how he'd trailed his fingers over the stretch marks while they were making love. Did he find them ugly?

'They're stretch marks. I got them when I was pregnant,' she said, bluntly, refusing to be embarrassed about the changes having his baby had made to her body—whatever he thought of them.

His Adam's apple bobbed as his throat contracted, and a muscle in his jaw hardened. He looked stricken, and she had no idea why.

'I was pretty huge when I got to the end of my pregnancy,' she offered, unable to read his reaction, suddenly needing to fill the silence—and take that stricken look out of his eyes. 'Mac was a big baby, nearly eleven pounds when he finally appeared. And, well, I slathered my belly in all sorts of concoctions, but it didn't...'

'Was it very painful?' he asked, interrupting the babbled stream of information with a direct look that could only be described as tortured.

'The stretch marks?' she asked.

'No, the birth.'

'Oh, yes, six hours of absolute agony,' she said with a small laugh, in a bid to lift the mood. But she realised her attempt at humour had backfired spectacularly when he paled.

She touched his arm, instinctively. 'Ross, what's wrong?'

'I'm sorry,' he said, the words brittle with self-loathing. A self-loathing she didn't understand.

'What for?' she asked.

'For putting you through that.' He stood, his whole body rigid with tension now.

'No need for an apology. I had a child I adore. The pain was totally worth it,' she said.

'That's not the point. I put your life at risk.'

'My…? *What?* No, you didn't.' She was so stumped now she didn't know what to say. He was totally over-reacting, but his face had become an implacable mask again, rigid and unrelenting.

'I was only joking when I said it was total agony.' She paused, needing to be forthright now in the face of his… Well, she wasn't even sure what this was, or where it was coming from. But the emotion had been wiped off his face, to be replaced by the same intransigence she'd seen before. She didn't like it. 'Okay, to be fair it hurt, a lot, but I had every pain relief known to woman by the end of it. And my life was never in danger.'

He rewrapped the towel around his waist, making her far too aware of his nakedness and hers—the ripple of sensation tearing through what was left of her composure.

'I need to get to work,' he said, abruptly changing the subject. 'We can discuss the details later, but compensating you for your pain and suffering because of my carelessness is non-negotiable.'

'But…that's madness.' She sputtered, but then he

grasped her chin, leaned down and pressed a kiss to her lips so possessive it cut off her thought processes entirely.

'We should probably also set some ground rules for the next week,' he added, letting her go. 'Sex-wise.'

The pragmatic comment had the blush firing into her cheeks.

How did he do that? Throw her completely for a loop without even trying? Because it was mortifying.

'What…what do you mean?' she said.

One dark eyebrow arched, and his gaze skimmed over her. She tightened her grip on the duvet—wondering for one panicked moment if he could see the hot weight lodged between her thighs that had started to pulse… *Again.*

'It's clear from what just happened that the exceptional chemistry between us is still very much there,' he said, the conversational, pragmatic tone belying the heat in his gaze and the brutal throbbing between her thighs. 'I figure we have two choices. We can either see that as a problem while you're here, in which case you should probably move into a hotel. Or we can enjoy it.'

'I…?' She stuttered, not sure what to say, or how to react. Was it really that easy for him to completely separate the sex from the emotion? 'You'd be okay with that?'

Was that possible? To treat this urge as purely biological? She'd wanted to believe she could be as pragmatic as he was about the sex, but could she? How would she even know if she was capable of that, when she'd never had a relationship with any man before now? Never even had a fling. Except for her one night with him—which was basically a micro-fling.

'Of course,' he said, as if there was no doubt in his mind whatsoever.

Had he ever had a committed relationship? Because from the insouciance in his tone now, it seemed doubtful.

'But it would be your choice, obviously,' he said. 'Why don't you think about how you want to proceed, and we can discuss it tonight? I'll make sure I'm back at a reasonable hour...' His gaze dipped again, making her ribs squeeze uncomfortably and her nipples tighten. 'And we can have dinner together.'

'Umm... Okay,' she managed as he strolled out of the room.

As the door closed behind him, the soft thud echoed in her chest.

She flopped back on the bed, her whole body humming again from just the thought of 'discussing' their options 'sex-wise' tonight.

She had no idea what to think any more, or feel. But as she turned her head to gaze out of the paned-glass window, one thing she did know for sure...

Thinking about him, and her choices, was going to keep her brain tied in knots, and her body alive with sensation, for the hours until she saw him again.

CHAPTER NINE

A car will be arriving at seven p.m. to pick you up. I thought it would be best if we discuss our options over dinner on neutral ground. Any problems text me.

CARMEL PLACED HER brush down on the paint table, wiped her hands on the cloth she kept tucked into the waistband of her jeans and picked up her phone as if it were loaded with nitroglycerine.

She reread the message from Ross. Then read it again, struggling to absorb the shot of heat and panic. And something else entirely. Something that felt disturbingly like exhilaration. Which could not be good.

Then she checked the time.

It was already five. She only had two hours before she would see him again...

Where was he taking her? Because he hadn't bothered to specify.

For goodness' sake, she didn't even have a single clue what to wear. Was he taking her to a restaurant? To talk about their sex life *in public*? Her cheeks burned... Was that the way of things in these situations? Did people do that in New York? Because they certainly didn't in rural Ireland.

She tapped out a reply as the panic—which she had

spent six solid hours immersed in her art to try and control—tightened around her ribs again…

Where are we going?

But as she went to press 'send', her thumb hovered over the button.

She reread her reply, twice, and could hear her own lack of social savvy and confidence revealed in the words. Ross didn't know she'd been a virtual recluse since Mac was born, rebuilding her life from the ground up.

And she didn't want him to know. Would he blame himself for that too? And want to 'recompense' her for the fact she'd chosen to spend the last four years living a quiet life in County Galway learning how to be a mother?

She loved her quiet life. It worked for her, and Mac. And she'd found an outlet for her art that she loved too, she thought, glancing at the portrait she had lost herself in as she attempted to capture the winsome intelligence of a two-year-old cockapoo called Orwell.

She hadn't missed the social whirl she'd only glimpsed in passing in the few weeks she'd been in London at art school, and the night she'd first met Ross, once she'd returned home pregnant…

But somehow having him know how unsophisticated, and unsure she was about going for dinner in a fancy restaurant in New York—where everyone seemed to ooze confidence and style from every pore—would just add to her feelings of inadequacy where he was concerned. And make her feel as if she was at even more of a disadvantage when it came to discussing Mac's future relationship with his daddy… And what they were going to do 'sex-wise' over the coming week.

So don't ask him where you're going tonight, you eejit.
After all, talking about Mac would not be hard. There

was so much she wanted to tell him about his son. And he seemed to have turned an important corner there this morning. When it came to the sex, all he was proposing was some fun while they got to know each other better and discussed their child's future. If they decided to go for it over the next week, to indulge themselves while she was here, it would be nothing more than a chance to blow off steam, to scratch an itch that had been there for four years—a quick fling with an end date already stamped on it. She needed to remember that above all else.

She deleted the reply and typed another.

Is there a dress code? What should I be wearing?

There now, that sounded less clueless, didn't it? Surely any woman would want to know that. But then the heavy weight sank into her sex and began to glow like a hot coal at the recollection of what she'd been wearing...or rather not wearing...when Ross had marched out of her room wearing nothing but a towel that morning.

And the innocent question suddenly seemed loaded with unintended innuendo.

'Oh, for the love of...'

She hissed, deleting the text. Then wrote another.

Cool, see you there.

She pressed 'send', before she could third-guess herself, and dumped the offending phone back on the paint table as if it were a grenade. Then she gathered up her brushes and palette so she could put aside her work for the day. She had two whole hours if she got a move on to scope out the cool little boutiques and vintage shops in the neighbourhood and find an outfit. Something that made her look and feel good, but which also suited her own sense of style.

She swallowed, convulsively. At the very least her quest should help distract her for the next two hours from the panic still closing her throat and the hot rock now pulsing in her panties at the thought of seeing him again.

Hallelujah for neutral ground!

'Would you like another beer, sir?'

'No, I'm good.' Ross glanced at the waiter who had been hovering for the last ten minutes in the private terrace he'd hired in the chic rooftop restaurant—which was one of Manhattan's most popular eateries, apparently, not that he'd ever dined here before.

He winced slightly at how stunning the space looked with the sun setting on the horizon, casting a reddish glow over the dramatic view of Manhattan's skyline through the terrace's tall brick arches.

Terrific, the wait staff probably thought he was about to propose. When all he had wanted to do was to make absolutely sure they didn't give into the chemistry again before they got a few important things straight about his responsibilities to his son, and what any liaison between them while Carmel was in New York would and would not entail.

He cleared his throat. 'By the way, once you've taken our drinks order, could you give us twenty minutes alone?'

'Absolutely, sir, and good luck,' the young man said, positively beaming. Ross bit back a groan.

But then Carmel appeared at the terrace entrance—and the groan got locked in his throat. The hum of arousal that had been tormenting him most of the day hit first, swiftly followed by what could only be described as awe.

He stood as she walked towards him.

Her vibrant red hair flowed out behind her in the light spring breeze, which also caught the floaty material of the short dress she wore, which was decorated with lavish red roses and clung to her torso, defining each and every one of the curves he had explored that morning.

A pair of combat boots and a leather jacket completed the original look. But as she approached his gaze rose to her face, and his pragmatism took another fatal hit. The make-up she wore—cherry-red lipstick to match the dress, smoky black eye liner and some kind of golden glitter on the lids, which sparkled in the light—made her look like a fairy queen, or a Valkyrie, stunningly beautiful, strikingly cool and so hot it hurt.

'Hi,' she said breathlessly as she reached him. 'Sorry I'm late. I wanted to walk the last couple of blocks.'

'Not a problem,' he murmured, trying to control the brutal reaction as he caught a lungful of her scent—something sultry and yet summery and as addictive as everything else about her.

'Wow, what a spectacular view,' she said, her voice rich with awe, the glittery eye shadow making her lids sparkle like rare gems.

There's only one spectacular view here, and it's not downtown Manhattan.

He swallowed round the lust swelling in his throat and held out her chair, silently cursing the decision to have this conversation in a restaurant.

Because the urge to lick every inch of her delicate flesh, taste the sweet sultry scent of her arousal, swallow the broken sobs of her pleasure again had already turned the hum of arousal into a roar.

'Is this a private space?' she said, glancing around.

He had to shake his head slightly, to unglue his gaze from her mouth and process the question.

Damn, De Courtney, get a grip.

'I thought you might prefer to talk without an audience,' he said.

Except talking is the last damn thing I want to do now.
He dragged his gaze away from those full lips.
Will her mouth taste like cherry?

'Really? That's so thoughtful of you,' she said, sounding as if she meant it as she seated herself. He walked back to his own chair and sat. He picked up his beer and finished it in one gulp to unstick his dry throat and give himself a moment to concentrate on easing the painful pulsing in his pants.

'More practical than thoughtful,' he said, desperately trying to regain his equilibrium and some semblance of control.

She blinked, the pure blue of her irises almost as breathtaking as the light blush on her pale skin.

'Thoughtful or not, I appreciate the privacy,' she said. 'I'm not gonna lie, I was nervous about meeting you here. I guess I'm too much of an unsophisticated Irish country lass to feel comfortable talking about my sex life over cocktails and cordon bleu cuisine with other people around.'

His gaze dipped of its own accord to the bodice of her dress, which cupped her breasts, the words 'sex life' delivered in that soft Irish burr detonating in his lap.

'You don't look unsophisticated,' he said. 'You look stunning.'

A bright smile curved her lips and lit her gaze, while the becoming blush spread across her collarbone. Something twisted deep inside him at the realisation of how much the offhand compliment had pleased her.

'Good to know the hour I spent scouring the vintage shops in Tribeca wasn't wasted,' she said as she shucked the leather jacket and handed it to the waiter, who had reappeared. The movement made the silky dress drift off her shoulder. The shot of adrenaline became turbo-charged as he glimpsed a purple lace bra strap before she tugged the dress back up.

Just kill me now.

'Hiya,' she said to the waiter, who Ross noticed was staring at his date with his tongue practically hanging out of his mouth.

Possessiveness shot through him and he glared at the kid. 'Perhaps you'd like to take our drinks order?'

The young man jerked. 'Umm, yes, of course. What can I get for you, ma'am?' he said, not taking his eyes off Carmel. Apparently Ross had become invisible.

'What's good here?' she asked, and the waiter proceeded to stammer his way through a complex list of cocktails.

Ross's irritation increased.

What could only have been a few minutes but felt like several hours later, Carmel's new number one fan had finally left them alone together, as Ross had requested.

'So I take it you had a productive day,' he said, struggling to make small talk—not his greatest strength at the best of times.

'Yes, very. Your apartment has so much light, it's a glorious place to paint,' she replied. 'And I'm particularly fond of my current subject. He's an adorable cockapoo with an abundance of personality. It's never hard to capture that on canvas. Plus, Nina dropped by to take Rocky out and we had a chat. She suggested introducing me to some of her other clients and their dogs while I'm here, which could be a great opportunity. She feels sure a lot of them would love a portrait of their pet.'

But I want you all to myself.

'I see,' he said, more curtly than he had intended, surprised by the strength of his disapproval. Where exactly was it coming from? Because it felt more than a little unreasonable... Just like the spike of possessiveness when he had caught the waiter staring at her. But he couldn't seem to shake it, even as the flushed excitement on her face dimmed.

'Do you have a problem with that?' she asked, the tone clipped as her smile died.

'Not precisely.' He shrugged, trying to make himself believe it. 'Obviously you're a free agent while you're here, and your career is your concern.' If painting pet portraits could really be called a career.

She'd had to drop out of art school to have his child. It seemed her brother hadn't stepped in to offer her any financial support—which seemed callous in the extreme, given that the guy was a billionaire—but ultimately, Ross knew, Conall O'Riordan wasn't the one responsible for supporting her and his son, he was.

Suddenly his knee-jerk reaction made perfect sense. This wasn't about some Neanderthal desire to keep her all to himself as 'his woman' while she was here, it was simply his desire to right the many wrongs he'd done her, with his thoughtless reply to that text.

'Just so you know, I've worked out a generous maintenance package for you and Cormac with my financial team today, which means you won't have to continue shouldering the financial burden of his care any longer. Or, I hope, making compromises with your art based on that burden.'

Instead of her looking pleased with the news though, her brows drew down and those lush lips tightened into a thin line of disapproval. The blue of her irises turned to flame as outrage sparked in her eyes.

He braced himself for what he suspected was going to be a fairly spectacular argument. Discord was not something he usually enjoyed in a relationship. But as he watched her anger build, the arousal became razor sharp.

And it occurred to him that, unlike any other woman he had ever dated, Carmel O'Riordan totally lived up to that age-old cliché, that she was even more stunningly beautiful when she was mad.

'Oh, have you now?' Carmel snapped, managing to temper her tone, just about.

But she could do absolutely nothing about the breathless rage threatening to blow her head off at his condescending and arrogant assumptions. And the prickle of fear beneath it. She'd spent the last four years refusing to take the many handouts Conall had offered her to help support her and Mac. So why should Ross's offer be any different?

His money didn't mean that he cared. She already knew that. So why should his persistence bother her so much? Or threaten to undermine the independence she'd worked so hard for?

'Since when has Mac become a burden to me?' she asked, because there were so many things wrong with his statement she didn't know where to start.

She knew she looked good in the fabulous vintage dress she'd found in a tiny shop off West Fourth Street, but still she'd been nervous at the thought of seeing him again, especially in the chic, uber-hip restaurant in the Murray Hill area of the city, which she'd immediately checked out on the Internet when the driver had told her of their destination. So nervous, in fact, she'd had to get out of the car a block early, even though she was already a few minutes late. Consequently, she'd been stunned... and moved...to find he'd booked this private space when she arrived, the view almost as staggeringly gorgeous as the sight of him in the twilight. His eyes had darkened, that searching gaze making bonfires ignite all over her skin, and the compliment had gone straight to her head.

The nerves hadn't died, exactly, but they'd shifted, making her focus on *them*—and the rare chemistry that she was becoming increasingly sure she wanted to indulge.

Where was the harm in taking him up on his offer? If he could be pragmatic, why couldn't she? Her life was in Ireland after all, and his in New York. And while they shared a child, apart from Mac they had nothing else in common, having never shared more than a few hot, stolen moments together. She wasn't the artless, foolish, lovestruck girl she'd once been. She had believed herself in love once and it had all been a lie, based on chemistry and heat and one enchanting night. She wouldn't fall for that romantic nonsense again—that little wobble after they'd made love again was just that, nothing more than a wobble, an echo, of a girl long gone. This man had captivated her four years ago. But she knew now he couldn't be further from her ideal partner...

Surely his insulting offer of 'compensation' for her pain and suffering only confirmed that? So why couldn't she control the stupid emotion pushing against her ribs?

'I didn't say that,' he said, even though he'd said exactly as much.

'And if you'll recall I have never asked you for money,' she said, reiterating the point yet again, annoyed the fury she wanted to feel had become something a great deal more disturbing.

How could she be moved by his desire to support her—when she didn't want or need his support?

He leaned back in his chair, the appreciation in his gaze unmistakable. The top buttons of his shirt were undone, and the movement drew her gaze down to where his chest hair peeked out.

Heat settled like a hot brick in her belly, tangling with the nerves and the fury and the unwanted emotion to create a cocktail of sensations she seemed unable to extinguish.

'I know,' he said, the calm tone only adding to her agitation. 'You've been consistently clear on that point. But that doesn't mean I don't owe you for the upkeep of my son. And the things you have clearly sacrificed in the last four years.'

'I've sacrificed nothing I did not wish to sacrifice. And I'm perfectly happy with the life I have now,' she said. 'Maybe doing pet portraits seems like a waste of my talent to you, but I like it and I'm good—'

'I didn't say it was,' he cut her off.

'Yes, but you implied it,' she said, because he totally had.

But then he leaned forward and covered the fist she had resting on the table with his hand. 'I didn't mean to,' he said. 'I'm proud of you, and everything you've done to make a life for our child. But I remember the smart, witty, brilliant girl I met that night who captivated me with her dreams. You had ambitions for your future, which I destroyed. I want to give them back to you.'

The statement—delivered in that deep husky, forceful voice—cut off the outrage at the knees, the hot brick in her belly rising up to pulse painfully in her chest.

She tugged her hand out from under his as the fury disappeared to be replaced by the deep yearning she knew had no place in this relationship.

He felt beholden to her. She had to make it very clear to him, he wasn't. But why did the thought he would even want to give her back dreams that had died long ago seem so dangerous?

She shook her head, stupidly close to tears. He didn't understand that those dreams didn't matter any more, because he had given her something far more precious.

Making him understand that was what she had to concentrate on now.

'I don't want those dreams back,' she said. 'And I don't want your money, Ross. I thought I made that clear when I came here.'

He settled back in his chair, his gaze studying her with an intensity she remembered from that night—as if she were a puzzle he was determined to solve.

She'd found it exhilarating then. It scared her that look could still trigger the giddy bumps in her heart rate now.

She placed her hand in her lap, her skin still burning from the touch of his palm.

'As I understood it, you wanted me to form a relationship with Mac,' he said. 'I've said I'm willing to do that. I doubt I'll be much of a father, but I'm willing to try.'

'Okay,' she said.

'But you have to meet me halfway, Carmel. You have to let me provide financial security for you both.'

'Why?'

'Because it's important to me.'

'But *why* is it so important?' she asked again, almost as tired of his evasions as she was of her own see-sawing emotions.

He simply stared at her, but then he looked away. And she knew he was debating whether to tell her more.

The waiter chose that precise moment to arrive with their drinks and the menus.

She spent several minutes checking the array of eclectic and delicious-sounding dishes, taking the opportunity to calm her racing heartbeat. But once they'd ordered and the waiter had left them alone again, she knew she had to find out why he was so obsessed with providing for her and Mac to stop herself from misconstruing his motivations again.

'You didn't answer my question,' she said.

He took a sip of the beer he'd ordered.

But just when she thought there was no way he would tell her more, he murmured, 'Because I spent my whole childhood watching my father exploit and abuse the women he slept with… And never live up to the responsibility of being a father to his own children. I vowed to myself then, I would be better than him.' He sighed, and for a moment she could see the turmoil in his eyes, devastating memories lurking there that she suspected he had no intention of sharing… 'What I did to you, and Mac, means I have broken that vow. Do you understand?'

Emotion pulsed hard in her chest at his forthright, honest answer. And the misery she glimpsed in his eyes.

It saddened her and moved her… But it also made the fear release its grip on her throat. His offer, his need to provide for her wasn't really about her, about *them*. This was about his past, his childhood, his dysfunctional relationship with his father.

'You didn't exploit me, Ross. Or abuse me,' she said, knowing she couldn't let him take responsibility for her choices. Because it would make her a victim, and she never had been one. 'And you've offered to try and be a father to Mac, even though you're not confident in the role…' A lack of confidence she was beginning to understand now stemmed from his unhappy relationship with his own father. 'So you certainly haven't abandoned your responsibility towards him. And while it's touching you would want to give my dreams back to me, only I can decide what my dreams are, and only I can make them come true. The girl you met that night doesn't exist any more. She's not who I am now. And I'm glad of that. Having Mac has turned me into a stronger, smarter, less impulsive person. I was forced to grow up, for sure, but I've no regrets about that. And neither should you.'

He stared at her for the longest time, the silence only

broken by the distant sound of sirens from the street below. She could feel her breath squeezing in her lungs, the moment somehow so significant—a battle of wills between his honour and her independence, which she knew she had to win.

But at last he broke eye contact and swore under his breath.

When his gaze met hers again, she saw rueful amusement, the feelings she had glimpsed earlier carefully masked again. But something had shifted between them, something important, because now she knew she had his respect.

'You're not going to accept the maintenance settlement, are you?' he said, giving it one last try, but he didn't seem surprised when she shook her head.

He thrust his fingers through his hair, which she had begun to recognise as a sign of his frustration, but then he let out a rough chuckle, which seemed to wrap around her heart. Why did she get the impression Ross De Courtney didn't laugh often enough?

'Do you have any idea how ironic it is that I wrote that unforgivable text four years ago convinced you were a conniving little gold-digger, and here I am now, frustrated beyond belief that you have point-blank refused— over and over again—to take the money I want to throw at you?'

She laughed, stupidly relieved they could finally share a joke about it. 'Actually, I'd call it poetic justice for that text, but then Conall has always said I've got a cruel sense of humour.'

'The fact I find myself agreeing with your brother only compounds the irony,' he said, the rueful tone intensified by the rich appreciation in his gaze.

Her heart bobbed into her throat. She swallowed it down ruthlessly, determined to concentrate on the pulse pounding in the sweet spot between her thighs, which he had exploited so comprehensively that morning—and nothing else.

'Doesn't it just?' she said, then wondered if she was enjoying the moment of connection a bit too much.

Whoa, girl. Don't go complicating this. Not again.

The sun had set on one of the most spectacular views she'd ever seen in her life, and it felt as if a huge hurdle to their future association as Mac's parents had been overcome. Plus she'd seen a crucial bit more about the man behind the mask. Maybe it had only been a glimpse, grudgingly given, but she could see now Ross's relationship with his father was the key to why he believed he would struggle to parent Mac, and she could give him some solace on that score at least, from her own experience. No need to make this new accord mean anything more.

'Would you let me at least set up a trust fund for Mac?' he said.

'I don't need your…' she began, but he held up his hand.

'I know you don't need my money,' he said. 'And I know now my money is no substitute for me attempting to be some kind of father to him. But it would make me feel a little bit better about abandoning him for the first three years of his life.'

She wanted to tell him no again. But she could see she needed to compromise now. Relinquishing even this much control over her son's life was hard, but how could she let Ross be a father to Mac, if she couldn't even allow him to set up a trust fund for his son?

'Okay, I can accept that,' she said. 'As long as you promise not to let him buy a motorcycle with the money when he's sixteen,' she added, desperately trying to make light of a difficult concession on her part.

She'd wanted Ross to consider being a real daddy to Mac. Why hadn't she realised, until this minute, everything that would entail?

He laughed. 'I'll tell my legal team to make his mother the primary trustee until he's thirty-five, how's that?'

'Perfect,' she said, just as the waiter arrived with the dishes they'd ordered.

The delicious aroma of grilled chicken and delicate spices filled her nostrils, and the tension that had been tying her gut in knots since getting his text that afternoon unravelled enough to make her realise she was absolutely ravenous.

Ross watched Carmel tuck into her food with the same take-no-prisoners gusto with which she appeared to tackle everything in her life—from motherhood, to art, to sex.

The woman certainly drove a hard bargain, he thought, as he sliced off a chunk of the succulent steak he'd ordered.

He let the juices melt on his tongue—while struggling to forget how much better she had tasted that morning. And how much he had been forced to reveal about his childhood, and his father.

He never talked about that time in his life. Or the man who had sired him. The flashbacks and nightmares he sometimes still suffered from were just one reason not to dwell on it. He'd had a disturbed night's sleep last night, thanks to the night terrors that had visited him in dreams and woken him up in a cold sweat—the shame of his own weakness almost as vivid as the brittle fear. But surely it was inevitable discovering he was a father would naturally bring the nightmares back again—at least for a little while.

Was that why he'd dived into a sexual relationship

this morning that could effectively blow up in his face? Perhaps. But he was past caring about the consequences now. All he knew was that he had to have her again. But that still didn't stop him hating the pity in her eyes when he'd been forced to tell her the real reason providing for her and her son's financial needs was so important to him.

He tried to shrug it off as they finished their meal and talked easily about the day's business. Or easily enough, if you didn't count the ticking bomb in his lap ready to explode every time she licked the dark chocolate and sea-salt mousse off her spoon. Or he noticed that vintage dress slipping off her shoulder again and he got another glimpse of that damn bra strap.

As soon as she had licked the final drops of chocolate off her spoon, the waiter arrived to whisk their dishes away and offer them coffee. Ross waited patiently, or patiently enough, but when the waiter began to walk away, he opened his mouth to bring up the subject of their sleeping arrangements for the rest of the week when she beat him to the punch.

'My mother died when I was eight years old,' she said, her gaze fixed on his face.

'I'm sorry,' he said automatically, nonplussed not just by the complete non-sequitur but also the wealth of emotion in those bottomless sapphire eyes. And the twist of anguish in his gut, at the thought of her, as such a young child, losing her mother.

He ought to know how that felt—after all he had lost his own mother when he was even younger... He tensed. Not true. Although his mother had died when he was five, he barely remembered her.

'It's okay, we weren't particularly close,' she said, still watching him with a disturbing level of intimacy.

'Are you sure?' he said, because he didn't believe her. He could hear the hollow tone of loss in her voice.

She gave him a weak smile. Then nodded. 'She suffered from depression. Had been battling it for all of my life—she had two miscarriages before I was born and that's when it struck. It got much worse when my daddy died in a farm accident. Then one Christmas morning, two years almost to the day of his death, she decided to end it. Con went to her room to wake her up... And found her dead.'

'Hell.' He whispered the word, shocked not just by the devastating picture she painted of her family's tragedy, but also the pragmatism with which she delivered the news. 'That's horrendous.'

'Yes...' She let out a small laugh completely devoid of humour. 'Yes, it is horrendous. For so many reasons. It's horrendous that my daddy died the way he did. It's horrendous that my mammy couldn't cope without him. It's horrendous she never got the help she needed. And that Conall had to live with the trauma of finding her like that. And then had to take on so much responsibility when he was little more than a lad himself.'

'I'd say it's also horrendous you had to grow up without a mother,' he murmured.

'Yes, that too,' she said, almost as if her own loss was an afterthought. 'I suppose,' she added. 'But I didn't tell you so you'd feel sorry for me. I told you because...' She paused, sighed. 'Here's the thing—when I got pregnant with Mac my biggest fear was that I wouldn't be able to be a mother to him, because my own mother had been...' She hesitated again, then took a breath, and let it out slowly. 'Well, not much of a mother to me. I had no frame of reference. She hadn't been able to show love or even affection towards the end. She was in far too much pain to focus on anything other than the big black hole she couldn't climb out of. I worried constantly, while I watched my belly getting bigger, that I would have the same trouble bonding with my baby she had had bonding with me. Con and Imelda tried to explain to me it wasn't the same thing at all. That mam had been ill. But I'd always been secretly, even subconsciously, convinced there was something very wrong with me. And that's why she couldn't bond with me. That somehow I wasn't worthy of love. And what if that same thing was going to stop me loving Mac?'

He frowned. 'But that's absurd. What does one thing have to do with the other?' And anyway, he'd seen how she interacted with the boy. She obviously adored the child and he adored her. If anything, the closeness of their relationship had only intimidated him more.

'Nothing,' she said. 'Just like your father's inadequacies as a husband and a parent and, by the sounds of it, a human being have nothing whatsoever to do with you.'

He stared at her, the statement delivered in such a firm, no-nonsense tone, it took him a moment to realise they weren't talking about her family and her relationship with Mac any more. They were talking about him.

'That's not what I said,' he murmured, annoyed she had turned the tables on him so neatly, and annoyed even more by the fact he hadn't seen it coming.

'It's what you were thinking though,' she said.

Damn, she had him there.

'All I'm saying,' she said, leaning across the table to cover his hand with hers, 'is that it's okay to be scared of becoming a parent. Believe me, I was terrified. But don't let whatever cruel things he did to you influence your relationship with Mac. Because it's not relevant, unless you let it be.'

He stiffened and drew his hand out from under hers. The empathy in her voice and the compassion in her gaze made his stomach flip.

'I never said he was cruel to *me*,' he murmured, even

as the brutal memories clawed at the edges of his consciousness.

She watched him, her expression doubtful, but just when he thought she would call him out on his lie, her lips curved in a sweet and unbearably sympathetic smile. 'Then I'm glad.'

But he suspected she knew he wasn't telling the truth.

Reaching back across the table, he grasped her hand, then threaded his fingers through hers, suddenly determined to get back to a connection he understood.

She didn't resist, looking him squarely in the eyes. Her heartbeat punched her wrist as he rubbed his thumb across the pulse point.

'How about we stop talking about our pasts and start talking about what we plan to do for the rest of the night?' he said.

Being a parent was a role he doubted he would excel at for a number of reasons, but he was prepared to take her lead on that and hope for the best. Sex, however, was simple and something they both appeared to excel at, with each other. And it would defuse the tension currently twisting his gut into hard, angry knots.

'You didn't give me an answer,' he added, seeing the indecision in her eyes, which he was beginning to realise was unlike her. The woman seemed to have a natural inclination to rush headlong into everything. But not this. He wondered why that only made him want to convince her more.

'Because I haven't made up my mind,' she said, the words delivered on a tortured breath.

Smiling, as the shot of arousal echoed sharply in his groin, he opened her hand and lifted her palm to his mouth.

'Then let's see if I can persuade you,' he said, before biting gently into the soft flesh beneath her thumb.

She let out a soft moan, her vicious shiver of reaction making his own pulse dance.

But then she tugged her hand free and buried her fist in her lap. 'I want to sleep with you again,' she said boldly, her gaze direct. 'That's pretty obvious.'

'Ditto,' he said, unable to hide his grin as the dress slipped off her shoulder again.

She yanked it back up.

'I can see there's a but coming,' he said, determined to persuade her.

'But I don't want this…' She paused, and chewed her bottom lip, turning the trickle of heat into a flood. She thrust her thumb backwards and forwards between them. 'This *thing* between us to impact on your relationship with Mac.'

'It won't,' he said. 'Just to be clear, Carmel,' he added, astonished to realise he had yet to give her the 'hooking up' speech he gave every woman—usually long before he slept with them. Why he hadn't got around to it until now with her was something he would have to analyse at a later date, but the first order of business was to remedy the situation.

'All we're talking about is a short-term arrangement for the duration of your stay. I don't do long-term, it's just not in my make-up.'

'I know,' she said, completely unfazed. 'Your sister said as much. Don't worry, I'm certainly not looking for long-term either. Especially not with a guy like you.'

He frowned, taken aback not just by her pragmatic reply but also by the spurt of annoyance. 'Katie said that?' he asked, not sure why his sister's candour felt like disloyalty.

Given the history of their sibling relationship, why would Katie say any different? And why should he care? But what the hell did Carmel mean by a 'guy like you'…

What *kind* of a guy was he? Because he'd always considered himself fairly unique.

'Yes,' she answered. Then added, 'It's okay. Just sex works best for me, too.'

'Well, good,' he said, not quite able to keep the snap out of his voice as the annoyance and indignation combined. 'I'd hate to think you were expecting more from me than just orgasms on demand.'

Her gaze narrowed slightly. 'What's the problem? Isn't that the only thing you're offering?'

He forced himself to breathe and control the urge to contradict her... After all, it *was* all he could offer her, he'd just said so himself. It was all he had ever wanted to offer any woman.

But that didn't stop the questions queuing up in his head. Inappropriate questions which, intellectually, he knew he shouldn't want to ask her, had no right to ask her, but...

Who exactly had she slept with after losing her virginity to him? How many other men had there been in the past four years? Had they ever met his son? Formed a relationship with the boy when he had not? And what *kind* of guys *did* she consider worthy of more than just orgasm-supply duty? Because all of a sudden he wanted to know.

'Yes, precisely,' he said, through gritted teeth, holding onto the questions with an effort.

He'd get over his curiosity. This was just some weird reaction to spending all evening enthralled by those tantalising glimpses of her bra strap, the intermittent whiffs of her scent—fresh and sultry—and the torturous sight of her licking chocolate mousse off her spoon. Not to mention a much more revealing conversation about his past—and hers—than he had anticipated or was comfortable with. That was all.

She was still frowning at him. As if she was somehow aware he was struggling to keep his cool—which made the fact he was even more infuriating. What was it about this woman? How did she manage to push all his buttons without even trying? Buttons he hadn't even known he possessed till now...

No, he thought, that wasn't strictly speaking true. Because she'd pushed quite a few of his buttons that night four years ago, when he'd found himself haring after her escaping figure through the crowd of partygoers like a man possessed.

'So if orgasms on demand is all you want, what exactly is the problem with us going for it?' he managed, trying to finally ask a question that mattered, instead of all the ones that did not.

She heaved a deep sigh, which naturally made that damn dress slip off her shoulder again. Then glanced away from him. The fairy lights reflected in the glittery make-up on her eyelids. And he found himself catching his breath again, to stem the sharp flow of heat. She really was exquisite. This was all this was, an overpowering attraction to an extremely beautiful woman. Why was he complicating it? When he didn't want to and neither did she?

But then she turned towards him and he got momentarily lost in her sapphire eyes.

'I don't want it to be awkward, that's all. After it's over. Mac has to be my priority. As long as you're sure that won't be a problem?'

'A problem how?' he asked, because he was genuinely confused now.

'You know, that you won't get too attached. To me. And the orgasms.'

He wanted to laugh. Was she actually serious? Hadn't he just told her he didn't get attached? But the laugh died on his tongue, her dewy skin and large blue eyes suddenly making her look impossibly young... And vulnerable. When she'd never seemed that vulnerable before.

What a fool he'd been. He had been her first lover. And she was the mother of his child. Of course, that made her unlike any of the other women he had slept with, whatever her dating history since that night.

Not only that, but if he was to keep the promise he had made to her, about their son, he would never be able to sever this relationship the way he had severed every other relationship in his life before her when the woman he was dating had threatened to get too close.

For a moment, he considered forgoing the pleasure they could have during the coming days, and nights. To protect her, as well as himself, from the awkwardness she was referring to. But the rush of need came from nowhere, and he couldn't seem to say the words. Because it wasn't just sex he wanted, he realised. He wanted to know more about her. So much more.

He frowned, disturbed at how fascinated he was with her.

But surely, as long as he was well aware of the pitfalls of deepening this relationship over the next few days, he should be able to avoid falling into any of them?

After all, while he knew very little about real intimacy, so was naturally cautious about encouraging too much of it, he happened to be an expert at avoiding it.

'I guarantee, I won't get too attached,' he said, sure of this much at least.

And neither will you. Not when you realise how little I have to offer.

'Okay, then,' she said. 'I'd like to stay at your apartment for the rest of the week. And take you up on your orgasms-on-demand service.'

He gave a gruff chuckle, the rush of need making him a little giddy. He called the waiter over. 'Cancel the coffee order,' he said. 'And get the lady's jacket. We're leaving.'

CHAPTER TEN

CARMEL SHIVERED VIOLENTLY, but the cool spring breeze wasn't the only thing making goosebumps riot over her skin as the chauffeur-driven car drew up to the kerb in front of the restaurant entrance.

'Are you cold?' Ross asked, his hand settling on her back and making the silk of her dress feel like sandpaper.

She shook her head, aware of the heat slickening the heavy weight between her thighs.

She felt like that reckless girl again—intoxicated by the adrenaline rush. But she couldn't seem to stop herself from taking this opportunity to feed the hunger.

The driver opened the passenger door for them and Ross directed her into the warm interior. The scent of garbage from the street was replaced by the aroma of new leather and sandalwood cologne as Ross folded his tall body into the seat next to her.

'Put the partition up and take the scenic route, Jerry, slowly,' he said.

The hum of the screen lifting cocooned them into the shadowy space. She reached for her seat belt as the car pulled away, aware of her hand trembling. But as she went to snap the buckle in place, he caught her wrist.

'How about we live dangerously?' he said, the purpose and determination in his gaze accelerating her heartbeat.

She let the belt go, aware of the tension drawing tight

in her abdomen, and the heat firing up a few thousand extra degrees.

She nodded, giving him permission to pull her up and over his lap.

Suddenly she was perched above him. Her hands on his shoulders, her legs spread wide, her knees digging into the soft leather on either side of him, the short silk dress riding up to her hips. Excitement rippled and glowed at her core, making the hot nub burn as his large hands captured her bottom to drag her down, until she settled onto the hard ridge in his pants. His fingers kneaded and caressed, as urgent, desperate desire pounded through her body. Every one of her pulse points throbbed in unison, the rhythm in sync with the painful ache at her centre. She rubbed herself against the thick ridge as he caught her neck, lifting the hair away to tug her face down to his.

He captured her moan, the kiss firm and demanding. Her lips opened instinctively, giving him greater access, letting his tongue drive into her mouth, exploring, exploiting.

A harsh groan rumbled up from his chest as he cradled her cheek and tugged her head back to stare into her eyes. 'Take off the jacket,' he said, or rather commanded.

She did as she was told, scrambling out of the garment. The dress fell off her shoulder, as it had done so many times during the evening, but when she went to yank it back up he murmured, 'Don't.'

His thumb trailed across her collarbone, rubbing over the frantic pulse, then slipped under her exposed bra strap to draw it off her shoulder with the dress. The material tightened, snagging on the stiff peaks of her nipples. He cursed softly and undid the buttons on the dress's bodice, his other hand still caressing her bottom, his thumb sliding across the seam of flesh at the top of her thigh.

She gasped, thrusting her hips forward, the contact

too much and yet not enough, as she struggled to ride the ridge in his pants and release the coil tightening in her abdomen.

'Shh,' he murmured, the hint of amusement as rough and raw as she felt. 'We'll get to that in a minute.'

Just when she was gathering the words to protest, the bodice of the dress fell open to her waist, revealing the purple lace bra. Then his devilish fingers delved behind her back. The sharp snap of the hook releasing moments later startled her.

'What the…?' she murmured, shocked by his dexterity, as she whipped her hands off his shoulders to catch her breasts before she exposed herself to the whole of Manhattan.

He chuckled again, the low sound more than a little arrogant. He ran his thumb under the heavy flesh, making her nipples tighten painfully. Then pressed his face into her neck, kissing, licking. With her hands trapped trying to preserve her modesty, she shuddered, forced to absorb the onslaught of sensation, his tongue and teeth cruising across her collarbone, his other thumb still gliding backwards and forwards across that over-sensitised seam—too close and yet not close enough to where she needed him.

'Let go of the bra, Carmel,' he murmured, his hot breath making her nipples hurt even more.

'I can't, I don't want everyone to see,' she managed, aware of the sparkle of lights outside as the car crossed the busy junction at Times Square and Broadway. 'We might get arrested.'

He laughed, apparently delighted by her gaucheness, the rat.

'The glass is treated. The only one who can see you is me.'

She shuddered again, his thumb dipping beneath

the leg of her panties now, inching closer and closer to heaven.

'Are you...?' She swallowed around the lump of radioactive fuel suddenly jammed into her throat and throbbing between her legs. 'Are you sure?'

'Positive,' he said. 'Let go,' he demanded again.

Her hands released and seconds later he had pulled her arms out of the dress's sleeves, tugged her bra free and flung it away. She sat perched on his lap, naked to the waist, panting with need, but instead of covering herself, she forced herself to let him look his fill.

He groaned again, his gaze scorching the turgid flesh, before his hand cradled one heavy breast and his mouth captured the aching peak.

He licked and nipped, hardening the swollen flesh even more, making it pound and throb, before switching to the other breast. She had never realised she was so sensitive there. Her breasts had always been nothing more than functional. She'd loved feeding Mac when he was a baby, but this was so different, the arrows of need firing down to the hot spot at her core, building the brutal ache there with startling speed.

She cried out, barely able to breathe now around the torturous sensations firing through her body. Cupping her bottom and lifting her slightly, he kept his mouth on her breasts, sucking, nipping, caressing, her sobs echoing round the car, and slipped his fingers inside her panties to find the slick seam of her sex.

She jolted, bowed back, as he touched the heart of her.

The moan built from her core, slamming through her as the orgasm ripped into her, firing up from her toes and cascading through her in undulating waves. She rode his fingers, panting, sobbing, every part of her obliterated in the storm of sensation.

At last the orgasm ebbed, releasing her from its grip.

She collapsed onto him, washed out, worn through, damp and sweaty, and shaking with the intensity of her pleasure, aware of her naked breasts pressed against the fabric of his suit jacket, the nipples wet and sore from his attention.

Damn, he was still fully clothed.

Perhaps she would have been embarrassed that she was virtually naked and draped over him like a limp dishrag, but she couldn't think about anything in the moment, her mind floating in a shiny haze somewhere between bliss and consternation.

The last throes of the orgasm rippled through her as he finally slid his fingers from her swollen flesh. His hand caressed her neck, pressing her face into his shoulder, murmuring something in that deep, husky voice that made her feel cherished, important to him, when she knew she wasn't.

She clung on, breathing in the subtle scent of sandalwood and clean pine soap, the huge wave of afterglow at odds with the heavy weight settling on her chest.

How did he know just how to touch her, to make her fly? And how was she going to separate that from the painful pressure making her heartbeat stutter and stumble, and her ribs contract around her lungs?

He drew her head back at last, ran his thumb down the side of her neck as the car drew to a stop outside his loft. 'Ready for round two?'

She forced her lips to curve into what she hoped was a cocky grin, to cover the empty space opening up in her heart, then wriggled against the hard ridge in his pants while she pulled her dress back up. 'Bring it on.'

He laughed, but the sound reverberated in her chest, and did nothing to release the brutal stranglehold on her heart.

CHAPTER ELEVEN

CARMEL DABBED THE brush over the canvas one last time, to add texture to the paint layers, then lifted it away.

Enough. The portrait is finished.

She dropped the brush in the turpentine and shifted to glance past the easel at her model, who had taken to flopping out on the atrium's stone floor every morning after his first walk of the day with Nina.

Maybe he wasn't the prettiest dog in the universe, but he had so much character and charisma she had been unable to resist painting him when she'd finished the portrait of Orwell three days ago.

And you want to give Ross something tangible to remember this week by.

She frowned, pushing aside the sentimental thought.

'Hey, boy, want to look at yourself?' she asked, the sadness—at the thought her time with Ross was nearly over—squeezing her chest as Rocky's ears popped up, then his whole body followed.

The dog lopped over to the easel and stuffed his snout into her belly. She rubbed his head, giving a soft laugh. 'Not interested, eh?'

She was going to miss Rocky almost as much as his master when she returned to Ireland tomorrow.

Almost.

Who was she kidding? As much as she adored the

dog, she was going to miss Ross, so much more. Too much more.

She glanced at the sun beginning to slide towards the New Jersey shoreline in the distance, the turmoil of her thoughts deepening.

This shouldn't have happened. How had she become so attached to a moment—and a man—which was only supposed to be fleeting?

Ross would be home soon from work—for their last night together.

Her body quickened. The last six days, ever since they'd made their devil's bargain at the hip Murray Hill restaurant, had gone by in a haze of confused emotions and insatiable desire.

They made love two or three times each night, but why did it never seem to be enough? He would even wake her each morning from dreams, the heady touches triggering an instant and unstoppable response. They'd got into the habit of showering and eating breakfast together in the mornings. And then he was gone for the day. The hours she spent without him seemed to stretch into an agony of panicked thoughts and painful longing, peppered with a ton of 'what ifs' which had become harder and harder to shut away when he returned from work each day. And then there was that brutal shot of exhilaration, excitement, when he came back—always with some delicious takeout food they could dive into before diving into each other—which had stopped being all about the sex days ago.

Why couldn't she stop thinking about him? Not just the things he could do to her body, but the way he looked at her when she spoke about her day, or about her latest video call with Mac, or about a thousand other minute details of her life—that look, as if he was truly interested in what she had to say about herself, about their son, had come to mean far too much too.

And that was before she even factored in all the questions she wanted answers to, but had become too afraid to ask. Because that would only increase the sense of intimacy—an intimacy she knew she shouldn't need, shouldn't encourage, but seemed unable to resist.

The truth was, the only thing anchoring her to reality for the last few days had been her work, and Mac. Her brave happy little boy still wasn't showing any signs of missing her much, Imelda insisting he went to bed without a problem each night and was having lots of fun not just on the farm but also at Kildaragh—with Katie and Con who, to everyone's astonishment given Con's love of a grand gesture, had decided to stay in Galway for the first couple of weeks of their honeymoon.

She would have to thank them both when she got home for allowing her three-year-old terminator to gatecrash their romantic break.

But even as she thought of Katie and Con, she felt the pang of jealousy too at the settled, happy, wonderful future they had ahead of them together.

What was that even about?

They deserved their happiness. And this interlude with Ross was never supposed to have a future, they'd agreed as much in the Murray Hill restaurant a week ago. She didn't even want a future with him. This stupid yearning was nothing more than fanciful nonsense... And probably way too much great sex. She'd become addicted to the endorphin rush, that had to be it.

She cleaned the brushes and draped a clean sheet over the portrait, which she had decided to present to Ross tonight as a parting gift.

Not a romantic gesture, simply an acknowledgement of the fun we've had over this past week.

She gulped down the raw spot in her throat, knowing it was past time to leave New York.

Mac had asked for the first time this morning when she was coming home, igniting the yearning she always felt when she was away from him. She needed to return to Ireland now—to her real life again. Her little boy missed her and she missed him. Desperately. He grounded her and gave her life strength and purpose.

The last week had been filled with the heady excitement she had craved as a girl—a conflagration of physical fireworks—which Ross seemed capable of igniting simply by looking at her a certain way—but with it had come the emotional roller coaster she remembered all too well.

She'd become way too invested in falling asleep each night in his arms, or sparring with him about everything from politics to rugby to the latest gala at the Met over a bowl of Lucky Charms in the morning, or their impromptu picnics on the roof terrace each evening—and that look, which made her feel special, cherished, important to him, when she knew she wasn't, not really.

The domesticity, the simplicity of their routine in the last week had given her a fake insight into what it might be like to live with this hot, charismatic and taciturn man for real—but he wasn't her man, and she didn't want him to be.

She huffed out a breath. As the week had worn on, and the evenings and the mornings they spent together had become more intense, she'd lost perspective, that was all, become that girl again, who wanted something she couldn't have. Just like the little girl before her, who had craved her mother's attention, her mother's love, precisely because it was unavailable. It was a self-destructive notion that she needed to get a handle on.

Even if this could have been more, she knew Ross wasn't right for her... He was still so guarded, so wary, so unwilling to open himself to her or anyone else, but it horrified her to think that might be why she was so attracted to him. He presented a challenge, and she'd always had a bad habit of taking on challenges she couldn't win.

Rocky barked and shot out into the living area. Her heart thundered into her throat at the sound of the apartment's door opening, and the excited yips as Rocky gave his master his customarily insane greeting.

He's back early.

She held her ground, swallowed past the ball of anguish in her throat and finished putting away her paints, holding back the foolish urge to run out and give Ross an equally enthusiastic greeting.

Don't go soft now. Be cool, be calm, be smart. Protect yourself. Tonight's your last night... This is the way it has to be...

But as she listened to Ross's low voice talking to his pet and then he shouted, 'Hey, Carmel, where are you?' her heart ricocheted against her chest wall like a cannonball and the surge of sensory excitement was followed by the deep-seated yearning she still had no clue how to ignore.

She walked out into the living area, her thundering heart lifting into her throat as she spotted him, tall and indomitable and so hot in his business suit, with one hand caressing the dog's head and the other ripping off his tie.

His gaze locked on hers, possessive and intense—as always. And the heady rush of adrenaline and need shot through her on cue.

'Hey, how are you?' she said, disconcerted when her voice broke.

'Good,' he said. 'Now I'm finally home.'

The word *home* echoed in her chest, with far more resonance than she knew it deserved.

This isn't your home, or Mac's, it's his—he doesn't want you here, not in the long term. Why can't you get that through your eejit head?

'Sit, Rocky,' he demanded in a voice that brooked no argument. The dog planted his butt on the floor, his tail swishing against the polished wood, as Ross marched past him towards her.

Grasping her chin, he lifted her gaze to his, and the need on his face stabbed into her gut.

'Let's go to bed.'

It wasn't really a question, but she nodded anyway, the sensation flooding her system helping her to ignore the pulse of longing beneath.

He boosted her into his arms and strode across the room towards the curving metal staircase in the middle of the large space. She wrapped her legs around his waist and kissed him hungrily, channelling all the yearning into the promise of release.

Sex will make this better. Sex will take this ache away. Because sex is all this was ever meant to be.

But as they crashed into his bedroom together, and began to rip off each other's clothes, the brutal pain in her chest—and the frantic feeling of desperation and confusion and need—refused to go away.

Ross drew out slowly, the last spasms of another titanic orgasm still pulsing through his system as her swollen flesh released him. He rolled off her, flopped down, exhausted, sated—or as sated as he could be when he didn't seem able to completely satisfy his endless craving for her. He covered his eyes with his arm, holding back a staggered groan.

He could hear her breathing beside him, her deep sighs as shattered as he felt.

He'd taken her like a madman. Again. Hadn't even had the decency to wait until they'd eaten. Hell, he hadn't even been able to stop on the way home tonight long enough to pick up takeout for their evening meal, the way he'd been forcing himself to do up to now—just to prove he could be civilised enough to feed her before jumping her.

Why did this hunger keep getting worse? More insistent? Why couldn't he stop thinking about her? All day. Every day.

He'd lost focus at work in the last week, stopped caring about most of it, had curtailed his standard fourteen-hour days to eight hours, because he couldn't bear to be away from her a minute longer.

Today he'd been caught daydreaming about the sound of her sobs in the shower that morning while doing a conference call about a container ship emergency in the Gulf of Mexico—and made a fool of himself in front of the head of De Courtney's South American division and her two assistants because he'd had absolutely no clue what they were discussing when she asked him a direct question.

But as his breathing finally evened out and his heartbeat slowed, he knew it wasn't just this insatiable hunger that was the problem. It was so much more.

It was the sight of her each morning, her long legs crossed as she perched on one of the stools at his breakfast bar and tucked into the cereal she'd become as addicted to as he was.

It was the soft glow that seemed to light up her face every time she told him some new story or detail about their son—a soft glow he had become addicted to as well. So addicted he wasn't even sure any more if it was the insights she was giving him about his son—such as his obsession with horses and dogs, his love of arranging his toys in long lines all over her living room, his hatred of eating anything green despite her attempts to hide it in everything she cooked for him—which fascinated and captivated him, or the joyous light in her eyes when she was talking about Cormac.

It was the feel of her—so warm and soft in his arms as he fell asleep each night—that had managed to chase away the nightmares.

It was the dabs of bright colour in her hair from her work, which he enjoyed washing out after they had made love, the smell of turpentine and oil paint that lingered on her, and around the apartment now.

It was even the thought of knowing she would be there in the evening, waiting with Rocky, when he got back from the office. Making him realise he'd never really considered his condo a home until this week—which was ludicrous, seeing as he had owned the duplex loft for over six years, ever since moving to Manhattan.

But worst of all, it was the knowledge of how much he was going to miss all those things when she left tomorrow morning.

She stirred beside him and sat up. 'Did you bring anything home for supper?' she asked.

He dropped his arm, the inevitable hunger resurfacing as he absorbed the sight of her naked back, his gaze drifting down to her buttocks. 'Not today,' he said, unable to stop himself reaching out to caress the soft swell. She shivered and he lifted his fingers, aware of the heat settling in his groin again. 'I've run out of ideas. We've tried out pretty much every place I usually use,' he lied to cover the truth—that he hadn't wanted to wait a moment longer than necessary to see her again. 'How about I take you out for supper?' he made himself ask, even though the last thing he wanted to do right now was leave the apartment. Or this bed.

The truth was, if he could, he would happily spend the next fourteen hours, before her flight home, buried deep inside her, losing himself in this incendiary physical connection so he wouldn't have to dwell on all the other things he was going to miss when she was gone.

And the powerful urge to ask her to stay a while longer. He'd even come up with a plan to make that happen. Had asked his assistant to rearrange his schedule and have the staff at his estate in Long Island open up the house, simply so he could take a whole week off for the first time since his father's death ten years ago.

But he'd nixed the idea on the way home.

When the hell had he become so obsessed with her? It would be laughable, if it weren't so damn disturbing. And would it really be wise to spend twenty-four hours a day with her, when he was already spending every waking minute thinking about her?

She glanced over her shoulder at him, holding the duvet up to cover her breasts, breasts he had just spent several insatiable minutes devouring because he knew exactly how sensitive they were—and how she loved his attention there. A warm flush highlighted the freckles that covered her nose. Funny how he found the surprising glimpses of modesty as captivating as everything else about her. It enchanted him, probably because it reminded him so forcefully of the girl he had met that first night. The girl she had insisted was long gone. The girl who had been bold and beautiful, brutally honest and artlessly arousing, and yet at the same time had an innocence, a fragility beneath the boldness that had captivated him then, and made him want to protect her now... Even though he was fairly sure the only person she needed protecting from was him.

She smiled, that quick, generous smile that always made his heartbeat bounce in his chest. 'Okay, that would be grand. I've not seen much these past few days except the inside of this apartment,' she said. The little dig made him laugh, but he could see something else in her eyes that had his bouncing heart swelling in his throat.

'But I've got something to show you first,' she added, then threw off the duvet and got off the bed.

She hunted around for her clothing as he watched her, unable to deny himself the simple pleasure of studying her as she dressed in quick, efficient movements. First her panties went on, then the bra, which she hooked in the front then swivelled round so she could loop the straps over her shoulders. She wiggled back into the faded jeans—speckled with paint—which he knew she wore while she worked, then threw on a baggy green T-shirt with the insignia of the Irish Rugby Union Team, which was speckled with even more paint.

He stretched, and adjusted himself, grateful the heavy duvet hid the insistent erection already making a second appearance.

Since when had he found watching a woman dress so hot?

She swept back her wild red hair and tied it into a knot behind her head, then looked over her shoulder. 'You'll have to get out of bed, you know, if you're to see your surprise... And we're to eat before midnight.'

He chuckled, her sharp tongue as alluring as the rest of her. And forced himself to sit up. 'I'm going to have a quick shower. Do you want to join me?'

Arousal darkened her eyes, but she shook her head. 'If I do that we'll never get out of the apartment and you know it.'

'True,' he said, trying to keep his voice light and unconcerned, despite the brutal pulse of disappointment and yearning. And the knowledge that he was even going to miss her attitude.

Time to back off, De Courtney. This obsession is getting out of hand.

He dropped his feet off the bed, keeping the duvet firmly over his lap.

'I'll shower downstairs and meet you in the atrium,' she said, rushing out of the room before he could change his mind, and attempt to seduce her back into his bed.

He took care of the insistent desire in the shower—while he tried not to dwell on the humiliating fact he hadn't had to resort to such antics since he was a desperate teenager in an all-boys boarding school in the Scottish Highlands and the chance to interact with girls had been rarer than the chance to interact with Martians.

He took his time shaving and getting dressed in more casual clothes, determined not to let the yearning get the better of him again. Perhaps it was a good thing Carmel was leaving tomorrow. He'd become fixated on her, that much was obvious. Establishing his relationship with his son was what mattered now. Avoiding hard conversations about that had been all too easy while he was focussed on feeding the hunger—perhaps that was why it had resolutely refused to be fed.

He finally made his way downstairs. Rocky greeted him with his usual over-the-top enthusiasm. 'Hey, fella,' he said, his voice strangely raw as he knelt down to give the hound a tummy rub.

Thank God for the dog. He'll keep me company when she's gone. I'll be fine.

He'd never had any trouble being alone before now. This was all in his head.

But then he walked into the atrium and saw her standing in front of her easel, the evening light turning her damp red hair to a burnished gold. And the yearning dropped into his stomach like a stone.

I don't want her to go. Not yet. I'm not ready. And there's the boy to consider, I need to meet him, but I need her help with that.

Then she turned and stepped aside. 'Here, what do you think?' she said, directing his gaze to the painting on the easel beside her. 'I thought you might like a portrait of Rocky.'

He stared, so stunned for a moment, he was utterly speechless. The portrait was exquisite of course, the likeness striking, the dopey adoration in the dog's expression so expertly captured, it was hard to believe his pet wasn't embedded in the canvas instead of by his side, busy licking the back of his hand.

But as his gaze met hers, again, it wasn't the exquisite artistry of the portrait—the evidence of her incredible talent—that had the stone in his stomach turning into a boulder the size of El Capitan.

'You painted that? For me?' he said, the boulder rising up to scratch against his larynx. So astonished, he could barely speak.

He couldn't remember the last time he had received a gift. His father had never been a gift giver—believing his son's birthdays were simply another chance to drum into him his responsibility to the De Courtney name, while his Christmases had always been spent at school as a child. He didn't currently have any friends close enough to know when his birthday was, let alone celebrate it with him. Plus he avoided dating over the holiday season simply to avoid the kind of sentimentality that was now all but choking him.

Not only was this gift rare, though, it was also so thoughtful.

How had she captured what he saw in his pet so perfectly? Did she know how much he relied on Rocky for the warmth and companionship he had convinced himself he didn't need?

And suddenly he knew. He couldn't let her go. Because he needed time to find a way back from the precipice he was standing on the edge of as she stared at him now with the same soft glow he had seen on her face when she talked about their son... And the yearning in his chest turned into a black hole.

'Ross? Is everything okay?' Carmel's heart slammed into her throat. He looked stricken, his gaze jerking to hers—the flash of panic in it disturbing her almost as much as the melting pain in her own heart as she absorbed his visceral and transparent reaction to her gift. One minute he'd been his usual guarded self, his defences very much back in place, as she knew they would be, because they always seemed to return after they made love. She would glimpse something in the throes of passion that she had become as addicted to as the endorphin rush of good, hard, sweaty sex. But as soon as they collapsed on top of each other, each joining more frantic and furious than the last, the mask would return, and she was sure she had imagined that intense moment of connection.

But as his gaze rose to hers now, and she watched the shutters go down again, she knew she hadn't imagined it this time. Because for one terrifying moment he had been totally transparent and what she'd seen had broken her heart—yearning, desperation, confusion and panic, but most of all need.

And in that split second, she had the devastating thought that she was falling in love with him. That this yearning wasn't about sex, or the unfulfilled needs of that emotionally abandoned little girl, it was so much more dangerous than that.

'Do you like it?' she asked, her voice raw, terrified that her heart was already lost to him and knowing that, even if it was, it didn't really change anything. Because he had given her no indication that his heart was available to her. Or would ever be. That he was even capable of ever letting down the guard he had built around it.

Maybe he could love his dog. A dog's love was unconditional, and uncomplicated. But what indication had he given her he could love her? Or that he was even willing to try? None whatsoever.

She'd spent her childhood beating her head against that brick wall—trying to make her mother love her—and it had made her into someone reckless and impulsive and ultimately afraid. She couldn't spend her adulthood doing the same with him. But even knowing that, she couldn't seem to stop the giddy rush of pleasure when he spoke again, his voice rich with awe.

'It's incredible.'

'I thought I could give it to you as a parting gift,' she said, determined to remember their time was nearly over. She couldn't give into this yearning, this hope, this foolish need. Not again.

'Don't go.'

'What?' she asked, sure she hadn't heard him correctly. Wishing she hadn't felt her heart jolt.

'Don't go back to Ireland tomorrow,' he said. 'I have an estate in Long Island, which I mostly use for occasional weekend breaks and business hospitality purposes. But I haven't taken a proper holiday in ten years. The forecast is for warm weather. I'd like to take you there.'

'I can't stay,' she said, upset that for a second she'd even considered accepting his invitation. How far gone was she, that she would even want to pursue a reckless pipe dream when she'd missed her little boy so much? 'I need to go home. Mac needs me. And I need him.'

To ground me again and make me realise this isn't real.

'I thought we could fly him over, so he could spend the time with us there.'

'Are you...? Are you serious?' she asked, so shocked by his suggestion she couldn't think over the pounding in her chest.

He'd listened when she'd regaled him with stories about Mac, had asked a lot of questions about their child, but she hadn't expected this.

'Absolutely. If I'm going to form a relationship with him, I think we both know I'm going to need your help. I know nothing about children. This is a big step for us all. I don't want to make a mistake.'

'That's... I'm overwhelmed,' she said, because she was. But she forced the foolish bubble of hope down—knew it had no place in this arrangement. She needed to be practical now... And most of all she needed to protect herself, not just from these foolish, fanciful notions about Ross and her, but from the devastating prospect of letting that insecure girl reappear again, who had thought she could make someone love her just by wanting it enough.

'I'd have to go back and get him,' she said. If they were going to do this thing, it had to be about Mac—not them. Because there was no them. 'He's only three, I couldn't send him over on his own.'

'How about I ask Katie if she will accompany him?' he said. 'I need to repair things with her anyway. It's been five years and, after my behaviour at the wedding, I think perhaps more than a ten-minute conversation is required.'

Again, she was surprised, at his willingness to consider such an option. And at how open he was being to having a proper conversation with his sister. Surely this was a huge sign he was willing to do much more than simply go through the motions in his relationship with Mac?

'Okay, that could work,' she said, not sure Katie would go for it—after all, she was on her honeymoon at the moment. If anything, she was fairly sure Conall would insist on using the Rio Corp jet and accompanying his wife to New York, but if Ross was serious about repairing this rift, he would eventually have to talk to Con too. And involving her brother and his wife would be a good way of helping her to keep things in perspective and focus on what mattered now—Ross forming a relationship with his son.

'Good, I'll make the arrangements,' he said, in his usual no-nonsense fashion. But then he stepped forward and cupped her cheek. 'How about we order takeout? I'm not sure I want to leave the apartment tonight.'

She made herself smile, but the gesture felt desperately bittersweet as her abdomen pulsed at the purpose in his gaze. She covered his hand with hers, to draw it away from her face. 'That would be good, but, Ross...' She swallowed, knowing she had to make a clean break from him and the intimacy they had shared, before their son arrived. The danger to her heart was all too apparent now. 'We can't continue sleeping together while Cormac is with us. It would confuse him.'

It was a cop-out. Cormac wouldn't be confused. He didn't need to know they were even sleeping together if they were discreet. A part of her hated the lie and using her son to reinforce that lie. But she had no choice. Not if she was to keep her heart secure for the week ahead. Watching Ross bond with his son would be hard enough, without introducing the intimacy they had already shared into the equation. An intimacy she hadn't been as good at dealing with as she had believed.

'Why?' he asked. 'Hasn't he seen you dating before?'

'No, there hasn't been anyone...' She stopped. But his eyes narrowed, his gaze seeing much more than she wanted him to see. The flush burned in her cheeks, but it was already too late to disguise the truth.

Damn my Irish colouring.

'There hasn't been anyone but me?' he asked.

She could lie again. She wanted to lie, only feeling more exposed and wary at what the truth revealed, aware of the sudden intensity in his gaze. But a bigger part of her knew lying would only give the truth—that he was the only man she had ever slept with—more power.

She shrugged, even though the movement felt stiff. 'Being a single mum is a full-time job. I haven't had the time,' she said, trying to make it seem less of a big deal. Knowing in her heart it was just more evidence of how careful she needed to be now.

She had expected him to look spooked by the admission. Would have welcomed that reaction—because it would have given her at least some of the distance she so desperately craved.

But instead of looking spooked, he just looked even more intense. So intense she could feel the adrenaline rush over her skin.

'I see,' he murmured, then framed her face and pulled her close.

He slanted his lips across hers, his tongue thrusting deep, demanding a response. A response she was powerless to stop. The kiss was raw and possessive, and heart-breakingly intense.

She held his waist and kissed him back, letting the fear go, to indulge in the moment.

She wasn't that reckless girl any more. She would never jeopardise Mac's happiness, or her own, on a pipe dream—which was why she couldn't sleep with him again after tonight.

But as he lifted her easily into his arms to carry her upstairs she groaned, and gave herself permission to indulge that reckless girl, one last time.

CHAPTER TWELVE

'THANK YOU FOR interrupting your honeymoon, Katie. And bringing Mac over,' Ross said as he headed towards the liquor cabinet, needing a stiff drink. The evening sunlight shone off the water in the distance, the scent of sea air helping to calm his racing heartbeat.

He'd held his son for the first time ten minutes ago. His hands shook as he lifted the whisky bottle and splashed a few fingers in his glass.

'You're welcome, Ross. He was extremely excited during the flight over. But I think it was all too much for him and he crashed out on the helicopter ride to the estate,' Katie said.

He'd forgotten how little his child was. When the helicopter had touched down at the Long Island estate's heliport twenty minutes ago and his brother-in-law had emerged from it with Ross's sister by his side, carrying the sleeping boy—the child had looked so small and defenceless Ross's ribs had tightened.

Cormac had woken up momentarily, and smiled sleepily at his mother, reaching out to be held. She had scooped him into her arms with practised ease—but then she'd turned to Ross and said, 'He's heavy. Do you want to hold him?'

He'd reached to take the boy, only realising as he lifted

the sleeping child into his arms that he had no idea what he was doing.

But Mac had settled his head against his shoulder without complaint, his small arms wrapping around Ross's neck—the sweet scent of talcum powder and kid sweat invading his senses as the child dropped back into sleep.

Ross's heartbeat had accelerated as a boulder formed in his throat. Part panic, part fear, but mostly a fierce determination that he would do anything to protect this child. It had reminded him a little of how he had felt when he had lifted Rocky as an injured and abused puppy out of that dumpster, but this time the feeling had been a thousand times more intense.

But that moment had also brought the reason why he had invited Mac…and Carmel to Long Island into sharp and damning focus.

He took a gulp of the fiery Scotch, let the liquor burn his throat to suppress the jolt of annoyance at the memory of the assessing look in Conall O'Riordan's eyes as he had lifted the boy back out of Ross's arms so he and Carmel could settle him in his new bed, while Ross and Katie talked.

The knowledge O'Riordan had effectively taken Ross's place in Cormac's life for the last three years had been a sobering thought. But what was worse was the knowledge he had no right—not yet—to stake any kind of claim to being the boy's father. And that his reasons for inviting the boy here—with his mother—had been far from altruistic.

He'd resented Carmel's suggestion they stop having sex yesterday evening, had been filled with an almost visceral urge to change her mind, especially when she had told him he was the only man she had ever slept with. That swift surge of possessiveness, of ownership almost, had made their joining even more intense, even more desperate, but this afternoon when they'd arrived at the estate—and this evening when they'd waited together for O'Riordan's helicopter to arrive—he'd forced himself to back off. To give her space. And now—after holding his son for the first time—he realised that attempting to seduce her back into his bed would be a mistake.

He'd waited far too long to take on the responsibility of parenthood. He could not afford to mess it up. But more than that, what more did he really have to offer Carmel?

He splashed another finger of Scotch into a tumbler. 'Would you like something to drink, Katie?'

'Nothing for me, thanks,' his sister said, but then he noticed the flush on her cheeks, and the way her hand swept down to cover her stomach.

He frowned, his gaze meeting hers. 'My God, you're pregnant.'

The colour intensified, and her eyes widened. 'How did you know?'

He choked out a laugh, the stunned surprise on her face somehow helping to break the tension gathering in his stomach.

It made him remember how transparent she'd always been. Even as a lonely, grief-stricken teenager, the first time he'd met her. She'd run up to him that day—a complete stranger—and wrapped her arms around him, her eyes flooding as she told him how grateful she was to have a brother.

He could remember at the time being extremely uncomfortable. Patting her stiffly on the shoulder and wondering what the hell he was supposed to do with a grieving teenage girl who he did not know from Adam.

In the end, he'd abrogated the responsibility to a series of expensive boarding schools. He'd failed Katie that day. He couldn't afford to fail Mac in the same way. Surely that was where he had to concentrate his energies, not on the kinetic sexual connection he shared with the boy's mother, however tempting.

'You're an open book, Katie,' he said.

The knots in his stomach tightened again as the news of her pregnancy echoed in his chest.

His baby sister was having a baby of her own. But how much better prepared for that role was she than he was? Katie, even as a girl, had always been open and compassionate and generous. All things he would have to learn, if he was going to have any hope of living up to the task of being a father.

'Or you're a mind reader,' she countered, sounding disgruntled.

He smiled and poured her a soda water, added ice and a slice of lime. He handed her the drink. 'I guess congratulations are in order. When is the baby due?'

She took the glass and grinned, all the love she already felt for this unborn life shining in her eyes. 'We had the dating scan two days ago and they basically put the due date on Christmas Eve,' she said, her excitement suffusing her whole face now. 'Dreadful timing really—who wants to be born on Christmas Eve? But we got pregnant quicker than we thought. Poor Con's still in shock, actually. He was convinced it would take several months—he had worked out a whole schedule for when exactly we should stop taking contraception so we'd have a spring baby, which he thought was the perfect time for a birthday.' She cradled her still flat belly, her grin widening. 'But apparently baby didn't get the memo.'

'Bummer,' he said, his smile becoming genuine at the thought of 'poor Con' having his carefully laid plans shot to hell.

Welcome to the chaos, bro.

But then the empty space opened up again.

When was his own son's birthday? How could he even

pretend to be a father when he didn't know something so fundamental…and had never thought to ask?

'You should have told me you were pregnant,' he said, as it occurred to him she hadn't just changed her honeymoon plans to make the trip to the US at such short notice. 'Carmel and I could have made other arrangements.'

'Don't be silly, I'm perfectly fine,' she said, touching his arm. 'And we were happy to do it. Con has a house in Maine he's been waiting to show off to me for a while and then we're heading to his place in Monterey.'

He very much doubted her husband had been quite as happy to accommodate him—as he recalled the frown on O'Riordan's face when he'd first spotted Carmel and him standing together at the heliport.

He suspected the guy was even now grilling Carmel about what exactly the two of them had been doing together in the last week, but he kept his opinion of O'Riordan's reaction to himself, the enthusiasm in Katie's eyes both humbling, and painfully bittersweet—because his affair with Carmel was now over.

'I'm so excited you've made the decision to be a part of Mac's life. He's an incredible little boy. You won't regret it,' she added.

'I just hope he doesn't,' he mumbled.

'He won't,' Katie said and touched his arm. 'I think you're going to make an incredible father.'

'Thanks,' he said, humbled all over again by her belief in him, as it occurred to him he'd done absolutely nothing to deserve it.

The truth was he'd been a piss-poor brother. And it was way past time to change that too. *Really* change it.

'I'm sorry, Katie,' he said, realising how long overdue the apology was when she tilted her head, her gaze puzzled, her smile fading.

'What for?' she asked softly.

'Everything.' He huffed out a breath, looked away, because he couldn't bear to see the scepticism he knew he *would* deserve.

His gaze tracked towards the horizon, across the manicured lawn, the tennis courts, the guest house where Carmel and Mac would be staying, the pool—surrounded now by new railings, which he'd had installed before Mac's arrival.

He'd spent a small fortune refurbishing the estate buildings three years ago—the mansion had originally been constructed by a railroad baron in the nineteen-tens but had fallen into disrepair since the eighties. But how much time had he spent here? Virtually none. In many ways, the lavish but unlived-in property was a symbol for his life. He'd worked so hard, spent so much time and effort building De Courtney's, but with every goal he had achieved his life had only become emptier as he'd shed all his personal responsibilities, and shunned companionship and love.

The L word made him shudder.

Did he love his son? Already? Was that possible? The thought had his heart rate ramping up again.

He breathed deeply, trying to counter his haphazard pulse.

Calm down. You can handle this.

The twinkle of lights from the pool house reflected off the surface of the water as the sun sank into the ripple of surf in the distance, casting a red glow over the wooden walkway that tracked past the tennis courts and into the dunes. Whatever happened now, whatever he was capable of feeling for the boy, he made a vow never to shirk his responsibilities again. He would learn to be a good father. And maybe finally fulfil the promise he had made all those years ago to be a better man than his own father.

And he would keep his hands off Carmel, even if it killed him.

He turned back to his sister. 'I'm sorry for treating you like an inconvenience, a debt to be paid, rather than a sister,' he said in reply to her question.

She stood, watching him. But, weirdly, he didn't see scepticism, all he saw was compassion.

'You deserved—needed—so much more than I was ever capable of giving you. So I'm sorry for that too,' he finished.

She shook her head. But the all-inclusive smile, the unconditional love he knew he did not deserve, still suffused her features—and tore a hole in his chest.

'You did the best you could, Ross. But I also think you're capable of much more than you think,' she said, so simply it had fear slicing into his heart.

No, he wasn't. He knew he wasn't. He was selfish and entitled and absolutely terrified of love... Or he would have been a much better brother to her all those years ago.

And he would never have asked his sister to bring his son all the way to America, primarily so he would have a chance to sleep with the boy's mother for another week.

'I think you're ready now to open your heart to Mac...' Her smile widened, her eyes twinkling with excitement. 'And maybe his mum too, because it's pretty obvious there's a lot more going on between you and Carmel than just figuring out your new parenting arrangements.' She laughed, the sound light and soft and devoid of judgement. 'And that makes me so happy. Carmel's an amazing woman, brave and honest and talented and...' Her smile widened. 'Well, I'll stop being a matchmaker, but I think you two could make a great couple—even without factoring in Mac.'

'I'm not sure your husband agrees,' he managed as the shaft of fear twisted and turned in his gut.

Maybe he could love his son. He already felt the fierce need to protect him. But Carmel? That wasn't going to happen. Ever.

'Ignore Conall,' Katie said, still beaming, still so sure he would make a good partner for Carmel... On no evidence whatsoever.

Katie wasn't just sweet, and generous and kind, he realised, she was also irrepressibly optimistic and hopelessly naïve. Why else would she have forgiven him so easily after the way he'd treated her?

'My husband has been known to be chronically wrong about affairs of the heart,' she continued, the secret smile tugging at her lips suggesting her courtship with O'Riordan hadn't been quite as blissful as Ross had assumed.

Yeah, but O'Riordan's dead right about this.

'And he's more like a father to Mel and Immy than a brother,' she added. 'So he has a tendency to be a tad overprotective. But, believe me, Carmel is her own woman. And if she trusts you enough to let you form a relationship with Mac, my guess is she's probably already halfway in love with you.'

The guilt plunged like a knife deep into his gut.

No way. She can't be in love with me.

'I see,' he said, taking another sip of his whisky as he hoped like hell Katie was wrong.

CHAPTER THIRTEEN

'MR ROSS, CAN WE play more?'

'No way, slugger, it's time to get out of the water before you turn into a fish.'

Carmel grinned as she listened to Ross and Mac in the pool. Her little boy giggled and she lowered her book to see Ross hoist Mac out of the water—where they'd been playing together all afternoon—and sling him over his shoulder to stride out of the pool.

Rocky joined in the fun, barking uproariously and dashing over from his spot beside Carmel's lounger. Ross stood on the pool tiles—the water running in distracting rivulets down his broad shoulders and making his swimming shorts cling to his backside.

The inevitable endorphin rush joined the painful pounding in her chest that was always there when she watched the two of them together.

She blinked, her skin heating—her heart hurting in ways she hadn't expected and couldn't afford to acknowledge.

Ross lowered the giggling, squirming Mac to his feet, and she found herself enchanted by the tableau they made together. He wrapped a towel around his son and began to dry him with a confidence she was sure would have surprised them both six days ago—when she had handed him their sleeping son at the heliport, and she had seen the stunned emotion as he'd held Mac for the first time.

Mac's giggles got considerably louder as the dog helped out with the drying routine using his tongue.

'Rocky, sit!' Ross said.

The dog stopped licking Mac's face and planted its butt on the tiles—having learned to obey his master's voice. Mac wrapped his arms round Rocky's neck, burying his face in his fur.

'I love Rocky,' he said.

The dog sat obediently. Any worries they'd had about introducing Rocky to their child had quickly been dispelled. The pressure on her chest increased. The rescue dog had turned out to be a natural with children—his usually excitable temperament placid and protective with Mac.

But Rocky was not as much of a natural with children as Ross had turned out to be.

'I know you do,' Ross replied. 'I think he loves you too,' he added, the roughness in his voice making Carmel's eyes sting.

Ross loved his son. And Mac absolutely adored his father.

The weight on her chest grew as she thought back over the events of the past week. Which had been easy in some ways and incredibly hard in others.

Ross had thrown himself into fatherhood with a determination and purpose—and a hands-on approach—she hadn't expected, but she realised now, she should have.

He was a pragmatic, goal-oriented man, who knew how to pay attention to details. From the moment they'd arrived at the estate, the morning before Conall and Katie were due to fly in to drop Mac off, Carmel had known she had made the right choice to take this extra week and the opportunities it held… To finally give her son a father, however painful this week had promised to be for her.

The estate itself had been the first surprise. She'd expected something sleek and stylish and glaringly modern.

Instead, what she'd found was a lovingly restored Italianate mansion—reminiscent of something straight out of *The Great Gatsby*—which had been meticulously prepared for their son's arrival. Not only had Ross had a room repainted next to hers in the large guest house by the pool, and fitted with everything a little boy could possibly want—including a bed shaped like a pirate ship and a box full of age-appropriate toys—he'd even thought to have the estate's pool fenced in.

The workmen had been finishing off the railings when they had arrived, and he'd simply said, 'I thought it would be best to make sure he couldn't hurt himself.'

At that moment, she'd had to force herself not to allow that foolish bubble of hope to get wedged in her throat again. Not to give into the emotions that had derailed her during their week together in New York.

The interrogation she'd had from Con during his flying visit had helped. Her brother had questioned her about whether there was 'something going on' between them as soon as they'd been alone together after putting Mac to bed. And she'd been able to tell him the truth, or as much of the truth as he deserved to know, that there was nothing going on between them, not any more.

He'd looked at her suspiciously, no doubt picking up on the qualification in the statement, but to her surprise, instead of giving her another earful about how wrong Ross De Courtney was for her—something she was already well aware of—her brother had simply sighed, then given her a hard hug and whispered:

'Be careful, Mel. You and Mac are precious to me—and I don't want to see either one of you hurt.'

Conall's capitulation had empowered her despite the pain. That her brother had finally accepted she had the right to make her own choices felt important, like a validation, that she was doing the right thing now by stepping back, taking stock, instead of rushing headlong into feelings that would never be reciprocated.

The only problem was, knowing she was doing the right thing hadn't made it any easier to deal with the news that Con was about to become a father himself.

She'd been overjoyed for him and Katie, of course she had. She knew he would make a magnificent father and Katie a wonderful mother. But a secret, shameful, mean-spirited part of her had also resented the fact her brother was going to have it all, when she could not.

And as she'd watched Ross begin to establish a strong, loving relationship with their son, that niggling, mean-spirited, resentful part of herself had refused to go away.

Which was of course ludicrous, because the man had surprised her in the best way possible.

He'd talked to Mac so carefully, so practically, and increasingly taken on the more difficult elements of child-care without hesitation—had even, she could admit now, established a rapport with their son that was very different from her own. Where she tended to baby Mac, to worry about the risks rather than see the reward of allowing her son more independence, Ross was firmer with him, but also bolder. He was protective but also pragmatic and she'd been forced to admit that it had allowed Mac to gain in confidence, particularly in the swimming pool, where he'd been tentative at the beginning of the week to put his head under the water, but was now happy to leap in and go under, as long as he knew Ross would be there to scoop him up if he struggled.

She hated that she'd even resented a little bit seeing Mac grow to rely on his father, but she had. Up till now it had only ever been her and Mac. She'd held all the cards, made all the decisions. And while on the one hand it had been good at the end of each day to have someone else to talk to about Mac, it had also been much harder than she had expected to let go of that control. To know that she wasn't the only one who would have a say in Mac's upbringing from now on.

They hadn't had any conversations about visitation rights, formal custody agreements—perhaps because she had been careful to keep the evening meals they shared to an absolute minimum, the torture of being alone with Ross, and knowing she had no right to touch him, to indulge the pulsing ache in her sex as well as her heart, quite hard enough without being forced to talk about the permanent relationship she was going to have to share with him now.

Unfortunately, she doubted Ross would let her get away with that again tonight. She was already dreading the thought of spending the evening talking about the legalities of their continued relationship—in sterile, unemotional detail, when unemotional was the last thing she felt.

'Okay, buster, how about we feed you and the dog?' Ross said as he lifted Mac back into his arms, and the boy wrapped his arm around his neck.

'I want pizza.'

'What? Again?' Ross did a comical double take.

Mac nodded enthusiastically.

Ross laughed. 'I guess we'll have to ask Ellie if she has any left,' he said, talking about the chef who Mac had charmed just like everyone else on the six-person staff.

'Yes, please, Mr Ross,' he said, playing with Ross's hair now, in the way he had always done with her when she held him like that.

Mr Ross.

The name echoed miserably in Carmel's heart. Like

a symbol of her cowardice and selfishness in the last six days. It was way past time Mac knew who Ross really was. Not just Mammy's friend, but his father.

They hadn't had a chance to discuss it in the last six days, like so much else about Ross's permanent relationship with his son, because she'd avoided it. The same way she'd avoided being alone with Mac's daddy.

She swallowed heavily as Ross walked towards her toting their son, the surge of desire at the sight of his long limbs and naked chest prickling across her skin like wildfire—and making her feel like even more of a failure. Even more of a fraud.

Ross had scrupulously observed her request to end their intimate relationship while Mac was here. He'd escorted her to the guest house, after they had their meal together on the nearby terrace each evening. And had made no move to even touch her, let alone kiss her, since they'd arrived at the mansion.

And in a weird way, she'd even resented that too—that it was so easy for him to end their physical relationship, when it was so hard for her.

Her gaze took in the toned skin glistening in the afternoon sunlight, the bunched muscles of his biceps as he held their son aloft, the rakish beard scruff shadowing his jaw, which she'd watched appear in the last few days and had been itching to run her nails through.

Each night she woke from dreams, sweaty and aroused, the longing so intense she'd often had to resort to finding her own release.

The demands of navigating the massive adjustments when it came to co-parenting their child had taken some of the edge off that insistent, endless yearning in the early days, but every time she was near Ross now, she felt the pull. And she knew he felt it too.

She'd seen him watching her, when he thought she wasn't looking.

But what was worse, she couldn't seem to separate the physical yearning from the emotional yearning any more. Instead of their enforced abstinence making it go away, it seemed to have made it gather and grow, to become this huge lump of need and longing.

'I'm going to take Mac in now. He wants pizza again, is that okay?' Ross stood before her in all his glory, the prickles of heat now both damning her and terrifying her.

'Please, Mammy, can I now?' Mac chimed in.

'I don't suppose another pizza night would do any harm,' she said.

Mac started cheering.

'Cool,' Ross said, his voice roughening as his gaze flicked to her cleavage and back up again. 'You want me to handle his bath and bedtime routine?' he asked.

'Why don't we do it together?' she said. She should tell Mac Ross was his daddy. What was she waiting for? This wasn't about her and Ross, and it never had been. Perhaps if she finally acknowledged that—told her little boy who Ross really was—it would make the craving shrink, instead of grow.

He nodded and headed off with their baby in his arms, Rocky following on their heels.

Her gaze dipped to admire his glutes in the wet shorts. She forced it back up.

Focus, Mel, on what's best for Mac. And only Mac.

'Mammy, Mammy, Mr Ross said if Rocky has a puppy we can have him. Can we?'

Ross watched Mac reach out from his bed as his mother walked into the little boy's bedroom.

'Oh, did he now?' she said as she perched on the edge of the bed and gave their son an easy hug. She sent Ross a tense smile, and he caught a whiff of her scent—earthy and hopelessly seductive—the surge of need shot through him, vicious, unstoppable and unrelenting.

Only one more night to keep your hands to yourself.

They'd managed to stick to their no-sex rule, had focussed on their son these past few days—he couldn't afford to give into the need now. He dragged his gaze away from her to concentrate on the boy.

'It's okay, I doubt Rocky will be having pups any time soon,' he said, determined to keep his mind on what mattered, instead of what shouldn't.

The last six days had been a revelation in so many ways. He had fallen completely and utterly under the spell of the little boy who he still couldn't quite believe was a part of him. And fatherhood, much to his astonishment, hadn't been nearly as much of a struggle as he'd assumed. It was intense and disturbing on one level, the emotional independence he'd clung to for so long now utterly shot to hell. Every time he held the child's soft, sturdy body in his arms, listened to him giggle, or even whine, watched his small round face light up with excitement or frown with intelligence, or breathed in the scent of talcum powder and bubblegum shampoo, the fierceness of what he felt still shocked him, but it didn't terrify him any more.

His feelings about Mac were surprisingly simple and straightforward and, once he'd let them in without hesitation, were much easier to handle than to deny... His feelings for the boy's mother, though, remained a minefield that had only got worse as the week wore on.

Especially as he watched her struggle with the new reality of letting him be a father to her son.

He wanted her incessantly, of course. The effort to stay away from her, not to let their quiet evening meals lead to more, had been pure torture. But far worse was the yearning, the desire to be with her constantly, the fascination of simply watching her. It made him feel like the small boy he'd once been, giving ownership of his happiness to someone else.

But it was that struggle to share her son, the moments when he could see the doubts and fears cross her face, and realised how hard she must have had to strive to do this all alone, that had really crucified him.

Because it had made him realise how strong and how brave she really was.

The nightmares, not surprisingly, now he could no longer hold her in his arms each night, had also come back with a vengeance. Haunting his dreams and waking him up, confused, alone and yet painfully aroused.

'Can we have a puppy, Mammy, please?' Mac held her cheeks, forcing her to look directly at him.

Ross huffed out a laugh, trying to ease the tension in his gut. And force the sweet, simple feelings for the child to the fore. Because they made so much more sense than his obsession with Carmel.

'Mr Ross said so. Can we?'

Carmel tugged her face away and laughed. The first real laugh he'd heard from her in days. The light musical sound arrowed into Ross's gut, as it always did.

'We'll see, but before you go to sleep, I have something important to tell you,' she said, deflecting the boy's attention with an ease that always impressed him. 'Or rather, *we* have something important to tell you,' she said, glancing his way and sending him a look that made his heart thunder even harder.

He frowned, confused by the direction of the conversation, and the fierce glow in her eyes… He'd seen it before, on the pool terrace that afternoon, and so many other times in the past few days, often when he was with Mac. It disturbed him how it only increased the yearning.

She's not yours…she can't be…you don't want her to be.

'What, Mammy?' Mac said at the exact same time as he asked.

'We do?'

She nodded at him, then turned back to their son, but her hand reached out and covered his on the bedspread. The touch was electric, sparking so many reactions, not one of them safe, or subtle, or secure.

'Do you remember, you once asked me why you didn't have a daddy, Mac?' she said.

Mac nodded as Ross's heart began to pound painfully. Was she about to tell the boy who he really was? Damn it, he wasn't prepared for this.

'You said I did, but he couldn't be with me,' the little boy said as the pain in Ross's chest twisted with guilt, his grip on his emotions slipping even further.

Carmel nodded. So calm, when he could feel himself falling apart inside.

'He's with us now. Mr Ross is your father, Mac. And he wants to be a part of your life now, very much.'

Mac blinked sleepily, then his eyes widened, the spark of joy and instant acceptance making Ross's heart slam against his rib in hard heavy thumps.

'*Really?*' he asked, his little brows launching up his forehead.

Ross leaned forward, his hand shaking as he cupped his son's cheek. The boy's skin felt warm and impossibly soft beneath his palm. 'Yes, really,' he confirmed, his words coming out on a husky breath, the emotion all but choking him now.

'I'm sorry I wasn't here sooner,' he said, trying to concentrate on the child, and not the fissure opening up in his chest.

The boy was a smart, sweet, bright, brilliant child—who loved dogs and playing in the pool, who could eat a whole slice of pizza without taking a breath, and charm the pants off everyone he met—and he couldn't have been prouder to be his father. So why did he feel as if the black hole were opening up to swallow him whole?

'Can I call you Daddy?' the little boy asked, looking hesitant for the first time since Ross had met him.

'Of course, I would love for you to call me Daddy,' he replied. 'If you want to,' he finished, as it occurred to him he'd never called his own father by such a familiar name.

As much as he hated to think of the man who had frightened him so much as a child, and whom he had despised as an adult, he clung to that distinction.

Carmel had told him once his own father's failings as a human being didn't have to be his failings, and she'd been right about that. He would strive now to earn this child's trust and respect, the way his own father had never earned his.

But as the little boy flung his arms around his neck and whispered into his ear, 'Daddy, don't forget now, I want a puppy,' the aching hole in his heart refused to go away.

He blinked, the stinging sensation in his eyes making the hole bigger as he lifted the child out of his arms and placed him back in the bed.

'We'll have to talk about that more with your mother, and Rocky, but your request has been duly noted,' he said, the words scraping against his larynx. 'I think it's time for you to go to sleep now. You have a long journey home tomorrow,' he added, the thought crucifying him even more.

But as he pulled away, to let Carmel finish tucking their son in, the word *home* echoed in his chest and seemed to scrape against his throat.

The thought of how much he was going to miss his son, how much he was going to miss them both once they were gone tomorrow, only compounded the sense of loss, of pain and confusion.

He'd thought about it, of course he had, but until this moment he hadn't realised that they had turned this huge, palatial estate into a home in the last week. The way Carmel had turned his loft in Tribeca into a home too. The thought terrified him.

How had he let that happen? When had he ever been anything but self-sufficient? How come it only made him feel emptier inside?

Ross lifted off the bed, his steps heavy as he walked to the door, to give Carmel time to settle the boy, but then he heard the small sleepy voice say, 'Goodnight, Daddy.'

'Goodnight, son,' he replied.

He left the guest house and walked out onto the lawn beside the pool terrace to relieve the choking sensation in his throat. He looked up at the stars, and felt the deep sense of loss at the thought of returning to the city tomorrow. Without them.

He had to get out of here, to get away, from the pain in his chest and the hole she had made in his heart.

Resentment flared. She shouldn't have told Mac like that. Without his input. Shouldn't have hijacked him.

He spotted Rocky sleeping on one of the loungers, headed towards the small gate into the pool area ready to take the dog back to the main house, when he heard the guest house's door open behind him.

Longing shot through him. Swiftly followed by anger. Because the black hole in his stomach remained, which he had no idea how to repair now.

He turned, to see her walking towards him, the summery dress she'd changed into fluttering around her legs in the evening breeze. She had the baby monitor in her hand, which she always brought with her when they ate out on the garden terrace in view of the guest house.

'Why did you tell him?' he said, making no effort to keep the brittle edge of anger out of his voice—to disguise all the other emotions churning in his gut, which he had no idea now how to control… Longing, need, desire and a fear so huge it all but consumed him.

'I thought it was past time,' she said, with a flippancy that infuriated him even more.

How was this so easy for her?

'You don't think we should have talked about it first?' he said, still trying to control the brutal turmoil she had triggered.

She tilted her head to one side, considering, her whole face suffused by that ethereal glow that had captivated him and terrified him. *Always.* Ever since that sultry summer night so long ago when she'd mesmerised him with her soft lilting accent, her smart, erudite and impulsive personality and the rich scent of her arousal. She was looking at him now the way she'd looked at him then, as if she saw right through him. Knew all the things about him he didn't want her to know. Could see the frightened boy he'd once been, inside the man.

Exposed was too small a word for how it made him feel.

Exposed, and wary and… Needy. Damn it.

'I suppose,' she said. 'But we've only this one more night together, so I saw no point in waiting.'

We've only this one more night together.

The yearning reverberated through him, twisting something deep inside. Yanking at that empty space that had been growing ever since he'd seen her again… And he was very much afraid only she would ever fill.

The desire surged through him again, but this time it was sure and solid and elemental. And simple, unlike all the thoughts and feelings queuing up in his throat.

He stepped towards her, not sure what he was doing any more, but knowing he needed to taste her again, just once more. This enforced celibacy had been her idea, but he'd embraced it after his conversation with Katie, believing it was the best way, hell, the only way, to create the distance he needed to let her go…

But somehow it had backfired on him—because not having her had only made him want her more.

'Don't tempt me, Carmel,' he murmured, seeing her ragged pulse punch her collarbone and hearing the shattered pants of her breathing. She felt it too, this hunger, this need. That was all this was, a physical connection so intense they'd only increased it by keeping their hands to themselves… 'I'm not in the mood,' he finished, the statement closer to the truth than he wanted it to be.

He was on edge, the emotions he didn't understand, for her as much as the child, too close to the surface, threatening to tip him over into the abyss.

He heard the shattered sigh, felt her hands brace against his waist, saw her gaze darken with awareness… He braced himself, expecting her to pull back, even as her spicy scent filled his nostrils and the desire, so fierce, so urgent, beat in his groin.

But instead, she lifted her chin, the challenge in her gaze unmistakable as her fingers fisted in his shirt, the stars reflected in her eyes bottomless enough to drown him as she leaned into him.

'Kiss me, Ross,' she whispered, bold, provocative and as tortured as he was. 'We've only this one night, why should we waste it?'

His control snapped, like a high-tension wire winched too tightly.

He thrust his fingers into her hair, tugged her head back and slanted his mouth across hers, capturing her sigh of surrender and plunging his tongue deep into her mouth.

He took command of the kiss, absorbing her sighs, dragging her into his arms, grinding the hard weight of his arousal against her sex. Forcing back the turmoil of emotions lodged in his gut at the thought that he had to let her go tomorrow.

With the knowledge that, tonight, she was all his.

Heat spread through her body like wildfire, but it was the emotion closing her throat that made her groan as Ross's tongue invaded her mouth, claiming her sighs for the first time in six days. She tried to focus on the need, that brutal endorphin rush, but the terrible truth kept echoing in her brain.

You're not just falling, you've fallen. This man is it for you. There's no going back now. There never was.

His hands cupped her bottom, pressing her against the prominent ridge of his arousal, letting her know how much he needed her, how much he wanted her too. Clasping her waist, he lifted her easily into his arms, and wrenched his mouth away. She missed it instantly, the longing already at fever pitch.

'Where?' he rasped.

'My room,' she gasped. 'But we'll have to be quiet.' She'd dropped the baby monitor in the grass. But they would hear Mac if he woke up.

'Quiet? Yeah…' he said, his lips doing diabolical things to her neck, and her heart rate.

'Mammy? I had a bad dream.'

Mac's cry didn't register at first through the fog of dazed heat and terrifying emotion, until Ross froze, his fingers digging into her hips. His head jerked up and she saw the stricken look in his eyes before he gasped. 'Oh, God.'

He put her down so suddenly she stumbled. Looking over her shoulder, she saw Mac standing in the doorway of the guest house, in his PJs, his hair rumpled, rubbing his eyes.

The flames that had been burning in her abdomen died

down as she tried to switch into mummy mode. The heat continued to burn in her cheeks, though, as she scooped up their son. 'It's okay, baby. Mammy's here.'

Her little boy wrapped his arms round her neck, snuggled his face into her shoulder, still mostly asleep, thank goodness. She couldn't help the pounding in her chest as she carted him back to bed and tucked him in—getting a sleepy rendition of his nightmare, which had involved an enormous pizza and a puppy who kept eating Mac's share.

After kissing him, and promising that when they got a puppy they'd make sure it didn't like pizza, she levered herself off the bed.

Mac was already asleep as she rechecked the room's monitor, giving herself time before she returned outside.

What had they just been about to do? Because it had been so much more than just the fever of desire.

'I love him.'

She whispered the words to herself, forcing herself to face them, knowing them to be true, despite the fear still gripping her chest.

She closed the door to her little boy's room, stood with her back to it and tried to focus. She'd tried to deny her feelings for Ross, for six days, maybe even longer than that. Tried to make this need, this connection, about nothing but sex and her own insecurities. She'd been so scared before, terrified even, of admitting the truth to herself.

But how could it be so wrong? He'd shown himself to be a good father, a good man in the last week. She'd come to know him for who he really was. He wasn't the man she'd fallen for that night four years ago. Not a romantic notion, but flesh and blood, with fears and insecurities just like hers. He could make mistakes, try and fail, just as she had, but she admired him for that now. And yes, there were many things he seemed incapable or unwilling to share, about his past, his childhood, but she knew he had struggled to overcome them. Surely that was what mattered now.

How could she know how Ross really felt about her, about them, about the chance for them to make a future together with their son, instead of apart, if she didn't tell him she loved him? Her fear of her feelings had never really been about Ross and her—it had simply been an echo of that little girl. Who had become so scared to fail she'd refused to try.

She took a deep breath, the fear still huge, but somehow not as black or impenetrable. Not as final. Because now, finally, she had a plan.

She walked back out of the guest house to see Ross standing with his back to her. Her heart did a giddy two-step, the emotion flooding her again.

God, he was so gorgeous, so hot, but he was also flawed, and human, just as she was.

He held the dropped monitor in his hand, the rigid set of his shoulders reminding her of the haunted, horrified look that had crossed his face when he had spotted Mac.

Her courage faltered a little as she approached him. With his head bowed, and his body radiating tension, he seemed a million miles away. What had caused that awful look? she wondered.

She touched his shoulder and he jerked. 'It's okay, Daddy,' she murmured as he turned towards her. 'We didn't scar him for life,' she added, trying to keep her voice light and even, and ignore the painful hope swelling in her chest.

'Ross, what's wrong?' she said when she got a look at his face.

Where was the man who had been devouring her moments ago with such urgency? The man she was finally ready to admit she loved? Because the man in front of her now looked like a ghost. The blank expression so rigid, it was starting to scare her.

'Nothing,' he murmured, his voice as controlled as the rest of him. 'I'm tired. And I'm sure you are too,' he said. 'I'll have the staff bring some food over for you. You've got a long day tomorrow—and I need to head back to Manhattan early. I'll be over in the morning to say goodbye to Mac.'

She'd barely absorbed the long list of details—which he must have been preparing while she was putting Mac back to bed—before he nodded and turned.

Everything inside her rebelled.

No.

She grasped his arm to stop him walking away. 'Wait. What? That's it?'

She could feel the frantic beat of her heart threatening to choke her. But ignored it. This couldn't be happening. How could he suddenly be so cold? When only moments before…?

His mildly puzzled frown—so distant, so vacant—made the pain in her chest increase. 'I think it's for the best we don't finish what we started—which would clearly have been a mistake.'

'A…a mistake?' she stuttered, still stunned by the sudden change in him from wild, passionate lover to cold robot. 'How can it be a mistake when I… I'm in love with you?'

The declaration burst out on a tortured breath. It wasn't how she'd planned to tell him. But that sudden dismissal had left her reeling. Frantic and scared and suddenly so unsure again.

She'd never been a person to temper her feelings. To judge and weigh all the pros and cons carefully, methodically, before making a move. She'd seen that impulsiveness as a weakness for so long. Something to be corrected and suppressed. But she didn't want to live like that any more. To try and deny rather than confront. She was sick of being a coward.

If she'd been wrong, about everything she thought had been happening between them, about where they might go from here, she needed to know now. She could deal with the worst, she told herself. She just couldn't deal with lying to herself any longer.

He blinked several times, clearly as shocked as she was by the whispered revelation. But then a muscle in his jaw tensed, and the first stirrings of nausea churned in her stomach, alongside a deep wave of sadness. The same sadness that had overwhelmed her once before, when she'd received that cold, cruel, cutting text. How could she have forgotten that feeling so easily? Enough to open herself to the same torment again?

'You don't love me, Carmel. What you feel for me is infatuation, believe me, it will pass.'

No, it won't, and I don't want it to. Why can't we be a family? Why can't you let me in?

It was what she wanted to say, what she wanted to shout at him so he would hear her. Her feelings were her own and he had no right to doubt them… But the sadness had spread like a black cloud, over the bright twinkle of hope, covering everything in a thick impenetrable shadow and she knew… This wasn't her decision, it was his. She couldn't make him love her, any more than she had been able to make her mother love her.

And it would only hurt her more to try.

When she fell in love it was fierce and true and she was very much afraid for ever. But she was also a realist. And what she had to do now was deal with the truth. Because if he couldn't love her back, couldn't even accept her feelings for him, what chance would they ever have?

So she said nothing, just stood dumbly, refusing to

fight, refusing to cry, but most of all refusing to beg, as he walked into the night.

And the next day, when he came to the guest house to say goodbye to his son, she applied her make-up carefully so he wouldn't see the tears she'd shed over him. And she forced herself to stay strong, to stay calm, to say nothing about the agony of longing and to focus on keeping things light and upbeat for their little boy.

She told herself she would get over it. And she forced herself to pack away all her half-formed dreams for them the same way she packed away her clothes.

But when they boarded the De Courtney Corp chopper at the estate's heliport and she watched Ross standing on the grass and waving goodbye, his dark hair flattened by the wind from the helicopter's blades, the beard scruff that had abraded her skin the night before during that ferocious kiss now shaved off, she held her little boy a bit too tightly, and knew it was going to take a lot more than expertly applied make-up to repair her shattered heart.

CHAPTER FOURTEEN

'MR DE COURTNEY, the conference video call with the European hub is due to start in five minutes.'

Ross stared aimlessly at the Manhattan skyline from his office at the top of De Courtney Corp's US headquarters, only vaguely aware of his assistant's voice, so exhausted he wasn't sure he even had the energy to switch on his computer, let alone conduct a two-hour video call. It was three days, three long days since he had left Long Island, since he had watched the chopper containing Carmel and his son disappear on the horizon, and he still couldn't get her face out of his mind. Or the words she'd whispered to him:

'I'm in love with you.'

But the surge of impossible hope that replaying those words in his mind over and over again brought with it faded into a morass of guilt and loathing, and horror, as he recalled the sight of his child, his son, so small, so vulnerable, witnessing that frantic kiss. And the terrible memories that sight had triggered, memories he had buried for so long, memories he had only ever grasped in nightmares until three days ago, had come slamming back into his consciousness ever since... And refused to leave him now.

The sick dread pressed against his throat again.

His father's voice cold, callous, cruel, his mother's pleading, the cries, the agony, the blood...

He thrust shaking fingers through his hair.

How could Carmel love him when he was only half a man? And that half was not that different from his own father after all...

'Would you like me to get you some coffee before you start, Mr De Courtney?'

'No,' he said, turning to see his personal assistant standing at the door, looking concerned. 'Actually, yes, but can you cancel the call, Daniel?' he said.

'Um...of course...certainly, sir,' the young man said, but he looked even more concerned and completely confused. Probably because Ross had never shirked a work responsibility in his life.

He turned back to the view he couldn't see as his PA left to get his coffee.

He couldn't go on like this. He needed help. He felt as if he were in a fog, a dark, cloying fog he would never find his way out of. Mostly, he needed Carmel. She was the light on the horizon, thoughts of her the only thing he seemed to be able to cling onto when those dark memories loomed.

But he also couldn't forget her shattered expression that night, and her listless behaviour the next morning. So calm, so controlled, so devoid of passion. And so unlike the woman he knew.

He'd done that to her. How could he ask her for help, when his knee-jerk reaction to her declaration of love had destroyed everything they might have had?

'Mr De Courtney, you have a video caller,' Daniel said, walking back into the office with a cup of coffee. 'A Mrs O'Riordan?'

Carmel? The brutal surge of adrenaline was painfully dispelled when Daniel added, 'She says she's your sister?'

Not Carmel, Katie.

But then a strange thing happened. The rush of need would have disturbed him three days ago, but he was too exhausted to resist it now. Or question it. 'Put her through to my mobile,' he said, his voice rough.

Maybe Katie would know what he could do, how to fix what was broken?

He scraped his fingers through his hair, sat down at his desk, and picked up his smartphone to click on the link his PA had sent through.

'Katie?' he said, shamed by the desperation in his own voice as her familiar face appeared on the screen.

'Ross, what on earth did you do?'

The forthright, even aggressive tone was so unlike his usually sweet and malleable sister, all he could do was blink. 'What?'

'To Carmel, you dolt?'

The mention of her name had the pain he had been keeping so carefully leashed charging through his system all over again.

'You've seen her? What's wrong with her? Is she sick?' he said, concern and panic taking hold and shaking him to his core.

'We spoke to her via video chat, last night. And yes, she's sick. Heartsick. Although...' Her eyes narrowed. 'Ross, you look even worse than she does. What happened between you two?' The soft concern in her voice made the guilt bloom like a mushroom cloud.

He swallowed convulsively, to control the new wave of nausea. 'She told me she loved me and I threw it back in her face,' he said, blurting out the truth. But he was past caring now, what Katie thought of him, what anyone thought of him. 'I want to fix it, but I don't know if I can.'

'Oh, Ross. Of course you can, if you want to enough,'

Katie said, the concern in her gaze turning to determination. 'Do you?' she asked.

'Yes, yes, I do,' he said—that much at least was simple. 'But I've made such a mess of everything.' He wanted to believe Katie, but how could he vanquish the demons from his childhood? After all this time? And how could he risk sullying Carmel with them? 'But I'm not sure it can be fixed. I'm not even sure I deserve to have it fixed. I certainly know I do not deserve Carmel.'

Katie stared at him. 'You do know that's nonsense, don't you?' she said, the matter-of-fact tone, and her undying faith in him, making him wonder why he had ever believed he didn't want a sister. Or need one.

Then she added with complete conviction. 'I'm sure between the two of us, we can figure out a way to fix it.'

He wasn't sure he believed her, but he knew that if nothing else Katie had given him the courage to try.

CHAPTER FIFTEEN

CARMEL STARED UP at the large detached mansion house tucked at the end of a blossom-strewn mews in London's Kensington as the chauffeur-driven limousine that had picked her up at Heathrow glided through iron gates and into a pebbled courtyard.

'Where are we?' she asked the driver as he opened the door, confused now as well as wary. But too tired to summon the anger that had fortified her during the flight from Galway in Ross's private jet, after the text she'd received two days ago. His personal assistant had requested that she attend a meeting with his legal team today in London—to discuss Mr De Courtney's visitation rights and other financial matters.

Ross hadn't contacted her himself, and that had hurt, at first. But then she had been grateful. Seeing him again would only draw out the agony, she thought miserably as she stepped out of the car. Was that why he hadn't mentioned this meeting when he was video calling Mac last Sunday from Manhattan? Their conversation had been short and stilted and… Well, agonising… Which surely proved it would have been too soon to see him again in the flesh.

'This is one of the De Courtneys' ancestral homes, I believe, Ms O'Riordan,' the chauffeur remarked, although he seemed unsure.

Strange. She had assumed she would meet with Ross's legal team in the company's London headquarters.

'Okay,' she said, forcing down the new wave of sadness. She didn't really want to spend time in his ancestral home, but she followed the driver up the steps to the imposing Georgian building without complaint.

She just wanted to get this over with.

She hadn't slept properly in close to two weeks. Ever since she and Mac had returned from New York. She'd been burying herself in work, and childcare, her go-to strategy when anything in her life was stressing her out. But it seemed this crisis was bigger than any she'd faced before.

Why couldn't she forget that last night, the hope she'd had—so quickly dashed—that she and Ross might build a family together? A future? It had always been a ludicrous pipe dream—one last hurrah for that starstruck girl who had fallen under his spell in an apple orchard a lifetime ago. She needed to pull herself together now and stop thinking about what might have been and instead face the reality... And concentrate on the callous ease with which he had rejected her again.

Mac was what mattered now, and on that subject at least, she knew they were in accord—because she'd heard her son's giggles from the other room as he had chatted with his father in Manhattan for over an hour on Sunday. There was no reason to believe the legal team were going to ambush her with any conditions she couldn't accept. And if they did, she had Con's number on speed dial.

She stepped into the musty interior of the house and shivered. The gloomy hallway, mostly devoid of furniture, was even more austere and forbidding than the outside, despite the sunlight coming in through the stained-glass window above the door and illuminating the dust motes in the stale air.

The chauffeur stood back to let her enter then pointed towards an open door at the end of the hallway. 'I was asked to direct you to the library, and then leave. But I will wait outside for you when you wish to depart.'

Huh?

'Okay.' Carmel frowned, the house's chilling stillness only broken by the loud ticking of an antique grandfather clock as the chauffeur closed the front door behind him.

She made her way down the hallway, the blip of irritation fortifying her. Seriously? Didn't they think she had better things to be doing than spending the day in an empty house?

She stepped into the library. And her heart stopped, then rammed into her throat. Instead of the team of solicitors she had been prepared for, there was only one man, silhouetted in the room's mullioned windows. A man who had delighted and devastated her in equal measure.

'Ross?' she whispered.

Was she dreaming now?

But then he turned from his contemplation of the house's overgrown gardens. And her battered heart threatened to choke her. Pain shot through her, as fresh and raw and real as it had been two weeks ago, and she recalled every single word of his rejection for the five thousandth time.

'You don't love me, Carmel. What you feel for me is infatuation, believe me, it will pass.'

If this was infatuation, she wanted no part of it any more.

'Carmel,' he said, his voice husky and strangely hesitant as he crossed the room's parquet flooring, his footsteps echoing in the empty room—the books that must once have been here long gone.

'What are you doing in London?' she asked, surprised her voice sounded so steady when her ribs had become a vice, squeezing her chest so tightly she was afraid her heart might burst.

She drank in the sight of him, but everything about him now seemed intimidating—his long legs, broad shoulders, that devastatingly handsome face, the planes and angles sharper than she remembered them, the waves of chestnut hair furrowed into haphazard rows, the dark business suit and white shirt, so unlike the man who had played with their son for hours in the pool.

She stepped back, and he stopped.

'Don't, don't come any closer,' she said, the inevitable surge of heat her enemy now, like the painful yearning in her heart. 'If you've brought me here just to tell me again you don't love me, I got the message the first time,' she said, brutally ashamed of the quiver in her voice.

Her eyes stung. She'd shed so many tears for him already, how could there still be more? God, could he not even leave her with this last scrap of dignity?

'I brought you here to show you the house where I grew up.' He glanced around the room, thrusting his hands into his pockets, the hunched shoulders matching the flash of pain and loathing she had seen that night.

She should tell him no, she wasn't interested any more. But she couldn't seem to get the words out, past the thunderous emotion still choking her.

'Why?' she managed to ask, suddenly unbearably weary. Unbearably tense. The struggle to hold onto her tears so hard.

'Because I want you to know everything. So you can understand what happened on our last night, when you told me you loved me.'

She frowned. What was this now? Did he want her to say it again? So he could reject her again? Why was he talking in riddles?

But even as the caustic thoughts assailed her, she could

see that wasn't it. He looked tormented, on edge—whatever ghosts had haunted him that night, this was where they dwelled. And suddenly she wanted to know—all those things he had been so unwilling to share with her. So all she said was, 'Okay.'

He gave a stiff nod, then glanced around the empty shelves. 'This is the room where my father destroyed the only photograph I had of my mother in front of me,' he said, his voice so flat and remote it was chilling. 'I was seven.'

She shuddered, reminded of how he had spoken to her two weeks ago in that same monotone.

'That's hideous,' she managed. 'Why would he do such a thing?'

He shrugged, the movement tense but somehow painfully resigned too, as if it didn't really matter, when it clearly still hurt.

'He was sending me to boarding school and he was furious that I was still wetting the bed at night, according to my governess. I'd been having night terrors ever since...' He hesitated, swallowed. 'Ever since her death, two years before. He was concerned I would embarrass the De Courtney name at school.' His lips lifted in a rueful smile, but there was no humour in it, only sadness. 'To be fair, it worked. I was more terrified of him than the nightmares.'

'I... I'm so sorry, Ross. He sounds like a terrible father.'

She wanted to go to him, to hold him, to console him, the way she would Mac when he had a nightmare, but she could see the brittle tension, and sense the struggle within him to hold the demons at bay so he could talk about them. So she kept her distance.

She had known his father had scarred him, but had she ever realised to what extent? She'd dismissed that haunted look two weeks ago when Mac had appeared so unexpectedly, too busy wallowing in the rejection that had followed, the desire to tell him how she felt... Why hadn't she asked questions, thought more about what he might be feeling, instead of focussing on her own?

'If it's hard for you to be here, we don't have to stay,' she added. Suddenly wanting to leave this place. Sure, if he was going to reject her again, to tell her this was why he could never love her, she didn't want it to be here.

But he shook his head slowly, the small quirk of his lips somehow devastatingly poignant. 'Don't let me off the hook so easily, Carmel.'

She nodded slowly, realising that, for whatever reason, she had to let him show her the rest.

He led her out of the library, and up the stairs, reaching a large landing, his movements stiff and mechanical and comprehensively lacking his usual grace. He stopped on the threshold of the first room on the left. A huge piece of furniture—from the shape of it under the dustsheet, probably a four-poster bed—stood in the middle of the room. He hesitated, took in a lungful of air, then stepped inside.

'This is where the night terrors came from. This is the room where I watched my mother and her baby die. And where, the therapist believes, nine months before I may have watched him assault her.'

'Oh, God.' Carmel gasped beside him, then pressed her fingers to her lips. Ross tucked his hands into his pockets to stop them shaking.

One lone tear skimmed down her cheek, crucifying him. He could see pity in her gaze as she turned towards him. But more than that he could see compassion.

The nausea in his gut rose in a wave to push into his throat.

The sick, weightless feeling in his stomach reminded

him of those moments—between sleep and waking—when he could see it all again so clearly. But he knew he had to keep talking. He owed her this. So he forced himself to channel the advice the therapist he had employed a week ago at Katie's suggestion had given him.

You're not responsible for her death, Ross. But what you saw between your parents would cause a deep trauma for anyone—let alone a five-year-old child—and that's what we need to address.

He needed to tell her the truth, about the baggage he might well carry with him always—and the truth about his heritage, and the legacy he was terribly afraid might lurk inside him.

'She used to like me to sleep with her,' he said. 'I suspect now to stop him visiting her at night. But I can remember one night. I woke and he was there, beside the bed, kissing her, hurting her, she was crying and he wouldn't stop…' He couldn't say any more, the vision terrifying him even now.

'Ross…' She reached out her hand, grasped his fingers, held on. 'Is that why you freaked out, when Mac woke up and saw us kissing that night?' she asked.

'I… I suppose yes. It brought it all back. But…' He hesitated, scared to say the truth out loud. She squeezed his fingers, giving him the courage he so desperately needed to continue. He forced himself to turn, to look at her, to give it to her straight. 'I wanted you so damn much in that moment. I'm not sure I could have stopped, if you'd asked me. She begged him to stop and he wouldn't and I can't bear the thought that I might… That Mac might have witnessed the same depraved—'

'Ross…' She cut him off, pressed a gentle palm to his cheek, to stop the rambling confession. A lone teardrop fell from her lid. 'What Mac witnessed, if he witnessed anything at all, was a kiss between two consenting adults.

It's not the same thing at all,' she said so simply it pierced through the fog at last. The feel of her palm stroking his face felt so soft, so warm, soothing the brutal knots in his belly. 'And anyway, you did stop, so fast you almost dropped me,' she said, the humorous quirk of her lips warming the brutal chill that had overcome him the moment he had walked into this room.

But then she added, 'Can you tell me what happened when she died?'

He dipped his head. He didn't want to talk about it. But somehow it was easier now, knowing she didn't blame him, the way he had blamed himself, for his father's sins.

'I wasn't supposed to be in here,' he said. 'No one saw me, they were too busy trying to save her... But her cries had woken me up,' he said, but then the words simply ground to a halt.

'You don't need to tell me,' she said softly beside him. Weirdly, the fact she would let him stop, if he needed to, gave him the courage to carry on.

'I do... I want to,' he said, knowing it wasn't pity he saw in those stunning blue eyes, but a fierce compassion. 'I want you to know what you'll be dealing with, because... I still have the nightmares. They came back, after I discovered I had a son. And once I couldn't hold you at night. And they've been much worse, since we left Long Island.'

'Why didn't you tell me, Ross?' Her voice broke on his name, another tear slipping down her cheek.

'Because I was so ashamed,' he said simply.

She shook her head, then gripped his wrist and tugged his hand out of his pocket. She threaded her fingers through his and held on. The contact was like a balm again, releasing the renewed pressure in his chest.

'Is that why you had the vasectomy?' she asked, with

an emotional intelligence that he now knew he found as captivating as the rest of her.

He nodded. Funny she should figure that out when he never had.

'Yes, I think it was. I guess it all got jumbled up in my mind. He was there, in the room, demanding they save the baby, no matter what. It was another boy, another male heir, and I expect that was why he had assaulted her in the first place. Because that was always his priority. Continuing the De Courtney legacy.' He gathered in a painful breath, let it out again. 'There was so much blood,' he murmured, seeing it all again. The private medical team rushing around, the metallic smell suffocating him, the silent scream tearing a hole in his chest.

His breathing became laboured, but her hand gripped his, reassuring, empowering, making the nightmare vision retreat.

'So you had yourself sterilised as a young man, so you would never put a woman through what he had put your mother through,' she said softly. 'Can't you see how different that makes you from him?'

'Yes,' he said, because finally he did see. But then he dropped his chin, swallowed round the rawness in his own throat. 'Although it's kind of screwed up, especially as I never properly checked to find out if the damn procedure had actually worked.'

'Well, thank goodness it didn't or we wouldn't have Mac,' she said.

He chuckled at the force of feeling in the remark, his relief almost as glorious as the sudden feeling of lightness. The realisation she had lifted a weight that had burdened him for far too long.

He dragged her out of the room, slammed the door. Feeling strangely empowered at the thought of shutting out that part of his past. It would always be there, he knew that, but there was no reason to believe it could control him any more. Not if he could do this next bit.

'I spoke to Katie ten days ago.' He clasped her cheeks, no longer able to deny the wealth of feeling moving through him. Desperation yes, but also determination, and a strange sort of acceptance. 'I told her everything, and she suggested I get a therapist. I've had a couple of sessions already, and...' He paused, swallowed. 'It may take me a long time to finally get the nightmares to stop.' Although oddly, after this conversation with Carmel, he already felt as if he had turned an important corner.

Identifying your demons was one thing, but defeating them was another, and she had already helped him with that. He'd managed to laugh in a room that had once filled him with terror. Until today, he would never have believed that was even possible.

'I'm so sorry, Ross,' she said. 'I didn't ask what had spooked you that night and I should have. Instead I burdened you with my feelings when you were struggling to handle your own. It was selfish and immature and—'

'Stop.' He pressed his finger to her lips. 'No, it wasn't, Carmel,' he said. 'You were honest with me.' God, how he hoped that was still how she felt about him. 'And instead of being honest with you, I protected myself. That's not okay.'

'But, Ross...' She began again, grasping his hands, and looking at him with the same glow in her eyes that had captivated and terrified him so much.

And suddenly he knew... She still loved him. She hadn't changed her mind, even knowing the darkness that lurked inside him and might never be vanquished.

He let go of her cheeks and dropped to one knee, taking her hands in his.

'Ross?' She looked stunned. 'What are you doing?'

'What I should have done two weeks ago,' he said,

then swallowed down the last of his fear. 'When you told me you loved me.'

'But—' she said.

'Shh, now,' he said, but he grinned. Damn, but he adored the way she always needed to have the last word. But not this time. This time it was his turn to bare his soul. And her turn to listen. 'What I should have said, what I know now was already in my heart, was that I love you, too. And I love our little boy. And I would really like to marry you.'

Her big blue eyes widened even further, her mouth opening, then closing again.

For the second time ever he'd left her speechless. But this time felt so much better than the last.

'I know you will probably want to wait, until I've had a lot more therapy,' he qualified. 'But I'm planning to relocate to Galway—to buy a house near you and Mac so we can begin to—'

'No,' she interrupted him.

No? His heart jumped, stuttered, but before the panic could set in, she continued.

'No, I don't want to wait,' she declared, tugging him up off his knees as his heart soared. 'We've waited long enough. And so has Mac. And no, you don't need to buy a house. Because we already have one that we can share. It's only two bedrooms, but perhaps, if it's too small, we can—'

'Shut up, Carmel,' he groaned, dragging her into his arms, the weight of emotion all but choking him, but in a good way. In the right way. 'I don't care about the house, as long as you and Mac are in it… And Rocky,' he said.

She chuckled. 'And all his puppies.'

'Because then it will be home,' he finished.

Grasping his shoulders, she boosted herself into his

arms. He caught her easily as she wrapped her legs around his waist and began kissing his face.

He kissed her back with all the love bursting in his heart, the heat pounding through his veins as fierce and strong as the happiness enveloping him.

She reared back and gripped his cheeks. 'Now please tell me there's another bedroom in this place so we don't have to seal this deal in the hallway.'

He was still laughing as he sank into her a minute later, on the floor.

EPILOGUE

One year later

ROSS HEARD THE crowd hush and then the strains of the wedding march build at the back of Kildaragh's chapel. He imagined the bridal procession beginning to make their way down the aisle, the very same aisle he had marched down twelve months ago to stop a wedding.

Not yet...don't look yet.

He smiled, appreciating the irony—and the glorious swell of anticipation—as the melodic Celtic tune Carmel had chosen for her entrance matched the heavy thuds of his heartbeat.

Twelve months. Twelve long, endless months it had taken to get to this day. Because apparently he and Carmel had very different opinions about what 'not waiting' a moment longer than necessary to get married actually meant. But in a few minutes the waiting would finally be over.

Carmel, of course, had insisted everything had to be just right. So there'd been the wait for Immy and Donal's baby boy, Ronan, to be born, then another longer wait for Katie and Conall's daughter, Caitlyn, to finally arrive on Christmas Day. Then there had been a new house to build—so he could move his business headquarters here, as well as

having room for his family. He'd put up with all the delays
with remarkable patience and fortitude. Given that he'd
been desperate to make her his wife—legally, officially,
in every way that was humanly possible—as soon as she
agreed to marry him. In the end, he'd brought Katie in to
help plan the wedding and speed things along. But still it
had taken one never-ending year to finally get to this day.

'Daddy, Mammy's coming now,' his little boy and
best man—who looked particularly grown up with his
blond curls slicked back and wearing a miniature wedding suit—announced loudly beside him. Ross smiled
despite the nerves and looked down at his son, who had
his arm wrapped around the neck of Ross's other best
man, or rather his best dog.

'She looks so pretty,' Mac murmured, the awe in his
tone making Ross realise he couldn't wait one damn moment longer.

He shifted round. And his thundering heartbeat got
wedged in his throat—virtually cutting off his air supply.

Mac is wrong.

With her russet hair perched precariously on her head
and threaded through with wildflowers, the sleek fall of
cream silk accentuating her slender curves as she headed
down the aisle towards him on her brother's arm, and that
stunning bone structure, fair skin and pure blue eyes—
only made more bewitching by the wisp of lace covering her face—Mac's mammy wasn't just pretty, she was
absolutely stunning.

He had to force himself to keep breathing. Stunning,
both inside and out.

At last, his bride and her brother reached them.

Katie and Imelda arrived behind them in their maid-of-
honour dresses. His sister and his soon-to-be sister-in-law
positively beamed with pleasure while Donal looked on from

his spot in the front row, holding little Ronan securely on his lap and guarding a bassinet with the sleeping Caitlyn in it.

Conall presented Carmel's hand to Ross, then stepped back, winking at him. Incredible to think Con and he had actually become friends over the last year—more than friends, brothers—bonding over the chaos of new fatherhood and their shared dismay at exactly how they were supposed to handle the two extremely strong-willed women they'd chosen to share their lives with.

He took Carmel's hand, felt her fingers tremble in his—and suddenly the only thing he could concentrate on was her. She grinned at him, but the power and poignancy of the moment was reflected in her misty sapphire eyes.

He stroked his thumb across the soft skin and grinned back at her as the powerful thought squeezed his chest too. Tonight, they would be a family, in every sense of the word, before God and man.

'About time you showed up,' he murmured.

She gave a low chuckle, which struck him deep in his abdomen. 'Don't you worry, you'll not be getting rid of me or Mac now.'

He smiled back at her, the elation making his heart swell against his ribs. 'Don't *you* worry, I intend to hold you both to that promise, for all eternity.'

She blinked, the happy sheen in her eyes making his own sting.

But then Mac squeezed himself between them both, holding up the band of white gold Ross had given him not ten minutes ago and shouted, 'Can Rocky and me give you the ring now, Daddy?'

And the whole assembly dissolved into laughter.

'I now declare you man and wife. You may kiss your bride, Ross,' Father Meehan finally announced.

Carmel couldn't stop grinning, her heart so buoyant it was all but flying as Ross finally got around to lifting her veil.

Spontaneous applause swelled under the roof of the old chapel. She could hear Mac cheering like a lunatic as his uncle Conall boosted him into his arms, Rocky's excited barking, and a baby wailing—probably poor Caitlyn woken by all the commotion—and feel the confetti fluttering onto her cheeks. But all she could see was the love dancing in Ross's eyes—pure, true, strong, for ever—exactly the way it was dancing in her heart.

He placed callused palms on her warm cheeks, lifted her face to his, and pressed his mouth to hers at last.

She let out a soft sob, the exquisite sensation gathering in her belly nothing compared to the storm of emotion singing in her heart. The kiss went from sweet to carnal as his tongue delved deep, exploring, exploiting and claiming every inch of her as his. She pressed her hands to his waist and kissed him back with the same force and fury, claiming him right back as hers.

The applause, the barking, the shouting and baby cries faded until all she could hear was the sure solid beat of her heart. But then as her brand-new husband pulled away—forced to come up for air—she leaned up on tiptoes, held him close and whispered in his ear. 'By the way, you should know, in about seven and a bit months' time, it'll not just be me and Mac and Rocky you're stuck with for all eternity.'

His eyes popped wide, his hands tightening on her waist as she watched the emotions—emotions he no longer felt the need to hide from her—flicker across his face. Confusion, surprise, shock, awe... And uninhibited joy.

Then he lifted her off her feet, spun her round and

threw his head back to add yet more noise to their wild Irish wedding commotion.

Needless to say it took close to another whole eternity to calm down the dog and their son again long enough to tell them the good news, too.

* * * * *

HIS SECRETLY PREGNANT CINDERELLA

MILLIE ADAMS

MILLS & BOON

To the Modern line.

For all the joy, fantasy and escape it's provided me, both as a reader and a writer.

CHAPTER ONE

MORGAN STANFIELD HAD never taken seriously the idea that a person could die of embarrassment. But from where she was crouched currently, dressed in nothing but a black lace bodysuit, watching her boyfriend of approximately six months laying another woman down onto the bed, she was sure that she was close.

And that, perhaps, should have been the first clue that it was actually a good thing that Alex was cheating on her. Really, she should've known.

She should have known that whatever patience he seemed to have for her desire to wait, he would not defer his own pleasure endlessly. She should have known he didn't actually love her quite so much.

And Morgan had always wondered why he'd been with her. She had always wondered why Alex was interested in her. She had met him when she was waitressing at a bar near her university, and she had been shocked when he'd approached her. He was tall and beautiful with arresting dark eyes and an easy smile. His Greek accent had sent shivers down her spine.

Morgan had worked for everything that she'd ever received in her life, and she was not working at the bar by the university because she went to the university. It was because she wanted to. Because she was saving up all of her precious money to get herself a better future. And when she'd started dating Alex, that future had suddenly been dropped in her lap. He'd given her the funds to go to school immediately, even though she had protested. He had brought her to family functions, bought her clothes and paid for her to be transported to luxurious affairs, and never once had he pressured her for sex.

Well, now she could see why.

He was getting it elsewhere.

And she was… Devastated.

She was also trapped. Trapped in her boyfriend's bedroom at his parents' house, their estate, actually, about to see a whole lot more sex than she'd ever had in her life. And she really thought she might die. She really did. And that was when she turned and saw the door that led out onto the balcony. The alcove she was in was quite separate from the bedroom. These rooms were more like suites, with separate compartments. And she had a feeling that if she crawled over to the door, and worked her way out onto the balcony, she would be able to go unnoticed.

Granted, once she was out there she might be stuck, but she would prefer that to being stuck indoors with a full pornographic scene happening within earshot. She took a breath. She turned and began to crawl across the floor. Literally crawl on her belly. Well, her friends had been right. Men like him were too good to be true, and it could only end in humiliation.

Of course, she hadn't confessed to her friends that she hadn't given him her virginity yet.

They thought she was silly being a virgin as it was, much less when she had a gorgeous, rich boyfriend. It was just that she'd seen the way that men had taken advantage of her mother over the years, and she had never wanted to... She had never wanted to lose herself like that. Had never wanted to lose her mind quite to that degree.

That worked out well, didn't it?

She could finally touch the door. She reached up and prayed that the handle would pull. It did. Easily, and she was able to get it open silently. Staying low, she wiggled through the crack she created in the doorway, then once she was outside, keeping the handle pressed down, reached up and close it as silently as she had opened it to begin with.

She sat crouched on the balcony.

This was stupid. It was absolutely stupid. She had finally thought to...to give herself to him and he was giving himself to someone else. She wondered if his parents had any idea he had a woman here...

She knew who probably did. A dark rage expanded in her chest. Oh, yes, she was sure that there was one person who was well aware that Alex was locked away in his suite with some blond beauty.

His older brother.

The man who hated her most of all.

The man whose name she would not even think. Because he didn't deserve it.

In her moment of humiliation, acknowledging his existence would be too great a burden to bear.

She looked down below. She was four stories up, and she did not relish the idea of trying to climb down.

Then, she really would be dead ostensibly of humiliation, and that seemed a fate too ignominious to contend with.

She looked across and saw that she was very close to the next balcony. She was trying to remember what the room might be, based on her time spent in the manor. A library, maybe. Or was that on the other side? Honestly, it didn't much matter. She just needed to look in and see if it was occupied.

She stood up slowly, certain that Alex and his lover would be too occupied to notice if there was movement outside, and looked across the space between the stone railings. Honestly, in any other circumstance, she would have called herself crazy, curled up in a ball and lain there on the floor of the balcony until someone came to rescue her. But, no one was going to rescue her. Not from this, not from the site of her own folly. She would have to rescue herself. There was no rescuing her pride. It was already on the ground. So, she would think nothing about crossing the two spaces. She would have not a care in the world about falling.

"Don't do that," she said to herself, "if you fall to the ground you won't die, it's grass. You'll only be maimed. And that's really only compounding the problem, isn't it?"

She gritted her teeth, and before she could talk herself out of it, lifted herself up and slung one leg across the railing on her balcony, and over the railing on the next, not quite able to plant her foot on the floor of the next balcony, but feeling somewhat secure that she at least had herself partially there. Then she lifted herself with her arms, and planted the next leg over, rocking forward and pitching herself safely to the ground. Thank God.

She really didn't want to have to do that again. She looked next door and saw that the room was dim. There was no movement, though, she could not tell quite which room it was. There were bookcases, so perhaps she was right, and it was the library. Her only hope was that the door was also unlocked to this balcony. And it was. She slipped in quickly and quietly, cursing that she had left all of her clothes behind. She moaned. He was going to wonder about the clothes. Later, it was going to be clear someone else had been there. Or maybe he wouldn't notice. Maybe he would attribute it to some other fling. Or maybe the maid would clean it up before he ever saw them.

It didn't much matter, because she was never going to see him again. Not him or anyone from this family. For a moment, she felt utterly, desolately sad. Because she had been convinced that... That she'd found a dream.

But dreams did not come true for girls like her. Not dreams like this. There was no Prince Charming. There was no magical happy ending; there was just not going to be any getting out of this with her dignity. But all she needed to do was get down the stairs. And out the front door. And if she had to run... Well, there could only ever be a rumor of a crazed redhead running through the halls. She would never look back, she would never call back, and she would go back to being alone... It was just all over. All of it.

She took a step deeper into the room and heard a sound. A glass clicking against a hard surface.

"Well. When I ordered a nightcap, I can honestly say I did not expect this."

"Constantine."

Because of course it was him. Of course, he would be the one to see. Of course, he would be the one in this room.

She was surprised he didn't bring with him hell's very fire and all the demons. Or maybe he had, because she was suddenly hot.

He's always made you hot...

She ignored that. As she'd ignored the heat for six months. Because Constantine wasn't her knight in shining armor. Her Prince Charming.

Constantine was something shameful, dark and awful she pretended she didn't harbor inside of herself.

Alex isn't your Prince Charming either...

"So it is you. I thought that I recognized you." His dark gaze swept over her, the contempt there so...

Obvious.

Scathing.

Hot.

"I see you've abandoned your fresh-faced ingenue look for the evening." The expression on his face was almost bland. If you didn't know him.

And, sadly, she did.

She had made an effort to not know him, but it was unavoidable.

Over the past six months she had been taken into the family with enthusiasm. She loved Alex's parents.

She did not love Constantine. And he did not love her.

But she was fascinated by him. She had learned to read a lot of things in one quirk of his arrogant eyebrow, had become well acquainted with the disapproval inherent in the slightest adjustment of his jacket cuff. He did not look at her so much as through her, so at this moment, as he looked at her with that burning intensity, she felt it. Down to the very center of her soul.

"Your brother is otherwise occupied," she said.

And if a person could die of humiliation then she was well on her way.

Because to have to admit to Constantine Kamaras of all people, that she was... That she had been replaced... Not even replaced, as she had never even been in Alex's bed.

Your choice, Morgan.

Yes, it was her choice. Born out of extreme paranoia, to be sure. A fear that if she were to fall pregnant she wouldn't be taken care of, that she would end up like her mother.

But she had gotten so... So confident in Alex. And what they had. And she had been ready to...

It was more than humiliation that had her reeling now.

It was the stunning clarity that in her confidence in another person she had still been wrong. But she had been cautious all this time and so certain of him…

And she had been wrong.

"He is otherwise occupied?"

He shifted in his chair, affecting a more languid pose than she ever typically associated with Constantine. He was rigid. Hard like a mountain. And yet at the moment he looked… Approachable. Which made him all the more terrifying.

His shirt collar was open, revealing a wedge of chest, a bit of dark hair. His sleeves were pushed up to his elbows, and she couldn't help but take stock of his muscular forearms.

He had the sculpted face of a fallen angel. His eyes black as midnight, and his hair like a raven's wing.

He was every gothic fantasy a lonely girl growing up with books and little else for comfort could have ever wanted.

Pity he hated her.

Pity he was the older brother of the love of her life.

Pity the love of her life was a faithless scoundrel.

And really, the biggest pity of all was the fact that she was standing there in her underwear.

"What an effect," he said, his tone dark. "You in that, and with the man you intended to seduce occupied. I feel I must ask. Is it another woman who occupies his attentions?"

"Yes." She did her best to copy his uncaring pose. "And I think you know that."

She let one shoulder drop, and with it went the strap on the shockingly scandalous teddy she was wearing. Absurdly one piece and all lace so you could see her body peeking from beneath rose petals in a rather strategic fashion.

It had seemed so daring and sensual earlier.

Now it just seemed dangerous.

"I know nothing of the comings and goings of my brother, mainly because if I had to keep tabs on every creature he took into his bed I would do nothing else. You must understand, Morgan, my objection to you has always been that you were simply another in a long line of questionable choices my brother seems to enjoy making."

She refused to let the words stab her.

"He loves you, you know," Morgan said. "He thinks you are the most brilliant, wonderful man in the entire world."

"What is it they say?" Constantine said, looking down at his hands for a moment, and then back up at her. "Yes. Imitation is the sincerest form of flattery. And my younger brother is hardly even a pantomime of me. And I think *you* know that."

There was something about that dark, disdainful note in his voice that sent a shiver directly down her spine. And to her horror, her nipples beaded tight behind the lace bra that did not do an effective job of covering her breasts.

"I think I would like to hear the story of how you came to be standing here without your clothes."

"I told you. I… Well. I…" And this was where it was going to be tricky to keep her pride.

Your pride is shot to hell, Morgan, you might as well tell him. He thinks the worst of you. Go ahead and give him a story.

"I decided to sneak in his room tonight. To surprise him. Unfortunately I learned the hard way that there are some men you should not surprise. I went into the bathroom to change… And I was in the corner of his room in the dark when he arrived with… Whoever she is." Her stomach was like acid. "And my clothing was in a different room. I could not bear the thought of him seeing me so I slipped out the balcony. I could not climb straight down, so I decided to seek another room that I might enter... And as you can see it turned out to be occupied. So. Surprises all around."

"That is quite the tale," he said. And there was nothing but silence between them as he looked at her. Behind every petal, she felt. "It would be a shame to waste the outfit, don't you think?"

Her stomach plummeted, that place between her legs began to pulse in a strange and greedy fashion.

She had been ready to sleep with Alex, and she had not felt like this. But one look of intent from Constantine and her entire body was thrown into a tailspin.

You read too many fantastical novels when you were a girl. You are being a fool.

No. Maybe she wasn't being a fool. After all, she had been certain of Alex, and it was over. It was over. And that realization washed over her like a wave. Insistent and terrible.

He was sleeping with another woman. And she could never...

She could never subject herself to that. And it did not matter that he had paid for her schooling. It did not matter that she loved his family.

She wanted to be loved.

Morgan Stanfield had never been beloved in her entire life. She had been a burden to her mother, nothing to whoever her father was... And she had been certain she had finally found love with Alex. With his family.

But he did not love her. She didn't know what game he was playing with her, but it was clear that it had to be a game. It had to be.

And she was an idiot who did not have any kind of special insight into other people. Who was not more responsible than other women, than her mother. She had been ready to fling herself on that ghastly altar of love because she had finally thought that she had found... The one.

And she took such great pride in her ability to assess people. Because she did not feel that she was wide-eyed. She did not feel that she was naive. She had always felt that she was exceptionally realistic and pragmatic, and where had that gotten her?

Naked on a balcony.

Well, *nearly* naked.

And there was a man before her that called to fantasies that she had long tried to suppress.

He despised her. He did not love her as she had imagined Alex did.

And she did not love him.

But regardless, he had captivated her from the first moment she had seen him.

Alex had an ease about him, and Constantine was nothing like that. Constantine was every inch the man you might expect to have a mad wife in the attic. Constantine was...

"Do you think?" she asked, the question coming out much more breathless than she intended.

"I hate to see a woman all dressed up with nowhere to go."

His voice had become a seductive purr now, nothing like the interactions she'd had with him prior. His tone was usually hard, deep and clipped. And now it washed over her like a wave.

Leaving her feeling restless.

"You're very beautiful, Morgan."

He thought she was beautiful? She was pretty. She knew that, but it had always felt a little bit like an inconvenience more than anything else. Her flame red hair and translucent skin drew a lot of attention, as did the vividness of her green eyes, but for a woman who had always wanted to keep her head down and get on with school and work, it had felt an uneasy burden to bear.

She had never much cared whether or not a man thought she was beautiful, but for some reason the revelation that Constantine did was... Well it was heady indeed.

"You think I'm beautiful?"

"Yes. But I would bet you know you're beautiful."

"Perhaps. But I imagine you despise everything about me. I did not ever consider that you might apply any sort of virtue to me."

"Do you think beauty is a virtue?"

She blinked. "No. Not... That isn't what I meant."

"Beauty," he said, his voice hard, "is a vice. Were it not, I would have grabbed hold of you by now and shipped you straight out the bedroom door, flinging you to your ass out in the corridor. However. Your beauty is a particular vice of mine. When I find I am not a man given to questioning a gift when it shows up in my room trussed up and ready to be unwrapped."

"And if I don't want you?"

He stood slowly, never breaking eye contact with her, never wavering. Then he made his way to her, and she felt her breath go more and more shallow.

"Darling," he said. "Do not lie. It insults us both. You have wanted me from the very moment you first set foot in my parents' house. And the more cruel I am to you, the more you seem to want it."

Her breathing was truly labored now, and she hated it. Mostly because he was right.

She could recall easily that first encounter they'd had six months ago. When he looked at her as if she was something vile that he had to scrape off the bottom of his shoe. And she had found him beautiful.

She had been thankful, then, for Alex and his easy charm. For the feeling she had for him. Because they had done something to shield her from the scalding heat that came from his older brother's disdainful gaze.

But there was nothing between them now. No feelings for Alex. Nothing.

"And you must know," he said. "How I have wanted you."

He did not grab her and haul her into his arms. Instead, he extended his hand, and with just the barest edge of his thumb he traced the line along the top of her cheekbone. And it was like a match, struck slowly and painfully before igniting the flame.

Her breasts felt painfully heavy, and she was so aware of what she was wearing.

"I knew you were beautiful," he said. "But I was not prepared for a sight such as this. Even veiled, you're glorious—something to behold."

She did not know why it made her heart flutter so, because compliments about one's appearance were cheap and easy. And they shouldn't mean a thing. She had decided as a young girl to never let her head be swayed by such things. By romance and beautiful words.

But something twisted in her stomach then, hard and painful, and a voice inside of her spoke the shameful truth.

That she knew this wasn't romance. Or beautiful words, or anything quite so floral.

It was desire. And from the beginning there had never been anything she could do about it. Never been anything that she could do to minimize what she felt for him.

It simply was.

And, oh, how she wished it were not.

"Show me, Morgan," he said, his voice going rough. "Show me what I want to see."

He wanted her to strip. She understood that. She waited for him to sit back down, a king reclining, but he did not. Instead, he stood there, his gaze far too intense, far too intent. And he felt so large. He was broader and taller than his brother, by at least three inches.

And quite near to a foot taller than she was.

She ought to feel frail and shockingly vulnerable, and yet, she did not.

He had not an ounce of fat on his body. Not that she had seen his body, it was just that... Well she had been helpless to not take a visual tour of him anytime she had seen him in the family home. In his custom fitted suit that lovingly held his broad shoulders, muscular chest and slim waist.

And now, every ounce of his power, every ounce of his beauty was all directed at her. His gaze keen, his muscles bunched as if he were a predator ready to attack.

And she found that she did not fear it. Before she could decide what to do, before she could think it through, she reached around and unhooked the lace top. It went loose, and she pressed her hand over her breasts as it went slack. Her forearm neatly covering her from his view. She had certainly never done a striptease in her life. And it wasn't so much that she was being a tease now as she was feeling... Dazed. Wondering what the hell she was thinking.

A fantasy. He is a fantasy.

And should he not be the thing that you get on the way out the door?

Because it was always him, hadn't it been?

He was the one that had appealed to her in this darkly sexual way that had always felt shameful to her.

She had always been so ashamed of this part of herself. The part of herself that didn't simply want sweet and wonderful words but wanted a man who wanted her. A man who would grab hold of her with big, strong hands. A man who would kiss her, taste her…

She had pushed all that down and told herself that she didn't need that sort of thing.

Because it kept her safe.

Because it felt like something that was too close to her mother and all of her vices.

There was that word again.

Vices.

Perhaps *beauty* was his. And *he* was hers.

And she would make herself a slave to it. For tonight. Just tonight.

It emboldened her, and she dropped her arm, letting the top fall free and expose her breasts to him.

His jaw went tight, a muscle jumping there, and arousal speared her between the thighs.

She had forgotten about Alex and whatever he was doing in the next room. Because one look from Constantine and her entire body was alight. And it had never been thus with Alex. Oh, she had thought him handsome. She had felt comfortable with the idea of sleeping with him. It would be no hardship.

But it had not been like this. This sickness. And perhaps that was one reason she had wanted Alex.

Because this was the very thing she had always feared. But the beautiful thing was she didn't like Constantine. So she would never be like her mother pining after a man far after he had moved on. She would never pine after Constantine.

She would heal from the disappointment of losing Alex.

Just like she would heal from missing the sheer sexual connection she felt right now with Constantine.

But at least she would never miss the man himself.

So her recovery would be quite a lot easier than it might've been otherwise.

"Stop," he said.

"What?" she asked, feeling confused now.

"Thinking. I do not need you to think. You simply need to feel."

She focused on the glide of the lace fabric against her skin as she began to tug the bodysuit down over her hips, exposing the rest of her body to his hungry gaze. She swished her hair and focused on the feeling of it skimming over her shoulders.

She felt the breath fill her lungs, felt her heart beating a hard and steady rhythm. Felt that place between her legs go liquid with longing, aching for his touch. For his possession.

And she didn't think. Not at all.

He appraised her openly, his gaze taking in the most intimate places on her body. He took a step toward her, and then moved to the side, around behind her. He put his hands on her shoulders, let them skim down her arms, and then he placed them on her hips and pulled her against him, and she felt the hard ridge of his desire pushing insistently against the curve of her buttocks. "I want you," he growled.

"Oh," she said.

"You are truly beautiful," he said.

"Now who's thinking too much," she said. She turned her head slightly, and then he kissed her, light, teasing. Not enough. She wiggled in his hold and turned toward him, and he deepened the kiss. And it was like fire.

His mouth was firm and hot, his tongue insistent and clever as he licked deeper and deeper into her mouth with each pass of his lips over hers.

She arched against him, completely naked, aware of the silken fabric of his shirt, of a button skimming over her nipple and making her gasp. She could feel the belt buckle on his pants pressing against her stomach, and beneath that the insistent evidence of his desire. He kissed her, and backed her against the wall, the plaster cool beneath her skin, with him hot and hard at her front. She clung to his shoulders as he kissed down her neck, to her collarbone, to her breast, where he took one distended bud into his mouth and sucked hard, making her cry out in a ragged gasp of joy.

She wanted him. And she was going to have him. Because tonight, she would not lose everything. She would not walk away a broken, demeaned woman who had been made a fool of.

She would embrace this darkest part of herself that she had always denied, and she would claim her power once and for all. She was tired of being afraid. She would not allow this to be a lesson in how she could not trust herself. It was other people she couldn't trust. She was not to blame. She wasn't.

And in Constantine's arms that felt true and possible and real.

Because he made her feel like she was everything. He made her feel like she was perfect. He growled, his hands hard on her hips as he thrust forward, making sure that she felt how much he desired her.

"I want you to know," he growled against her lips, grinding his hips against hers. "I do not behave in such a fashion. I like sophisticated women. Close to my age. With cultured experience. I do not like twenty-two-year-old waitresses with dangerous sexuality they do not know how to control."

And something in her sparked. She felt the corner of her mouth turn upward into a smile. "Stop then. If you don't like me. If you don't want me. Stop."

He cursed, something vile in Greek, and grabbed hold

of her chin, his eyes meeting hers. "Little cat," he said. "I cannot walk away. Or I would have done so already."

"Then I suppose this is something you do now. You have painted me with quite the brush, Constantine, it is hardly fair that you get to excuse yourself, exclude yourself, from your own judgment by pretending that this is somehow an aberration, and therefore excusable. If I am an aberration, then perhaps it is because I am singular. A sea change in the world of the most immovable Kamaras."

"Then I will drown."

He kissed her again, and hauled her against his body, as he moved them across the vast chamber, toward his bed. He flung her down on the center of the mattress, and stood back, his eyes wild on hers as he undid the buttons on his shirt, as he stripped it off and let it fall to the floor, his pants and underwear following. And Morgan was faced with the sight of a naked man for the first time in her life. He was… Glorious. An Adonis carved from golden marble. Except he was not cold. He was hot. And that most masculine part of him was… Cruelly, dangerously beautiful. He made her ache with desire, even while she battled her virgin's nerves.

But there was something about the wildness in him that only increased her confidence. She was made to take him. She knew. Because he was made to need her. If it was deniable, then they would have denied it, that was the thing. That was the truth. If there was a way for the two of them to not want each other, then they simply wouldn't want each other.

Of that she was deeply certain.

He held her in no esteem whatsoever, and while she respected a great many things about him, she never wanted to sit down with him at a dinner party with only him as a conversation piece.

And so, this moment must be, as she had thought, singular. And inevitable. And that meant that she would take him. Yes. She would.

He joined her on the bed, but he was down at her feet. He kissed her ankle, her calf, the inside of her knee. And she began to tremble as she realized his intent. She had fantasized about this. Not him specifically, but only because she had gotten a handle on her fantasies in the last couple of years. Knowing that she needed to get through this last year of school, knowing that she couldn't go sleeping around for her own protection, she had done her best to banish her sexual desires. But there had been times… Late at night, when she had been unable to sleep that she had thought of a man, dark haired and intense, putting his head between her thighs and tasting her like she was the sweetest of desserts.

His breath was hot at the apex of her thighs, and she whimpered as he hovered there, glorious anticipation tightening her stomach into an impossible knot.

And then he took her, his lips and tongue slick and clever as he composed the symphony of desire that built to a crescendo, and then eased again, before finding its way to a crest, and waning into something slow and soft and steady.

Again and again he took her to that edge, again and again he took her there, but denied her the cymbal crash.

Again and again he made her mindless with desire as she twisted and writhed beneath him.

Constantine.

There was no doubt that it was him. For his mouth, the lyrics traced against her skin by his tongue, were wicked in a way that no other man's ever could be.

At least, wicked for her.

The most perfect expression of the rebellion that she had always tried to deny.

She was sobbing, begging as he took her to another swell in the masterpiece. "Please," she begged. "Please."

And finally, he gave her what she desired. He pushed two fingers inside of her, and the shock of the penetration sent her hips up off the bed. There was a slight stinging sensation, but her orgasm was hard on the heels of it, pulsing and demanding, drawing a scream up from her throat as her release went on and on, more than a cymbal crash, an entire finale with fireworks.

And she lay there gasping for air, barely able to move, completely unable to breathe. And she found herself staring up into his dark eyes, and she felt exposed just then.

Terrified.

Because in that moment he did not feel like a man she couldn't make conversation with at a dinner party. He felt like a man she could bare her entire soul to.

She felt as if he could see her. And for one fleeting moment she thought she might've seen him.

But then a veil was drawn back up and he was himself again. Hard and remote, but no less beautiful for it. She reached up and touched his face. Just as he positioned himself between her legs and thrust inside of her.

She gasped, and he groaned as he sank deep.

She felt like she couldn't breathe. Almost certain that she would be torn in two by the size of him. She was gasping, clinging to his shoulders for all that she was worth.

And then he began to move, the slick friction that she had found beneath his mouth and fingers returning, the pain beginning to ease.

She looked up at his beautiful face and saw that his eyes were clouded with pleasure. He had not noticed her moment of discomfort, and for that she was grateful. Because she did not want him to stop and ease her fears. Did not want him to stop and treat her like an inexperienced virgin.

She felt like a seductress in his arms and she did not want to lose that sense of power.

He gripped her hips and thrust into her with ferocity, the act of making love so much more physical, so much more feral than she had realized it would be.

Man and woman. Hardness and softness. The slick slide of their skin, the sensual overflow of his hardness inside of her. And with each thrust he carried her higher. Higher and higher. And when her pleasure broke, like a damn, spilling pleasure over her in a wave, his movements increased, until he shouted out his pleasure, the mountain fracturing above her, the shock of it sending her hurtling toward another release.

And afterwards she lay gasping and unbearably conscious of her nudity. Because it was done now. She had given herself to Constantine, and she had done it not simply out of duress or any kind of desire for revenge, but because she had wanted to. And there was no denying that.

"I will see you out," he said, moving away from her and getting out of the bed.

His broad, muscular back filled her vision, that sleek waist and muscular backside.

"Of course," he said. "I will get your clothes."

"Surely not *my* clothes." Alex's room could still be… occupied.

"Clothes that will be fitting." He dressed, methodically, and she felt slightly ashamed of watching him.

Then when he was finished, he left the room.

She crawled beneath the covers in his bed, feeling like it was the wrong thing to do. He'd taken her on the top of his bedspread, he had not allowed her to be underneath it, and it felt like perhaps an intimacy she should not have taken.

And because he was not there, she gave in to her momentary desire to weep. Just a little bit. Just to let tears fall from her eyes enough to try and ease the pressure, around her tender heart.

He returned a moment later with clothes that were definitely not hers.

"Did you drive yourself?"

She shook her head. "I did a… A rideshare."

"That will not do. My driver will take you home."

"It's late…"

"It does not matter," he said. "My driver will take you home."

She got out of bed, and he turned around as she dressed in the clothes that he had brought her. "The car is ready," he said.

And then he walked her out of the bedroom, as if he were some sort of gentleman walking her to the door after a date.

She smiled weakly as he opened the entry, and she saw his sleek town car sitting there.

"Whatever business you decide to conclude with my brother or not, that is up to you. I will speak to no one about tonight."

"Thank you."

Preserving his pride as much as hers.

"Be safe."

"Right. Well. You too." She cringed as she said that as she got into the car and pressed her head against the cool glass window.

Tonight had been a spectacular failure.

She had lost Alex… And she had lost her mind.

She had given in and given herself to Constantine.

Except even as tears slipped down her cheeks, a slight smile curved her lips.

Because for just a moment, Morgan Stanfield had had a pure and perfect fantasy.

It was just a pity that it was over.

A knock woke Constantine around five a.m.

His first inclination was that it was her.

Her.

His stomach tightened viciously.

Morgan.

He should not have done that. He was a man who wasted little time regretting his actions. After all, what was the point. But Morgan...

"What?" He threw his covers off and went to the door, not bothering to cover himself before he opened it.

But it was not Morgan.

It was the family business manager.

And of course if there was urgent business it would be his door that the man knocked on. And not Constantine's father. His father was useless when it came to anything half so demanding as his business.

"Yes?"

"We had a call from the police," he said.

"What?"

"It is..." The older man's words became choked. "Alex. He was in an accident. He's dead."

CHAPTER TWO

"I DON'T BELIEVE IT." Morgan felt like she was made of stone, and she'd said these four words countless times in the past week. Now here she was, standing in the antechamber of the massive Kamaras home all in black, feeling faint.

She said it to herself. The staff was walking around brusquely, Alex's mother had taken to her bed, his father was in his study.

Constantine was...

As if her thoughts had conjured him he appeared, dressed all in black, as she was, his dark hair brushed back off his forehead, his eyes like chips of obsidian, glinting in the dim light.

"You came," he said.

"Of course."

"My parents will be glad."

"Will they?" She shifted where she stood, her heart beating so hard she was sure that he could hear it.

His lips shifted slightly. The ghost of a rueful smile. "As glad as they are of anything at the moment."

"You don't have to entertain me. I was ushered to the house, but I can go and join the rest of the funeral party out on the grounds..."

"Nonsense," he said, his voice hard. "You were my brother's girlfriend and he cared for you a great deal. Everyone knows that Alex never stayed with one woman for more than a night. And he was with you for six months."

"If he'd stayed with that last woman more than a night perhaps he'd still be here." She immediately regretted the venomous statement.

Alex was dead. She hardly needed to try to score points.

"You're not wrong," Constantine said, his mouth firming.

She took a deep breath and regretted it immediately because the air smelled of Constantine, and to her he smelled of sex. And it reminded her too much of that night.

His hands.

His mouth.

His body.

Him.

"My mother will wish for you to join us. To sit with the family. Come, have a drink."

Thinking of alcohol made her want to gag. She was already so unsteady the idea of adding a mood-altering substance to the mix didn't work for her.

"I'd rather have something soft, if you don't mind."

"A soda for the bartender?"

"I was a waitress at a bar," she said. "That isn't the same thing."

"All right."

He led the way, to a small—if you could call any room in the palatial home small—room off the main foyer, with dark wood and navy colored carpet. It was cozy, in a very old-fashioned interpretation of the masculine.

"This was once my grandfather's favorite room to occupy when he would come and visit from Greece."

"Did he visit often?" she asked.

"Yes."

"You were close with him. Alex mentioned that."

His eyes went cold. "Yes."

Of course he wouldn't want to talk about his grandfather. He was gone too. Just like Alex.

It made her heart squeeze tight. She wanted to go to him. Wanted to touch him.

The inclination made her breath catch. Hard.

She took a step away from him for good measure.

He went over to a wooden cabinet and opened it, to reveal a small refrigerator inside. He took out a can of soda and poured it into a glass, over ice. When he handed it to her, their fingers brushed, and her whole body shivered.

His eyes met hers, just for a moment, and it was...

It was like being back there that night.

Had it only been last week?

Alex had been alive and she'd been so hurt by him.

But Constantine had been there and...

He was Constantine.

She could remember the first time she had ever seen him. So brooding and gorgeous and she couldn't explain the way he'd been beautiful to her, not when compared to Alex, who was so bright and sunny. But it had been different.

It hadn't been butterflies. It had been something darker. Grittier. A call to a part of her sensuality she'd tried to ignore.

But he'd woken it up.

Loud. Insistent.

He had ruined her.

Shredded her every belief about herself.

She had felt so confident in her stance on life. In her choices. She was better, smarter than her mother, who had made such bad decisions when it came to men. And Morgan had been certain she'd never do the same. That she'd never be derailed by something like that.

But she had been.

He'd touched her and all of her convictions had gone up in smoke.

He was her last remaining conviction.

It made her feel so small, but even now, even after everything...

She wanted him.

He did not step away from her. He stood there. So close she could breathe him in. So close it would be easy...so easy to reach out and touch him...

She suddenly felt lightheaded and she swayed in place, then put her glass down with a resounding click. She felt her feet go unsteady and he moved quickly, his hand going to her face, his arm curved around her waist, holding her upright.

His mouth was barely a whisper from hers and she thought her heart...

"Are you all right?" he asked.

"Yes." Of course he had only gone to her because he was worried she would fall.

Of course that was all.

Her whole body felt like it was on fire. And she wanted nothing more than to close the distance between them. To taste him again. She wanted it so much she could cry, and it made a mockery of everything she'd ever thought about herself.

That she was controlled.

That she was smarter than her mother.

Better than her mother.

No. She just hadn't met her weakness yet.

But here he was, dressed in a black suit.

Her sin nature incarnate.

She wiggled out of his hold because she needed sanity. She needed to breathe.

And just then, his mother and father walked in.

"I'm glad you're here, Morgan," his mother said, walking across the room to greet her with an air kiss to both cheeks.

Morgan felt scalded. Shamed.

"Of course," she said.

"Let us go and…honor him."

She looked up and her eyes met Constantine's, and the fire she saw there was black as night, and she feared if she looked at him for too long, it would burn her alive.

It was the graveside he could not stand.

This, he supposed, was the cost of having a family burial plot on the estate.

You had to bear witness to your brother being buried where you once played as children.

There was a memorial to Athena, but it was different. They had not done this. Had not done graveside sadness and finality.

With her it was almost as if she could still be out there, even though he knew that was not the case.

There was no chance at believing in such things for Alex, though.

It was a heaviness that sat on his chest like a stone. And only Morgan, with her red hair stark against the gray clouds and the black coat she was wearing, provided any brightness.

"I thought I taught you better, boy."

His grandfather's voice sounded in his head—always in Greek.

I thought so too, Pappoús. But perhaps I am as I always was.

Weak.

Weak in his grief. Weak for her.

He was a man who prized control above all else. But what was the point of it? He could not control this. He had not. He had not saved Alex, any more than he had saved Athena.

He had all this power, all this money. He had not kept his family from tragedy, not again. Everything his grandfather had made him into in the aftermath of the kidnapping, of Athena's loss…

It had changed everything. They had been happy children. They'd had each other. He had loved his siblings. Had felt protective of them. Athena might have been his twin, but she'd been a few moments younger, and he'd felt like…

He had felt like he would conquer the world for her if necessary.

But then they'd been taken, and when her salvation had been tied to his strength, he had not proven strong enough.

When Constantine had been liberated from his kidnappers, it was not the miracle of that rescue that had shaped his life.

It was the guilt of Athena's loss.

The grief his parents had suffered.

This grief with biting teeth that had taken what was a chaotic, but happy family and turned small moments into battlegrounds he had not always been able to understand as a child. But he had felt the blows nonetheless.

They had not been able to look at him at first. For he and Athena had always been together, and sometimes he was certain they did not see him, but only the space where she should have stood beside him.

That was what he saw. So how could they not?

His parents…

They remained as ever. Fun and flighty, gregarious people, until tensions rose or anniversaries passed.

His birthday wasn't his own. On what should have been

his and Athena's birthdays…he could remember there was no celebration anymore and he could never figure out if it was to mourn her or punish him.

He could remember hearing his parents once, in their study, on the night of his sixteenth birthday.

How different would it be if she had lived? If we still had her?

How different, he heard echo in his soul, if he had been the one to die instead.

They would avoid him for days.

Then his parents would compensate by buying him things. Cars, a private plane. And the cycle would begin again. This strange wheel of grief that spun ever on, a series of highs and lows, and always hoping they weren't crushed to death by it.

And he had his own anger.

That his parents had been consumed in themselves when their children were taken…

His parents were now all he had left, and it might not be an easy relationship, but in the cracks of it, there was love, even if there was also resentment, guilt, and he suspected a dark wish that their daughter had been the one to survive.

As for himself?

Constantine's life was nothing more than a series of complicated relationships and failed vows. It was in isolation that his weakness had been exposed. It was isolation that had led to his failure of Athena.

All he had been able to do was establish charities in her honor, try to find ways to protect other women in her name. So that her name mattered.

So that it lived on.

And he had sworn to live a life of certain isolation.

There was no love, no wife, no child, on any horizon in his future.

And this was another example of why. Yet again he had failed to protect someone who mattered.

Yet again, he had to swear to honor the legacy that Alex would not have the chance to build.

Though not just now.

Morgan was here.

And she made him burn.

One last time.

He would never see her again. She had been his brother's woman and she was only here now because to do anything other than pay her respects would be to needlessly uncover Alex's weaknesses.

He understood that without her having to say it, because when his parents had spoken to him about including her as family, he'd not voiced an objection to it for the very same reason.

When the service ended, it was only himself, Morgan and his parents at the grave.

"Morgan," he said, keeping his voice even-keeled. "Would you like me to give you a ride home?"

She looked up at him, her gaze questioning. And then in a breath, he saw his answer.

She knew going with him was a mistake. He wasn't going to give her a ride home. Or, rather maybe he was. But he wasn't going to simply drop her and leave her. And this was something she knew, something she knew innately now because she'd crossed that threshold from innocent to woman who knew.

And she wasn't going to put a stop to it.

He did drive her home.

"My apartment is small," she said, as soon as they were out on the sidewalk.

But her words were cut off by his kiss. Hard and dark

and she wanted to weep because this was what she'd needed all day.

This was somehow different than the first time they were together. They were both so raw.

And he was...

He was something else entirely.

There was no cool detachment, no control.

None at all.

And she couldn't pretend it was an aberration because it was happening again. She couldn't pretend she'd make a better choice, a smarter choice next time.

Because next time was here, and she was diving in head-first.

And she was afraid she might drown.

"Upstairs," she whispered, because they were dangerously close to getting indecent on the street, and there were still people milling around in spite of the cold.

The North End of Boston always had people out late nights, going to bars and Italian bakeries and pizzerias. She didn't need to put on a show.

"There isn't an elevator," she said when they went into the building and she started up the stairs.

He didn't pause, he simply followed her up the staircase and to her apartment door. She shoved her key in the lock and jiggled it until it opened. "It's a little tricky," she said.

She was embarrassed. She hadn't expected him to come over. She hadn't ever had a man over at all. Alex had picked her up, but never come in.

But he didn't seem to care about the size or state of the apartment. Instead, he was kissing her again, walking her back to her tiny bedroom and smaller bed, and laying her down on the narrow mattress.

She kissed him, arching her back against him as he pushed his hand up beneath her dress.

Her mourning clothes.

This was wrong and she didn't care.

She wanted him.

And after tonight she would probably never see him again.

She was being driven by grief, but also by need. It had never been Alex for her, not like this, something that had been made clear the night she'd gone to Constantine's bed, and even while she'd wept tears over the loss of Alex, over the unfairness of his death. The cruelty of a life that had burned so bright cut so awfully short…

She had dreamed of Constantine. And the guilt had mixed with hunger, deep down inside her, and had created a monster that was raging now, one she couldn't fight.

One she didn't want to fight.

Was that the same beast that drove Constantine now? Or were there other demons driving him now?

For they were both kissing each other as if hell was at their heels, and time was not on their side.

Time was not on their side.

When this ended, so would they. And she knew it.

She knew it.

Tears tracked down her cheeks as he stripped them both of their clothes, and if he thought they were tears for Alex, that was okay with her.

He never had to know her tears were for the two of them.

When he was inside her, she clung to his shoulders. She held him while he trembled, as he split apart at the seams, raw and feral. As he claimed her, over and over again, sending them both to the heights.

She lost track of how many times.

He was like a man possessed, and she a woman possessed of him.

They had opened Pandora's box, and let the wave of darkness sweep over them both. Let it consume them.

When she finally slept, her face was wet with sweat and tears. And when she woke in the morning, he was gone.

And she cried like she would never, ever stop.

In the five months since Alex's funeral, since Constantine had left her apartment, everything had changed.

She had graduated—another milestone missed by her mother, though there were so many it shouldn't surprise her. Graduation was one good thing she'd managed to do as she put her head down and pretended that the changes in her body were coincidence. Grief and stress.

But she knew it wasn't that.

Morgan needed to go and see a doctor. She knew it.

She knew she was pregnant because she was visibly pregnant. She needed to see a doctor. She probably needed to talk to Constantine.

But ever since…

Hideous grief and guilt assaulted her.

Alex.

Oh, the month after his death was a blur. Because she had never broken up with him. He had died that morning in an accident. Likely taking his lover back home. He had been driving his car too quickly, and had flipped it coming around the curve.

But he had been alone, and no one had known why he was out.

Sure he'd had some alcohol in his system, though barely above the legal limit. His parents had shrugged at that. A little bit of partying was hardly notable to them.

But they had not shrugged at the loss of him. Their grief had been a horrible thing to witness, and Morgan had felt absolutely bound to be part of it.

Because she had been his girlfriend, and they had not ended it… And… And she did care for them very much. She had worn black to the service, she had cried while holding his mother, sobs racking her thin frame.

And she had done her best to avoid Constantine's gaze through all of it.

That was when she had decided she had to get out of the Kamaras family's lives. Alex had betrayed her before he died, that much was true. But she couldn't tell his parents that. And if it ever came to light…

When she had found out she was pregnant, she was only more determined to stay away. Constantine didn't want her. What had happened between them wasn't romance. It had been an exorcism. And something beyond them both. It had been sharp and ugly, even as it had been beautiful. And she knew…she knew he would hate this. And added to that…

How would she ever explain it to Alex's parents? It would compound all the pain that they had been through that she had… That she had slept with Constantine. While she was still… She was still with Alex. It did not matter that he had been cheating on her, that she had decided to break it off, she had not done so yet. And he had given her so much. That was where things like the gift of tuition, and all of the wonderful, glorious things he had showered on her during the time they were together began to model things.

Because surely she owed Alex more than he ever owed her. And now he was dead. And she mourned him, even these months later, even with the way he had betrayed her. Because in the end, she would look upon that relationship with… With joy. How could she look upon it with anything else?

And if nothing else, it had led to this.

Of course you don't feel an overwhelming sense of joy about this.

She looked down at the undeniable bump that seemed prouder than necessary.

Yeah. It was true. She wasn't feeling joy right at the moment. She was still in the throes of denial.

But she knew that... Once the baby was born...

No. She didn't know any of that. And she was terrified.

Because her mother had not been suffused with an injection of maternal joy and delight, so how could she count on the same?

They'd moved apartments all the time when she was a child, living in small, rundown studios, or sometimes with whatever man her mother was dating. Often her memories blurred, the settings amalgams of one another.

Whenever she pictured herself, it was sitting in the kitchen with yellow, flowered wallpaper, by herself.

She had one memory in particular of sitting there, kicking her feet against the legs of the chair in time to the clock on the wall.

She'd been invited to a birthday party. They were supposed to go to the zoo and Morgan had never been.

Her mother hadn't wanted to take her to buy a gift for her friend, so Morgan had walked to the corner store and used money she'd earned from watching her neighbor's cat while they were out of town and bought her friend a small off-brand doll. She'd wrapped it in tissue and waited for her mother to come home to drive her to her friend's house.

She hadn't come home.

Morgan had sat in that chair, hoping, until long after the party was over. And then she'd cried as she'd made her own dinner.

When her mother had finally come home Morgan had asked why she'd forgotten and her mother had yelled at her about how she'd taken an extra work shift, and she didn't need Morgan making her feel guilty about silly things when she was already overworked.

Morgan had been eight.

The thing that scared her the most was the way her mother was…no matter how many other men there were, she was obsessively angry at Morgan's father.

And while Morgan had her own issues with having a father she'd never met, who didn't want her…

She could remember the time her mother had looked at her and said: It's a shame. You have his eyes.

Like a failure or an accusation.

It was no accident Morgan had lost touch with her mom.

She'd visited at first, after she'd moved out. Then she'd turned those visits into phone calls that were less and less frequent. She'd made excuses about school. She'd called on her mom's birthday, Mother's Day, Christmas. That was all.

Then she'd started dating Alex.

"Sorry, Mom, school and… I have a new boyfriend so I'm just really busy."

Since Alex's death she hadn't called her mother once.

What if she was a bitter, distant mother just like her own?

Perhaps realizing that you could be, and deciding not to be, is the real answer.

Maybe. Maybe. But in the meantime… In the meantime she worried.

And she really did need to go to a doctor.

She also felt guilty living off what Alex had given her already, but she had been violently ill in the first stages of her pregnancy, and waiting tables had not been an option. Not anymore. So she had ensconced herself in her apartment, and had rarely left, only to get groceries.

She could get delivery, it was true, and right at first she had done that. But…

Eventually, she had realized that she had to get off the couch. Eventually, she realized that she had to venture out. She was having her weekly shopping trip now. Wearing the only pair of black leggings that she could fit herself into, rolled down beneath her stomach, and a white T-shirt.

She had thrown on a white baseball hat and a denim jacket, hands stuffed in her pockets as she strode down the street, eyes on her white tennis shoes, wondering why she had worn them, when she had to worry about the road grime getting on them.

She popped into her favorite bodega and got herself some milk, standing in front of the produce while she waited to see if a craving struck her. None did. She went to the freezer section and found herself putting ice cream in her cart. Then to the fridge where she grabbed cheese. And other than the crackers that she added later, she realized her little handcart was entirely dairy. And she would've felt shame if she weren't so blissfully, purely sorry for herself in the moment.

She suddenly had a strange sensation that she was being watched and looked over her shoulder to see two young girls staring at her. One had their phone slightly held raised like they were texting, but from a strange angle, and she had the strange feeling that they had taken her picture. But why would they do that?

She turned away, and then back again. And in a bid of strange paranoia she could not even quite understand, she put her sunglasses on. Then she got in line and paid for her things as quickly as possible, making her way back to her apartment. She spread her cheese out on the counter and chastised herself. She was being paranoid. And she really needed to get a hold of herself. There was no reason that anyone would know who she was. No reason they would be interested at all in her buying cheese.

Maybe they thought the guy running the counter was hot.

She thought about him. Tall and dark with an easy smile. He was hot, she supposed. She had been burned by Constantine Kamaras, and she did not think she would recover soon from the scalding. It made any other man seem… Tepid.

She was just being paranoid. She repeated that to herself while she made herself a lovely cheese platter.

And she felt a little bit better about herself and her life, given that she had gone out, and now she had made herself a dinner that was actually quite lovely, even if it was a little bit sketchy when it came to nutrition.

She would be all right. She would not become her mother.

Of that she was determined.

This was her mess.

She would not punish a child with it for the rest of their lives.

And right then she determined that she wouldn't punish herself either.

CHAPTER THREE

"HAVE YOU SEEN THIS?"

Constantine's blood ran cold as his father shoved his phone into Constantine's face.

"'The Late Kamaras's Lover Tries to Hide Baby Bump at Store.'" His father looked jubilant.

And Constantine was frozen.

For a moment…

For one moment, he had seen her and he'd forgotten. Everything. That she had been Alex's. That she was not only his.

And he had…

For just a moment a sense of total possessiveness had drowned out everything. She was there, she was pregnant.

And that night of the funeral loomed large in his mind. His hands on her body. Her mouth on his. Being inside her.

The pleasure of touching Morgan the only thing that drowned out the pain.

But then he looked more closely at the photo.

The article had arrows drawn to each element of her outfit, proclaiming her a low-key style icon.

He had no idea what it meant. And had no idea why she was being hounded like that.

Except…

Alex had been a darling of the tabloid media. So it stood to reason that Morgan would be as well.

He took the phone from his father's hand and began to scroll through the article. It gave an explanation of the fairy-tale romance between Morgan and Alex, along with a recap of Alex's untimely death. It talked about how Morgan had been "underground" in the months since, and that this was clearly why. That she was trying to keep a low profile to protect the child she was carrying.

She looked to be quite advanced in her pregnancy. Much more than five months.

The child wasn't his.

The child was Alex's.

He wondered if she had been intending to tell Alex that night she had caught him with another woman.

And then he'd died.

She was carrying Alex's child.

And his father looked… Overjoyed.

It did not surprise Constantine in the least.

His parents had favored Alex so. He was like them. He was carefree and bright, and everyone loved them.

Much harder to love the one who kept things running. That had been his grandfather's function as well, until his death ten years ago. When Constantine had taken over everything Kamaras.

Because God knew Cosmo Kamaras, his father, could not be trusted to do it.

It wasn't that he was a bad man. Far from it. He was gregarious, happy, and often generous with his wealth. Much of the same way that Alex had been.

But he was… He was at his core selfish. Even if he meant no harm with it. His mother was the same way. Delia Kamaras was a rare beauty, the toast of any social scene she found herself in. She liked parties and glitter. Glamour.

She had much preferred going out to nights spent at home. And they had thrown themselves into that even more after the loss of Athena. It was not a mystery to him why. They looked at him and saw ghosts.

And growing up might have been lonely if not for...

If not for Alex.

And that was the essence of the issue with his family.

Feckless. Reckless.

And perfectly wonderful to be around.

But someone had to do the work.

And someone had to pay the price. Always.

Someone had to.

But a child from Alex...

"I have not told your mother yet," his father said. "She would be... Do you know what this means? A grandchild? What if it's a little boy? We must bring her here."

"Yes," Constantine agreed. Because regardless of his entanglement with Morgan, of course, they must have Alex's child.

It felt...

There had been a moment where he had thought only of himself. Of Morgan carrying his child. And that would have been...

He had vowed he never would. He would never be a father.

Ever.

But this chance...this chance to have a piece of Alex here with them. That healed something in him.

They would have more than a cold stone with his name carved on it.

They would have his child.

"She is poor," Cosmo said. "Perhaps we can offer her money to give us the child."

"I very much doubt that Morgan is going to allow you to fight for her baby."

"You are so certain? I thought you had absolutely no esteem for her. I thought you imagine her to be a gold digger."

His parents had instantly welcomed Morgan, but they were like that. It was part of their complicated nature. They were not cynical people. They had no real reserve, that was the issue. They said what they thought and sometimes they said things that were painful for Constantine. And sometimes they spoke nothing but love and support.

They had certainly done so for Morgan. They had defended her no matter how cautious Constantine was about her.

Yet again, he'd felt he had to protect Alex where they were not…

Where they were only focused on the good and the glittering.

"I did," he said, clipped. "She could've come demanding money from you at any point over the course of this pregnancy, and she has not, has she?" Of course, that wasn't the real reason that he didn't think Morgan would go after his family money. Or at least, that she wouldn't trade her child for it.

No. It had been the hurt when she had discovered Alex was being unfaithful to her. And the passionate way she had gone up in flames in his arms.

She was not a woman of cold, calculated intent. Of that he was certain.

He knew that now.

If he were bracingly honest with himself the heart of his issue with Morgan had been the fact that he wanted her, and she had belonged to Alex, and at the first moment the opportunity had been there…

He had wanted her. So he had taken her. And it enraged

him that looking at her now, round with child, *not* his child, he felt the same sort of desire that had existed then. Only it felt feral now. Possessive.

As if it didn't before.

He gritted his teeth.

"You do present a good point. Perhaps she will consent to be part of the family. I don't see why not. Your mother… She was very fond of her. She was quite sad when Morgan faded out of our lives. It was so nice to see Alex as happy as he was with her. He was going to marry her."

Constantine wondered if that was true. He had no trouble believing that his brother could be unfaithful to the woman that he had wanted to marry, because Alex simply wouldn't think past the moment. He wouldn't take the emotion all that deep. It just wasn't in him.

At least it hadn't been.

He still found it very difficult to think of his brother in the past tense.

He wanted to rail at him. He had for these last five months. And now even more so.

You were going to be a father, you fool. Why did you need to drive that fast? Why did you need to drive drunk? Why could you not have settled? Why must you make me miss you like this? Why could you not have been more like me?

Athena had been taken, and nothing that had happened had been her choice. This was such a strange, complex pain. Alex had made his choices, and yet Constantine still felt he should have done something more.

And none of it fixed the hole inside of him. Not guilt, not anything.

Perhaps…

Perhaps this child would.

"I will go to her," Constantine said, on that he was clear. On that he was certain.

"Bring her here," his dad said. "And let her know that every offer is on the table. She's family now."

She's family now.

Those words rang sharply in his head as he drove his sleek sports car down to Morgan's brownstone. A location he knew too well.

The sight of his last downfall with her.

She would have been carrying Alex's baby, even then.

She would have been the first time too.

The thought of it made his blood burn.

He went inside the building and made his way up the narrow staircase, confident he remembered the exact details of which unit she was in. He might have been addled by grief and desire, but he was not a man who forgot such things.

He found it quickly enough.

The security in this place was shameful. The floors and walls scarred by God knew what.

He did not want her living here, that was certain.

Even now, he did not want that.

He did something he was deeply unaccustomed to and knocked.

"Yes?"

The question was muted.

"Morgan," he said. "Open the door."

"You must have the wrong unit."

"We both know I don't."

"No, we don't know that."

Frustration rocked through his veins, but still, he could not hate her. "We do."

He did not know why she was bothering with the pretense. He was a fool. But there was something so absurdly stubborn about this attempt at a charade, that he... Why was it always like this with her? Why could he never really quite hate her?

He had met her and they'd sparked off each other instantly.

"A bartender?"

"A waitress," she'd said. *"At a bar. It is different."*

"I imagine one makes it easier to meet rich men?"

"Are you accusing me of something?"

"Yes. Dating my brother for his money."

"I've only known you for a few minutes, but perhaps that is why women date you. Alex has a personality."

He'd grudgingly respected her then, even if he hadn't liked her being with his brother. But then, the real issue had been that he'd wanted her. From that moment.

"Maybe if you had your own dates at family functions you wouldn't be so concerned about me, Constantine."

"I don't date, Morgan."

"I wasn't aware you'd taken vows of celibacy."

His lips had curved and he'd had the strongest desire to see if he could make her blush. If he could prove what he suspected. That she always ended up talking to him when she came to his parents' home because she couldn't stay away. Because of the heat between them.

"I never said I was celibate. I don't have to play games. Women don't come to me for dinner dates. They simply come for dessert."

"And the witty banter I assume," she'd said, but her voice had sounded tight.

"No, it's for the orgasms."

And he'd realized in that moment he'd overstepped because the air between them had become thick, and the spark had been palpable. And knowing? It had fixed nothing.

Even now he should hate her. He should be angry at her. For concealing this from his family. And he was. He was angry about a lot of things.

But there were moments where she glimmered, even behind a scratched up old door, and that was the thing about Morgan that made everything difficult.

"I'm not going to leave," he said. "I can tell you I could break down this door in a matter of seconds, and I don't think that anyone would help you. This apartment is appalling."

"It is actually very nice for this area and reasonably priced."

"How nice for it. But it is not secure enough to keep you safe."

"You aren't going to do anything to me, Constantine."

"Funny how you suddenly speak English. And know who I am."

The door suddenly cracked open. "What do you want?"

"I should think it's quite obvious. I am here to claim my brother's child."

Morgan stared out of the crack, the door opened as wide as it could with the chain still on, utterly dumbfounded by what Constantine had just said.

His brother's child.

But surely he knew…

She looked up at his face, and it was clear that he didn't know. "My parents are overjoyed," Constantine said. "So thrilled that Alex is to have a child. It does not matter what passed between us, Morgan. What matters is that you have given them hope. You have given them joy when I thought it would not be possible for them to ever experience it again. When my father saw the article…"

"An article?"

"It was in the tabloids just yesterday."

"It was not!"

"It was," he said.

"I didn't see it."

"Do you read tabloids?"

"Well no. But I would if I thought that I was going to be in them."

"Open the door, Morgan. I will show you."

"I am quite capable of doing an Internet search without your interference." She closed the door, then went and grabbed her phone off the couch and did a quick search for her own name.

And there it was. In the bodega. And of course the picture they used was the one after she had put her sunglasses on, which was when she had become paranoid. She hadn't gone out incognito, but they'd certainly made it sound like she had. Like she knew that she might be followed.

"Style icon…"

She zoomed in slightly on the photo, she supposed she did look quite cute. "This is very strange," she shouted back.

"Irregular," he said, as if agreeing. "Now open the door so that we might speak.

"Please come back with me," he said. "My mother has not been this happy since Alex died. You cannot take this from them."

Morgan hesitated, guilt turning through her.

Constantine clearly had no idea that she'd been a virgin when they'd slept together. He thought this was Alex's child and… She had given him her virginity.

He'd been her first.

The only man she'd ever really wanted, and he had no idea. He had no real idea who she was at all.

How special their connection had been for her, and how

unique it was. How it defied everything she'd ever known about herself before.

It doesn't matter what he thinks. He won't want the child. And maybe this is a way to...to give them some joy, while maintaining freedom.

It was clear that this was the narrative that Constantine wanted to believe.

Does it really surprise you?

No.

Because she knew how he felt about having children. A memory she'd buried because she couldn't bear to unspool it. And she'd become very, very good at denial these last months.

Doing her best to turn that hot, glorious night with Constantine into a gauzy blur even though she remembered it all far too clearly.

And all the days she'd spent at the Kamaras Estate during her time with Alex. It was strange how those memories centered on Constantine. They always had. It hadn't mattered that she wasn't supposed to be there for him. They'd always found each other. They'd always ended up talking.

It was like they'd been pulled together by forces stronger than themselves. Even when other people had been in the room, he was at the center of the memory.

"I personally will be an excellent father, as I am an expert in all of life's important skills. Drinking fine alcohol..." Alex had lifted his glass *"...driving fast cars and ensnaring the most beautiful women."*

He'd gestured to Morgan when he said that.

"And if you were to have a daughter?"

"I am equal opportunity, Morgan, perhaps my daughter will appreciate those skills? One never knows."

His eyes had shone with humor and Morgan's stomach had fluttered. Then Constantine had turned his dark eyes on her and her stomach had clamped down tight. She hadn't been able to breathe.

"A fine role model then," he'd said, his gaze flickering to his brother.

"And you, Constantine?" Alex had asked. *"What will you teach your children? To glower, isolate yourself for days at a time and miss the punchline of most jokes lobbed your way?"*

"A glower when pointed well is a useful tool. I think you mean work, not isolate, and if a joke is poor, I do not laugh. Which could be why you never hear it, little brother. But I will never have children," he'd said, his tone definitive, *"so it does not matter either way if I have useful skills to pass on."*

"Never?" she asked.

She hadn't meant to ask. But she felt...sad hearing him say that. Constantine, for all that he perplexed her, bothered her, was one of the most beautiful men she'd ever seen. There was something magnetic about him. Something strong and infinitely...appealing.

The image of him holding a baby in his strong arms made her breath catch.

He looked at her and made her wish she hadn't spoken. *"Never."*

And she stood there, grappling with herself. With how much of this was her looking for an easy way out of her connection with him, and how much was a genuine desire to not disappoint his parents.

And would he even believe her if she told him it was his?

Two nights, they'd been together. And even though they'd made love many times that last night... He must think she'd been with Alex countless times prior...

"What happens if I don't go with you?"

"I think you will find that it is a legal battle that you do not want," he said, his voice grim.

And that she knew to be true. Because she didn't have any power, not in the face of the Kamaras family. It wouldn't be a fight. Not at all. She might have been unburdened of her student loans, but that didn't mean that she was wealthy by any standards. She lived in this apartment, which was truly not childproof, and she...

She would just never be able to fight his family, she knew that.

And part of her...

A small part.

That girl sitting in the yellow wallpapered kitchen in the recesses of her memory, whispered: *And this way you won't be all alone, not anymore.*

Oh, she desperately didn't want to be so alone.

Did that make her weak?

Maybe.

But she was so tired of it. That was the hardest thing. She hadn't loved Alex. But being with him had given her a family, in a way. Even when she'd been sparring with Constantine at those gatherings, it had given her something. Connection.

With his loss, she had lost them.

"I will go with you."

She went to get her purse.

"Do you intend to open the door?"

No. Not until the very last minute. She didn't want to any sooner than she needed to.

She grabbed her bag, and opened the door, her heart thundering as she came face-to-face with him.

"I'm ready."

"Damn," he said, looking down at her. "When are you due?"

"I don't know," she said.

And that wasn't entirely true. Using the dates of her last period. And the date of their intercourse, she had calculated the due date on the Internet. But it wasn't confirmed by a doctor or anything.

And she should just tell him. But his denial in wanting children stuck in her mind, and it mixed with what she knew of her own father. And if she told him…

Would she end up alone? Would he react the same as he was now in his bid to…?

He was preserving Alex's memory, protecting Alex's legacy. If he thought the child was his…

If his parents thought she'd betrayed Alex, if Constantine didn't have that drive to protect Alex, then what would this mean?

Would her child be rejected, just like she'd been?

Are you worried about your child being rejected, or yourself?

She refused to think about it.

"Why do you not know?"

"I haven't gone to a doctor."

"You haven't been to a doctor. Dammit, Morgan. That is the first thing you will do."

"Wait a second," she said, feeling panicked. "You don't get to tell me what to do."

"I'm afraid that isn't true. You were behaving irresponsibly. By not telling my family about the child, by not ensuring that you've been cared for medically… Come with me."

She followed him down the stairs. "And I don't like you taking the stairs."

"I'm not a soap opera heroine," she said. "I'm not going to get shoved down them by an angry rival and lose the pregnancy."

But she put her hand on the bump protectively then, because as a flippant remark, it might have been humorous, but in reality it made her feel slightly paranoid. She had never ridden in Constantine's car. It was red and fast looking, and not at all what she had thought he would drive.

"This seems out of character," she said.

"What did you expect?"

She shrugged a shoulder. "A hearse?"

"As I said," he returned, teeth gritted. "We all have vices."

She was shocked to learn that fast cars were one of his.

"I hope you drive more carefully than Alex."

He looked at her, his dark gaze pointed, and she felt the full impact of him down to her toes. "I do everything more carefully than Alex does. Did."

She did not correct him on that. Because the fact of the matter was, he had not been careful when they'd had sex.

They had not used protection, something she hadn't realized until she'd missed her period. The entire night was such a blur that it had not sunk in. Maybe it never really would.

She still couldn't quite believe it was her life.

A Cinderella fantasy turned upside down. Prince Charming was nowhere in sight. She had Prince Brooding and a precarious fairy tale that could be broken as easily as a glass slipper. And still she wanted to cling to it, even as she knew she was doing something wrong.

But she was doing the wrong thing while doing some right things, and that had to count for something?

In some ways, she was protecting the baby, and Constantine, and his parents.

Still…

Bravery took hold just for a moment, and she got the courage to test it. To test him.

"Did you ever think that it might be your child?" she

asked once they were driving down the road. "We didn't use condoms. We never even talked about it."

Her mouth was dry as she laid that out there. Seeing what he'd do, what he'd say. If he seized on it, or if he'd deny it.

He looked over at her. There was something dark radiating from him. The same emotion she'd sensed when he'd told her he'd never have children.

Never?

Never.

"No," he said. "You are far too advanced in your pregnancy for that."

She wasn't though. Whatever it looked like, she knew she wasn't.

"Are you an expert in the appearance of women during various gestational stages?"

"No," he said. "But I can see the obvious."

"Or is it just that you don't want to entertain the idea because it's inconvenient for you. Because then you have to admit that… That something happened between us. We both know that you were doing your best to pretend that was not the case."

It was dangerous to push him, and she knew it. And she didn't know why she was doing it. Didn't know what result she was after.

He didn't want a child.

She knew what it was to be an unwanted child.

And she would never…

She would never.

"What exactly would you like me to do? Did you wish me to grab you and kiss you at my brother's funeral while you played the grieving widow? You and I know the truth. That you were done with him, and rightly so. That he had betrayed you. We also know that we had an indiscretion.

And I regret that. But none of it matters. Alex is gone, and he does not have the ability to defend himself or share his side of the story. His reputation is set in stone, and we are the keepers of it. The only way that it changes is if we tell stories about him, is that not so?"

"I… I suppose so."

"He cannot defend himself, nor can he make amends."

That seemed so entirely sad to her.

Because there was so much to love about Alex. He had made mistakes. A lot of them.

"A lot of people make mistakes," Constantine said, as if he could read her mind. Suddenly, the sound of the tires on the asphalt seemed almost deafening.

"The difference is that Alex's opportunity to atone for them has been taken from him. The difference is, that his mistake killed him. Without giving him a second chance."

"I'm so sorry…"

And it was true. She was sorry. Because he had been full of life and lovely, and even if she realized now that he was not the love of her life, she had loved him quite a bit.

"Tell me," Constantine said. "About how you met."

"You know how I met him."

"Yes, I know how you met him but only in the way that I allowed myself to hear the story. I assumed that you wanted him only for his money. But the fact that you did not come chasing after a paycheck for carrying his child when you absolutely could have… It has made me question things, and I would like to relearn your relationship with him."

"I really did just… I was so utterly charmed by him." She looked out the window and watched the city fly by. "How could I not be? He came to the bar, and he seemed so entirely out of place. His suit was so much more expensive and cut so much more nicely than anyone else's in there. But he wasn't a snob. He was gregarious, and he bought rounds of drinks for people. And when he complimented me, it didn't feel like he only wanted sex. It felt like he meant it. And I cannot tell you how... How rare that was. Men flirted with me all the time. Made overt passes, but it was different with him. He said he wanted to get to know me, and I swear to you that is what he did. He got to know me. He treated me with the utmost respect. He treated me as I had never been treated before. How could I be anything but in love with him?

"I didn't discover that he was... Alex Kamaras, *that* Alex Kamaras, for a couple of weeks. I'm not connected to the social scene, and I confess I didn't really know much of anything about him beyond seeing his name mentioned occasionally in entertainment round up articles. But I still wasn't familiar enough to actually understand who he was. And once I did... It kind of scared me. I'm just a normal girl. I never expected to meet someone like him."

It was true. All of it. But she left out the part where she came home to meet his family and met Constantine.

She had felt nothing but joyous warmth around Alex. And of course she thought he was handsome. He made her flutter when he smiled, he did that to every woman.

But she had met Constantine, and something had happened. Something she understood now was raw chemistry.

What was a crush with Alex, was utterly sexual with Constantine. And being a virgin, she had not fully understood that. And she had preferred the light happy feelings that she got from being near Alex.

"I find the story so hard to believe."

"I know you do. And I even understand why. It must be difficult. Feeling as if everybody wants to use you for your money and power."

She felt him go stiff beside her. It was as if a wall had

been thrown up, and the emotion radiating from behind it was… It was intense.

"Yes. It is true. A family such as mine, older, carrying history that dates back as far as it does… We are targeted. The Kamaras family is nobility in Greece."

"Yes," she said. "I know. Because Alex took great delight in telling me that he was a count."

"Indeed."

"Though I imagine it's the billions that really causes problems, the title just seems decorative."

"In a fashion," he agreed.

"I know it sounds silly to say that I know what it feels like. But I do. You see, I have nothing. Nothing to offer any man except…"

"Your beauty."

She nodded. "Yes. I'm not rich, I'm not influential. I waited tables in a bar. And men saw me and thought that my body was a commodity. That is all any of them wanted from me. And the first man to not simply want that was Alex."

"You know, he treated every other woman differently. He did simply want sex."

"Yes, and I'm beginning to think he perhaps had an entirely different… Maybe he was different with me than he was with everyone else. It's an attractive thing to tell myself anyway."

"It's true."

And it made her feel… She didn't really know. Happier, maybe. Or sadder. To know that the truth was she had been different for him. It was just that he had made a mistake.

Would she have forgiven him, if he had lived?

No. Not after what happened with Constantine. There was no question.

She would've lost him, more because of her own understanding about desire, than because of his betrayal.

They finally made their way to the grand estate outside the city that the Kamaras family lived at.

She had learned, from listening to conversations in the Kamaras household, that Constantine had his own residence in Boston, and also in New York, LA and Greece.

One thing she had never done was look him up on the Internet though, and she hadn't just to spite Constantine. Since he'd accused her of targeting his brother from the beginning, of knowing who he was and so she had vowed to herself she would never go searching for information about him or his family that wasn't given directly.

The magnificent manor house came into view, and her stomach fluttered. Or perhaps that was the baby kicking her. Which had become more and more common lately. As soon as Constantine pulled the car up to the front of the estate, the doors flew open. It wasn't the butler who greeted them, but Delia.

She had tears streaming down her face, and when Morgan got out of the car, the other woman flew across the empty space and hugged her. "Agape," she said, smoothing Morgan's hair back from her face. "Daughter. You have no idea how happy I am."

And Morgan's heart contracted in on itself.

Her own mother had never looked at her with this much joy. With this much excitement. With this much love.

No. Not even her own mother.

But Delia Kamaras was looking at her like she was miraculous.

And what would they think if she knew?

Yes, it would still be their grandchild, but it would not be a piece of their beloved Alex.

And they would know that she and Constantine...

"I didn't know what to do," she said.

Because that was true. She still didn't know what to do, but the choice had been taken away from her. And right then she knew that she could never lie directly to Alex's parents. She was going to have to figure out exactly how she was going to handle this. But she would not lie while she thought of it. "You will stay here," Delia said. "We will take care of you."

"My apartment is perfectly adequate," she said. "You really don't need…"

"It is not adequate," Constantine said. "Not in the least. It is dangerous, in my opinion, and not suitable for any child of the Kamarases."

"Of course not," Delia said, ushering her inside. "You will stay here. We will have servants at your beck and call. Food prepared for you. Everything handled. That is how the child of the Kamarases is treated, and it is how you will be treated. You will never have to lift a finger again. You… You are… An angel. Salvation. You are to be coddled and protected at all costs."

She looked over at Constantine, whose expression was something like thunder, but he did not speak.

"We will ready a suite for you. When are you due?"

"I…"

"She does not know," Constantine said. "She has not yet been to the doctor."

"Well that will not do," Delia said. "We will make a doctor's appointment for you immediately. And we will have him come here. And then you will let us know, because, we are about to leave. Our summer home in Saint-Tropez is waiting. And we of course never rest."

"Oh…"

"You will be cared for here. And we will of course be here for the child's birth."

She looked over at Constantine again, whose expression was utterly unreadable.

"Constantine can show you to your quarters."

Delia hugged her, and then fluttered off.

"My parents are very much cut from the same cloth as Alex."

"What does that mean?"

"They're thrilled you're here. They will see you want for nothing. But they will not interrupt their partying."

"Partying?"

"They are... Professional socialites. They do not work for the firm. That would allow them too much time to sit and think and they...prefer to run from their problems. Straight into bottles of alcohol and loud clubs." She knew what pain they'd suffered recently, but the way he'd said that...it sounded like there was more. But he moved on before she could marinate on that too much. "For my part, I run the business. That is something that I inherited directly from my grandfather. I oversee Kamaras Industries."

"I see."

"It does not run itself."

For the first time, she fully appreciated the difference between Alex and Constantine.

Constantine was continuing to make money. To keep the family business going.

His family... Spent it. No wonder he seemed different. More grounded. No wonder he seemed to carry a weight inside of him that the rest of them didn't.

She had been in the Kamaras family estate many times, the beautiful well-kept grounds and the stunning architecture both in and out never failing to amaze her. But she had never stayed here. Not overnight.

And now she was being shown to a bedroom that was personally hers. A horrible thought stole over her.

"I'm not being put in Alex's room."

He stopped. "No," he said, his voice hard. "You and I both know how inappropriate that would be."

"Yes," she said.

"Anyway, it is being preserved. My parents do not want anything touched or moved. Understandable."

"Yes," she said, her voice hoarse. Choked.

"I loved my brother a great deal," Constantine said. "In spite of his shortcomings."

"Whether you believe it or not," she said, looking up at him. "I loved your brother a great deal."

"I do believe it. Now."

Tension seemed to stretch between them, an impossibly thick and difficult thing. It was nearly impossible to breathe. She struggled against the weight of it. And if Constantine struggled, he did not show it. She did not believe he was unaffected, and yet, he seemed to absorb the impact of all of it into his muscular body. Take it all on in a way that she just didn't know how to do. And that was when she suddenly felt angry. She was out of her depth. She had been from the moment she had met Constantine. She had never known how to be around him.

He had seemed as if he hated her and yet he always spent the evening talking to her. Even if his words were hard and sharp. And she had been hungry for every interaction.

She couldn't remember the point where she had begun to look forward to sparring with him more than she'd looked forward to seeing Alex. She had never fully admitted that to herself. But she had always found Constantine. And she might have complained bitterly inside about how much he seemed to despise her, and still, she sought him out.

Every time.

As he did her.

This man who called to parts inside of her that she had wished might remain hidden.

Yes, there was Constantine. And he was...

He was impossible. Impossible for a woman like her. He could handle this, because he had bed partners before. Likely many, because he was beautiful as a fallen angel, and even if he was the more responsible of the brothers, the way he had made love to her...

The skill. Combined with the intensity of it all, it spoke to an experience that she never even wanted to achieve. It was a mess. All of it. And she was the one who would suffer for it. And she would never be free of them. Not ever.

She didn't know what would happen when the truth was revealed. If it would be. Or if Constantine's denial would smooth over reality. If she wanted it to.

What she wanted right now was a reprieve, even if it was temporary.

She didn't want to make the decision, that was the issue. If that made her cowardly, then right at the moment she would just have to accept that.

"Come," he said.

And she did, because she was out of energy. Unable to fight. Unable to... Anything.

They walked past his room, and her chest seized up, but then they kept on going. To a room that had ornately carved double doors. With flowers and fairies.

"What is this?"

"This is a very old estate, and at one time, the lady of the house kept this grand room for herself. No one in my family has ever used it. But my mother thought that it was interesting. So, she... Spent several years enhancing it."

He pushed the doors open, and what he revealed was... Stunning.

There were little paper butterflies and flowers all over

the wall, a cascade of color that climbed up the ceiling and spread out to a glorious golden chandelier at its center. The bed was opulent, four posters with gauzy fabric wrapped around it. A gilded birdcage hung in the corner with…

"Are those doves?"

"Yes," he said. "My mother's pets. You may… Have them be homed if it does not please you for them to be in here."

"This is like a forest."

"That was the idea. A fairy wood, I believe."

"Well, it is that."

"My mother thought you would enjoy it."

Yet again she became completely overcome by the reality of the gulf between herself and the Kamarases, and she wondered how she had ever thought that she and Alex could… How they could ever meet.

And when she looked across the space between herself and Constantine, she at least had to congratulate herself on the good sense of knowing when they made love that it could only be temporary. Of knowing that the two of them could never, ever bridge the gulf between them. Because it was not simply that he was a wealthy man. A powerful man. There was more than that. He was Constantine Kamaras, and she was Morgan Stanfield. And they would never be on the same side of this unimaginable canyon. He would always be on one, and she always on the other.

And it only made her feel all the more isolated. All the more precarious.

"What is it?"

"Nothing. I just… I don't know how to be a person who might sleep in this room."

"It is simple. You need only to lie on the bed."

They stared at each other and sparks ignited between the two of them.

"I don't think it is that simple, Constantine."

"It matters not. The doctor will be here shortly to see you."

"The doctor. Wait a minute. Wait a minute. I have an apartment, I left all of my things and…"

"A member of staff has already been designated to handle the management of your belongings. But, I imagine you will not need many of them. We will provide you with whatever you need."

"I'm not… I'm not for sale, Constantine, you cannot simply… Pack me up in a bag and make me one of your belongings."

"Make no mistake, Morgan, you are not mine. But you are my family's. Take a rest. The doctor will be here shortly."

Then he turned and left her standing there in the opulent forest. And she could not escape the feeling that she was lost in the woods.

CHAPTER FOUR

WHEN THE DOCTOR ARRIVED, Constantine knew that he should let the man see to his business, but he could not help himself. He wished to be in the room. He wished to be there to hear everything. And he told himself it was a necessity. A responsibility. One that his parents had left to him. Along with the innumerable other responsibilities that fell in his lap.

The business, everything else.

But he just wanted to be there. That was the truth of it.

When he led the man up to the room, along with the nurse, and the ultrasound equipment, and knocked, it took a while for him to get a response.

And then when he did, desire was a living, growling beast inside of him. And he could not hide his reaction. Not even in front of the doctor.

Because when Morgan answered the door, she was bright red and scrubbed clean, as if she had been in a warm bath. And she was wearing nothing but a white robe.

When she saw him, her eyes widened. "Oh."

"The doctor's here," he said.

"All right." She blinked. "I see."

"Do not worry, child," the doctor said. "I have a great amount of experience with this. I was Delia's doctor when she had her children."

Which of course betrayed the doctor's advanced age. But, Constantine had thought that it was appropriate. To make sure that the heir of Alex had the exact same amount of preferential treatment as Alex had had. As Constantine himself had had.

"Oh. I see. Well…"

"We will begin with some simple questions."

Dr. Papasifakis had a gentle bedside manner, and as they all eased their way into the room, he could see that when Morgan looked at the doctor, she began to relax slightly.

"Go ahead and sit," Dr. Papasifakis said.

She did, in the lush, magenta chair in the corner, that was cast in gold like everything else in the ridiculous room.

And somehow, Morgan looked like a fairy in the surroundings. And it did not look ridiculous. He gritted his teeth and turned his attention to the doctor.

"And when was the date of your last menstrual cycle?"

Morgan gave it, and Constantine did his best to ignore the answers that she gave.

He let the dates, including the projected due date that the doctor mentioned, blur in his mind. He thought of Alex. Of all he was missing. That he was standing here when his brother should be. That he was doing all he could to honor his brother, to protect his legacy going forward.

It had to be that.

And then the doctor instructed her to lie down on the bed for the ultrasound.

"Could you…? Constantine…?"

"I will turn away," he said.

"I…"

"It is…" He bit back the scathing comment he was going to make about how he had already seen the whole of her, so there was no use being modest now. Nobody needed to know. And even as his body was gripped with the desire to see her, he turned away, while the doctor and the nurse readied her for the scan.

He heard the preparations, but he did not allow himself to look, instead he focused on one of the butterflies on the wall. A delicate, lavender colored paper creation. It was fragile, like Morgan. And far more intricate than he had ever truly noticed before. He did not spend a great deal of time in this room, or rather any. And so he had not realized how much detail had gone into each and every thing. Amazing, how you could see something hundreds of times, and never truly understand what it was you were looking at.

He thought again of Morgan, and his stomach went tight.

"Here we are," the doctor said, as a strange watery sound filled the room. Followed by a steady beat. "We have the heartbeat. And a boy."

"Oh," Morgan said, the sound fractured. And still, he did not turn.

A boy. A boy like Alex.

His mother and father would be thrilled.

"And here we have another heartbeat. And this one… A girl. A girl and a boy for you."

And everything inside of Constantine turned to ice. And this time, he did turn. "Twins?"

Twins.

Twins.

Everything in him went dark.

"Yes," Dr.Papasifakis said. "Twins. It is why she looked like she was at such an advanced gestational age. She is just barely five months along."

He looked down at her, at the exposed, pale skin of her stomach, that rounded bump. Two babies.

Five months.

"Five months," he said.

No. It could not be. Twins. That was a sick joke brought about by the universe. He did not want children, not ever.

Twins.

Alex had. He had wanted to be a father, and now he was gone, and these children were his last chance.

And if they were Alex's, they were, in many ways, Constantine's last chance for atonement.

If they were his?

Another sin.

No. It could not be.

He had spent two nights with her and, knowing Alex as he did, his brother had likely had her countless times.

The image of such a thing made his vision go black with rage.

She was his. She was his *and you were the one who took what wasn't yours.*

But they had to be Alex's. Alex needed this.

Perhaps you need it.

He hadn't protected Athena. And she was gone, there was no trace of her. His family had never even had a body to bury.

Now Alex was gone.

"Yes," the doctor confirmed. "What a great blessing this is for the Kamaras family. After all they have lost…" the doctor said. "And Alex. Such a blessing that he has two children to carry out his legacy in the world."

Two children. *Alex's children.*

Everyone needed them to be Alex's children.

And yet…

"Thank you," Constantine said. "What must we know now that we are aware that it is twins? Is there anything…"

"Everything looks good. And she seems quite healthy. She is young and strong, and I have no reason to believe that she is at any great risk of anything. It is likely the children will deliver early. But that is to be expected with twins. And it is no cause for concern. We will just keep that in mind as we set expectations."

The doctor spoke as a man who had in excess of forty years' experience in the field, because he did. And Constantine knew that he should trust him, but he found himself seized by an inability to do so. Perhaps because he had lost even the ability to breathe.

And the suspicion that existed inside of him began to grow, and while he knew…

"What about a paternity test," Constantine said. "Simply for the formality of it all."

"Well, that we can't do until after the babies are born. With multiples, you cannot take a risk like that."

"I see."

"But I imagine that is not a real concern of yours."

"Of course not," Constantine said, smiling. "The staff will show you out."

When the doctor left the room, Constantine turned to Morgan, who had wrapped her robe firmly around herself and was sitting on the edge of the bed.

"Did you know?"

"My due date? I suspected, yes. It is not a mystery to a woman when she had her last cycle, Constantine."

"Of course not. And yet you let me believe you were further advanced in the pregnancy than you are."

"I told you I had not been to a doctor. I also asked you if you were willing to entertain the idea that the child might be…"

"Children," he said.

"I didn't know that," she said. "Tell you the truth, I didn't know why I was so big. I just thought that it was perhaps how I was carrying them… Him… I didn't know."

"You have a history of twins in your family?"

"I don't know. My mother was always isolated from her family, and I don't know my father at all. I don't know anything about myself, and this is… Driving that home. I underestimated… Everything. I underestimated everything."

"My parents need these children to be Alex's."

A tear tracked down her cheek. "I think *you* need these children to belong to Alex." She took a sharp breath. "After they are born we can do a paternity test if you need…"

"They are *his*," Constantine said, his voice hard. "There is next to no chance they wouldn't be, and they would be better for it."

She said nothing to that, her face going pale.

Surely she didn't *want* the children to be his?

Why should she want that?

Because Alex had betrayed her?

At least Alex had cared for her, in his fashion.

Constantine felt nothing. Nothing but a dark, bleeding intensity that had replaced his heart when he was eight years old.

That night, he went to his penthouse in the middle of the city, and he paced back and forth, thinking that he might find answers if he wore a long enough trail into the carpet.

He was not a man accustomed to indecision. It did not do to dwell on that which one could not change. A man was not defined by his good intentions. Nor was he defined by his beliefs if he did not act on them. One thing he knew to be true for certain. Morgan must become a Kamaras. Whatever the truth of the parentage of the babies in her womb…

Rage built inside of him, and he honestly could not say

where it came from. It was primarily directed at the fact that the children might not be Alex's...

Or that they should be his.

Morgan was in shock for the rest of the evening. Two children. A boy and a girl. She was numb. She didn't know what to feel. She knew they were Constantine's babies, of course. And she should've just said something. Should've told him that... She should've told him the truth. Not that she had lied, it was only that she had not insisted that no test was needed.

What is it exactly you want? You want him to know without having to be told?

No. She wasn't that petty. It was just...

She was a burden. To her mother. She always had been.

But now she was having two children, and for the first time in so long...she wouldn't be alone.

It rocked her, to her core.

Two children.

And she should tell him. Flat out. She should not ask him about possibilities or skirt the issue. But she was...

She was afraid, and it made no real sense.

It does. You are so afraid he'll reject you. Them.

He wanted the children to be Alex's so very much, and what if she told him and that loss—another loss for him—made him resent the children?

And she did not possess the ability to burden the Kamaras family financially. There was no way. Their pockets were far too deep. But it was still different than being chosen. Of course it was. She just felt like she would never be chosen.

And he was just so adamant they be his brother's.

I will never have children. Never.

She wondered why. And wondering about him felt so dangerous.

She was linked to him. Forever. Whether she wondered about him or not. The danger had already happened, in that sense.

The thought of it made her shiver.

By the time she went to sleep, her dreams were filled with images of him. Dark and brooding. Avenging.

But also the way he'd been as a lover.

No less dark or brooding, and there had been something avenging about the way he'd thrust inside of her body, but he'd been...tender at moments. Intense, too. Rough.

He'd contained everything and given it all to her and the last five months without him had been torturous.

She woke up early and crying.

Wondering if the grief that had invaded her chest five months ago was really from the tragedy of the loss of a man like Alex, or if it was simply her personal grief over tasting Constantine once, and then never having him again.

There was a firm knock on the door and she sat upright in bed, even as the double doors to her fairy world opened wide.

And it was not a servant pushing a gilded tray into the improbable bedroom, no. It was Constantine.

Even at dawn he was in a dark suit.

Clean-shaven, perfectly put together.

The only indicator that all was not well was a faint shadow beneath his eyes. And she wondered...

She wondered if he'd slept at all.

"Good morning," he said.

Such a benign greeting didn't seem right coming from him. It made her laugh.

"What?" he asked, frowning.

"Sorry," she said. "You brought me breakfast and you said good morning. You seem almost human."

He straightened, his mouth firming into a grim line. "Do not make the mistake of thinking me human."

"You seemed like a man to me," she said, her throat going tight. "That night."

"Haven't you ever read mythology, Morgan? Even monsters can make love."

Her breath caught as she thought of him as he'd been that night. Strong and powerful above her, a bronzed god, powerful and dangerous.

Ruinous.

But he was not a monster. Of that she was certain.

Are you? Or do you just want it to be true.

She had never seen evidence that he was a monster. Ever.

He was firm, and he was...

He was something else entirely.

But he was not a monster.

He was not entirely mortal, either. Of that she was certain.

"I have come to a decision," he said.

Her breath caught and held. She wondered if he was going to acknowledge it. The children might be his.

They were his. She knew that. With certainty.

"We will be married," he said.

"What?"

"There is nothing else for it, Morgan. These children are part of my family. And they must be bound to the family in the name. There's no question that I will offer them my full protection."

"As their uncle? Or as their father?"

His jaw firmed. "I will make sure that they know about Alex. That they know who their father is."

"And if it's you?"

"It isn't."

"So certain?"

And she could see in the fathomless darkness of his eyes, that it wasn't certainty, it was pain. Pain and denial so desperate it made her chest ache. "What good does it do? Alex is gone. He has no other chance. I will be their protector. I will make sure that they understand where they come from. Alex was... He was a man with many faults. As you know. He betrayed you, and I do not take that lightly. But he was... In many ways, the best of us. He was funny, and he was..." He faltered. That mountain of a man. The first show of emotion she had ever seen in him.

Other than when he was inside you...

"I know," she said. Because she did.

Alex had been the sun. The entire sky lit up.

Handsome and glowing and far too much.

And she probably would've had a miserable life had she chosen to marry him.

Because like the sun, he could not be contained to one room. And he would've continued to shine himself down over all the land. Over everyone and everything.

He would never have committed himself solely to her, and that was what she wanted.

And she knew that Alex would never have meant to hurt her. He was not a cruel man. He was simply... As captivated by himself as everyone else was, when it came right down to it. She had found that to be part of his charm in many ways. He possessed absolutely no modesty, no humility of any kind, but it had all been expressed with such joy. At living.

And it really did feel wrong that he was gone.

But that didn't make the children in her womb any more his just because she also thought he was good.

But the way that Constantine seemed to need it. The way that he clung to it. As if he couldn't even acknowledge that their time together might've produced children…

He needed this. And she felt caught between impossible truths. Her need to let him know it had only been him. That it had only been him for her from the beginning, even though she'd been too cowardly to acknowledge it.

Her need to protect the babies, protect herself.

Her desperate need to both speak the truth and hide it.

Caught between fear and need.

"I'm not angry with him," she said. "For what happened. How can I be? In the end, how can I be?"

That much was true. If he had died while she was still in the throes of being in love with him, it would've been unbearable. But she had seen that she couldn't spend her life with him, and in that way… His betrayal had been a gift.

As to what else she had learned about herself that night… Well, that was where things became complicated. Because some of the lessons she had learned about herself were less than flattering. And they had almost certainly landed her in water that was too hot for her to handle. Because here she was, staring him down, staring down his marriage proposal…

Proposal. That was the wrong word.

It was a demand. Clearly.

"But you will not be a father figure to them, is that what you're telling me?"

"I will be their protector. And I will make sure they know…"

"Do I have a choice in this?" She wasn't a fool. Constantine was a powerful man, and at the end of the day…

What she knew was that he actually had a lot more leverage than he was allowing himself to believe. He was a billionaire, he was…wealthy and titled on more than one continent and she was…

Up until recently a waitress. And everything she had was because of his family.

And if a DNA test was done it would prove that he was in fact the father of the children, and his leverage would only increase. As an uncle trying to gain custody of them, he would've had a challenge.

But she knew what he would discover if she took it too far.

She knew what would happen if she refused.

Because she knew that Constantine was the only man she had ever given her body to.

She knew that the children in her womb were his.

And she knew that resisting him was…

"My parents are overjoyed," he said. "And think of all that they will have if we marry. Alex's children. Family vacations. They will be able to watch them grow. Twins."

He said that last word softly, but there was a roughness to it that was strange.

"Why marriage? I… I can still go on vacations with you I…"

"What else do you have, Morgan? You have finished school, yes, but do you have a job?"

"No," she said, thinking of her hard-earned hospitality degree. She had left working at the bar when she had begun dating Alex and he had paid off her debts, and she hadn't gone back to work since she'd found out she was pregnant—she'd had enough savings.

For the future she had imagined herself as a manager of one of the nice, historic boutique hotels in Boston, or something similar. A high-paying job that allowed her to interact with people, earn a living and have independence. She had been so proud of the work she had put in to accomplish it, because no one had helped her. Until Alex. Alex had helped.

And where would that leave her dreams? Were they even her dreams if she didn't need them?

If she was financially cared for, what would she do? What did she even want? Especially with the impending arrival of the twins. The twins.

Twins.

It really was a lot to take in.

"You don't have a choice, Morgan. It was not a request."

She knew that. She knew that it was true. That he wasn't asking her for her hand, he was demanding it.

"When?"

"As soon as possible. You are already great with child, and it is better that we marry sooner than later."

"Of course."

"We will marry at the family estate."

"Well, that will be easy…"

"In Greece."

"Greece?"

"Yes."

"I don't even have a passport…"

"A small thing. And not an issue. I will get you the necessary paperwork you require immediately."

"You can't do that. Surely not even you can force the United States government to move at a speedy pace."

"I think, *agape*, that you will find I can do whatever it is I please. I am not a man of patience. I am not a man who waits. I am a man who gets things done.

"You will be my wife. And you will be my wife as quickly as possible."

"In Greece," she said.

"Yes."

He finally lifted the tray on the cart that he had wheeled

in, to reveal a mound of pastries. "Perhaps this will put you in a better frame of mind."

"Are you… Bribing me with butter?"

Her stomach growled when she looked down at the croissants.

"Yes," he said.

He might as well have said he was bribing her with sex. Honestly, both sounded good right now.

Looking at him made her ache. Even now.

Even now.

"But then," he said, thrusting a croissant her way. "You and I both know that I don't need to bribe you."

"Because the blackmail is unspoken?"

"Yes."

She thought of her own father, who didn't even know her. Who hadn't wanted her. He was willing to strong-arm her into marriage to keep the children close. But not because he wanted to be their father.

She couldn't quite figure out what he thought was happening. What he thought he was doing.

But there was something haunted and tortured in his dark eyes, and she could see it even as she hesitated to take the pastry from his hands.

"All right," she said. "We will be married."

"In name only," he said.

That hurt. Like a knife driven through her chest. Because she had given herself to him. Because she hadn't been able to control herself. Because she had wanted him more than she had ever wanted anyone or anything in her entire life, and he was easily making proclamations about how it could be nothing more than a marriage on paper.

You will have freedom. You have your children, and you will be provided for.

And she waited to feel something like elation, but she

still felt like she was underwater. She still felt like she was in shock.

Because the one thing that she wanted, she couldn't give voice to. She couldn't allow herself to think. Because the one thing that she really wanted...

"Good," she said.

"Prepare yourself."

"How?" She took a bite of the croissant.

"Pack whatever it is you think you'll need."

"I don't have any of my own things."

"Then I will pack for you."

And she felt very much like this was a metaphor for her life now. Constantine was in charge. And she did not know what that made her. Did not know where that left her.

And she had never been simultaneously more excited or more terrified in her whole life.

CHAPTER FIVE

"I AM MARRYING HER."

"Are you?" his father asked, a chuckle in his voice.

"How else will we have the children in our family to our satisfaction?"

"I take it she did not wish to sell them."

"No, she did not," Constantine said.

And he bit back his commentary on the fact that not everyone saw children as tradable commodities. And not everyone prized a good time over their children, either.

Their recent behavior was triggered by the loss of Alex, he knew that. The increase again, in their partying.

They had changed their parenting after Athena's death. Their relationship to Alex especially standing as a testament to that.

However, when it came to Constantine...

He knew what they saw when they looked at him.

It was the same thing he saw when he looked at them.

Their failure.

Although, more and more, Constantine saw his own.

His grandfather had driven into him the need to change. To become harder. To distance himself from his parents and their hedonistic ways.

And he had tried.

His grandfather would likely tell him to feel no guilt

or sorrow for Alex, since his excess was the cause of his death.

A man must have control at all times...

He had succeeded, until Morgan.

"She is beautiful," his father said. "It is not a bad idea to take her for your own. You shall enjoy having her in your bed, I should think. Keep her with us, we've lost enough. Let us keep the family together."

He gritted his teeth. "It is to be a marriage in name only. This is strictly for Alex, his legacy, his children." He would not touch her again.

Alex would have called him a martyr. And right then he felt like one. As if flames were burning him alive.

Was that the truth of it?

He had punished himself with a measure of isolation for the loss of Athena. Had promised himself he would not have certain things his sister would never grow up to have. Had wrapped it all in the harsh but necessary lessons his grandfather had given him.

But in the end perhaps what he really wanted was to make himself suffer for being the one to survive.

"Why must you be so exhaustively noble?" his father asked with a laugh. "You could do both. You could protect your brother's legacy, and taste of her beauty."

"Marriage does not appeal to me," he said. "Not in that sense."

"Marriage to the right woman can be wonderful," his father said.

"I prefer variety."

His father laughed. "Did anyone say you cannot have variety while married? It simply depends on the arrangements that you make with your wife."

He did not want to know about that either. What his parents did in their spare time was their business, and Constantine wished that it was never his.

"You will come from where you are vacationing to the wedding, I trust. We will be at the estate in Athens."

"If you wish."

"It is right," he said.

"Yes. We will be there. It is... It is appreciated, the way that you have cared for Alex in the aftermath of all this." As if Alex was still alive to be cared for. "There is still something of him to protect, and that is a gift."

But it felt like a commission being given. To continue to care for him even in his death. Something he could not do for Athena, who he had failed.

His father had said that to him once. Ragingly drunk and weeping bitterly. *"You should have protected her."*

Constantine had not shouted back, *"You should have protected us both."* But it had burned in him, and even still...

Even still he had felt his own failure.

After that his father and mother had gone away for weeks, partying their way through Europe.

Trying to forget the pain of Athena, and possibly the pain of what Cosmo had said to him. It was why, even though his relationship with them was difficult at times, he never hated them.

It all came from pain.

So much pain.

He never wanted to cause more.

Athena.

He had been meant to protect Athena.

He had failed.

And in that same way, he felt he had failed to protect Alex. From himself, if nothing else. And then of course he had taken Alex's woman...

What if they are yours?

No. It was unacceptable. Unforgivable.

He had made his own vows. About what would not be his.

Love, marriage. Children.

Those were things Athena would never have. How could he have them?

And this marriage... It was different. It would be different.

"We will see you there," his father said, and he hung up the phone.

He was ready to leave, and he had not seen Morgan yet.

He stomped up the stairs and flung open the door to her bedroom.

She was standing there, holding a sundress up against her body, and he caught a glimpse of pale flesh. She was wearing a set of pale lilac underwear, and nothing more.

And he cursed the dress for providing such an effective shield for her.

"I'm getting dressed," she said.

"I'm ready to go," he said. "The car is waiting."

"I'm sorry. You didn't give me a time. You only said we were leaving this morning."

"The time is now."

"Can you turn around."

He found himself doing so obediently, and he heard the rustle of fabric, and when he turned again, she was wearing a white dress that barely came to her knees. Her red hair was like a coppery halo around her, and her curves were...

It was a strange thing, to find a pregnant woman so attractive. He would not say he had ever noticed such a thing being appealing to him sexually before. But she was. A fertility goddess, and he thought there could be nothing more appropriate than having her like this.

She looked like sex to him. All rounded curves and feminine glory.

He gritted his teeth.

In name only.

"Let's go."

They got into the car, both sitting in the back. "What about my things…"

"Everything is been sent ahead to the villa in Greece. You do not need anything."

"How convenient. Have you chosen my wedding dress as well?"

He looked at her. "Yes."

And he knew that it would be resplendent on her. He had simply asked the designer—a woman world-renowned—to make a gown fit for a goddess. And he knew that she would.

"And what will the world think, with you marrying your brother's girlfriend?"

"They will think what my parents think. That I am preserving Alex's legacy."

"Is it what you think?"

"Yes," he answered.

"It has nothing to do with the fact that you want me?"

"I wanted you," he said. "And I had you."

He could see the way that landed. Like a slap across her face, and he knew a moment's guilt for talking to her in such a manner.

She had been vulnerable and open when she had made love with him. And he could not accuse her of being manipulative in that way, not at all. She had simply… Wanted him. And had given herself to him with openness and sweetness. It had been the best sex of his life.

And he had told himself for a while it was because of the forbidden nature of it. He was not a man that indulged himself in the forbidden. Very few things were off-limits to him. He had money and power and women flung themselves his direction, and when he wished to do so he availed himself of their offerings. But Morgan had been off-limits. And that, he told himself, was why she was so delectable.

But he knew now it wasn't that. It was her.

And trying to reduce the thing that had transpired between them to something past tense and tawdry was... It was small of him, and he was not a man given to smallness.

"Well," she said. "How nice to be such an easy box on a checklist. Sex with Morgan. Done and dusted. Double check."

She was pushing him. As if they were back in his parents' study at one of their regular evenings, back before everything had fallen apart.

"I've no need to experience it again."

"Then you won't mind when I begin to take lovers of my own," she said, as the car carried them quickly down the highway toward the airport.

"Not at all," he said, rage building in his chest.

"I think I will enjoy that," she said. "I had of course imagined that I would be headed for a lifetime of monogamy when I met Alex, but things have changed. So maybe I will begin to sample freely. I didn't really experiment in college the way many do. Perhaps this is my moment."

"You can do whatever pleases you," he said, tension creeping up the back of his neck. "I am not your keeper."

"No. Clearly not. And obviously deeply unconcerned with what I might choose to do."

"And you with me, I imagine?"

"As you said," she pointed out, "even monsters make love. Feel free to spread it around the world. I'm sure you already have. I was nothing to you, after all. Just one more novelty for you to experience. And you've experienced it."

"Quite so," he said.

His private plane was waiting for them, and the driver pulled straight up to the steps.

"Oh," she said.

He laughed. "Did you think we would be flying commercial?"

"Well, I did imagine that you likely had first class..."

"I've never flown first class," he said. "I've never flown commercial."

"I've never flown," she said.

"Absurd, this, isn't it?" And he was struck by just how different their worlds were. And how little he knew of her.

It suddenly seemed not enough.

He wanted her. Desperately. All of her. The history of who she was.

Yet, she was not supposed to be his. Not in that sense.

"Yes. I would say that this is all patently absurd."

He walked behind her up the steps, and he regretted that, because when they got onto the plane, she stopped, turning her head to look around in broad movements, and he wished that he could see the expression on her face.

The plane was richly appointed, with a grand seating area with couches of plush leather, and a private bedroom and bathroom at the back.

"This is amazing," she said.

"Tell me," he said, putting his hand on her lower back and encouraging her to take a seat as he went over to the bar to pour her a glass of sparkling water. "Tell me why you have not been anywhere?"

They would have no attendant for this flight because he had wanted privacy, and he questioned that motivation now. His body went tight, and that told him exactly why he had wanted to be alone with her.

The very thought of it made the monster within him growl.

Possessively.

"Well, I've never had the chance to be anywhere but where I am. I grew up poor. And I got a combination of scholarships and loans to go to school. Alex paid those off. But before that, it was just… All I've done is go to school and work. All of my life. I've never done anything adventurous or fun."

It was a strange to look at her, and to understand. To look at her and feel…kinship. But he knew what it was to have a life consumed by responsibility, marked by a heavy weight, from the time he was a boy.

"What?"

She had looked very much like she wanted to say something, but hadn't.

"Until this. Until you, really."

She must mean until she had met Alex.

Because surely that was the beginning of her adventure.

A current of electricity arced between them, and he felt his desire for her growing.

"Don't look at me like that," she said.

"Like what?"

"You know like what. It's the way that you always looked at me, Constantine. From the moment that we met. I felt silly, I felt like it was just me. Until that night in your room… I thought it was only me. I thought I was crazy, and fashioning fantasies out of nothing. A girl who had read too many gothic novels and wanted to dance with darkness, rather than standing in the sun."

And her honesty shamed him. But then, what would the purpose be in lies? They could not hide their responses to each other.

"Tell me what you mean by that?"

"Surely you know."

"Surely I know what?"

"That I wanted you. From the first moment I saw you. And I felt so hideously guilty, because Alex was beautiful and lovely and was so good to me. So very kind. And I wanted his brother. Who showed nothing but disinterest toward me from the moment we met. And why should I want you? Why should I have ever wanted you? And now you look at me like that now. Like a wolf who wants to eat me whole, when you know already that nothing good comes of it. When you told me that you already checked the box. Choose a story and go with that. But stop making things up. Stop making it confusing."

"You wanted me?" He did not know why that made him feel as if he had won a victory.

"Yes. Though, don't sound so triumphant about it. We all want things that are bad for us, don't we? It's human nature."

"So I am just human nature, and you are simply a box I needed to check. I'm glad that we had this conversation."

If nothing else, he was grateful that the moment had been fractured. Because otherwise...

He might've reached across the distance and taken her into his arms, and that was not a good beginning for their marriage in name only, he supposed.

"Yes," she said. "Wonderful."

They sat across from each other, he with whiskey, and her with sparkling water.

"I need to use a bathroom," she said softly.

"It's toward the back. You will find there is a shower and bath as well. You may avail yourself of the use of the facilities if need be."

"I might just do that," she said.

She vanished, and he took a moment to draw in a full

breath, which he realized he had not done, not since they had entered the plane. What was it about her? He was a man of quite a bit of experience sexually. He should not be quite so tempted by this woman. This woman that he had already had. In truth, what he'd said should be accurate. He had her. And it should be done with.

Instead, his body growled with need.

She was pregnant with his brother's children.

Twins.

A reminder.

Unless they are yours...

No. Fury fueled him. And he stood from where he sat on the plane, and he found himself stalking back toward the bedroom and bathroom.

He did not know what he was thinking. And that was a strange thing, because he always knew what he was thinking. He never had the luxury of being impulsive. Not until that night he had taken her in his arms and she had come into his bedroom.

Of course, it could be argued, that the impulsive choice had been made for him the moment she had stumbled in there wearing nothing but lingerie. Few men would've refused her.

No. He could not push it off like that. He could not make it as if he had not been a willing participant.

He gritted his teeth.

She was not in the bedroom. And he flung the bathroom door open, and she gasped, sinking down beneath the water, as if it could hide her pale, lovely curves.

His body got hard, and he stood there for a moment, and he was at a loss for what to say. He had done this, not knowing what he would do when he got there. And it was... Intoxicating. This moment of not knowing. When had he ever not known? He always knew. He was Constantine Kamaras. And he knew everything. Because he made it his business to know everything. He did not let other people handle things, he got them done. Because his family tripped about like they had no responsibilities, and someone had to shoulder it all. Because he knew that when things went badly, people died. Because he knew these things, he was never uncertain.

And he was torn between yelling at her, for what, he didn't know, and reaching down and lifting her up out of the tub and taking her into his arms. Flinging her down onto the bed and making her his again.

And he simply stood there. Inactive. And he despised it, because it reminded him of another time when he had not been active. A time when he'd been afraid.

She was only a woman. And he was not afraid.

"What are you doing?"

"Tell me," he said. "What is it you want?"

"I told you I'd..."

"No. What is it you want? From the world. From your life?"

"I don't know anymore," she said. "I do not even know what to hope for or what to ask for. I did not imagine this being my life."

And that, he imagined, was as honest as anything ever could be.

She had lost the man she thought she would be with, even before his death. Though he did wonder if Alex would have actually managed to talk her back around to being with him. He had been persuasive like that. But they would never know. Not now.

A beast growled inside of him. And he could not take his eyes off her.

Her breathing went shallow, her eyes dark. And then she braced her hands on either side of the tub and stood.

Water cascaded down her bare body, the glorious bump that housed those precious lives inside of her a site that he could not take his eyes away from.

His body throbbed with need. He moved to her then, quickly, and pressed her naked, wet body against his, kissing her, fierce and deep. She sighed, wrapping her arms around his neck, kissing him. He lifted her up out of the water and set her down onto the ground in front of him. She was petite, and he wanted to shield her. Protect her.

She made him want to rage at anything that might threaten to harm her. She made him want…

She made him want. In ways he had not, for a very long time. If ever.

His heart was pounding so hard he thought it might burst through the front of his chest. And then she placed one small delicate hand there, as if to soothe the raging inside of him, and it made him growl. He backed her up against the wall, kissing her neck, his hands moved over her slick curves, his need a living thing.

And then he swore, pulling away from her. "This is not to be," he said.

"Why not? You clearly still want me. You *want* me."

"What difference does it make?" he asked, his voice fractured.

"It could make all the difference if you would only let it."

"What do you want, Morgan?"

And he realized why he had come in and asked that question. Because he felt like she had come into his life, his world, perfectly ordered and controlled, always, and upended it. And he wanted to rage at her as if she was an uncaring goddess in the sky and ask her what the hell she wanted from him.

Why she had the audacity.

"I'm afraid I want the same thing you do. I'm just not as afraid to admit it."

"It is not to be."

"Fine," she said, and he felt her words hit him in the back as if she had thrown something. "But if this is your decision, then it's your decision. Marriage in name only. And we will take other lovers. And you will not touch me. But you cannot have me and others. You cannot give in to temptation and touch me, kiss me, and then fling recriminations my way, I will not live that way. You want me, or you don't. But you don't get the choice to have part of me. You don't get the choice to play games."

"I'm not the one who plays games. That was Alex. And he is dead. I'm cleaning up his mess. As ever."

"How convenient. No acknowledgment of your own part in the mess. Of what the truth might actually be."

"We will land soon. I suggest you get dressed and get yourself together."

"Yes. I would hate for anything to look out of place. And that is, after all, your primary concern. How things look."

He left her then, heart raging, fury pouring through his veins, but it was at himself.

It would not happen again. He was not a man given to indecision, and yet, he had indulged in it. He would not do that again.

He refused.

She would be his wife.

And she would not be his.

She would be his wife, and he would not take her to his bed.

Because she was pregnant with his brother's children.

And they would never be his.

CHAPTER SIX

WHEN THEY LANDED in Greece it had been dark, and he had instructed her to try and sleep.

She had been given more milk and honey, and she had done her best. It surprised her that she had managed to sleep. Given the time change, and the fact that she was... She felt raw. Raw and endangered.

The way that he had kissed her, the way that he had held her... *And you tempted him to it.*

When she had looked at his eyes, she had seen that he wanted her. And there had been something so potent in that, because it teased the thing that she feared the most. Being unwanted. And in that moment she had felt... She had felt renewed. And she had wanted to make him prove just how much he wanted her, and she had done it.

Of course, the end result had been unsatisfying.

What did he want?

He had asked her that.

And she was afraid of the answer. Desperately.

When she woke the next morning, she took in the beauty of the villa for the first time. It was nearly palatial, made entirely of white marble. Everything was bright and airy, giving way to views of the Aegean Sea. It was a blue she'd never seen before. One photographs could never display.

The house itself was lovely, but it paled compared to the natural beauty that surrounded them.

She went out onto the balcony and stared out at the sea. It was silent except for the sound of the waves, the birds, the wind.

And for a moment, she simply stood there, soaking in the fact that she was in a different country. That she was living a life she would never have thought possible. That she was experiencing something wholly different than she had ever imagined she would or could.

And she tried to let that be enough.

Because the scary thing was when she thought about what she wanted…

Constantine was what she saw.

There was a brisk knock on the door and she knew immediately that it wasn't him.

"Come in."

She walked in from the balcony, wrapping the white robe she was wearing more firmly around her.

"You must be the bride," the woman said.

"Yes. I am."

Though she could hardly believe it.

"I will be fitting you for your dress."

"I just woke up and…"

And in came a tray with tea and cakes. It was funny how he seemed to know that she had a strong preference for carbohydrates at the moment.

The woman began preparing her fitting station, and Morgan ate, drinking her tea and savoring the sweet tartness of the lemon cakes.

Then she found herself being swathed in beautiful, draping silk. A dress that did nothing to disguise her pregnancy, yet rather seemed to enhance it, and her curves. The straps went off the shoulder, the Grecian drape of the fabrics making her look like a statue, and it went around her stomach in such a fashion as to highlight it.

"It is as he asked for," the designer said. "And you look incredible. So bold."

She had to admit, it was quite bold. To wear white and highlight a pregnancy the entire world thought was another man's.

Of course, the truth was, she was much closer to being a bride who could wear white than even Constantine might think. Pregnancy notwithstanding.

She thought of him again, of that kiss, and she throbbed. She was no innocent. That was for certain. Not anymore.

She was far too well acquainted with what her body wanted.

But it was more than simply what her body wanted. She was more in tune with herself. Admitting it was Constantine she wanted, admitting it was him that she wanted, admitting it wasn't Alex, it had brought about a deeper honesty with herself.

She was hiding and she knew it.

Knew not outright telling him there was no chance the babies were Alex's was...

Protecting herself.

Yourself. Not your children. Yourself. Not him. Not really him.

"It is a good thing the wedding is to be this evening. Otherwise we might have to have another dress fitting between now and then. Pregnancy is so volatile."

"This evening?"

"Of course."

And after that, the whole day became a whirlwind. Her hair was fixed, her nails done, skincare treatments and peels applied. She was scrubbed and moisturized and buffed and masked and left glowing and tingling in the aftermath.

She hadn't even had a chance to look at herself in the mirror when she was bundled into a limousine and whisked down the side of the hill.

She didn't even know if she had a groom. She had not seen evidence that he existed the entire day.

The limo stopped in front of the church, perched on the edge of a rock, right on the sea.

"I don't…"

The doors opened, and a woman helped her from the car. "You are to come and stand here in the antechamber. And wait for the music."

"I…"

"My name is Agatha. I'm the wedding coordinator."

Wedding coordinator. So she was here at a wedding. And presumably the groom was somewhere.

She pinched herself.

"What did you do that for?" Agatha asked.

"Because the entire day is starting to feel like a strange fever dream."

"Well, considering I pulled the entire wedding together in less than two days, I'm inclined to agree."

But she wasn't the one marrying a man under false pretenses, so Morgan didn't have a whole lot of sympathy for the other woman.

Maybe that wasn't fair.

And when the doors parted to reveal a cascading palace of flowers inside the sanctuary, she thought she really was being unfair to the other woman, who had clearly worked much harder than Morgan could've imagined.

It was… Astonishing.

Pale pink and lavender flowers were strung from the

floor all the way to the very top of the rafters, it was as if the entire building had been reconstructed of them.

It made the bedroom she'd been installed in back in Boston pale in comparison. For this was something else entirely. This was… It was magnificent. A marvel.

And then she looked at the head of the altar, and she saw him.

There were spare few people in attendance, and she knew none of them.

She knew a momentary stab in her heart over the fact that her own mother was not here. And why would she ever be here? Her mother didn't care about a single thing she did. She hadn't even told her mother she was pregnant, much less that she was getting married.

She wondered if she would see it in the news.

Her throat went tight with emotion, and she began to move down the aisle. And she focused on him. Because he was all there was. And it terrified her.

But it grounded her also. Because she knew she was marrying the father of her children. Even if he didn't.

You have to tell him.

Did she?

Yes. You're being a coward.

She was. She was being a coward. She wanted so much to be wanted and… She was playing a game. Seeing what would make him happier. She didn't want that icy, terrible look that he got on his face when she suggested the children might be his. And she felt filled with disquiet when he seemed to look at his own children as a mission of atonement, as he talked of telling them about their father. Their father was here. He lived. And he was a good man. A good man who deserved to know…

And of course his parents should know. They should know that they weren't Alex's children.

The ruse had never been to protect them. It had been to protect Morgan.

Because she didn't want them to be his responsibility in that way. Because she didn't want to be his grim responsibility in that way.

Because you want him to want you. That's what you want.

And she nearly burst into tears then and there because it was true.

She wanted him to care for her. She wanted the mountain to bend. She wanted him to look at her with more than desire. With more than that kind of angry need in his dark eyes. It wasn't Alex she had wanted to love her.

No. She would not let it be that. She would not let it be so intense.

And a tear did fall down her cheek then and there was nothing she could do to stop it. Because why was she really so sad? A girl desperately seeking love, and in such a silly place. From this man who didn't want children, from this man who didn't want her. At least not in any way that went beyond the sexual.

And at that point she had made it to the altar, and there was no more time to think about those things.

And so in her heart, when she spoke her vows, she did so with honesty.

Because she would forsake all others. Dammit, she would. Because she wanted him. Because actually, she wanted this.

It terrified her how much.

"With this ring," she said, her throat getting tight. "I take you as my husband."

And then it was time for them to kiss. And she didn't hesitate. She wrapped her arms around his neck and kissed him. And she knew that she had made a miscalculation, because the ripple that went through the room was palpable. It was clear, from the way she kissed him, that she was not simply grieving his brother. That she was not simply doing this for the sake of the children. Not in the way people thought.

And he would be angry. So for now, she would simply kiss him, because it was better than facing any of that anger.

But pushing him was the only way to get him to lose that control of his. It was the only way to shake him.

And when they parted, his expression was thunderous.

But he took her hand, and led her down the aisle, and out of the church to the same car that had brought her there.

"I think that was a bit much," he said.

"You kissed me back," she said.

The car began to carry them away from the church. "Where are we going?"

"We have a reception to get to, of course."

"Why bother with the show of a wedding?"

"Because we have an old family, because many in attendance are family, and I am making a show of this union."

"Yes. Clearly. And I made the wrong show of it, didn't I?"

"You did not make the right one, that is for certain."

"Yes, I feel terribly sorry for that."

"Somehow, I don't think you do."

"Well, you will have to survive the indignity."

The reception venue was a series of large tents out in an open field. And it was even more beautiful than the spectacle that had been inside the sanctuary. And there were more guests there than had been at the church.

"All business associates and extended family. Here in Greece, of course that number is legion."

"I see."

"And many of Alex's... Mourners."

"Ex-lovers, you mean?"

"In a fashion. He had many friends."

When they arrived, people stared at them. But Constantine held her hand and took her to a banquet table, where they sat next to one another. His parents sat down at the end of the table, and guilt lurched inside of her. She couldn't do this. She simply couldn't do it.

Not without telling him.

She had been wrapped in fear, so much fear it was hard to sort out exactly what scared her most. But she had to be better than that. Stronger. And she felt it now.

"Constantine..."

"Yes?"

"I have to tell you... I have to tell you. They're not Alex's children."

"I know you think they might not be..."

"No," she said, her voice growing stronger. "I know they are not."

"How is it you know that?"

"Because I never slept with Alex. Constantine, I was a virgin when I came to your bed."

A hush fell inside of him. She could be lying. But why? They were married already. It made no earthly sense for her to tell him this now.

The children were his. And she was his wife.

They were not Alex's.

She had never slept with Alex.

And of course all the world believed that the children

were his brother's, because that was what had been reported. Because nobody knew that the two of them had ever been together. But apparently, he was the only one she had ever been with.

It seemed impossible. Almost laughably so.

"Do not lie to me."

"I'm not. But there was never space to tell you this definitively because…"

"Yes," he said. "Give me your excuses. For why you lied."

"You were in denial, and I didn't outright lie. You didn't use protection and you know it. I did suggest to you that they could be yours and…"

"You did not say they were."

"You said you didn't want children. Not ever."

"And I don't," he said.

"You didn't want to know, Constantine, admit it. You've been lost in this desperate idea that you were doing Alex a service and it made it all feel better to you, and I…part of me didn't want to take that away. Part of me was just afraid of the rejection…"

"If you are pregnant with my children…"

"You'll what? Marry me? You already have. It's only that I realize that I had to tell you the truth. I cannot allow you to spend their entire lives memorializing a man to them who was their uncle, certainly, and who I cared for a great deal, but who I never…"

"They're my children?"

"Yes," she said.

"My twins," he said, the words catching hard in his throat.

"Yes," she confirmed.

"A boy. And a girl."

"Yes," she said.

And then, without pausing to think, without pausing to do anything at all, he stood from the table, and picked her up, throwing her over his shoulder. "The festivities will have to continue without us. I am eager to claim my wedding night."

CHAPTER SEVEN

IT WAS FURY that drove him. That poured through his veins like fire. It was rage that fueled him now. He was beyond madness. Beyond reason. He was beyond anything.

His children. His. Morgan was pregnant with his children.

She had never been with his brother.

She had been a virgin when she had come into his bed.

Everything in him roared.

He couldn't see the guests. His parents. Anyone. And he didn't care to. All he cared about was the need that fired through his veins. The reckless, raging desire that drove him now.

Morgan said nothing. She simply hung over his shoulder, as if in shock, and he strode toward his car.

"We won't be needing a driver," he said, and then he put her in the passenger seat, and commandeered the driver spot.

"Constantine…"

"Yes?" he said.

"I didn't know how to handle this. And I'm sorry. I get the sense that you…"

"They are mine," he said. "And you are mine."

"Yes," she said.

And it was all he needed to hear.

He drove away from the venue, the tires squealing on the asphalt as he did. Only he didn't drive back to the estate.

"Where are we going?"

"Somewhere else." He needed to take her away. And he knew exactly where.

He pushed a button on the dash of the car. "Have the boat prepared."

"A boat?"

He would take her to the island. And there… There they could sort this out. There, they would get to the truth of it.

But first…

First, he had his wedding night claim.

"We have a lot of talking to do."

"You didn't listen," she said. "I did ask you…"

"You did ask me if I had entertained the idea that they might be mine. What you did not say was that you definitively knew. That you were a virgin, who had never been with a man before coming to my bed. Isn't that true?"

"It is a hypocrisy to be so angry at me."

"You could've cleared all of it up. There were talks of paternity tests that we could not get because they were twins. *Twins*."

"I knew we didn't need a test. I let you talk, yes. But you wanted the story, Constantine. You wanted the lie."

It hit him hard. Bitterly so, because what she said was true. "It would have been better if it were the truth."

"And I know you felt that way, so why would I feel… I was afraid. I knew it would hurt your parents, and I knew it would hurt you. I knew it would…hurt me. To be in this conversation. To feel the sting of your rejection. I knew. So yes, I didn't come out and say it. But you must understand why."

"I…"

"Is it so hard for you to bend?"

He didn't understand bending. Only standing tall or breaking. And he refused to break.

"Yes," he said, his voice rough. "It is impossible."

"An acknowledgment of the truth doesn't have to be bending. It can just look like acceptance. Or so I am learning."

He paused for a long moment. "I am well aware of the fact fantasy serves no purpose. I am a believer in reality. I...thought. You are right. The force of my..."

"You can say it's denial."

"I don't want to."

"Oh. Well. Denial about your denial—that really is something."

"*Twins*, Morgan."

"No one is more surprised about that than I am," she said.

"I'm not surprised," he said. "I wish I could be. And I know that... I know that this is another part of why I...why I could not entertain the idea that they belonged to me."

"Why aren't you surprised?"

"Did no one tell you, *agape*? I am a twin."

Her eyes went wide, and she turned her head sharply. "I didn't know that."

"You really had no designs on his money, did you?"

"No. I told you that. I really didn't know who he was when I first met him in the bar. I thought he was outrageously handsome and I was charmed by the fact that he didn't immediately try to sleep with me. And even after he'd gone out with me a couple of times, when I told him that I was a virgin he... He seemed to respect the fact that there were reasons I had not... This isn't about me. I did not know you were a twin."

"I was," he said, and he determined that he would not be speaking about Athena. Not now.

"I'm sorry…"

"Now you will tell me about you," he said.

"You know about me."

"Apparently I do not."

He'd called it a boat, but it was a yacht. A sleek vessel fashioned to look like it was moving fast, even while moored in the harbor.

"I've never been out on a boat before." She looked pale and wide-eyed and he was regretful of that.

He had frightened her.

He did not wish to frighten her. He was driven now by the need to get her away from here. By the need to have her to himself.

"I have medication for seasickness on board." His gut went tight. "I do hope you won't find yourself indisposed."

Because tonight… Tonight he would have her. And tomorrow they would speak. There were many things to discuss. But tonight, she would be his.

"Who's going to handle your car…"

"It will be handled."

"I have no idea what that must be like. To just trust that all the details will come together the way that you wish them to. I've never been able to bank on that. And I hope… I hope that you can understand that. I hope that you can understand that in my world things don't just work out. And when I found out that I was pregnant…"

"You think that things in my world simply work out? No. What I have is money and a staff that know exactly how I want things. And if I am taking myself to the boat, that I will obviously need something to be done with my car. It will be handled, because I hire people who think in that fashion. But that does not mean the broader world bends itself to my will. My brother is dead." He could feel himself beginning to break apart. This reality was so bleak, and he would have never said he was a man who clung to fairy tales, but he could see now…he did have them. He did cling to things. "And how do you think that affects me?" he asked, his voice sounding as broken as his soul.

"I…"

"I *was* a twin," he said. "I am no longer." It was only him now. Him, his parents. These children. The children she carried. "So you tell me, how is it that you think the world bends to my will? How is it that you think everything works out for me? Whenever I can wield my power and money, I do. But I do not control the whims of fate. I cannot stay the hand of bloodthirsty men, and I cannot stop… I cannot stop my idiot younger brother from taking a turn too fast. There are great many things I cannot control. With you, *agape*. You are mine. And this boat, is private. Both of those things, are certainties."

He was in desperate need of certainty. Something to hold on to.

The back of the vessel was wide and flat, with a large lounge—big enough for at least ten people—and pillows on a raised platform. Morgan went and took a seat in the center of it, pale in her wedding gown, the silken fabric spread out around her. Like a selkie who had escaped the water and found a soft respite.

He turned away from her.

He unmoored the boat, and then took his position at the wheel, maneuvering them out of the harbor. Once they were in open water, he charted the course for the island, and turned on the autopilot.

He walked to the back of the yacht and stood, looking down at her.

"I'm sorry," she said. "I spoke out of turn. Shouldn't have said that about your brother. About you."

"It is no matter. I'm not sensitive. I have dealt with real struggle, and money makes a great deal of things easier. Both of those things are true."

"I have mostly thought about myself," she said. "Through all of this. I'm sorry. I didn't give enough weight to your loss, and I'm sorry."

A bleakness washed itself over him. His children.

The fierce possessiveness that had risen up when he'd made that realization had quieted some now.

But this was not a chance of atonement. It was simply evidence of another sin.

And he would've married her regardless. He would be here, regardless. Because he would not compound one sin with another. He would not leave his own children without a father simply because...

Simply because he had vowed not to have them.

It was too late for that. He had taken his brother's woman in a moment of weakness, and now he had even stripped Alex of his legacy.

No. It wasn't that you took anything from him. She was never with him.

She was his.

"Why were you a virgin?"

She laughed. "What a question. You said we would talk tomorrow."

"I did. But I have things we must discuss before."

Heat streaked through him like a lightning bolt. And she understood. He could see when she did.

She looked away, her cheeks turning red.

"Why were you a virgin?"

"I was afraid of this," she said, putting her hand on her stomach. "Desperately. All of my life. My mother was young, barely out of high school, and my father got her pregnant. He wanted nothing to do with me. He left, and she could never even find him. She never got a cent of child support, she spent my entire childhood talking about how much easier her life would have been if not for me. About how she regretted ever meeting my father. She was bitter. She said raising me ruined her dreams."

"No," he said, anger welling in his chest. "She ruined her own dreams. People are in charge of their own actions, and perhaps they have unforeseen effects. It does not matter, though. What your father did, that was his fault. His sin. But she could have given you up for adoption, perhaps that wouldn't have been easy either, but it would have solved the issue of her resenting you. She didn't make that decision. She chose to keep you with her, and she chose to live in that resentment. That was her own decision."

"What would you know about that, considering you're a man who didn't even want children. How can you say what my mother should've done?"

"I'm a man who owns his decisions."

"That's a lie. You were ready to pretend that there was no way these children could be yours."

"I assumed," he said. "That you had been in my brother's bed for months. I assumed that the likelihood that it was his seed that had taken root inside of your womb was much higher than the reality of my own doing the same."

"Well. Now you know. Now you know the truth of it."

"You were going to sleep with Alex that night," he said. She nodded. "I was ready. I trusted him."

And something inside of him broke. Because he had not known how vulnerable a place Morgan was in when she had come to his bed. He had thought that he had been looking at an entirely different situation than the one he was.

She had been a virgin. Heartbroken because her instincts had been so very wrong.

"He must've loved you, though," he said. "To not sleep with you. To want you in his life anyway."

"That's a terrible thing," Morgan said. "I think he did. But in the end of it all, I don't think I loved him. I think I didn't know what love was. He was handsome, and he turned my head. And he was kind to me. And no, I wasn't interested in his money in the beginning, but I really appreciated how much easier my life was with it. I was tired. I was tired of the person I had the strongest connection to—my mother—resenting me. I was tired of working so hard. And suddenly, I had Alex. And he was fun and wonderful. He made me laugh. He made me feel like I wasn't a burden. He gave gifts to me happily. And I... If that's what being a gold digger is, I suppose I actually am one. Because I met you, Constantine, and I knew that it wasn't really Alex's bed I wanted to be in. I wanted to want him. And he was easy to feel an attraction to. But it wasn't the same. It never was."

She was so brave in this moment it shamed him.

It made him want to be more for her.

He stepped down to where she sat and gripping her chin, tilted her face up at his. "Tell me more about how you want me."

She was pregnant with his children. And there were serious things to deal with. There was outrage, and a fair amount of recrimination for the universe. But... It would wait. It would wait until this was through. It would wait until he was finished with her.

"Your intensity. I... The moment I saw you..."

"You know why I hated you so, Morgan?"

She shook her head.

"Because the only time I have ever wanted anything

in the universe that I could not have was when a person died. When they were taken from me by forces much more powerful than I could ever be. But you… You were there. Flesh and blood in the most beautiful woman I had ever seen. And you were his. Alex is my younger brother, and he is… He was… So full of life, and I… I pledged to care for him. To look out for him. And I coveted his woman beyond all else. And I despised you for it. Because from the moment I first saw you I wanted you beyond all else."

"Why?" There was something hungry in the question. Greedy. And his body responded to it. He wanted to satiate it. That question. That raw need in her eyes.

"Maybe your beauty. Perhaps your innocence."

"You knew I was innocent."

"No. And I did not properly get to enjoy it. Tell me, had you ever seen a naked man?"

"No," she whispered. "Only you."

The monster within him gloried in that answer.

"Have you ever taken a man into your mouth?"

She shook her head. "No."

And all these months he had been tortured by the image of her pleasuring his brother, his brother having the thing that he could not, and in fact, she had never given herself to Alex. Only to Constantine. And the guilt that came along with the triumph of it all stunned him.

The water around them was clear, glimmering bright in the sun. And he had the desperate urge to see her body, bare beneath the sky. With no secrets. No lies.

He took her hand and had her stand, then reached around and pulled the zipper tab on her dress, drawing it down her body. It fell slack, revealing her pale, glimmering curves. She had on a pair of white panties beneath the dress, no bra. His need for her was a beast. Those curves—always so tempting to him—enhanced now by her pregnancy.

His children.

A surge of possessiveness went through him and he dropped to his knees, putting his hand on her stomach, desire and pure, masculine pride vying for pride of place.

He pressed his lips to her stomach and felt her shiver. Then he moved lower, gripping her underwear and drawing them down her thighs, leaning in and pressing his face to the cleft there, inhaling the scent of her arousal.

She was wearing heels now, and nothing more. And he had never seen anything more beautiful in his life.

Morgan. His.

No one else's.

Not ever.

His children.

And he knew then that he would die for them. For her. He would also kill for them. For her.

Self-sacrifice and violence were armor that he put over himself just then. The truth, a reality as incontrovertible as if the items had been forged in the fire, and not simply in the intensity of his own need to keep the world at bay.

Because he would not lose them. He would lose nothing. Not anymore. Never again.

Never again.

And this was what he had tried to avoid for all of these years. And this was why he had vowed that he would never…

This was why.

Because there was no certainty here. There was nothing but the vast stretch of terror that was the universe, that was fate. For he had not lied when he said that to her.

He had no illusions that he was all-powerful. He never had.

He had no illusions that things would be all right, because they often were not.

And what he'd said about her mother was true as well. He was a man who owned his choices. He had made the wrong choices.

He had failed.

And he accepted that punishment as his.

You even failed at punishing yourself. Here she is. In your arms. Pregnant.

And he pushed all that aside, because now, right now, he was going to seize it. Right now, she would be his. Right now, this reality was his, and he would not let guilt or doubt or recrimination creep in. This was what happened, and he could not rail at it any more than he could rail at the fact that he was the last remaining of his siblings.

It was simply what was.

And he let everything go. Everything except the dark need to possess her. Everything.

He looked at her. Ate into her with a dark need that had taken over everything.

She gasped, and he clung to her, his hands splayed over the globes of her buttocks as he licked deeper and deeper between her thighs, as he made her tremble, shake and moan.

No man had ever done this for her. Only he had tasted this honey delight between her legs.

And only he ever would. No man would ever touch her. There was to be no marriage on paper. This was a marriage between their bodies. They were joined together in this desire. In this truth that she belonged to only him. She was his.

She was his.

The sun shone high above, the open sky watching.

Do you see? He asked the powers that be. *Do you see that she is mine. She is mine, and you will not come for her.*

He laid her down on the deck of the boat, knowing that

it was hard, knowing that he should take her down to the bed. That he should lay her on soft sheets.

But there was nothing but heat now, no consideration for comfort.

He stripped his clothes from his body, pressing his palms down to her knees and spreading her legs wide, taking a long, leisurely look at her. Every inch of her.

Her breasts were pale, tipped with light pink crests that made his mouth water. That place between her thighs was the color of strawberries and cream, and he knew it tasted just as good.

Her fiery hair fanned out around her, and she looked delicate, innocent and carnal all at once.

And then she opened her eyes, the emerald green there shocking out here in the middle of all this blue.

"Constantine."

"Tell me," he said, leaning over her, hovering above her lips. "For which of my bad qualities did you first want me?"

"Your outright unfriendliness," she said. "The scorn with which you looked at me. The hardness. The cruelty of your mouth. The way that it would never smile. Not for me. Oh, how I wanted to taste it. How I wanted to drink in all of your ire for me. I had a man who was sunny and warm, and he would've given me the world. But I wanted the one out of my reach. The one who would not smile."

"Because we are all of us broken," he said. "Wanting what we cannot have. And look at us. Here. Together. What we have is because Alex was broken."

She reached up and touched his face. "No. It's not. I would not have stayed with him. It would've been you. I would've been pregnant either way. And this is where we would be. Don't you think so?"

He growled, pushing the tip of his masculinity into her waiting softness. She gasped, lifting her hips off the deck and he wrapped his arm around her, lifting her toward him as he thrust home, deep and hard. This time knowing that he was the only man to ever be inside of her. This time knowing that she was his, and his alone.

Her rounded belly was between them, a reminder of what had passed through them before.

A reminder of what lay ahead.

But mostly, there was nothing but sensation. But the perfection of being inside of her body.

She moaned, arching up toward him and he leaned down, capturing one nipple into his mouth and sucking hard. A raw gasp escaped her lips, and when he lifted his head, she put her hand on the back of his neck and brought his head down so that he was made to kiss her. And she consumed him. Her tongue searching as their mouths fused, as their desire sparked wildly between them.

She was a wild thing in his arms, and he became a savage.

His thrusts were without tempo or beat. They followed only the roar of his blood.

She gripped his shoulders, her fingernails digging deep as she found her release, as she screamed, a ragged sound in his ear, her internal muscles gripping him tightly, drawing him in deeper. And then, he exploded. On a roar he gave himself up to the desire between them, his jagged breath mingling with hers as he tried to come back to reality. Come back to the present.

He had intended to give her a wedding night. To take her down into the luxurious cabin below and show her what it meant to be his wife.

Perhaps you showed her exactly what it means to be your wife.

Well. Perhaps he had.

And why shouldn't it begin with such honesty? He had no control where she was concerned.

None at all.

She blinked against the harsh light, and he suddenly felt as if he needed to cover her. Protect her.

He picked her up from the deck, cradling her close to his chest as he carried her down below deck. She barely moved as he spread her over the silken sheets in the well appointed cabin.

It had been his priority that the yacht be luxurious. But he was not the playboy that his brother was. There were many places he entertained women. But not personal places such as this. And certainly not on the island.

She curled partway into a ball, her red hair cascading over her face.

She was his.

There was no question of that now.

And as she drifted off to sleep, and the boat continued on toward the island, he had the feeling that if he could keep her there, separate from the world forever, he might come close to finding happiness.

CHAPTER EIGHT

MORGAN HAD A strange feeling of déjà vu when she opened
her eyes and had the distinct sensation that she was in a
different place.

This was how it had been when they'd gone to Greece,
and again… Wherever they were.

She was lying in bed on Constantine's yacht.

She was sore because he had taken her so roughly on
the deck.

Not that it had been unpleasant. It had been… Lovely.
Really. He had been…

Everything.

He wanted her. And maybe even wanted the babies.

It had change something for him to know. And not in
the way that she had imagined.

She had thought that he would be… Angry. But that
wasn't how he was acting. He was acting like a man who
had a deep need to possess.

And she was… She wanted to be possessed by him. That
was the thing. It had always been the thing.

He was a twin…

That reality was hovering around the edges of her consciousness and had been ever since he'd said it.

She could look it up. On something. Though, she realized just then that she didn't have her phone. They

didn't have anything. She had her wedding dress. And that was all.

But she was naked now.

The door to the cabin opened then, and she scrambled back down to the bed, covering herself with the sheets.

"What are you doing that for?" he asked, his gaze raking over her with hot intent.

"I didn't know who was opening the door."

"There is no one else here. Indeed, there is no one else on the island either."

"The island?"

"Yes. My private island. There is no one else here, and there will not be for the duration, other than when people drop off supplies, and we will have ample warning. It was stocked in preparation for our arrival."

"It was…"

He handed her a lovely, delicately beaded bag. "I believe you will find clothing in there."

He left then, though in the bag she did not really find clothing. Rather she found a lovely if wholly impractical swimsuit, the bottoms resting low below her baby bump, the top barely covering her ample breasts. There was a diaphanous cover that went with it, but it was nearly completely see-through. Still, when she exited the cabin she found it was extremely warm, and if no one else was here…

He was bent over on the deck, wrapping ropes quickly and efficiently into coils. He was wearing a pair of shorts, his shirt discarded. His dark hair looked like he'd been running his fingers through it. Or perhaps like she had been running her fingers through it. And he was… He was gorgeous like this. Out in the wild, not contained in a suit. This was how he looked when he made love. But it was somehow… Illicit and thrilling to see him like this while he was doing something as orderly as working on a yacht.

"You are ready?" He straightened, and her mouth watered as she took in the sight of his broad chest, his flat abs, his bronze skin, covered with just the right amount of hair. She had never really considered herself a fan of chest hair, but Constantine's was a work of art. As indeed was his entire body.

The island itself was glorious. The white sand, palm and cypress trees, along with groves of olives providing shade for the landscape. High up on a hilltop she could just barely see the gleam of glass nestled in the trees.

The house?

Maybe.

"No one is here?"

"No," he said.

"Why?"

He looked at her. "I prize my privacy. I learned that from my grandfather. That a man must protect the space around him, if he is going to work hard, he must hold space."

"Does your father do anything with your family business?"

"No."

He led the way, off the boat, but he did not stop to put on a shirt. Or shoes. He was barefoot, walking up the sandy trail that cut through all those trees, and leading them up toward the house.

He seemed so different here. Relaxed. At home.

"It has all been my responsibility since the death of my grandfather. But he groomed me for this."

"Does it frustrate you?"

His eyes went blank for a moment. "My parents are lovely people. Much in the same way my brother is a lovely person. Was. Gregarious and fun, and not always reliable in the ways that one might like."

"Right," she said softly.

"I learned at a very early age that it was up to me. That I could not count on anyone but myself. Somebody had to take hold of the family fortune. Somebody had to take hold of the family business. It was me. I do not resent that lot in life. There are... There are people who shine brighter, but they do burn out quicker."

She looked at him, at the dark fire that was banked in his eyes. Did he not know that he shone brightly all on his own? He did. He was brilliant.

And yet, she had a feeling if she said that he would reject it. Ignore it. Perhaps even deny it.

"I never had anyone counting on me. Not really. My mother told me that my existence had already failed her. Everything I've ever done has been for me. I don't know what it's like to live for someone else." She put her hand on her stomach. "I wonder if that makes me inherently selfish."

"I see no evidence of your selfishness."

"I don't suppose you've ever seen any evidence of my selflessness either."

He shrugged. "No. But then... You are here."

"You kidnapped me."

"I married you."

"I was going to keep the baby myself. I didn't want you to resent them. Because I know what that's like. That is the most important thing to me, Constantine. That you... That you find it in yourself to love them. Please. Because I know what it's like to be raised by a mother who doesn't love me."

He nodded slowly. "My parents love me very much. And even still, they have done a considerable amount of damage."

"Then I beg you, I beg you to ask yourself what a lack of love might do." She looked at him, beseeching, because she really needed him to understand this. She needed him to know. "Without love, it doesn't mean anything. None of it does. My mother... She was so cold to me. And when I moved out... It was like she was just finished. Done with me. She hasn't spoken to me since. I've gotten in touch with her, and we had a couple of awkward phone calls. But she's never reached out. There's this... Detachment there, and it is brutal. And all I've ever wanted..." Suddenly, tears sprang to her eyes, and she felt ashamed. "All I've ever wanted is for someone to care for me. It is to have people in my life that I cared for. These babies..." And for the first time she felt it. For the first time, she felt her heart swell with love. Felt her chest expand with a deep desire to have these children. With the knowledge that she needed them. That she needed this.

"They will be my chance. My chance to... They're my family. And it is so important to me that you... I do not want you to be like my mother. Not to them. Not to these children. They didn't ask for this, Constantine. They didn't. They didn't ask for me, a girl who's never been loved by anybody. And they didn't ask for..."

"For me?" he asked, working a brow. "No, you're right. They did not ask for a brick wall as a father."

"I didn't mean that. I just mean whatever your baggage, and whatever mine, it is not their fault we carry it."

"You are correct, of course. And I would never want to pass on my particular trauma to anyone, let alone my own children. But that is why I didn't wish to have them."

"I wish that I understood a little bit better. Because we have to do this. Because we're in this together..."

"I told you I was a twin," he said, his voice hard. "Not identical. Fraternal. My sister, Athena... When we were eight years old we were on a beach. My mother was there, and my father. And a nanny, who was chasing Alex around. But not us. My parents were drinking. Partying with friends. It was their favorite sort of vacation, the kind that they were on just before they came to our wedding, in fact. Athena and I were kidnapped. Taken by some of my grandfather's enemies."

She stopped walking. "You what?"

"We were held. For two months."

"Constantine…"

"No one came for us. We waited, and we waited, no one came. There was… We were separated from one another, sometimes. Brought back together when we were terrified and hungry. So that we could see just how much terror was being wrought on the other. And they finally took Athena away from me. And they told me I would never see her again. Not if I didn't pass a test. But I failed. You see, I was left alone in the dark for days. And they told me not to cry, or they would know. But I thought I was alone. And so I cried. Alone by myself, an eight-year-old boy with no hope. With nothing. I cried like a baby. And when my grandfather found us. When he paid the ransom… Athena was nowhere to be found. Yes, whatever happened… My parents' neglect which allow the kidnapping, however long the discussions took place about whether or not they would pay… None of it mattered. Because Athena was gone. And it was because of me."

"You cannot blame yourself. They were evil, vile people."

"It is like your mother," he said. "Your father was a villain, that much is true. But she did not have to punish you. She could have made a different choice. I could have made a different choice. I could've been stronger. But I was weak. I have never been weak, not again. Not since then. I failed her, Morgan. And later I failed Alex. I will never fail my family again. Not ever."

"That's why you said I really wasn't after Alex for his money. Because this was in the news. Wasn't it."

"'Course it was. Athena's death was worldwide news."

"Are you sure she's…"

"She was never seen again. They never found her body, of course. But then… These are the kinds of people that leave no evidence when they wish."

"I'm so sorry. I'm so sorry that you ever felt like that was your fault. That you…"

"It was my fault. That part of it. I'm not afraid."

But he was. Maybe not of taking blame, but of what he might have to do if he didn't. She could see that, clearly. She tried to reconcile the pain he'd been through with the man that was standing in front of her. But of course he'd been through pain. Of course he had. He was not an easy man. And of course he was different than Alex, who would've been so young he wouldn't remember the loss of his sister.

"Alex didn't remember her."

As if he had read her mind. He let out a sharp breath. "It is its own grief. To not remember."

"It must be its own grief to lose a twin. I don't even have a sibling, let alone understand the connection…"

"It is funny," he said. "Because I always imagined that we had a magical bond. So you would think that I would feel as though a limb had been torn from my body because she is gone from this earth. But instead, I still feel the connection there. And I don't know what that means."

"That some bonds are stronger than life and death?"

He shrugged a shoulder.

And just then, the trail rounded the corner, and revealed the front of a massive garden. There were citrus trees and large, broadleaf plants with spots of pink and red. It was magnificent. And behind it, the house, a marvel of design.

Glass and large wooden beams. It looked like a part of the landscape, reflecting the ocean down below. Nearly hidden, constructed as it was.

"This is mine. Every other place you've been... It was the family's. But this is mine."

And she had the sense that she now knew him better than just about anyone else on earth.

Athena would've known him.

Her heart ached for him. For that loneliness and being the one left behind. What a horrible thing. A horrible fate. A horrible tragedy. And she had thought that he was a mountain who felt nothing. That maybe the truth was he was a man who had felt far too much pain. Far too much loss, after so much love. And he had closed himself down because it was more than he could bear. Because it was more than anyone could ever be expected to bear.

"Let's go."

They walked through the garden, and up the front steps and the doors parted as he approached.

"Facial recognition," he said.

Her mouth dropped in awe as they stepped inside to the tropical oasis. The floors were made of stone, plants climbing up the walls inside, over beams that ran across the ceiling. There was warm wood, a sharp contrast to all the glass around them, the pristine beauty outside.

It was quiet. They really were the only ones here.

"This is not at all what I expected."

"What did you expect?"

"More marble, I suppose."

"Marble is what my parents like. I... Especially here, I wanted it to be about our surroundings."

"If you could live anywhere it would be here, wouldn't it?"

"When I was kidnapped, being kept alone was terrify-

ing. In the end, I learned something from it. That sometimes solitude is the only way to find peace, and if a man
can learn to be alone with himself, then he can do anything. I learned to find purpose in solitude."

And to never cry, she imagined. To never let himself
feel anything unfettered. To conquer the deepest fear that
he held because he could not ever let himself be controlled
by it. Not again.

He didn't have to say that. But she knew all the same.
She just did.

"You spend a lot of time alone," she said.

He grinned. "It is how I like it."

No. It was how it had to be. That was another thing she
could clearly see. Why deny himself simply because he
was paying a penance? She grabbed his hand, put it on her
stomach. "They're yours."

He nodded slowly. "I know. I do not doubt."

"Why don't you doubt me now, Constantine, when you
did before? I could easily be lying to you about the fact
that I was a virgin."

His expression turned fierce. "You are not, though."

"No," she said softly. "I'm not."

"My desire for you is beyond measure," he said. "This is
my sanctuary, and I do not bring anyone here. But I wished
to bring you. Just like myself on your beautiful body. And
to… Keep you from the world."

And why wouldn't he? The world had been so unbearably cruel to him.

"Aren't you angry," she asked. "With your parents. For
allowing you to be kidnapped?"

His eyes went blank. "It does no good. And they are all
the family I have."

"Not anymore," she said softly.

They weren't alone. He knew her secrets, and she knew his. They weren't alone.

"I must go. I have some work to see to."

"Work?"

"I have an office upstairs. There is Internet here."

"Oh. Of course. I will…"

"There is food prepared in the fridge. You are welcome to it. It should be prepared and ready for you. You may also swim in any one of the pools, and explore the gardens. You will find many fresh fruits there that you may help yourself to. You may also take a nap. There is a room prepared for you."

"Thank you. It means something to me, that you always have a place for me."

His face went hard. "I take care of what's mine."

And then he went upstairs, his footsteps echoing against the wood as he went. And left alone, she could hear the sound of the waves beyond the windows, and nothing more.

This was the kind of isolation Constantine preferred. And she understood why.

And she had to wonder if he had to carry so much anger at himself because…

Because of the family he had left. *We will be his family now.*

She held that truth close, wishing that she could make it his truth as well.

CHAPTER NINE

"WHAT THE HELL HAPPENED?"

"It's complicated."

"Hell, boy," his father said. "I have time for complicated."

Funny, because he rarely seemed to have time for anything but indulgence, but now that there was a hint of a scandal, he had time. He banished that thought. He was simply raw because he had been talking about Athena. Because it was so clear that Morgan had not understood why he had to bear the burden of his own culpability in the situation. Why it was important.

"It will not make you happy," he said, and something dark and gleeful rose up inside of him.

Aren't you angry at them...?

"Don't tell me the babies are not Alex's," his father said.

"No," Constantine said. "They are not."

"Dammit. I don't know what we'll tell your mother. She's going to be heartbroken..."

"Oh," Constantine said. "They're still your grandchildren."

A pause settled between them.

"What are you saying?"

"They're mine."

"Yours?"

"Twins, father. And mine."

"How is that possible?"

"The usual way these things are possible. Your golden boy betrayed her. She went to his room, and he was already with another woman. And so she came to my room."

"And you could not leave your brother's girlfriend alone? She was the love of his life, Constantine."

"So much so that he was with another woman the night he died," Constantine said. "I know you love Alex, I do too. But that does not make him perfect, and it certainly does not absolve him of his betrayal of Morgan."

"Did you not betray him? You could've waited for the dust to settle."

"But I didn't. I wanted her. And I had her. I had still imagined that they were Alex's children. But they are not."

"This…"

"You can say it. You were disappointed because you prefer Alex to me."

"And I am disappointed because your brother will never get another chance to have children. You could've had children with anyone."

"And Alex could've chosen to fuck his girlfriend and not someone else. And had he not been with someone else, he would still be alive."

Barely leashed rage rose up inside of him.

"It is perhaps best if your mother does not know."

"You would have me deny my own children to my mother to preserve the fantasy you have."

There was a long uncomfortable silence on the other end of the phone. His father was not a cool man, but he was confronting him head-on, and he knew his father did not care for such things.

"Well?"

"I will think about it."

"I may not give you the choice."

"Alex…"

"You think about things for too long," Constantine said. "You are inactive for too long."

"I was not there," his father said, his voice suddenly turning to ice. "You were the one that was there. You were the one that failed the test."

His father had never been cruel to him before, but this was certainly edging close to it. Of course…he had fired the first shot.

"I've accepted my part in it," Constantine said. "I do not deny my own weakness. But that is not a skill I learned from you."

His father made a wrenching sound that chilled Constantine's soul. "I know it. Don't you think I don't know my own weakness, Constantine? To have lost two children as I have… I thought… I did believe that we would have this part of your brother."

"Sadly," Constantine said. "It is only me."

"Your mother…"

"Leave it for now," he said.

He hung up the phone and went to the window, looking out at the sea below. He had known they would not take this well. He was not taking it well.

For this very reason.

There was a strange, cloying fear that threatened to choke him. Something in the way that he breathed and moved.

These children were to be his responsibility. And then there was Morgan. Morgan who…

None of this was her fault. He had been angry with her. For appealing to him. Angry with her for daring to be beautiful when she belonged to his brother. When the fact of the matter was, she had been his downfall from the very beginning, simply by breathing. And it was more than her belonging to his brother, it was…

But now she's yours. She is yours, and you can keep her separate from the world.

Perhaps… Perhaps his father was right. Perhaps allowing the world to believe that these were his brother's children…

Maybe it would be better. Maybe it would keep them safe.

Because one thing Constantine knew for sure.

That which he loved ended up lost.

He could not bear for that fate to meet his children.

Morgan hadn't seen Constantine all day. She had found a fruit tray in the fridge, and she had spent the day grazing on it, and she would have said that she couldn't be satisfied by something so alarmingly healthy, not in this state where she craved carbs and cheese, but here on the island it felt somehow glamorous, and she found she enjoyed it.

She didn't bother to change out of the bikini that he had given her, because why? There was no one here.

She was beginning to feel like he wasn't here either. She missed him.

She had told him, and his response had been… So not what she had expected. He seemed angry with her, but desirous at the same time, and her own feelings had been thrown into a wild wind and whipped around until she couldn't sort them out.

And the longer she sat by herself the more she wondered if she… She did not want to. But the more she sat by herself the more she wondered if she needed to contact her own mother.

She was becoming a mother.

And it made her ache to reach out to the woman who had given birth to her. The woman who had not nurtured her.

The woman who had left her feeling scarred and tragic, but who had also… Given life to her. It was so complicated, and there was part of her that wanted to understand the complication as deeply as she could.

She didn't have her phone.

Everything had been left at the wedding. And she knew that meant seeking out Constantine.

She walked up the stairs, wood planks that seemed to float in midair, held there by taut wire, and stood on the landing for a long while, looking out the vast windows at the jewel bright sea below.

She did not know how she had come to be in this place. A waitress who had wanted little more than to survive, a woman who had been so desperate not to repeat the mistakes of her mother. But she had. It was only because the man was wealthy and insisted on claiming his children. That was the difference.

It made her feel… Shamed.

Because she wasn't better than her mother, she had made an easier mistake, fallen into a happier accident.

She had been ruled entirely by her desires the night that she was with Constantine for the first time. And she hadn't behaved much better since. She had not resisted him at all when he had taken her down on the yacht deck. She had resisted him at no point. She had seen him, and she had wanted him. She had thought nothing for the future.

She heard the door open, and as they were the only two people on the whole of the island, she knew it was him. She went toward the sound, down a long corridor that stretched over the first floor, a suspension bridge that lent itself to the open-air feeling of the house.

And then it was closed off, a few doors leading to other

rooms undoubtedly. And around the corner, she met Constantine. It was strange, to be in this enclosed place where there were so many other open spaces. And seeing him like this… She could barely breathe.

He was not wearing a suit, but he had put a shirt on. A white one, only buttoned up partway. She took a visual tour of his masculine beauty. All of that skin and black chest hair.

He was truly a stunning specimen of a man. And oh, how she wanted him. Even now, grappling with these hard truths.

The whims of fate. Accidents.

Her own lack of superiority.

"I need to call my mother," she said.

"I see."

"All of my things are back on the mainland. I don't have my phone."

"Do you know her number?"

She did. Only because her mother had had the same number since Morgan was a child.

"Yes."

"You may use my phone."

"Okay. Thank you."

"I spoke to my father."

She winced. "And?"

"He is not happy with me. That much is certain."

"I'm certain he is unhappy with me too."

His face took on a strange, serious cast. "No. His dissatisfaction lies wholly with me. Trust me."

She blinked, feeling emotion pooling at the corners of her eyes. "I am complicit in what happened between us. If they are angry at you…"

"He thinks it would be best if my mother didn't know

the truth. And I have thought about it, and I think that is perhaps for the best."

"Constantine… How can we possibly keep this to ourselves?"

"I wonder if… I do wonder if the children would be safer if they are not believed to be mine."

"Safer… Who do you think might come for them?"

"The same people who came for me when I was a child."

"But surely…"

"They are a powerful crime family. And the vendetta that they had against my grandfather was very real. I now occupy that position."

"Do you really think concealing the fact that you're their father will help?"

"I don't know. I have no way of knowing that. All I know is… My sister…"

"I understand," she said, even though she didn't. Not quite. Except he was afraid, this man. This rock. For the children that she carried, and perhaps, she simply needed to acknowledge that. Listen to it. But it hurt her. To think that he might not acknowledge them. Because that did skim far too close to her own truth. To her own life.

A father who never wanted anything to do with her…

But no. He would be there for them. He would.

"You are using this to distance yourself," she said.

He looked at her, his expression sharp. "What do you mean?"

"You never wanted children, Constantine, and I do think I understand why. I understand that you've been through things that… That would break lesser men. And you are not broken. But what I do wonder is this… What I do wonder is if this is an opportunity for you to pull away from being a father. And you are their father."

"I know that," he said, his voice hard.

"I didn't want to be a mother," she said. "I didn't. That relationship for me is… It is difficult, and it is complicated. And it hurts me. And I don't know if I will be a better mother to my children. Or maybe I will be, by default, because I don't have to worry about money. Because I don't have to worry about how we live. Maybe that's the only reason I'll be better. And does that really make me better?"

"I don't understand. Why would it matter. Better is better."

"Is it? I have spent so many years being angry at my own mother, and when I found out I was pregnant I could not muster one kernel of joy. Not in the deepest part of myself. I was so sad. Because I knew that I had done the exact same thing. Gotten pregnant by accident by a man who wanted nothing to do with his own child. Children. It never occurred to me of course that I might be pregnant with two. And if I had been left on my own to care for them, would I have sunk into bitterness just like her? Trying to care for two children on my own, trying to balance the demands of caring for them and having a job? And what would have kept me from that same bitterness?"

"I will," he said.

"Your money will?"

"Does it matter? Is it not all the same?"

He handed her his phone. "Call her."

And the thing that saddened and worried her the most was the fact that she really did think money might be the difference, and it felt so… It made her mouth taste like ash.

"Is there a place that I can go…"

"Your bedroom is just here."

He walked back around the corner and pushed open the door to a phenomenal glass room that stuck out high over the hillside, with trees all around it and the ocean at the front.

"Oh…"

"Every room in this home is designed to be part of nature."

"It's beautiful. Everything around me is beautiful all the time when I'm with you."

And she knew she sounded sad, because she was a little bit sad.

He regarded her for a long moment, and then closed the door behind her.

With trembling fingers, she called her mother. The phone rang three times, and she was not sure if she was hoping her mother would answer or… Or not.

But she did.

"Hello?"

"Hi, Mom," Morgan said.

"Morgan?" Her mother was questioning it, not because she had other children, but because Morgan hadn't spoken to her in a couple of years.

"Yeah. I just… I needed to tell you some things."

"Oh?"

It didn't surprise her that her mother hadn't seen the news. Why would she? She didn't follow the lifestyles of the rich and famous. It only upset her.

"I got married."

"Well," her mom said. "Good for you. Though, I would've thought you'd invite me to the wedding."

"It all happened really quickly. I'm… I'm pregnant."

"Oh," her mom said, and there was a wealth of hurt in that one sound. Maybe because the father of Morgan's children had married her.

"Twins," Morgan said.

"Twins don't run in the family," she said.

"They run in his," she said. "I'm due in four months. But they'll probably be early. I guess twins are like that."

"So it didn't happen all that quickly, then?" her mom said.

"Well. I guess not."

"Did you just want to share the news?"

"I wanted… I wanted to ask you something, but I don't know how to ask. I'm worried I…"

"What?"

"Did you love me ever? Or did I only ever just make your life hard? And was it the money? Was it that he didn't support you? What was it?"

"Of course I love you," her mom said. "I wouldn't have worked so hard to take care of you if I didn't."

Guilt overcame Morgan then, because she had always been so bitter about how hard her mother had made it seem, and that had made Morgan feel like a burden. But… She supposed that was true. Her mom hadn't had to take care of her. She had made a choice, and that choice had been to raise her.

And she made mistakes that had left Morgan feeling raw and wounded. And she was looking for something… Something magical in her own self that would make her know she wouldn't do the same thing to her own children. But right now she just felt… Well, she felt guilty. That she had judged her mother so harshly. That she had been so certain in her own superiority, and all of that was breaking down slowly as she faced the reality of her own situation, of her own limitations. But even more now that she was on the phone with her mother asking her directly if she loved her.

"It's just that you never seemed very happy to have me," Morgan said.

The words tripped clumsily off her tongue.

"I don't know that I've ever been very happy," her mom responded.

The words lanced Morgan. "Why?"

Her mother drew a tight breath in. "I've never thought about it. Not really."

"What do you live for?"

"I get up every day. I go to work. We had our apartment, and it was never much, but we had something. I felt like I did something by keeping you safe. And making sure you had food to eat. But I suppose I've always felt lonely. At least a bit."

"I'm sorry," Morgan said. "I'm sorry if I've been part of you being lonely. I guess I should've been there for you. But I didn't know if you wanted me to be."

"I've never liked asking for it," her mom said. "I begged your father to love me. And I've never felt so small in my life than when he refused. To ask for someone to care and to have them tell you they won't…"

"Did you love my father?"

"Yes. Because I was a fool. And I let that decide how I felt every day for far too long. And by the time I decided not to, keeping things closed down inside myself was a habit. I never wanted to ask for more. Not again."

"I want you to be involved with the kids," Morgan said. And that wasn't why she'd called. But she realized that it needed to be why. Because she was lonely too, and she still had her mother. Her mother wasn't evil, she was just… Sad. And now that Morgan had dispensed with any idea that she was superior, she couldn't look at her the same way. She was just human. Frail and fallible like Morgan was.

And Morgan didn't want anger or sadness to dictate the way she was with her own children. And she shouldn't let it dictate the way she was with her mother, either.

"Well I would like that."

"I'll have to tell you the whole story. Sometime. I'm in Greece, though. Well, I think I'm in Greece."

"Greece?"

"He's... He's from a very old family here. Actually, I'm on an island right now."

"An island?"

"Yes. And..." A big needy feeling opened up inside of her. One that she had always despised. "I do love you," she said to her mom.

"I love you too," she said. "I always have. It was hard. Raising you. But I did the best I could."

She believed it. She believed it then, because it felt right to believe it. She believed it then because what was the benefit of disbelieving? She believed it then because that was how she was going to look at it.

Because she wanted to begin to heal, and she thought this was the best way to do it.

Hanging on certainly wasn't going to do it. Being caught up in her own hurt wasn't going to do it. It was just going to keep that hurt fresh. It was just going to keep her right where she was, and she couldn't afford that. She had to move on. She had to. For the sake of her children. For the sake of herself.

"We'll... We'll talk more often," Morgan said.

"Okay," her mom responded.

"And I'll let you know when I get close to... When the babies are coming."

"Thank you."

They hung up the phone, and Morgan looked out at the water, and thought again about how far she'd come. But right then, she felt like she still had astronomically far to go. So many complicated things to sort out.

Constantine didn't want to claim the children as his, and she had talked to her mother about things she had never thought she would.

Her mother had been... Lonely for her father for so

many years, and she had been protecting herself. And that gave Morgan pause.

What would it be like to live with Constantine but not have his emotions? Would it begin to wear on her? Would holding herself back and trying to make herself not care affect the way she was with her children? She didn't want to do that with her mom, not anymore. Didn't want to hold back because she was hurt, because she had the feeling that that had been part of compounding their loneliness. She didn't blame herself. There were two people involved in the relationship, after all. She moved over to the closet in the room and opened it. And inside there was a bright blue dress, designed to flow and skim over the wearer's body.

And it made her want to be the woman that could wear it. That would look beautiful in it. That would tempt a man in it. That was the problem. In the middle of all these questions about motherhood, there was just this whole thing with him, and she wished they could've worked it out without… Marriage and children being in the mix. God knew it would've been easier.

Maybe that was what she needed to do. Maybe she needed to set aside the conversation with her mother. Maybe they needed to set aside the fact that they had married one another, the fact that they were having children, the fact that… All of the facts, actually. Maybe they needed to put it all away and simply be here. On an island. Two people alone. Perhaps the only people in the world. And see what happened.

And she proposed that she would do just that.

CHAPTER TEN

IT WAS TORTUROUS, working while here on the island. He didn't often do it. But it was the perfect vehicle by which to avoid Morgan, which was what he was doing at the moment.

Coward.

Perhaps.

But he had just told her that he might not claim the children.

Guilt ate at him. Because he wondered if she was right, and he rarely wondered if anyone but himself was right. If perhaps he had never considered himself a coward.

Not in the years since his kidnapping.

He had been weak then, and he had gone out of his way to never be in the years since.

He laughed at himself now.

He made his way down the stairs, and he smelled something phenomenal.

But what he saw when he made his way down to the landing was more exciting than the prospect of dinner. It was Morgan, standing by a set table that was surrounded by lush gardens, partly concealed. She was wearing a blue dress that hugged her curves, her red hair flowing freely. Her pale shoulders were exposed, and he felt a strong urge to count the freckles on them. To memorize her body. To make her his.

"What is all this?" he asked as he stepped outside.

"I thought that I would… Make us dinner. It's been a long couple of days. And we're here. On a private island. And there's nothing… There's nothing but you and me, Constantine. We called our parents. We did our duty. We…had the wedding. And now we're here. I am not your brother's girlfriend. And you are not my boyfriend's disapproving older brother. You are Constantine, and I'm Morgan. And maybe we need a moment to figure out what that means."

And he wanted that, he realized. Wanted to take that moment where it was only the two of them and exist in it. Put down the trauma from the past and let the memories recede into nothing. What if she was just a woman, a beautiful woman that he wanted. Standing there. Everything he'd ever desired. And he never gave in to temptation. It wasn't who he was.

But right then, he did.

He let her words paint a picture of a fantasy that he knew couldn't exist, and never would.

"You cooked?"

"There was some lovely steak, and beautiful vegetables, and I've had to cook for myself for a long time. I know my way around the kitchen, though I have to say yours is glorious."

"I do not cook," he said. "I didn't realize the kitchen was particularly glorious."

"What is the point of it," she asked, a funny little smile on her face. "Having so many glorious things when you don't even know how glorious they are?"

In spite of himself, he felt his mouth kick upward into

a smile. He crossed the space where she was and held her chair out for her. "Why don't you have a seat."

"All right."

The sky was low in the sky, and the pink light of it setting over the water suffused the air around them. Warm and close and intoxicating. The scent of flowers hung in the air, or maybe it was just her.

And he felt like he was under her spell for a moment. And he was not a man who had ever believed in such things.

She was right. He was surrounded by fantasy at all times. His mother's ridiculous fairy room, and all of the opulence they indulged themselves in. And yet he didn't... He didn't allow himself those moments. He did not allow himself fantasy.

So perhaps for just this moment.

Perhaps. All of his seriousness had not protected Alex, after all.

He had thought that it would. He had changed after the loss of Athena, and he had been certain he could keep harm from ever befalling his family again. But he hadn't managed it. Not with all of his determination and all of his strength, so what then did he think the result would be now?

The world was cruel.

And because of that cruelty he had not even allowed himself a moment to look at the beauty. Until her. He had looked at her and he had been unable to stop.

"I've never seen opulence as a gift," he said. "It was simply a fact of my existence. And I saw the hard things in the world early. And opulence did not save me from them."

"I understand that," she said. "I really do. But believe me when I tell you, the lack of it was something I always felt. In part because my mother was so keenly aware of it."

"I have been surrounded my entire life by opulence and remarkable beauty. And so private islands and stunning vistas, ornately themed rooms, and beautiful homes… They do not signify. But you… The moment that I saw you, Morgan, I felt like I was seeing something truly original. Truly new, and it was better than any gilded statue could ever be. And having you… What is forbidden to me? I'm a man with money and power. Nothing is forbidden to me. But you were. That is a novelty that far outstrips any well-appointed kitchen."

"Are you saying I'm your one indulgence?"

"You have been that, yes. And I… I have reveled in you, that much is certain."

"I don't think I've ever been anyone's indulgence," she said, her eyes looking glassy, and he did not know why such a… Such a basic compliment, borderline crude would produce that result.

"I'm sure many men would've liked you to be."

"But I didn't want to be theirs. I suppose. And it doesn't mean anything if you don't also want it. When I met you…"

"Why don't we pretend that you only just did?" Because he liked fantasy. Even if it was ridiculous.

"Okay. Then let's pretend I don't know anything about you. What was your favorite ice cream when you were a child?"

He laughed. He couldn't help himself. He was caught entirely off guard by the mischievous gleam in her eyes, by the little smile on her face, and by the mention of ice cream, of all things.

"I don't know," he said.

"That's ridiculous. Of course you know. Everyone had a favorite ice cream. What was it you ordered or asked for at the grocery store or…do billionaire children go to the grocery store?"

"No," he said, memories beginning to crowd his mind.

He realized he didn't know because he didn't allow himself to think about his childhood. Because in the before, there was Athena, and thinking of her was like a dagger in his soul. And in the after, he had no longer been a child. Not really.

But he could remember, he could remember his grandfather taking himself and Athena and little Alex to get an ice cream cone at a shop on the beach. The same beach that they had been taken from later. But he didn't focus on what had come after. And he didn't think about what had come before. He thought only of that moment. And the joy that he had felt in it. And he remembered the ice cream.

"Chocolate. With caramel. That's what I would get at this little place on the beach. And my grandfather would let us each get a cone. And I cannot think of ice cream without also thinking of the beach. Of sand, and of the sun melting it so quickly that we had to eat impossibly fast. Yes. That's what I think of." He could see the ice cream in his mind, rolling down the cone, down his hand, onto the gritty sand below.

"My mother would get me some sometimes when we went to the grocery store," she said. "It was only a quarter, and I never got a cone, because if you got a cup you got much more. They would overfill it. Praline pecan. That was my favorite. Also caramel, but with vanilla ice cream. And those candy nuts. That is a memory from my childhood where I felt truly happy."

"And me as well."

"Very different memories, but that makes us seem more the same than different, doesn't it?"

He nodded slowly. "Yes. It does."

"Favorite cartoon."

"Cartoons?"

"Yes."

"I don't… I do not think I watched cartoons."

"I am certain that you did," she said. "I personally love this entire block of cartoons on the public access channel. And actually, I suppose the one that I loved wasn't actually a cartoon. It was about a dog. And it was light action. He dressed up in costumes for every book that he went into. I loved that. I wanted my imagination to be that real. I think that's what captured me about the different things that I loved."

"I suppose my imagination did not have to be so strong," he said.

Though as he said that he had the impression of being in a playroom, early in the morning, snuggled up in blankets, with Athena next to him. "There was a cartoon about ponies. And they had magic powers. My sister liked to watch that. And I would sit with her. I did not enjoy it, of course."

"Of course not," Morgan said.

"I preferred cartoons that had some sword fighting."

"Naturally."

"We had quite the home theater. And we used to screen films down there. My parents were always like children with things like that. So excited to show us the latest big cartoon that could otherwise only be seen in theaters."

"Well, that is far beyond anything I could've imagined."

"There was one about a woman who dressed as a man to save her country. That had a lot of sword fighting and I liked it. It reminded me… You remind me of that."

"I have not dressed up as a man," Morgan said.

"Perhaps not. But you are willing to fight. No matter what. Every step of the way."

"I think that is one of the nicest compliments anyone has ever given me. Though sometimes I'm tired of fighting."

Me too.

But the word stuck in his throat. He didn't have the luxury of being tired of fighting. He didn't know why he felt that. What was he even fighting for? To atone for the dark and gritty things in the past that he could not make right, no matter how hard he tried.

To do what his grandfather had told him. When there had been no more ice cream and no more Athena. When he'd looked at him with fierce eyes and told him he had to be a man now. Hard. He had to have control. He had to handle things.

It was up to him to make things right.

To live right.

To be the Kamaras man that his grandfather needed him to be.

He just knew that it always felt like a fight. One that he seemed to continually lose. And he was not a man who was given to such things.

He had been a success taking over his family's business. He had been a success in managing his parents' spending and excesses, and Alex's too. But in the end he had not been able to keep Alex safe. So what did it all mean? And what did it all matter?

It was strange how not talking about it, housesitting with Morgan and trying to interact as strangers, brought up things that he tried not to think about any other time.

"We don't have to fight now," she said.

She smiled at him, and he realized they hadn't been eating. They had only been talking.

The dinner that she had made him was truly wonderful. "I don't know that anyone's ever made dinner for me before."

"That's ridiculous. Don't you have chefs? People make dinner for you all the time."

"That's different," he said. "They are paid to cook for

the family, or for me I suppose in the abstract sense. You just decided to cook for me."

She ducked her head, and color mounted in her cheeks, and he felt an answering desire rise inside of him. He did not have a name for what it was he wanted. He was reminded yet again of being a child. On that same day he'd gone and gotten the ice cream. And they had gone into an aquarium, and he stood on the other side of the glass staring at the colorful, teeming world of fish. And he had felt like he wanted to step through that glass, for beyond that was a true mystery. Something truly off-limits, something that he could not just be given. And that was how he felt now. As a little boy staring at something brilliant and wild and intangible and knowing that a thick sheet of glass separated him from it, and that even if it were not there, it was not something that he could possess. Not something that he could experience.

She was right there, and yet it felt like she was in another world. Felt like she was apart from him.

He wanted to rage, because he did not like things that were out of his control. He did not like things he could not understand.

And there was something about Morgan that he could not understand. Something about her that he could not touch.

"I wanted to cook for you," she said. "I wanted to give you something."

"Why? What have I ever given you?"

"You're giving me children." She smiled ruefully. "Sorry. I suppose I'm not doing a very good job of acting like we just met."

"I don't care. Enough games. Why would you do this for me? Why do you… Why do you care at all?"

"I don't know how not to, Constantine. If I did that I never would've slept with you."

"You were angry with Alex."

"I wanted you. I told you that already. Yes, I was angry with Alex, but I was a virgin, do you honestly think I would only sleep with you to get back at your brother? I did it because I wanted something that was mine. For me. I did it because I wanted to indulge myself after a lifetime of total control. And you were the gift that I wanted. You were… The ice cream. Just there to be an indulgence. So I suppose we're the same on that score. That you were my indulgence too."

"Morgan…"

"And now we are having these children. And nothing about the way we've begun is normal, or makes sense, or is a way that people should carry on. But I don't know how to go back and be like everyone else. And maybe we won't. Maybe we can't be. Maybe a billionaire who ends up with a waitress can never be…" She shook her head. "I'm sorry. Maybe those are the wrong words."

"What words?"

"Ends up with. I feel like that implies romance and happy endings. And that isn't necessarily us."

"What you are is mine," he said. "There will be no question of there being other people in this union, you understand that, don't you?"

"I don't want anyone else. I never have. You were the only man that I have ever wanted."

"You were ready to sleep with Alex."

"I liked him and I thought it was time. But I didn't think at all when it came to you. It was about desire, and I was completely overwhelmed by it."

But that wasn't it. It wasn't the answer. It wasn't what

he felt when he looked at her. That unsatisfied sensation that made him feel rocked to his core.

It wasn't just desire, because... Even if he had never experienced desire like this before, he knew what it was to want a woman.

Do you? Can you even remember what it's like to want anyone other than Morgan?

No. He couldn't. From the moment he had seen her he'd been consumed with her. He had not touched another woman since the first time he had seen Morgan almost a year ago.

The realization stunned him.

"I have not been with anyone else since the moment we met," he said, and he had not intended to say that to her, had not meant to say it out loud, but for some reason honesty had felt... It had felt necessary then. Perhaps because he was sitting there grappling with the truth of it in himself.

"You... You haven't been?"

"No. I haven't wanted anyone. Not since the moment my brother first brought you home. I thought it was quite a cruelty. That a woman on his arm should capture my attention so. But you must understand, I never expected to see you again after that first time. And still, you haunted me. You haunted my dreams. In a rather effortless fashion."

"And you wanted to have a marriage in name only?"

"I did not see what the alternative could possibly be."

"You didn't want me to be carrying his children."

"It doesn't matter. It would've been better. It would be right."

"You didn't want me to be carrying his children because you want them."

"I should not."

"Who cares about should and shouldn't, Constantine? We have never followed that guideline. It has never mattered to us. No matter that we might have wanted it to, it never has."

He could not deny the truth of what she was saying, even if it gouged at him. Of course he wanted the children to be his, the same as he wanted her to be his, but it didn't matter. Except it did. All of it mattered. No matter how he told himself it should not and could not. It did.

She was pregnant with his babies.

And he wanted to believe that redemption was what was on the other side of that glass. But did it matter if it was? He had her. She was here. They were his children, they were not Alex's. And just perhaps he did not owe his brother a legacy. Perhaps Alex should've guarded his own legacy. Perhaps his brother should have managed things, taken care of himself. Well, perhaps that. The children were his, and she was his. And she had wanted him above Alex. And suddenly, the beast inside of him roared.

He wanted her. In his bed. Tonight. Now.

"I hope there is no dessert," he said.

"Why not?"

"Because I do not have the patience to eat it."

He reached across the table then, drew her to him, and kissed her on the mouth.

She made a muffled cry as he did so, and then she stood, rounding the table quickly and scrabbling into his lap. He kissed her like he was dying. Like she was water and he was a man dying of thirst out in the middle of the desert.

He kissed her because there was nothing else he could do. He kissed her, because he wanted nothing else.

And she was like a flame in his arms, hot and perfect, and when he pressed his mouth to hers he whispered, "Mine."

He picked her up and carried her into the house, up the stairs, and he took her straight to his room. His room. Because he had been a fool to believe that he would ever keep her in her own room.

No. She was his.

And this was beyond the desire that he had felt for her on the deck. When he had claimed her on the yacht fresh with the knowledge in his mind that she had never been with another man.

He had been consumed then by the primal urge to claim her, but it had still not been this. This wholehearted acceptance of the fact that she was his.

That there was no part of her that belonged to Alex, least of all their children.

And that he was… And that he was glad of it. That he would want it no other way.

He laid her down on the white sheets, her dress like spilled ink across the pristine fabric. Her red hair as a flame.

She was exquisite. And he had never known such need.

"Please," she whispered.

Begging for him.

Morgan was begging for him.

And he felt…

She had made him dinner. And she begged for him.

He had no shortage of women in his life, in his bed. Women who came to him because they wanted a powerful man. And he was not foolish enough to be unaware of the fact that physically he was the sort of man women desired. It was simply the way he was put together, and he never had vanity about it, nor humility.

It was simply part of who he was, the same as the money, the same as the power. But that Morgan wanted him suddenly mattered.

That it was her begging for his touch, that mattered.

And why? She had said it herself. She was a waitress. He was a billionaire.

And yet, he felt in the moment that the power was with her. He stripped his clothes off, and came down to lie beside her, running his hands over her curves. Then slowly, ever so slowly, he pulled the strap on her dress down, displaying one pale breast for his enjoyment. And then the other.

He ran his hands slowly over them, flicking his thumbs over her nipples. Watching as she gasped with need. She arced up off the bed, a live wire of desire, and he pulled the dress down more, revealing the rounded curve of her stomach. And truly, in that moment it struck him, that she was carrying his children. His children. His blood. His blood in the way that Athena had been. And they were twins. A boy and a girl. He put his hands on her body then, watched as they covered the baby bump.

"I will protect you," he said.

And he kissed her there then, resting his forehead right there. "I swear upon my life. I will not let anything happen to you."

A vow. Both to Morgan, and to his children.

"You cannot take that all on yourself," she whispered. She ran her hand over his hair, down his jaw, and tilted his face up to look at her.

"Yes, I can," he said.

"You don't control everything," she said.

He growled, making his way over her body, grabbing her wrists and capturing them in one hand, trapping them up over her head, her breasts rising up toward him as he did so.

"I will protect you. Because you are mine. My wife. The mother of my children."

"And will you tell the world?"

"Yes," he said, his voice a growl. "Because I will not have anyone thinking that you were ever anyone's but mine."

"Constantine."

She said his name. His name. And on her lips it was like magic. And it ignited a piece of his soul, made him feel alive in a way he never had before.

He was overcome. By the desperate certainty that he would create a new heaven and a new earth all in the name of keeping her safe. Of keeping her with him.

He was powerful, and he had always taken it for granted. She made it feel essential. Because he would use that power, he would use any means necessary to bind her to him.

And he knew that beyond a shadow of a doubt.

He continued to trap her hands as he leaned in and kissed her mouth, pouring all of that intensity into her. He didn't have the words for it. *Nothing but mine.* That word echoed inside of him, over and over. Mine. He kissed her neck, her collarbone, down to the soft swell of her breasts, and he sucked her there until she moaned with desire.

He tormented her with his mouth, tormented them both. She was everything. Perfection. The most glorious, delectable treat he had ever tasted. And he was enthralled. He had to have her. He had to.

He thrust inside her then, the tight, wet heat of her body testing his control.

"Mine," he said. "Mine."

He claimed her like that, over and over again. Until they were both mindless. And just as her pleasure reached the boiling point, his own unraveled, and they both went over the edge together.

CHAPTER ELEVEN

MORGAN WAS SORE and sated the next day, her whole body replete from making love with Constantine all night.

She had stayed in his bed. It was the first time they had gone to sleep together. But when she woke up, he wasn't there. And she felt bereft. Wondering if the connection that she felt with him last night had just been something she'd imagined. She kept coming back to that thought she'd had earlier. That what she wanted was for him to have feelings for her. She was sitting with that, while considering all that it meant for her. Especially when taking into account the revelations that she'd gotten from her mother. It should have—almost—made her more afraid of her feelings. But that wasn't the effect. She was afraid of being hurt.

She didn't know if she could reach him. She just wasn't certain.

But she wanted… She wanted.

And last night had been… Well, she had loved their conversation. He had seemed younger. More human. And then a switch had flipped inside of him and he had gone all intense. But of course, he hadn't talked about that.

She got out of bed and realized she didn't have any clothes in here. And because there was no one else here… There was no reason to be concerned. She walked out of the bedroom, stark naked, and began to head toward her room. But there, of course, was Constantine, standing at the end of the hall, looking at her with dark, fathomless eyes.

"You're awake."

"Yes," she said, heat rising up in her body.

"I like you this way. If you aren't cold, perhaps this is how you should be for me all day."

"Possessive," she said.

Mine.

He had said that, repeatedly. Over and over again.

"Yes," he said.

"Why?"

"Because you're carrying my children, *agape*."

She knew enough to know that meant *love* in Greek.

But she was not his love.

No, what had passed between them last night had been something dark and intense, and nothing half so sweet. There had been a moment. When they had spoken of ice cream, and she had…

He was fathomless, this man who was her husband.

He had told her about his sister, about his deep pain. But she didn't feel closer to knowing him because of that. It was when he had stopped and spoken of things he'd enjoyed that she had found something she recognized. It was only then.

"I'm not certain you would get anything done," she said.

"What do I need to get done?"

She laughed at that. "I don't know. You were awfully busy yesterday."

"And now I'm not busy today."

And he wasn't. They spent the day at the beach, and after she got over her initial shyness, and her concern over being sunburned—which he dealt with by rubbing lotion all over her body—she enjoyed being bare underneath the sun. He joined her, only he looked like he was part of the landscape. Like he belonged. He looked as if he had been born there. Poseidon, maybe. A god of the sea…cut and bronzed and glorious.

And it was perfect like this. They spoke little, feeding each other fruit and making love in the sand. Swimming in the waves.

But the problem with that was it gave her a chance to interrogate her heart.

She loved him. And love, she realized then was the seed of joy.

That joy that had taken root in her spirit and begun to drive out the bitterness she'd been so afraid of.

She had been on the verge of admitting that to herself quite some time ago. But it was more complicated than that. She loved him, and she recognized that loving someone who was not prepared to love you in return could create all manner of hurt. That if she wasn't careful, she could become like her mother, and she didn't want that. Not in the least.

She wanted to avoid that at all costs.

Not because she didn't love her mother, but because she was able to recognize the mistakes her mother had made. She could recognize the things that had soured her, she hoped. Then try to avoid them.

But when she looked at him she worried. When she looked at him, she was concerned. Because what if he didn't… What if he couldn't. What if he would never love her in the way she loved him.

And what would that do to them. And what would it do to her, and to their relationship with their children.

She knew about his deep wound. She knew about his darkest pain. But she wasn't sure even he fully understood the way that it had affected him.

She was just now getting to the bottom of how her own

life had affected her, and all the things that she needed to put away. The things that her mother had been dealing with that she'd made about herself, because she was a child who hadn't known how to allow her mother to be human.

She could recognize that, and still also recognize that there were mistakes she didn't want to repeat with her own children. And the thing that she feared the most was becoming bitter over the lack of love. Except... She wondered if the key was being open. If it was being vulnerable. And that frightened her. How could it not. How could it not frighten her to ponder being open and vulnerable to a man who... Wasn't. He had moments of it. She felt that she had seen his truest self when he had thrust inside of her and growled and proclaimed that she was his.

She didn't want to be vulnerable alone. The thought was terrifying.

But also... She realized that she might have to be. She realized that what she could not do was close down.

It would keep her from opening her heart to her children, wasn't that why it had taken her so long to feel joy in her pregnancy?

Joy.

Constantine was lying on the beach, the sun making his perfect skin gleam. She was hot, and she waded out into the water, and let the waves wash over her bare skin. She threw her arms out wide and looked up at the sky. And for the first time, she felt like there were no chains on her. No limits. She wasn't struggling. She had been given a gift, and she had felt some guilt over the fact that it was possible she might only be a better mother because of the access and wealth she'd been given.

But she realized then that wasn't it. She would be better because she would make the choice. Because she would choose joy even when it was hard. Because she would choose vulnerability, even when she wanted to protect herself.

Because she would choose love, even when it was easier to choose anger. And then, right then, she felt it. Shining in her soul like the sun, a beacon of light that she didn't think she could contain. She was going to be a mother. She was having twins.

She was married to the father of her children and he was beautiful. An astonishing, wonderful man who had been through great pain. But who she knew had the capacity to care greatly too, because if he did not then his pain would not mark him so.

She gave herself permission. To feel all of her feelings. To luxuriate in them. She was having Constantine's babies. And she loved him. She loved him with everything that she was. And she would show him. Before she ever asked for anything else. She would show him. She would make herself vulnerable.

No matter the cost.

No matter the cost.

It was two days later that she asked to have an adventure.

"Am I not myself a great adventure, Morgan?" he asked.

She smiled. She loved him when he was arrogant. But now that she had given herself permission to use those words in her own heart, she found herself thinking she loved him all the time.

It was such an interesting thing, to be unfettered. And that was a gift from him. Not from his money, but from who he was innately.

This man who was so confident in and of himself, and who looked at her like she was the stars.

That she had the power to test him and tempt him mattered to her.

But there was more to it than that even. He seemed to like everything about her, and to never be happier than when she was walking about naked.

He accepted admonishments from her, and allowed her to put sunblock on him, even though he insisted he was inured to the Greek sun, as a child of these lands.

He shared with her, even when he didn't want to. And there was something about that which made her feel grounded in her own importance. Which gave her the confidence to open herself up to feelings and desires she had previously kept closed off.

There was a wholeness to herself now.

She felt comfortable in her skin even as it expanded to accommodate the children she carried. Felt comfortable in her skin when he touched her, tasted her, did things to her that no other man ever had, and that she had never wanted another man to do.

It was more than being with someone who completed her. She was with someone who gave her the courage to complete herself. To be all that she was and accept it.

"Tell me about the parts of your industry," she said, while she watched him pack snacks for their adventure.

"Have we not discussed the company?"

"Not at length. Manufacturing and…"

"Real estate. Hotels."

"Really?"

"Yes."

"My degree is in hospitality. I'm very interested in that industry."

"I have several high-end resorts."

"I would like to visit them."

"Certainly."

"What if I… If I had ideas for them."

"Then you would be free to explore them."

"Really?"

"I enjoy talking to you, Morgan, and I enjoy your ideas. I imagine I would like them when applied to the resorts also."

"You wouldn't feel like I was invading your space."

A strange expression crossed his face. "No one in my family, other than my grandfather, has ever evinced the slightest bit of interest in the way we make money. It has always been me. The fact that you are interested in helping with that... It pleases me."

And she felt warmed by that. And by the idea that she might find a way to use her degree, and her interests.

The island was such a beautiful jungle, and the hike they started out on was brilliant. Lush plants closing them in on the trail, making it all feel wild.

"You could be forgiven for thinking that a tiger might jump out at any moment," she said.

"The only predator here is me," he said, turning to flash a grin at her, and her stomach flipped. "I can guarantee you that."

"Funny how I'm not really afraid of you."

A shadow passed over his face, and he said nothing.

"It's a good thing we didn't hike naked," she said, dodging one of the plants. "It is a bit... Dense."

"Indeed. That is a recipe for certain disaster."

In fairness, nudity on sand could also be a bit of a disaster, but they had both risked it, and happily, to indulge themselves.

The trail wound deeper into the trees, until they were so thick the sun only peeked through in small patches, lending a prismatic effect to the jungle floor. The sound of the birds was held in by that canopy of trees, and they echoed loudly around them. There were bright blooms, pink and golden sapphire, a riot of color all around. And then she heard it. Rushing water.

"Where are we going?"

"You'll see."

When the trees cleared, her eyes widened.

It was a pool, clear as could be, with a massive, churning waterfall spilling into the depths of it from the top of the craggy rock.

The water was like crystal, and she could see little fish swimming down in the depths of it.

"This is…"

"This is the kind of opulence money does not buy," he said.

"In fairness, your money did buy the private island."

"But I have no control over this. I did not create it. Here my hand does not matter. There is no hand but God's."

"You don't like that, usually."

"I have been betrayed by it."

"But here you feel safe."

"It is not myself I fear for."

She put her hand on his face. "Of course not. I understand that."

They stood for a moment and looked at the water, and she knew, that this was the moment. She grabbed hold of the hem of her sundress and pulled it up over her head. She had no underwear on beneath.

She could feel his hot gaze on her as she kicked off her shoes and slipped like a nymph into the pool.

"The water is wonderful," she said, swimming on her back until she was out at the center of it.

He was already removing his own clothing, and he dove

in without making a splash, his movements neat and precise as always.

When he resurfaced, his dark eyes were intense. And she knew that she was looking at the predator. And she didn't mind. She swam away from him, kicking toward the waterfall. The water was a violent current at its base, and she avoided that, swimming behind it instead, where she found a massive, glimmering cavern.

"What is this?" she asked, and he came behind the falls with her.

"It's called Dead Man's Cove. Legend has it, there was a pirate treasure in here. But I believe the treasure is what's all around us."

"I believe it too." She got up out of the water, pleased to find the rock there smooth and sandy. He followed her, in all his naked glory. He was standing, and she on her knees. And she did not hesitate in her next action.

"I believe I found some treasure." She leaned in, sliding her tongue along the length of him, and his breath hissed through his teeth. He moaned as she took him into her mouth. As she began to pleasure him in the way that he had done for her so many times.

She had not been the boldest lover, but she was learning. He made her bold. In a way she had never been. She felt so changed, transformed. That she was the kind of woman who would take a man into her mouth outside. In a cave.

But it wasn't just because she wanted him. It wasn't that simple. It was because she loved him.

She pleasured him like that, her hands, her lips, her tongue. Until he was shaking. He grabbed hold of her hair, gritted his teeth. "Morgan. Wait."

But she didn't wait. She didn't stop. Until his control

had shattered, fractured, until she had taken in every last drop of him. A forfeit of his control that she needed. For she was about to be more vulnerable than she had ever been. She looked up at him, her eyes meeting his, his expression one of supreme torture. And she smiled.

"I love you."

CHAPTER TWELVE

CONSTANTINE COULDN'T CATCH his breath. She had destroyed him. This wicked fairy who had taken him out to the middle of nowhere—*you took her out here*. Maybe he had. But he could scarcely remember now, and it hardly mattered. Because the world had turned upside down, and he no longer knew where he fit in it. Because Morgan was telling him that she loved him, and that was something he simply could not fathom. Something he could not abide by. She loved him.

How was such a thing possible?

She loved him.

His heart was thundering hard, and it wasn't just from his release.

He hadn't wanted it to end that way. He had wanted to pull away and thrust inside of her tight, welcoming body, but instead she had swallowed him down.

And it felt like she had won something. Like she had stolen something he had fought his entire life for.

Control.

"I love you," she whispered.

"That is not necessary," he said.

"I don't care if it's necessary," she said. She looked up at him like he was... Pitiable. "Or rather, I don't care if you think it's necessary. It is. I've been thinking... I thought so much that I gave myself a headache. Trying to figure out how not to be the same sort of mother my own was. And then I talked to her. I did more thinking. And I found a lot of sympathy for her that I didn't have before. But it was when I stopped thinking and started feeling that I found the answers. She came across as bitter because she hardened herself. Because she let the things in her life that hurt her decide what she was allowed to feel. She let it put limits on her happiness. I don't want to do that. So this is me. Open and raw and vulnerable. This is me loving you. And I am better for it. I will be a better mother. And a better wife. And a better person."

"I can't," he said.

"I know you think you can't. But you don't have to know the answer. Not now. You don't need to tell me anything right now. And it wasn't… It wasn't an action item for you. It was a gift to myself."

"Morgan."

But she slipped away from the waterfall, back into the water, and she swam away, leaving him there, ragged and bloody and more uncertain than he had been since he was an eight-year-old boy, crying in the dungeon, uncertain if he would live to see tomorrow.

It took him time to figure out what he had to do. He sat up all night considering her words. She loved him. And the way that it had made him feel to hear it was disconcerting. It made his chest ache. And so did she. And he realized… He realized that he didn't need to be here with her. He needed to get his life in order. He had to deal with his parents head-on, and he had to go back to what he did best. Running the company. Here he had been on an endless vacation with her. Here, he had been ignoring who he was. He had allowed himself to get sucked into a fantasy.

He had acknowledged as much days ago, but he hadn't realized how much this place had been affecting them until she had given him her declaration. She could feel what she wished. But he could not afford to change. He had promised her nothing would happen to her. And he meant that. He would protect her. With all that he was.

And that meant leaving her. But she would be here. She would be safe. He would send fully vetted staff and the doctor to care for her. And he would continue on as he should have this entire time. Because he knew where his strengths were. He handled things. He did not take care of people, not directly. He did not...

He took one last look at the house. And then he slung his bag over his shoulder and walked outside, down toward the yacht.

CHAPTER THIRTEEN

THINGS WERE NOT easy after that. Constantine was taking great pains to avoid her, after all of his proclamations about her being his. After... After everything.

He certainly wasn't acting as if she was his. Rather he was behaving like she was on the private island by herself.

And she had said that she didn't need anything from him, but she was very afraid that she actually did.

She wanted him to love her. Was that so bad?

And that was the problem. What she wanted was to be patient. What she wanted was to give him time.

But she also wanted the feeling of having her love returned, because she had felt so... Dry and lonely for all of her life, and even knowing her mother loved her it... It hadn't been expressed in a way that she could understand it, and so she had often felt like... Like it wasn't there. When she looked at Constantine, she could not imagine what he was thinking.

She was brooding in her room, upset that Constantine had been avoiding her for the better part of the day.

When she heard a door, she went to it. Expecting that it would be Constantine, because who else would it be? She was shocked to discover that it was not Constantine, but a woman.

"Hello, miss," she said. "I am Cristela. I am part of the

household staff in Athens. I've been sent here to help care for you."

"What?"

"Mr. Kamaras has gone back home."

"He didn't."

"He did. He assures you that there is a phone waiting for you in what he was using as his office."

She ran straight upstairs to that office, and she looked in the phone to see if he had left his number. He had. She called him in absolute fury.

"Constantine," she said. "What is it you've done?"

"I'm leaving you on the island, where you are safe," he said. "But I… It was time for me to return back to work."

"You left me here."

"Yes."

"You're keeping me prisoner," she said.

"I am not. I'm making sure that you're safe. It is the only place on earth that I can make sure nothing will happen to you. And as the news of our relationship gets out…"

"This is… This is a lie. You were perfectly happy to be here with me until I told you that I loved you. And you left me. I think we both know it has more to do with that than it has to do with—"

"Are you calling me a coward?"

"Yes," she said. "I am. I'm calling you a coward because you deserve to be known as one. Because how dare you? How dare you leave me here?"

"You will be provided for. You will have everything that you could possibly want. And you have no reason to be upset."

"I have every reason to be upset," she said. "You have marooned me."

"On a private island with a beautiful house and a full staff. There is a doctor as well."

"Everything I could possibly want except the man that I love. You know that I… You had to know this would hurt me."

"The last thing I want to do is hurt you. I am protecting you."

"From yourself? Is this about your sister? Because I don't understand. You were a child, and you were kidnapped by very bad men. I can understand you being angry at your parents for not coming for you in time. Angry at your grandfather. I cannot understand you being angry at yourself for crying. You were a boy. A child."

"And the world does not care. The world does not care if you are innocent, if you are a child. It doesn't matter. There is great evil in the world, and it does not ask if you are prepared to grapple with it. It will be the same for our children. And I will protect you. Both of you, I will never fail again. Not as I have failed before."

"Do you really think that you failed? You didn't have control over those people. You didn't ask to have it happen to you. You never would have. They took you. They—"

"Enough. This is not a discussion. You are acting as if you've been abandoned, you have not been. I am taking care of you in the best way I ever could. That is my job. My task. It is not…distraction."

"Are you so afraid to be loved? Or are you just afraid of what it would be like if you love someone else again."

"I said it was enough. We do not need to have further discussion. You will remain on the island until after the birth of the children."

"And will you be here for the birth of the children?"

"I'm not a doctor. Such a thing is not necessary."

"And if it is for me?"

"You do not make the rules."

"And you don't care for me?"

"I did not say that."

"Then be honest with me. Be honest with yourself."

"We will speak again another time, Morgan. Perhaps I should've told you of my plans before I left. But I felt it would only result in unpleasantness."

"By unpleasantness you mean my feelings?"

"Feelings are unnecessary. What is necessary is protection."

He hung up the phone, and her heart felt scarred and bloodied. Bruised. She hadn't expected this. Of all the things, she hadn't expected this. She had been prepared. Prepared to love him with no certainty that he would love her back. Prepared to love him in spite of whether or not he loved her ever. But she had not been prepared to be abandoned. She had not been prepared to lose him.

She walked down the hall, and there was another member of staff, and then another. This place that had been theirs, the sanctuary, was now invaded with strangers, and she wanted to weep. It all felt wrong. Desperately, hideously wrong. She went into their room. His room, which had been theirs. And she lay down in the center of the bed and realized the linens had been changed and it didn't even smell like him anymore. And she gave in to her misery, clutching her belly and crying. How would she overcome this? How would she... How would this ever be okay?

It just would be. Because it had to be. Because she had to be. Because she would not let this wither her and make her bitter. She squeezed her eyes shut tight, and she tried to tell herself that, as she wept like she would never stop.

"And where is your wife?"

"Safe," Constantine said as he walked into the living room where his mother and father were already sitting. His mother would be upset. She would be devastated. But there was a reason he was doing this here. There was a reason he was doing it now.

"I'm here because I have to tell you something. Morgan's children are not Alex's. They are mine."

It was a truth that had to be told. He could not live in the lie. In the shelter of fantasy and neither should they.

They were his. And maybe the truth was... He needed his mother to know because he needed the children to matter. As his.

"Constantine," his father said, a warning tone that was almost funny on the old man who had never done an authoritative thing in his entire life.

"What are you saying?" his mother asked.

"I am saying that Morgan and I had an affair before Alex's death. The children are not his, they're mine."

"How can you be certain?"

"She was a virgin when she came to me."

"That makes no sense," his mother said.

"It may not make sense, but it is the truth."

"How dare you," his mother said. "How dare you take this from me."

And he knew it was time. To hear all of the things that he was certain his parents thought.

"You took Athena from us. You did. You took her. And now Alex's gone and..."

"And you wish it was me who were dead," he said. "I know. I have always known."

His mother's eyes went wide with horror. "I did not say that."

"But it is what you feel."

"No," she said. "I wish none of my children were dead. I wish none of my children were dead and I... I wish I could go back in time and change whatever I need to change in order to make it so that you... So that you are all okay."

"That isn't what you were going to say."

"No. It isn't. Because what I was going to say was hideously unfair and I didn't even mean it. Because I want to be angry at someone, and if you were the one in the grave then it would be Alex that I was yelling at, because I would be yelling at whoever remained. Because it is all bad. It is bad and horrible and nothing but grief, and there is nothing that fixes it."

"Except having Alex's children would have fixed it."

"No," she said. "They still wouldn't be Alex. And you... You're going to be a father."

"Yes," he said, gritting his teeth, not certain what the hell he was supposed to make of this new development. Because he had been waiting for the recriminations that had nearly come, but then they had stopped. Because he had been waiting to be told that he was a disgrace, and she had nearly said it. Because it would excuse him. If they blamed him, then it would excuse him from ever having to deal with any of this. Because blame was so much easier than the reality of what he had. Which was loss and fear and guilt. Which were all things he could not control. Blame was focused. Guilt was such an easy thing to keep. It was the other emotions he didn't want. The other emotions he didn't want to have a handle on.

"They are your children," she said. "And you will love them. Even if you don't want to. Even if it feels dangerous. And I will love them too."

"Mother..."

"It's true, Constantine. You will."

"I don't want this. I don't want any of it. I didn't set out to get his girlfriend pregnant. I never would have... I..."

"Where is she?"

"She's on the island. I have to keep her safe."

"So you've imprisoned her."

She was using that same word to describe what he'd done that Morgan had already used.

"I'm keeping her safe. I am doing what I was asked to do, and none of you understand that. You do not…take care of the family business. Just as you did not watch us when we were on the beach." His mother drew back as if he'd struck her. "Grandfather told me it was my job to be the man. To keep the family together and I have done so. I cannot afford to be distracted."

His mother looked away, then back at him. "Are you keeping her safe? The family? Or are you keeping yourself safe?"

"Enough. I needed to tell you the truth of the matter. She is my wife and she is my wife in truth. The children are mine. But that is all I came for."

"Your grandfather was a hard man," his father said. "I know. He raised me. He was broken by the loss of Athena, and he loved you very much, but he…he was worried. He was worried your experience would make you soft, traumatized, and I was furious at him when I heard him give you that command to be a man when you were only a boy."

"You were still acting as a boy," Constantine said, hard. "What was I to do?"

His father's shoulders slumped. "I have never been the man my father would have wanted. I admire you and your work ethic, Constantine. But surely…surely there must be balance? Perhaps I could have done more. But must you do everything?"

Yes.

"It is not a debate. It is simply what is," Constantine said.

"Will you go back to her now?" his father asked.

"I will go back to work."

He got into his car and he began to drive. And panic

overtook him. A strange, clawing panic he had not felt since he was a child.

And this, he realized was what was underneath the guilt all along. This, he realized was the real thing that drove him.

Fear.

Because you could be a child who had been getting ice cream one moment but was snatched off the streets the next. A child who watched early-morning cartoons with your sister, and then one day she was gone and you never saw her again. And they said it was your fault. *Your fault.*

A curve came up quicker than he expected and he swerved, his car spinning out and nearly going into a ditch. And he sat there in the middle of the road, clutching the steering wheel, his heart beating hard.

And he realized. He realized.

He would live with this fear for the rest of his life. And keeping her on an island wouldn't solve it.

And she was... She was brave enough to love him. She was brave enough, and she was... Brave enough to raise the children in a way that he never could.

The answer was not to keep her locked away tightly.

The answer was to let her go.

CHAPTER FOURTEEN

SHE HAD BEEN alone on the island for three weeks. Every day that she felt the babies move, that she ate breakfast alone and lunch and then dinner. That she swam by herself and felt nearly blinded by the constant beauty, she missed him. She was in a rage.

Every day.

She was furious that he had done this to her. But he had done it to them.

How dare he? Really, how very dare he.

But he wasn't here for her to yell at. And that just added to the indignation of it all.

And then, when she was taking her breakfast one morning, she saw a yacht in the distance and was certain that she was hallucinating. Absolutely certain.

But no, it kept coming, closer and closer. Until there he was. And it took all of her strength not to run out into the sea to greet him. But he wasn't smiling when he moored the boat. Rather his expression was grim. "I'm sorry," he said by way of greeting.

"You're sorry?"

"Yes. And I've come to… To apologize and set you free."

"Set me free?"

"I cannot keep you here on the island. I also cannot keep you with me."

"Why not?" She felt plaintive and silly and sad. Angry at herself for being hopeful, even for a moment.

"Because I cannot. Because to stay with you is to live with fear. And I cannot do it. Not anymore."

"Being with me makes you fearful?"

"Yes," he said. "Because if there's one thing I know, I cannot protect anyone from the cruelty of this world. And I thought to keep you prisoner. I thought to keep you safe that way. But then I realized... I am the one who cannot handle it. Not you. I will never... I will never take the children to learn to swim, or to the beach. Or to get ice cream. Because I will only ever be able to think of the terror that awaits them. And that is all. That is all their life will ever be. Living with a man who knows only how to keep people in chains to keep them safe."

"So you would keep yourself in chains instead?"

His eyes were wild, and she felt a great stab of horrible sympathy when he looked at her. "I'm not in chains." He shook his head. "I am a man in full control when you were not in my life. I never had an issue with this as long as you weren't there."

"You love me," she said.

"No," he said.

"You do. It's why you're afraid for me. The same reason you're afraid for the children. You love me, and you grieve the fact that you have feelings. But you do. And there's nothing that can be done about them. Except to give in to them."

"No."

"Why do you only trust fate when it's bad? Why are you so convinced there is evil under every rock, when there is love right here?"

"Because I cannot guarantee—"

"I never asked for your guarantees. I don't want them. I want you. We must live dangerous. We must live dangerous in order to live free. Or you become hard like my mother, you end up having everything, and being able to enjoy none of it. My mother had me, and I was desperate for her love, and she couldn't show it because of her fear. Because of the way that my father had hurt her. And you... You are letting the men that took you, the men that took your sister from you decide how happy you will be. Why would you give them that power?"

His throat worked, stark emotion filling his dark eyes.

"You are allowed to have feelings. It is not weak. You wept because you missed your sister. You wept out of fear for her. You were not wrong for doing that. You were not wrong for loving her any more than you are wrong for loving me."

"But this cannot be..."

"I'm afraid it is," she said. "I'm afraid you love me. And you can send me away, but you will still love me. And you can keep your children at a distance, and you will love them. It will just be locked in a cage inside of you. And what kind of a tribute is that? To your sister. To your brother. And to your own self. You're alive, Constantine. We are alive. Why can we not love?"

"I was tasked with being...with being the one to keep us all together. My grandfather told me..."

"And why do you care about doing what he said? Because you love him. But he was still wrong. My mother was wrong and she loved me. Love doesn't make people perfect. It doesn't make the world perfect. But we don't have to wait for perfection to find happiness."

And then Constantine fell to his knees and wrapped

his arms around her. "I love you," he said, the words broken. "I love you."

"I know," she said, smoothing his dark hair off his face. "I really do."

"But it opens you up to so much pain," he said.

"The pain is there, whether we protect ourselves from it or not. The only thing we ever managed to really keep out is the joy."

"No more," he said.

She nodded her head. "No more."

"I love you Morgan," he said.

"I love you too."

"Let us go to bed."

"Yes. I think that's a good idea."

The phone woke Constantine in the middle of the night. But he was too sated by his evening spent with Morgan to be angry. He answered, and it was his mother on the other end, her voice breathless and strained.

"What is it?"

"It's Athena," she said. "They've found Athena."

And the last bit of any defense he had built up inside of him crumbled completely. And the emotion he had been holding back for all those years poured out.

Athena was rescued by a man called Castor Xenakis who had been searching for his own sister for years. It was an incredible story of persistence, and he had apparently found his own love with a woman named Glory along the way. But when his work had come to fruition they had discovered that more than one girl had been kept by the wife of this particular crime lord, a woman who had always wanted daughters.

Apparently there had been a tip from a man known only

as Dante, which seemed a bit on the nose, if it was a reference to *The Inferno*. But the end result was simply that he'd helped save Athena, whether he was a devil or not.

Athena looked far younger than Constantine did, her glossy dark hair smooth and perfect, her skin golden like the rest of her family, but with a pale cast, as if she did not spend very much time in the sun.

"These are strange times," she said.

"Do you remember me?" Constantine asked, his voice rough.

And Morgan's heart felt bruised on behalf of her husband.

"Of course, Constantine." And though it was tentative, Athena smiled. "Do you remember, we used to watch that cartoon about ponies."

And Morgan wept. Her heart had never felt so full of joy.

And she was grateful. For the decision to open her heart in the first place. For her decision to love even when it was hard.

And she no longer worried about being a good mother. She knew she would be. She didn't worry, because she was happy with herself. Happy with the wife she was. And she had a sister-in-law. One that she was very excited to get to know.

She and Constantine went to bed that night in his room. The room where they had first made love.

"It is a miracle," he said.

"You see," she said. "Sometimes the miraculous is hiding just around the corner. Not everything is dark."

"And sometimes the miraculous is right in plain sight," he said, looking directly at her. "As you were, from the beginning. From the first moment I saw you."

"I love you."

"I love you too."

"Do you think this will help, with the fear?"

"You know, you already had."

"Me?"

"Yes. Love and fear cannot occupy the same space. And by choosing one I had already let go of the other. That was because of you. Athena is just an extra gift."

"And what an amazing gift."

"Yes. Indeed." He kissed her mouth. "It seems the gift of love is one that keeps on giving."

EPILOGUE

MORGAN WONDERED IF someone could burst from happiness. If they could, she would. When she gave birth to the twins, she was exhausted, but euphoric.

"And do you have names picked out for them?"

He nodded. "If you don't mind, I would like to name them Alexius and Athena."

Athena, the proud aunt, was in the room, beaming.

"I would like that," she said.

"We don't have to. If you fear the names might be cursed."

"I don't fear that. There's far too much love for a curse to continue to exist."

"On that, my dear wife, we can agree."

"Perhaps it is fate that we should be happy," she said.

"I heard it said once, we do not have to wait for perfection to claim happiness."

"I said that."

He smiled. "But I believe we may have found perfection."

She kissed him, all the love in her heart pouring out of her like a wave. She was vulnerable, and so was he. And she was overjoyed. "I believe, my dearest husband, you are right."

* * * * *

COMING SOON!

We really hope you enjoyed reading this book.
If you're looking for more romance, be sure to
head to the shops when new books are
available on

Thursday 3rd February

To see which titles are coming soon, please visit

millsandboon.co.uk/nextmonth

MILLS & BOON

MILLS & BOON

Coming next month

BOUND BY HER RIVAL'S BABY
Maya Blake

A breeze washed over Amelie and she shivered.

Within one moment and the next, Atu was shrugging off his shirt.

"W-what are you doing?" she blurted as he came towards her.

Another mirthless twist of his lips. "You may deem me an enemy but I don't want you catching cold and falling ill. Or worse."

She aimed a glare his way. "Not until I've signed on whatever dotted line you're determined to foist on me, you mean?"

That look of fury returned. This time accompanied by a flash of disappointment. As if he had the right to such a lofty emotion where she was concerned. She wanted, no *needed* to refuse this small offer of comfort.

Return to her room and come up with a definite plan that removed him from her life for good.

So why was she drawing the flaps of his shirt closer? Her fingers clinging to the warm cotton as if she'd never let it go?

She must have a made a sound at the back of her throat because his head swung to hers, his eyes holding hers for an age before he exhaled harshly.

His lips firmed and for a long stretch he didn't speak. "You need to accept that I'm the best bet you have right now. There's no use fighting. I'm going to win eventually. How soon depends entirely on you."

The implacable conclusion sent icy shivers coursing

through her. In that moment she regretted every moment of weakness. Regretted feeling bad for invoking that hint of disappointment in his eyes.

She had nothing to be ashamed of. Not when vanquishing her and her family was his sole, true purpose.

She snatched his shirt from her shoulders, crushing her body's instant insistence on its warmth as she tossed it back to him. "You should know by now that threats don't faze me. We're still here, still standing after all you and your family have done. So go ahead, do your worst."

Held head high, she whirled away. She only made it three steps before he captured her wrist. She spun around, intent on pushing him away.

But that ruthlessness was coupled with something else. Something hot and blazing and all-consuming in his eyes.

She belatedly read it as lust before he was tugging her closer, wrapping one hand around her waist and the other in her hair. "This stubborn determination is admirable. Hell, I'd go so far as to say it's a turn on because God knows I admire strong, wilful women," he muttered, his lips a hairsbreadth from hers, "but fiery passion will only get you so far."

"And what are you going to do about it?" she taunted a little too breathlessly. Every cell in her body traitorously strained towards him, yearning for things she knew she shouldn't want, but desperately needed anyway.

He froze, then a strangling sound leaving his throat, he slammed his lips on hers.

He kissed her like hc was starved for it. *For her*.

Continue reading
BOUND BY HER RIVAL'S BABY
Maya Blake

Available next month
www.millsandboon.co.uk

MILLS & BOON

THE HEART OF ROMANCE

A ROMANCE FOR EVERY READER

MODERN — Prepare to be swept off your feet by sophisticated, sexy and seductive heroes, in some of the world's most glamourous and romantic locations, where power and passion collide.

HISTORICAL — Escape with historical heroes from time gone by. Whether your passion i for wicked Regency Rakes, muscled Vikings or rugged Highlanders, awa the romance of the past.

MEDICAL — Set your pulse racing with dedicated, delectable doctors in the high-pressure world of medicine, where emotions run high and passion, comfort love are the best medicine.

True Love — Celebrate true love with tender stories of heartfelt romance, from the rush of falling in love to the joy a new baby can bring, and a focus on t emotional heart of a relationship.

Desire — Indulge in secrets and scandal, intense drama and plenty of sizzling hot action with powerful and passionate heroes who have it all: wealth, statu good looks…everything but the right woman.

HEROES — Experience all the excitement of a gripping thriller, with an intense romance at its heart. Resourceful, true-to-life women and strong, fearless face danger and desire - a killer combination!

To see which titles are coming soon, please visit

millsandboon.co.uk/nextmonth

LET'S TALK
Romance

For exclusive extracts, competitions
and special offers, find us online:

f facebook.com/millsandboon

🐦 @MillsandBoon

📷 @MillsandBoonUK

Get in touch on 01413 063232

For all the latest titles coming soon, visit
millsandboon.co.uk/nextmonth

MILLS & BOON
Desire

Indulge in secrets and scandal, intense drama and plenty of sizzling hot action with powerful and passionate heroes who have it all: wealth, status, good looks…everything but the right woman.

MILLS & BOON

HEROES

At Your Service

Experience all the excitement of a gripping thriller, with an intense romance at its heart. Resourceful, true-to-life women and strong, fearless men face danger and desire - a killer combination!

MILLS & BOON
MEDICAL
Pulse-Racing Passion

Set your pulse racing with dedicated, delectable doctors in the high-pressure world of medicine, where emotions run high and passion, comfort and love are the best medicine.